FOOL'S GOLD

FOOL'S GOLD

a novel

Jane S. Smith

𝒵

ZOLAND BOOKS

Cambridge, Massachusetts

First edition published in 2000 by
Zoland Books, Inc.
384 Huron Avenue
Cambridge, Massachusetts 02138

FIRST EDITION

Book design by Boskydell Studio
Printed in the United States of America

06 05 04 03 02 01 00   8 7 6 5 4 3 2 1

This book is printed on acid-free paper, and its binding materials
have been chosen for strength and durability.

Library of Congress Cataloguing-in-Publication Data
Smith, Jane S.
Fool's gold / by Jane S. Smith. — 1st ed.
p. cm.
ISBN 1-58195-019-5 (acid-free paper)
1. Americans — Travel — France — Provence — Fiction.
2. Family recreation — France — Provence — Fiction. I. Title.

PS3569.M5374 F66 2000
813'.54—dc21
99-089680

For Carl,
Stalwart Pathfinder

To the Reader

Imagine a crown. Start with gold dug from the sacred mines in Ireland and transported over the sea to France. Shape it into a broad, flat circle stamped with a series of mystic images: a horned demon, a skull, an owl with streaming hair, water that seems to give off steam, a sun that burns within a circle of stars. At the center, put a portrait of a fierce, spike-haired goddess. Have lightning shooting from her fingertips and spitting snakes coiled around her naked legs. Across her brow place a miniature duplicate of the golden crown, with another, smaller, equally fierce goddess at its center.

Now lose the whole thing for two thousand years. Let it turn up, quite by accident, in that part of Gaul so thoroughly colonized by the Romans that it is still called Provence. See what happens.

If that seems too obscure, start again. Imagine a number of Americans far from home, trying to make their varied reputations. Add a field of lavender, several hilltop villages, a touch of romance, and a great deal of self-delusion. Remember that art is long, life is short, and children, while infinitely precious, are not always to be trusted.

If you're ready, we can begin.

PART I

Lost and Found

The Lecturer on Art

L ATE AS USUAL, Vivian Hart rammed her car into the fast-
moving traffic heading west to New Jersey over the George
Washington Bridge. The aggressive driving was just a reflex, a
habit acquired during her thirty-eight years on Planet New York.
She was on her way to be fired, a situation that no degree of
promptness would improve.

She had received the call at nine that morning, a terse order to
attend her first faculty meeting in the ten years she had taught at
Malcolm College of Knowledge. The explanation came when she
turned on the car radio. Every day, just before the weather, her favorite station featured a one-minute exposé of the most glaring
case of capitalist malfeasance in the last twenty-four hours. Today's subject had been Vivian's boss.

Amos Malcolm, millionaire pioneer in drop-in education, the
genius who had transformed an evening class in auto-body repair into the largest privately owned school in the tri-state metropolitan area, had just been indicted for misappropriation of
federal funds. To keep their client out of jail, old Amos's lawyers
had agreed to an immediate suspension of operations. When she
finally arrived at the main campus, a converted freight depot just
off the New Jersey Turnpike, it was to hear a somewhat reworded
version of the same news. Malcolm College of Knowledge, Where
Northern New Jersey Learns What Earns, was beginning a sys-
temwide restructuring of its curriculum that necessitated a brief
interruption of classes. Starting today. Ending no time in the
foreseeable future.

None of this was Vivian's fault. She had not pressured students to apply for guaranteed student loans to pay for programs that would never, ever bring them a job. She had nothing to do with the Keyboarding Department, equipped with Underwood typewriters of a sort not seen in any office in North America for over thirty years, or with the Computer Servicing Department, where students were graded on their ability to crawl under tables and make sure that all plugs were firmly anchored in their sockets. She had never approved the program of the Interior Decorating Department, which offered a master's degree to anyone who could make a color wheel out of an ordinary paper plate, or of the extremely popular but apparently illegal Domestic Surveillance Certificate Course, where students were taught the best ways to spy through the windows of total strangers. For ten years she had lectured on art and architecture without ever once suggesting that anything she said would make her students more employable. The worst she had done was allow them to plaster her photo through the catalog to show that one could indeed be a student at Malcolm College of Knowledge and still learn something about the arts. Not much, as a brief consideration of the course offerings would show, but at least something.

And now she was out of a job. After the gray-faced accountant had explained there would be no final checks, there was not much more to say. Vivian had no office to clean out, no favorite piece of equipment to steal before the federal agents got there in the morning. Nodding briefly to her former colleagues, none of whom she had ever met, she returned to her car and headed back to Manhattan.

A Career Retrospective

VIVIAN'S FIRST FEELING was embarrassment at finding herself in so trite a situation. Malcolm College of Knowledge was certainly on the fringe of intellectual respectability, but it was a ragged edge she valued more than she had realized. She felt like a character in an academic farce.

In a sense, Vivian was a victim of her own success. Small, fair, and unremarkable in appearance, she had made the most of her agile mind, her facile tongue, and her passionate conviction that the salvation of modern woman (by whom she meant the middle-class, moderately educated woman of postindustrial urban centers) lay in the rediscovery of her connection with the primitive rhythms of the ancient earth. Her popularity came from her talent for titillating night school students with soft-core pornography presented as "eco-feminist art appreciation."

It was an accident at first. Hired at the last minute, recruited by a notice posted outside the office of the Graduate Program in Art History at CUNY, she had agreed to deliver an eight-week series of lectures which somebody in the marketing department had already titled "Making Sense of Impressionist Painting." Her husband was between photography assignments, her son was six weeks old, and she needed the money.

The day before she was to begin, a tired-sounding woman from the business office called to say that *sense* had somehow been changed to *sex* in the announcement that went out to two thousand people on their mailing list. It was too late to mail corrections, and, actually, preregistration had been pretty good, so did she think she could make her lectures fit the new title? Too confused to object, Vivian agreed.

The renamed course was a huge success. The class, twenty-three strong, found something deliciously hip in Vivian's way of pairing gorgeous color slides of everybody's favorite French paintings with biting attacks on the exploitation of female models. They lapped up her analysis of Renoir's boating party paintings as modern fertility rituals. They took notes when she showed how Cézanne's haystacks were really male-coded assertions of power. They were bemused when she described van Gogh's tortured fields as erotic fetishes, the landscape writhing in a frenzy of sterile titillation. For her final lecture she rehashed a seminar paper where she linked Monet's famous garden with Luther Burbank's experiments in hybridization, exposing both as capitalist-oppressor attempts to exploit nature for commercial use.

After "Making Sex of Impressionist Painting" came the even more popular "Making Sex of Urban Architecture." The growing audience, still almost entirely female, had giggled when Vivian announced she was going to trace the history of what she called "civic erections." They loved it when she talked about roads and bridges as a municipal chastity belt imposed upon the sexual organs of the earth. They howled with approval when she defined the male ideal of a public park as a grassy mound pierced at the center by a fat, upright column commemorating a particularly orgasmic moment of military penetration, and they nodded in solemn agreement when she described the long tradition of multi-stepped courthouses and public buildings as a conspiracy to deny access to stroller-pushing mothers.

By the third series, "Making Sex in the Garden," over a hundred women, and even a few men, were paying to hear Vivian's weekly diatribes. Soon a Thursday night session was added to the original Tuesday schedule. In a small but fervent circle, Vivian had many followers.

Over the years she had expanded her topics to include "Reclaiming Your Inner Gaia" (on landscape painting), "The Feminine Touch" (on autoeroticism), and "Women Who Run with Painters" (brief biographies of wives and mistresses illustrated with paintings for which they served as models). Every fall she repeated "Making Sex of Impressionist Painting." Putting it at the top of the mailing list was like having a license to print money, the business manager confessed.

For this Vivian received a decent salary and access to a group medical package that paid the bills when Lily was born four years after her brother, Justin. Vivian never finished her dissertation, but one of the charms of Malcolm was that nobody there cared about credentials.

Obviously, such bliss could not endure. As she flung her fat copper token into the hopper at the toll booth, Vivian decided to visit the Metropolitan Museum of Art, her favorite source for last-minute inspiration. Justin and Lily would not be home from school until 4:30. Surely four hours would be enough time for her to decide what to do with the rest of her life.

The Artist

W HILE VIVIAN is completing this patently symbolic journey from old life to new, we can take a moment to look in
on her husband.

Richard Hart was a photographer. It was in his blood. His
grandfather, a grim, quiet man who always traveled with a canvas
sack of flashbulbs, had taken crime-scene pictures for the police.
His father had worked at a well-known portrait studio in lower
Manhattan, cajoling smiles from a lifetime succession of fussy
babies, nervous newlyweds, and jowly executives who needed to
look purposeful for the pages of the annual report.

Richard liked to say he sought a broader range of subjects,
which sounded high-minded but meant he worked freelance,
one of those reliable hacks who filled the Rolodex of every advertising art director in the greater metropolitan area, available at
short notice to transform ordinary products into images of con-
sumer desire. His days passed in an overlighted room on the West
Side of Manhattan, unrolling and rerolling cascades of background paper while client and account executive squabbled over
which color looked best with dish detergent, or cat litter, or whatever it was they were shooting. Much of Richard's work appeared
in the color advertising inserts of local newspapers.

Richard's art was something else. Shot in black and white, ob-
sessively devoted to theme, these photographs were meant to cut
to the core of the modern urban experience. In his soul, hidden
beneath his somewhat paunchy exterior, was a biting social critic.
His earliest work, begun while he was still in art school, had been
a series of tightly focused images of ordinary shoes (and accom-

panying feet) descending the same two steps at the bottom of the Columbus Circle subway station. No gallery had been willing to exhibit the Shoe Series, a rejection Richard attributed to fear of foot fetishists. Undaunted, he had moved on to the Pretzel Series, which showed people eating the large soft pretzels sold by sidewalk vendors in central Manhattan. Here, too, his preferred shot was the close-up, which often showed people with their mouths open, bits of pretzel clearly visible inside. This purified his art, Richard claimed, stripping it of the social baggage of clothing or setting.

As before, no one was interested. One gallery owner, more candid than most, complained that Richard had achieved a style that was both revolting and pointless. Taking this as a call for clearer narrative content, he had then embarked on the Icon Series, which featured cheap plastic religious objects in disrespectful situations — Buddha squatting on a child's potty, Moses carrying the Ten Commandments down a mountain of sausage links, the Virgin Mary wearing a yellow vinyl sign that said "Baby on Board." But even loaded with ironic reference, his art failed to find an audience.

When he met Vivian, Richard had known at once she was his passion and his muse, there to raise his photography to a higher plane of meaning. Just out of Hunter College, she was working for a fancy Madison Avenue florist and had come to arrange the wildflowers needed to enhance the box of margarine he was shooting. While she poked and prodded her arrangement of daisies and buttercups, she had entranced him with an impromptu commentary on the transformation of sunflowers from nutritionally useful weeds to enormously expensive allusions to the lost world of pastoral, with examples ranging from Vincent van Gogh to Van Cleef & Arpels. Although frequently misinformed, Vivian was a good talker.

Plus she was small and thin and wore her blond hair pulled back like a ballerina, which was attractive to a large, hairy guy like Richard. Vivian liked large, hairy guys. He took her out to dinner, then back to his apartment, and then out to breakfast, and five weeks later they were off to city hall to get married. It was wildly romantic, they both agreed, very proud of themselves.

Two years later, when Richard inherited a few worthless stocks and a real gem of a rent-controlled apartment from his grandmother, Vivian quit her job with the florist and enrolled in the graduate program in art history that had brought her to Malcolm College of Knowledge.

Richard, meanwhile, waited to be discovered. He blamed his lack of success on bad timing. He had been seeking originality when the next big thing was copying older works and calling it Appropriation. He had missed the brief moment when reckless opportunists got famous fast by photographing their acts of self-mutilation in the name of performance art. He had taken no nudes, homoerotic or other. He had photographed his children, but not in provocative poses. He neither owned nor photographed large dogs.

Now he was forty. It was time to develop a name, a style, an identity beyond the generic black shirt and baseball hat that could describe any photographer in Manhattan. For ten years he had watched as Vivian, the facile popularizer, sailed home from her evening lectures so high from applause that she rarely got to sleep before midnight, while he endured the fate of the true artist, unappreciated in his time.

Richard had enough sense not to share this view with his wife, but he thought it often, especially when gazing at the samples of his art photography he had mounted on his studio wall. The only client who had ever mentioned them was a shoe manufacturer who had made it clear that his own product should have a classier presentation if Richard expected to get paid. On this particular morning, he was fingering a brochure advertising the International Exposition of Photography at Arles. If he registered by May 1, he would get a fifty-dollar discount. If he was one of the first hundred to send in his check, he would get his portfolio reviewed by a member of the curatorial panel. If pigs fly, he thought bitterly, I'll get to France this summer. Then the buzzer rang. It was the messenger service with another piece of shoddy merchandise for him to backlight so skillfully it would somehow look good enough to buy.

The Intersection of Commerce and Pastoral

VIVIAN PARKED in the underground lot of the Metropolitan Museum and walked out into the thin sunshine of Fifth Avenue in April. Clusters of exhausted tourists were already collapsing on the museum steps. Above them, a vividly blue banner of a shade never seen in the skies over Manhattan advertised the latest blockbuster show of Impressionist paintings.

My field, Vivian thought reflexively, pushing her way inside. Then she remembered. She didn't have a field anymore. She also didn't have a ticket, and only ticket holders could be admitted to the show. Those who were barred from seeing the real Impressionists often liked to visit the gift shop, according to the guard at the door.

How could they avoid it? In honor of the new exhibition, the already vast museum store had been enlarged to occupy even more of the main hall. A temporary annex had been constructed in a hallway that usually housed Greco-Roman funeral portraits. At the entrance was a large photograph of Hugo Bartello, curator of European painting and author of the catalog stacked on the table below. A screen on the other side showed the same man narrating the video tour, in which close-ups of paintings were matched with modern footage of the beaches, gardens, and color-drenched fields of an impossibly gorgeous France. Vivian studied his face, searching for something to hate in the suave, smooth-cheeked, enthusiastic features. Drawing a blank, she turned to study the merchandise.

The annex was crammed with every conceivable object that might bear or be an allusion to Impressionist art. Along with the usual posters, tote bags, cocktail napkins, and note cards, there were pot holders shaped like haystacks, pincushions silk-screened with Cézanne's apples, and refrigerator magnets imprinted with Renoir's nudes. There were seed packets designed to reproduce the famous gardens at Giverny (soil, sun, water, and gardeners not included), and a barometer that used a reproduction of van Gogh's sunflowers to indicate fair weather and Monet's water lilies to lend a pastel gloss to the possibility of rain. Tucked in a corner was a tiny metal table set with blue-and-yellow pottery whose pattern matched the hand-blocked cotton place mats. Leaning against a saucer was a writing portfolio covered in the same sublimely impractical pale, quilted cotton.

Dizzy from the scent of all the lavender sachet, Vivian began to fantasize. With all her heart she wished the gray actuality of Manhattan in April would melt away and she would find herself seated at precisely *that* green-painted café table, sipping coffee from precisely *that* blue-and-yellow cup, unfolding precisely *this* blue-flowered portfolio as (this was where the display tables, the guards, the shoppers, the great museum itself dissolved like a dream sequence in a sentimental movie) she glanced for one last moment over her very own vineyard before setting down today's brilliant insights on art, nature, and the meaning of life.

At that moment, Vivian was roused from her reverie by a clerk who asked, none too kindly, if she was planning to buy the portfolio she was stroking so fiercely. "Of course not," she snapped. "It's absurdly overpriced." And then, smiling seraphically, she swept out of the store.

She had had her vision.

Vivian's Vision

L IKE ALL GREAT ideas, Vivian's plan had the charm of extreme simplicity. She would rehash her lectures as a book,
stringing together her various disjointed observations on art and
politics as a feminist manifesto. The unifying thesis had come to
her in the museum gift shop. It went something like this:

1. Women had once been connected with the vital power of
the earth.

2. Culture had severed that connection.

3. The male-dominated hierarchy of professional artists had
worked to reinforce the division.

4. Women who bought art that depicted gardens (a category
which Vivian decided included everything from landscape paintings to flower-printed lampshades) were struggling to restore
their ancient bond.

5. In so doing, they were contributing money to their own oppression.

Driving back through Central Park, rushing to get home before she forgot her train of ideas, Vivian tried to picture the broad
outlines of her proposal. As she envisioned it, her book would be
intellectual but not academic (here she mentally excused herself
from the chore of footnotes), insightful but not definitive (here
the burden of biographical research fell away). Most important,
it would be extremely popular. After all, she would be combining
the three big interests of contemporary book buyers: sex, garden-
ing, and the recovery of the primal self.

As the road slanted upward, out of the sylvan paradise and
back to the concrete reality of modern-day Manhattan, she con-

sidered the link between nature and female sexuality, and how to turn it to a profit. Her approach would be feminist, of course. Her attitude would be confrontational, her language righteously vulgar, but with enough classical references thrown in to show that she was really very learned.

Pulling into her monthly parking space, Vivian rammed her tote bag on her shoulder and began the six-block hike to her apartment. As she walked, she made a mental outline of her chapters. She would begin with sex. Sex was basic. Sex was necessary. And yet sex was also the problem. Women were being denied the ancient power of their own fertility. Worse, they were being taught to buy the emblems of male oppression and hang them on the refrigerator door.

That was where she would swerve into her examples from French painting. The orchards and mountains that had once been accepted as Cézanne's sentimental homage to an agrarian ideal would now stand revealed as instruments of patriarchal oppression. Pissarro's farms would deconstruct to show the bleak connection between agriculture and hysterectomy. The female earth, besmirched by the male gaze (in complicity with the obviously phallic paintbrush), would turn in upon itself in a rejection of power politics that would lead to the deliberately sterile industrial landscapes of the next generation. Plus all that stuff she did every fall on Monet's seed stock and van Gogh's fields. And then, in conclusion, she would come back to sex. The ladies of New Jersey ate it right up. Why shouldn't everybody else?

Fate Cooperates

THE HARTS were people much influenced by random chance. Vivian took it as natural, then, when *The New York Review of Books,* folded neatly in her mailbox, offered exactly the opportunity she sought. "Ideal sabbatical retreat in the South of France," the ad whispered from the middle of the classified page. "Rustic farmhouse amid fields of lavender, 3 BR, swimming pool, family car, central location. Available June to December."

Nearly identical ads appeared in every issue of *The New York Review of Books.* Ordinarily, Vivian regarded them with the same suspicion she gave to the listings of Divorced White Males who were looking for intellectual companionship but seemed more curious about their future soul mates' height and weight.

This ad, however, was different. It spoke directly to *her,* Vivian Hart, in tones both dulcet and direct, telling her it was an opportunity not to be missed. In addition, it rubbed suggestively against another classified in the adjacent column seeking a three-bedroom Manhattan sublet for a German lawyer and his family. Two solutions within two inches of type. Snake eyes. Kismet. This was something that was meant to be.

Vivian imagined their half year in Provence. She would shut herself in a whitewashed bedroom and write with a broad-nibbed pen, just like Colette — though of course she would write about art as well as sex. She knew she would never get anything done if she just sat on West Eighty-sixth Street and waited for inspiration to come. To find the true power of Gaia and show how it had been suppressed by Impressionist painting, she needed to experience the landscape of France directly. She needed to smell the heady aroma of the vineyards, to feel the hard, bright sun of Provence, to find out where van Gogh was standing when he cut off his ear and what it was like to wake every morning, or at least one morning, in the shadow of Mont Ste-Victoire. If she could spend some time in the South of France, savoring the true essence of the Provençal sun and wind and soil, she was sure she could get a book finished. By the end of six months, she would have produced something that would make her rich and famous. Then she would be ready to come home.

The rest of the family would benefit, too. Richard would get away from alcoholic ad directors and rediscover pure photography. He was always talking about how limiting it was to do catalog shoots when his soul was out there on the cutting edge of art. Six months with no distractions would be the making of him. He could sell things to *Aperture*, or *Artforum*, or *Spin*. He could diversify his portfolio, find a gallery, get denounced on the floor of the Senate. It would be his breakthrough. He could find a better agent. He could become an artist.

For the children, it would be the opportunity of a lifetime. They would learn a second language (always an asset) and discover the joy of amusing themselves in the vastness of nature. Lily, a shy second-grader who lived in terror of lightning storms, shadows, loud noises, public events, and especially an imaginary ogre she called Lion Man, would learn to relax. Justin would lose his eleven-year-old swagger and get over his addiction to television cop shows. In September they would enroll at the little schoolhouse opposite the village church, where they would form lifelong friendships with their simple, rustic neighbors. Instead of taking field trips to the Museum of Natural History, they could run barefoot through reality.

The only real issue was money. Vivian did some quick mental calculations. Richard had just gotten paid for that shoe company's Christmas catalog. Their seven-room apartment, stabilized at the 1946 rent of $134 a month, could be quietly sublet for at least $3,000. That should be enough to squeak through till the end of the year. Considering what they would save by not sending the kids to Camp Ticonderoga or paying fall semester tuition at their ridiculously expensive school, they might even come out ahead. Exalted and determined, Vivian waited for her unsuspecting family to return home for the news.

The Co-conspirators

W HEN VIVIAN introduced the idea of going to France, she treated her sudden joblessness as a wonderful convenience. Now that she was free from the academic grind, they should seize the chance to have some fun. Who knew when they would have another opportunity?

It was the same old carpe diem argument people have been tossing out for centuries to justify all sorts of foolish self-indulgence, but it fell on fertile soil. Richard was already dreaming of Arles; he could hardly wait to send in his check and win the free consultation with a world-renowned curator. Justin had had his bicycle stolen from under his nose, right around the corner on West Eighty-sixth Street, and asked in a hopeful voice if they still used the guillotine on criminals in France. Lily wanted to stay home and play Barbies with her friend Martha, but she was too young to have a real voice in the matter. In half an hour, it was settled. They were going to France.

Once the decision was made, the practical details were surprisingly easy. Three days of harried negotiations with a tight-fisted French geologist currently at the University of Chicago left them the proud tenants of a fully updated stone farmhouse in Provence. They would be living in the historic village of St-Etang, apparently too tiny to be listed in any of Vivian's guidebooks but described by the geologist as offering easy access to urban centers while being conveniently close to the celebrated hill towns of tourist dreams. The house came with swimming pool, a groundskeeper, and a car waiting for them at the airport in Marseilles. They would arrive in the middle of June, so Vivian could experience the full intensity of the summer sun, and stay until the end of December, time enough for Richard to photograph the hidden Provence after the tourists had left. An art director who moonlighted as a photography dealer gave Richard a hundred rolls of film in return for first refusal on any work the trip produced. An extremely young woman at an extremely large literary agency boasted she could fax a contract overnight if she liked the sample draft of Vivian's book. The German lawyer didn't even blink at the rent or the stipulation that he keep his name off the mailbox.

With airy smiles that were supposed to excuse rudeness, Vivian announced to all their friends and relatives that they would not be receiving any guests. Six months of isolation and hard work. Everyone agreed it would be idyllic, but they would have to have a wonderful New Year's Eve party to make up for not entertaining in France.

The Village

IN THE OFFICE of the Truck Stop St-Etang, Didier Renard answered the telephone with some impatience.

"*Oui, allô*," he barked, watching through the gas station window as his red-haired giant of a daughter took a credit card from a car with Paris plates. Idiot. She should have demanded cash. Now he would have to pay the commission.

Allô, allô," he repeated, while a distant voice began to answer his first response. The only person whose calls came with a satellite delay was his brother Antoine, the brains of the family. Before he understood the words, he knew that the old dump of a place was rented.

"Didier," his brother repeated. "C'est moi, Antoine. I am freezing my ass in Chicago, but the rate of exchange continues to treat me well. Please embrace your family for me. I have arranged for the house to be rented, starting June fifteenth. It is a family of four, from New York. Do me the favor of airing the place before then, and remove anything of value. You know these Americans, they will steal the very rocks out of the fields if you let them. I leave it to you to choose a car for their arrival."

Didier Renard wrote down all the necessary information, his good humor restored. He had provided many cars to his brother's tenants over the years, starting with the first ancient Deux Chevaux he had sold and then refused to buy back when the lease was over. They had left it, of course, a wheezing hulk not worth hauling back to wherever they had come from. Since then, the sorriest junker stranded at his garage had been included in the rental, brought back just to the brink of life and towed down to meet the latest unsuspecting tenant at the airport. The drive from Marseilles always convinced the new arrivals that they could afford to rent another car for the duration of their stay.

"But of course. I will be happy to help them. And Marianne will show them around."

This was Renard's favorite joke. His wife had not crossed the boundaries of the truck stop parking lot for the last eight years. For one thing, she had grown undeniably fat, and it hurt her ankles to go further. For another, there was nowhere else she wanted to be. The world came to her door, and after her loving husband installed the television and the satellite dish, she had no need to leave.

In any case, there would have been little to show her new neighbors. St-Etang had existed since at least the first century B.C., when Caesar himself had commented on the brutish customs of the locals, but it had become a ghost town after all thirty-four of the village's adult men were killed in the Second World War. The widows and children had migrated, en masse, to Marseilles, the closest place that could accommodate a hundred extra hungry mouths in those lean days of 1945. In the 1970s, the new superhighway, the Autoroute du Soleil, destroyed what little of the village had not already gone to ruin. The construction foreman spared a single farmhouse to use as his office and a dormitory for his crew. It was this building, the sole remnant of the ancient hamlet, that the Harts had rented.

Didier and Antoine Renard were grandsons of St-Etang. Their mother had been part of the move to Marseilles in her youth, but she had always told her boys that the village would one day rise again. When they began to build the superhighway that connected Paris with the South of France, Antoine had first shown his gift for negotiation by persuading the construction foreman to rent the family farmhouse. Didier had decided to profit in a different way. Borrowing money from the displaced children of the old village, now elderly themselves, he had returned to the land of his ancestors to build a roadside oasis of gas station, restaurant, and two-room brothel. While the workmen were still pouring the concrete for the owner's apartment nestled behind the restaurant, he courted and married the daughter of the baker in the nearest village, a place linked to St. Etang through two millennia of intermarriage. The next year Clotilde, their only child, was born.

Twenty years later, Renard felt deeply rooted in St-Etang. He was blessed with a steady business, no permanent neighbors, a hardworking daughter, and a faithful if rather overweight wife. And despite the continued payments to his Marseilles backers, he was also getting rich. It was, altogether, a very pleasant dry dock he had chosen, so far from the harbor of his native port. And now he had the prospect of additional entertainment with the arrival of the tenants across the way.

The Welcome

GABRIELLE RENARD, daughter of the absent Antoine, waited in the lounge of the Marseilles airport with the sullen serenity that only a teenager can maintain. As she sat, she ran her palms over the backs of her calves. She was wondering if she should invest in one of those electric depilatory devices that pulls hairs out by the roots. She had heard an ad for one on the radio just before she left her mother's apartment in Marseilles; on the way back she would get off the bus downtown and see what they cost. For now she would simply sit and enjoy the air-conditioning, a luxury which her parents discussed every summer but had no intention of buying.

The connecting flight from Paris had arrived ten minutes ago, so she supposed the Americans would be emerging soon. They would be tired, she knew, and relieved to find she had come to meet them, though that wouldn't last long once they saw the car. In the two years she had been old enough to drive, she had become accustomed to the routine. Her job was to receive the car from her uncle Didier, get it to the airport, meet her father's latest tenants, escort them to the parking garage, and hand them the keys. The first time she had been so abashed at their reaction she had run to the kiosk and bought them a map from her own money. Now she was hardened. If they did not like the car, they could walk to St-Etang. How long it took them was their affair.

Shifting in her plastic chair, she watched the first arrivals come through the door. Businesspeople in their suits, grandmothers visiting for the summer, a party of students on some sort of school trip, and then, quite obviously, the people she was to meet. A fat man with all sorts of things bulging out of the pockets of his silly safari vest, a pale, bedraggled woman who could have used some lipstick, a dark-eyed boy whose socks did not match, and a little blond girl whose hair very much needed combing. Who but Americans would travel with such complete lack of style?

"Madame 'Art-ee?" she asked, dropping the initial consonant and adding an extra syllable at the end to show she was a loyal daughter of Provence. It was entirely an affectation, since the schoolteachers of Marseilles were uniformly strict in rooting out the country intonations of the Provençal dialect, but she thought it gave her speech a certain regional charm. Dimly, Gabrielle sensed she needed every charm she could muster. "Madame 'Artee? Please come. I go to show you your car."

As the girl had anticipated, the Harts were tired, disoriented, and extremely relieved to find her there. Justin hadn't slept at all on the flight from New York and then had thrown up in the main terminal of Charles de Gaulle Airport as they ran to make their connecting flight to Marseilles. In the confusion of finding him clean clothes, Vivian had lost the carry-on bag containing her three most useful guidebooks, the ones too essential to check through with the luggage. Lily, already disturbed by the strange arrival of daylight so much earlier than her body expected, was in the midst of a panic attack brought on by the realization that people here spoke much faster than the nice lady who taught French at school. Craving protection, she had insisted they stop at a Disney kiosk in the Paris airport and buy a long-brimmed baseball hat featuring the guileless eyes and floppy ears of Goofy. Her tantrum had not endeared her to her father, who had passed the night drinking cognac with the man across the aisle. During the entire flight from Paris to Marseilles, Richard had been click-ing his tongue, always a sign of extreme annoyance. By the time they emerged into the airport lounge, he sounded like a danger-ous parcel, the kind you call the police to open.

None of this was known by Gabrielle, but the combination of misadventures had produced precisely the state of woozy confusion by which she had expected to recognize her party. Just as predictably, their relief turned to horror when they saw what had been described to them as a family car. Uncle Didier had outdone himself this year. He had come down last weekend, towing a battered Renault in which some game-hunting owner had replaced the backseat with a rough wooden crate, perfect for hiding out-of-season quail but rather uncomfortable for passengers. There was a large vent in the roof, apparently sculpted with pruning shears, and only half a steering wheel. From beneath the chassis dangled several pieces of frayed rope, probably all that was holding the heap together. Personally, Gabrielle was looking forward to taking the bus back into town.

Richard had already pushed his way to the front of the family group, ready to assume his rightful position as leader of this expedition. As he realized where this unattractive young woman was leading them, he motioned to Vivian and the children to halt while he proceeded alone to meet the enemy. Silent and grim, he circled the vehicle, searching his somewhat rusty French for the best translation of the vivid phrases that were springing to mind.

Staring at the rusty holes that showed where a rear bumper should have been attached, he flung down his suitcase and turned on Gabrielle, ready to launch a bilingual tirade. The girl was looking off to the left, twirling a piece of hair over her shoulder, as round and impassive as the cement pillar next to which she stood.

Richard sighed. She was but a tool, a mindless agent of evil. Her father, the diabolical villain who had listed this car as one of the additional assets of his farmhouse, was safe in Chicago. If Richard didn't take this car, which was included in the rent he had already paid, he would have to either find another at some ruinous price or spend several hundred dollars on a taxi to take them all into the country — where they would then be stranded for the rest of the summer. Snatching the keys from Gabrielle's outstretched palm, he slammed the suitcases into the wooden box, hoisted Lily and Justin on top, and piled the backpacks and duffels around them.

Vivian climbed into the passenger seat. Clicking steadily, Richard handed her his camera bag and turned what was left of the steering wheel in the direction of the exit. Vivian leaned out to say good-bye to Gabrielle, but the girl had already made her escape.

Sunday Afternoon in the Country

THE AFTERNOON HEAT is brutal in June in Provence, and the Harts drove through the worst of it after they left the airport. Dust swirled up through the broken floor of the old Renault. The sun beat down through the jagged hole in the roof.

Sweaty and apprehensive, his head pounding in unison with the bouncing wooden box on which his precious children perched uncushioned and unbelted, Richard navigated the peculiar desolation of industrial suburbs on a Sunday afternoon. If he abandoned the clutch and pressed both feet on the gas pedal, he could get up to sixty kilometers per hour, almost half the speed limit. It would have to do.

According to the directions sent from Chicago, they were to drive north on the main highway, the Autoroute du Soleil, for precisely ninety minutes, until they saw the sign for St-Etang. From there, the landlord assured them, they would know where to go. As they began to cross a flat plain covered with vast plantings of immature crops, Richard willed himself to stay awake. Three hours later, they arrived.

Even from the highway, they had no trouble recognizing the farmhouse. It looked just like the photograph: a low stone building dominated by a broad tile roof, the clay tiles bleached down to a warm coral color that was radiant against the flowering lavender in the surrounding fields.

Yes, that was definitely their house. Reaching it, however, was another matter. There was the road sign: ST-ETANG. Across the highway was a gas station: TRUCK STOP ST-ETANG. But where was the exit for the farmhouse? Richard took one foot off the gas,

increasing their already excellent prospects for a rear-end colli-
sion, but there was nothing to see beyond an unbroken expanse
of fields.

"We must have missed it," he said finally. "I'll turn around at
the next chance."

Fifteen kilometers later they saw their first sign since St-Etang.
It was nothing but a blue circle with rays around it, like a child's
drawing of the sun, but it was followed directly by a well-paved
stretch of asphalt leading off to the right, so Richard turned in.
Almost at once, they jerked to a halt at the locked gate of a tall
chain-link fence. Vivian opened the car door so she would have
room to unfold the map.

"There's St-Etang," she said after a moment, pointing to the
spot she had circled in red marker back in Manhattan. "And this
must be where we are," she added. "See, that's the same mark as
there was on the road sign."

"So what does it mean?" Richard asked.

Vivian turned the Michelin map over to study the list of symbols on the back. "The sunburst mark indicates a *Fabbria*. No,
wait, that's the Italian version. Let's see. *Kraftwerk* . . . the English
must be here somewhere." Folding the map in another direction,
she readjusted her sunglasses and tried again. "Here we are!"

"Where?" asked Justin and his father together.

"It says right here, 'factory, power station.' That's what the sunburst sign means!"

Triumphant in her discovery, Vivian beamed at the children in
the backseat. Lily was sleeping , her little face mashed into a suitcase. Justin looked back at her, tired and confused.

"Are we living at a power station?" he asked.

Richard grabbed the map and studied it himself, clicking furiously. "We must have missed it," he announced again. "There's
nothing ahead for a good two inches."

Vivian stared at the chain-link fence, at least four feet away.

"On the map!" Richard snapped. "Two inches on the map. You
figure it out in kilometers. I'm turning around."

Home

THEY MISSED ST-ETANG again in the other direction, where the only exit dead-ended into the truck stop they had seen before. Passing it, Richard then had to go another twenty kilometers before he could turn around in a bedraggled little town with the inappropriate name of La Baronnerie. The third time they approached the house, Richard simply drove off the side of the highway, pushing the car through an open space in the tall grass that skirted the road and onto a narrow, unpaved road.

They were all jolted by the sudden transition from asphalt highway to hard-packed dirt. Richard hadn't even seen the ditch that ran along the side of the highway, much less braked for it, and the plank bridge provided a surprisingly hard bounce. For the first ten yards they were blinded by their own dust. Then, again, they were rewarded by their vision: the perfect farmhouse in Provence.

Coming closer, they could see the vine-roofed veranda running across the front of the building. On the second floor, a rustic array of windows was sealed against the sun with wooden shutters whose faded blue exactly matched the color of the summer sky. Richard pulled into a small, stone-paved courtyard, and they all sat for a moment, mesmerized by the colors. Ocher roof, blue shutters, walls the palest pink of fading blushes, deep purple flowers on the green vines over the veranda. On both sides of the house were rows and rows of lavender, converging in the distance like a child's exercise in perspective drawing.

"It's beautiful," Vivian sighed. "It looks . . ." She hesitated, searching for the right words. "It looks just like a picture."

Richard, fingering his camera bag, debated between Koda-chrome film, better at capturing reds and yellows, and Ekta-chrome for the blues and greens. Lily fluttered her eyes briefly, then fell back asleep, breathing heavily through her open mouth. Justin, hot and carsick, stuck his head through the gash in the roof.

"I'm trapped!" he shouted. "Let me outta here! I wanna watch TV!"

Another Artist

GLANCING OUT his office window, Didier Renard noticed a new cloud low on the horizon. Rain was out of the question at this time of year, so it must be dust. This was a good sign. Usually the arriving tenants came to his truck stop for directions, necessitating awkward explanations and often causing an unpleasant scene in front of his other customers. These people had managed to find the road by themselves. A very good sign. Their timing was also excellent. He could finish his paintings before he went across the road.

Renard devoted himself to art for thirty minutes every Sunday afternoon. His routine was always the same. As soon as the midday rush had cleared in the café, he retreated to his office, where he pinned a large sheet of the cheapest variety of watercolor paper to a board. Using a long wooden ruler he kept for this purpose, he then divided the paper into one hundred rectangles, each the size of a standard plastic credit card. He was ready to paint.

Loading a fat sable bush with marine blue, Renard swept an uneven wash of color across the top third of each of his ten rows of little rectangles. Another brush was used to sweep the rest of each row with a pale clay wash mixed from ocher and permanent rose. Turning back to the first brush, he then started at the midpoint of each rectangle and sketched six lumpy stripes fanning out below the vanishing point. As blue stripe met clay ground, the damp paints ran together, and the stripes turned interesting shades of lavender and olive green.

Five minutes in front of the electric fan dried the paper and gave Renard a chance to check on the bar. Returning to his office, he would then load his thinnest brush with dark brown paint and place a tiny gnarled tree on each horizon line, transforming the blurry rectangles into minute images of vineyards and fields. Then he would lean the board against the side of his desk while he turned to the business of the account books.

Every Wednesday, a dull-witted cousin of his wife, Marianne, came to the garage to cut the sheet into individual pictures and glue them to the postcard-size mat boards Renard bought pre-punched from the box factory in Apt. In the afternoon, as she watched her television programs, Marianne would scrawl an artistic looking signature on the mat board, clip the mounted painting to a rectangle of picture glass, and wrap it in tissue. Then on Thursdays, always slow at the café, Renard loaded his Peugeot 406 with carefully inventoried deliveries for the more elegant tourist boutiques of the area, where his charming watercolor landscapes sold quite well for fifty francs each. Renard charged only half that amount to the store owner, but at a hundred little paintings a week, this left a comfortable profit margin even after he had covered his costs. It was also helping him stop smoking, which Marianne assured him was the modern, sexy thing to do.

Finishing his Sunday ritual of creation, Renard stepped outside to visit the new tenants. As he glanced back to be sure he had closed the office door, he had a true aesthetic vision. Reduced to the size of a fingernail, the gas station would look like a shepherd's hut. To make it clear, he would put some sheep in the foreground. A few drops of clear water, removing the wash, should give the right effect, with four tiny dark lines to indicate legs.

It was wonderful to live at the dawn of the twenty-first century, he thought, fastening his seat belt for the short but perilous journey across the superhighway. If people hadn't gotten used to accepting fuzzy little sketches as finished art, he would have lacked sufficient skill to pursue this particular sideline.

The Neighbors

O NCE THEY PRIED themselves out of the car, the Hart family huddled, dazed and sweating, under the shade of the lone oak tree shielding the front of the house.

"Go see what's in back," Richard suggested to the children, after they had all caught their breath. "But don't fall in the swimming pool." As Lily and Justin stumbled off, he turned to Vivian. "Do you think there is a swimming pool? Or is it just another fraud, like this so-called family car?"

Vivian didn't answer. She was staring at the farmhouse. Slowly she walked across the stone-paved courtyard, back to the dirt lane that had led them so abruptly from the highway. If she stood there and looked at the property, as the owner had when taking photographs, she saw a rustic stone *mas,* the traditional farmhouse of Provence, surrounded by equally traditional fields of lavender. A gentle slope of grapevines stretched up behind it and, beyond that, the low, white hills of the Luberon.

In the other direction, it was a different story. Moving slowly, as though to give the view a chance to change, Vivian turned until her back was to the farmhouse. All remained as it had been the last time she looked. Their picture-book rental sat squarely by the side of a six-lane highway that sported mileage signs for every major shipping depot from Hamburg to Naples. On the other side of the highway was the only other structure visible in any direction, a large gas station topped by an even larger neon sign inviting travelers to pull into the TRUCK STOP ST-ETANG. Smaller letters below offered the added enticements of RESTAU-

RANT, BAR, and MASSAGE EXOTIQUE. A clever turnaround lane, a sort of figure eight inserted in the center of the highway, made it possible to reach the truck stop from either direction.

As though in response to her inspection, a shiny black Peugeot suddenly left the truck stop, looped the figure eight at high speed, bounced over the ditch, and continued up the dirt road. It was Monsieur Didier Renard, bringing the keys.

He had seen their arrival, he explained in rapid, heavily accented French, shaking hands without removing his cigarette from between his fingers. He had come to unlock the doors, to show them the location of the generator and the gas tank for the refrigerator, to explain the septic system, and to offer them any other service to make them welcome.

"Where's the town?" Vivian demanded.

She hadn't meant to be so abrupt, but there it was. St-Etang was listed on her Michelin map of Provence. In very small letters, but listed. It existed on the road sign. The landlord had assured her she would be able to buy all her provisions from the merchants outside her very door. So where was the town?

"The town?" Monsieur Renard echoed, with an expression of exaggerated incredulity. "But you are in the country! That is the point of the vacation, no?"

"How far is it to St-Etang?" Vivian persisted.

Renard shrugged. "In a manner of speaking, you are there. But then again. . . ."

"You mean there is no town?" By this time Vivian was almost shrieking.

"St-Etang was a sacrifice to the autoroute," Renard conceded. "The people had left anyway, so it was not so difficult a decision."

Perhaps she had misunderstood, or asked her question in the wrong tense. Giving a lecture at Malcolm College of Knowledge, Vivian could send her audience into a collective swoon with the Gallic quack she gave to the pronunciation of names like Renoir and Cézanne, but in truth her French was limited to four years of high school study, supplemented by an occasional foreign movie. Usually this was a source of secret embarrassment. Now it was a glimmer of hope.

"*St-Etang n'existe pas?*" she asked, pronouncing each syllable with care.

"*Non plus,*" Renard agreed cheerfully. "Me, I'm the boss here. Me, my wife, my daughter, we are St-Etang. And you, too," he added, graciously extending native status to the newcomers.

"But how can we live? Where can I do my shopping?" Vivian asked plaintively. How would she have time to become one with the land if she had to go all over creation just for groceries?

"Ah, the shopping," Renard answered. "But that is very simple. Every day the trucks come to my station. The baker's truck comes each morning at six thirty. The butcher comes every Tuesday and Friday. The poulterer comes Tuesday as well and brings the eggs, too. Wednesday and Saturday are the days of the vegetables and fruits, though in truth I would recommend that you go to Oppède-le-Percée for the farmers' market Saturday morning." Turning to Richard, he explained, "You get more selection, and also you can sample the wines."

Then he resumed his calendar of commercial arrivals, ticking them off on his fingers. "On Thursday there is the truck for all the little necessities of the kitchen, and on Friday the postal truck makes a longer stop, if you want to send a package for which you do not have the proper stamps. Gas, of course, you come to me, and also I hope you will try our restaurant. Not on Saturday night, however." Monsieur Renard glanced at Lily's pink backpack, which was lying on the ground. "If you bring the children, it is perhaps not the proper atmosphere then, when we have many clients who are relaxing at the end of the week. But now let me show you your home, where I think you will be very satisfied. And then I must go back to my business. The customer does not wait."

The Perfect Farmhouse in Provence

OUTSIDE, THERE WAS a blazing afternoon sun and long acres of fragrant green and purple bushes. Inside, the stone house had a dank, moldy smell, like the memory of a flood. It was also dark. Somewhere deep in Vivian's consciousness, a recollection stirred. When Colette had retreated to that whitewashed bedroom in the South of France, she'd applied the paint herself so it would be bright enough for her to see her papers.

Scattering cigarette ashes with every gesture, Renard started the tour upstairs with two dormitory-style bedrooms, each furnished with enough bunks to sleep eight, and a functional tiled bath with two toilets and two showers, none of them enclosed.

On the ground floor was another full bath, built into an alcove of a small room almost entirely filled by a gigantic brass bed that Richard suspected had first seen service in the "massage exotique" across the way. The main room, long and low, held nothing but a dusty purple futon facing the immense stone fireplace, six plastic lawn chairs, and a large trestle table with matching benches pushed up against the opposite wall.

Next they were introduced to the kitchen, whose pitted Formica counters and weary orange vinyl chairs were hailed by Monsieur Renard as a miracle of modern efficiency. Then came the hot-water system, which was really very easy to use once you understood the functions of the various meters. Reaching under the kitchen sink, Renard pulled out a small carton of what appeared to be scouring pads but turned out to be chlorine tablets for the pool. "Put one in the water every week," he instructed.

"The children will enjoy the water sports. And now I say good-bye."

Richard went to see him off. Vivian sat at the kitchen table and held a brief memorial service for her fond hopes and reasonable expectations. There would be no delightful breakfasts of steaming coffee and hot chocolate in the local café, for the simple reason that there was no local café, unless you counted a truck stop bar. There would be no pleasant chats with the local shopkeepers, or family dinners with the parents of Justin's and Lily's new friends. There would be no friends. The nearest settlements, let alone schools, were fifteen kilometers in either direction. Even the fields were not theirs to enjoy. They had been rented out to a farmer from Apt, who thus qualified as their "groundskeeper." Just last month, Renard informed them, the farmer had been acquitted of stabbing a tourist caught clipping some lavender from his field. He mentioned the trial twice. Vivian got the hint.

Nor was the farmhouse entirely what they had been led to expect from the photographs of the exterior. Instead of the Provençal cottons which should have draped the kitchen windows, there were dinghy nylon curtains imported from China. The original flagstone floor had been replaced with orange and brown vinyl tiles, worn in ways that clearly showed the favorite routes of previous occupants. The cabinets were some kind of laminate meant to imitate old oak, with wrought-iron hardware that nurtured twenty-odd years of accumulated cooking grease.

The first-floor bathroom, visible from both the kitchen and the salon, had its own, equally hideous decor. The sink and toilet were both made of some opalescent pink synthetic substance that matched the wall panels but not the mustard brown ceramic tub. The shower curtain was a darker shade of pink, with a floral pattern stamped in the plastic. Turning her head, Vivian noticed the living room curtains seemed to be made of the same material. She would have to go see, as soon as she regained her strength. In the meantime, she fingered the box of chlorine tablets, which were manufactured in California. "Use 3 to 6 tablets per day, to prevent the growth of algae and other disease-harboring organisms." Renard had recommended one tablet per week.

Vivian wondered bleakly what disease-harboring organisms were native to the region, and how soon it would take the children to develop recognizable symptoms. Then, more abruptly, she remembered Lily could not swim. Ignoring the cobwebs, she pushed open the back door. There was another rough-stone terrace. Beyond was an actual swimming pool, green with slime. Rushing across the terrace, Vivian peered into the depths. It was hard to tell, but the scum seemed undisturbed. Running back to the kitchen, she grabbed the household broom, sweeping the surface for a better look at the bottom. There was some strange stuff down there, but nothing that looked like a person. Relieved, she dropped the broom and started to call for her missing offspring.

"Justin? Lily? Justin! Lily!" Racing around the house, she crashed into Richard.

"Holy shit," he exclaimed, rubbing his arm where she had rammed him into the wall of the house. "They're in the car. They hate it here," he added. "They want to go home." Then he told her his good news. Monsieur Renard was willing to rent them a larger, newer car for not much money, as well as overhaul the original clunker so it would shift out of second gear. Surveying their isolation and weighing the charms of six months of total togetherness, Richard thought two cars sounded like a good idea.

Shopping

Over time, angry disappointment gave way to the more tempered emotion of resignation. The first day, they had been too tired to find another place to live. The second day, they had been shocked by the prices advertised for better-located vacation houses. The third day, Didier Renard had brought over some patio furniture and assured them that his brother, from whom he himself was completely estranged, was a stingy bastard who would never let them out of their lease.

For the better part of a week, the Harts moved through a haze of disbelief, the ghostly apparition of what they had expected lingering like a primal memory of a better world. Soon enough they settled into a routine — not as pleasant as the one they had imagined, but at least something that let them know where they were when they woke in the morning, in those few seconds of confusion when even the least introspective traveler feels beset by cosmic questions of identity. The rock upon which the Harts built their new reality became the trip to the nearest village, fifteen kilometers down the road.

Devoid in equal measure of natural beauty and historical significance, the village of Oppède-le-Percée had been spared the relentless commercialization of more attractive destinations in Provence. It offered no views or hiking trails, no Roman monuments or artistic festivals of any sort. It was neither picturesquely ruined nor fashionably renovated, and was too far from the highway to benefit from traffic. And so it remained what it had always been — a place one visited for business, not pleasure, populated by an ingrown society of people who had been born there and felt no pressing need to leave.

For the Harts, however, Oppède-le-Percée had the irresistible attraction of being the nearest commercial settlement of any kind. Their first visit was on the afternoon of their arrival, when the prospect of going without dinner pushed grocery shopping to the top of their agenda. Renard had provided directions, along with a caution that stores would open at four and close precisely at six. Monday they were back first thing in the morning, and then a second time for all the essentials they had forgotten on the earlier run, and then a third time because where else was there to go?

By Tuesday, the route was reassuringly familiar. Navigate the highway loop, exit at the truck stop, and take the local road that wandered off by the side of Renard's garage. Turn left at the wine co-op and right at the farm machinery dealer. Circle the old stone enclosure built in the sixteenth century for the annual shepherds' fair, now empty except for the Saturday farmers' market.

After the immense stone ruin, the streets narrowed quickly and the walls of Oppède-le-Percée shut off the view, until suddenly they were at the center of town, dominated by the blank facade of an undistinguished early Gothic church. The public laundry, once a center of community activity, had fallen into disrepair since the installation of water pipes some forty years before, but the public fountain, at the point where the single street branched in two directions, was still a gathering place of sorts.

When they had first come on the day of their arrival, there had been three old women seated on metal chairs around the fountain, hands folded, looking ready for whatever evil tidings the day might bring. The women had been there the next morning as well, and the next afternoon, and the day after. Richard referred to them as the Fates, which made no sense but seemed to amuse him. By the third visit Justin and Lily were allowed to stay by the fountain, watched by the Fates, while their parents wrung whatever charm they could from the brusque transactions of the local merchants. That was how the children met Marcel, standing in the doorway of his grandmother's house.

The Friend

MARCEL WAS A large, soft, amiable young man. He always wore the same long-sleeved undershirt and the same blue twill overalls, the waist hitched high over his round paunch so that he looked like a modern Tweedledee. A frayed piece of clothesline, his favorite toy, was never far from his hands. According to the baptism records, he was twenty-two. Mentally, he was the same age as Lily, and she was pulling ahead fast. He lived with his grandmother, who had cared for him since he was born. His mother had abandoned Marcel to marry a storekeeper in Avignon who knew nothing of the eternal child she had left at home. She never came to visit.

It didn't matter. Marcel was content with his life the way it was. He liked to stand in the doorway of his grandmother's house, watching the people going in and out of the bakery and feeling the morning sun on his face. Middays, when the stores were all closed for several hours, he would take long walks through the vineyards and into the forest, delivering messages to outlying houses along the way. Late afternoon found him back in his doorway. At night he sat with his grandmother and watched television, or else cut pictures of bicycle racers from the sporting magazines that people gave him. It was this skill that had persuaded his cousin Marianne to let him cut apart her husband's valuable watercolor efforts.

On Monday, Vivian had emerged from the bakery to find Lily trying to teach Marcel to use his clothesline to jump rope. On Tuesday they had played hopscotch, drawing squares in the hard-packed dirt in front of the fountain. On Wednesday morning

Justin had shown Marcel how to make a half-franc piece appear from behind Lily's ear. Or at least he had shown him that he, Justin, could do this. Marcel was never able to suspect a trick, much less master one.

Still, the children liked him. His slow, simple speech was much easier for them to understand than the French of most adults, and he never grew impatient with their many mistakes or omissions. They liked the grave seriousness with which he answered their questions, or showed them the various things he had collected on his walks, or simply stood in the sun, at ease with his idleness. Weighing enlightened social principles against maternal anxiety, Vivian told the children they could play with Marcel as long as they stayed within sight of the fountain. By then it was clear to all of them that Marcel was the only companion Justin and Lily were likely to find.

An Artistic Paradox

IT TOOK RICHARD one day to get used to the time change, two to get settled, and three to get bored. Tuesday afternoon, Renard had delivered a ten-year-old Citröen sedan whose major flaw was its very peculiar lime green color. As soon as they agreed on the terms, Richard handed the keys to Vivian with what he intended as a gallant bow. By this she understood that he would take the heap, as he called the first car, and be gone first thing in the morning. It was time to get to work.

Before they left New York, Richard had taken on a small photo assignment, just a little something to help them stay solvent until he and Vivian sold the breakthrough efforts they had come to France to produce. He was to provide the pictures for a desk calendar, page-a-week Scenes of Provence. The publisher was Extended Vistas, a West Coast outfit specializing in lavishly illustrated address books, diaries, and calendars for people who liked to hang around bookstores but preferred not to read. They were what his agent, Ken, called a Very Good Outlet. They were Money in the Bank.

Ken was right. Extended Vistas's offer was too good to refuse. The only wrinkle was the job order made it clear that the pictures had to be pretty.

This was a condition that gnawed at Richard's artistic principles. According to Richard, prettiness was available to any idiot with an automatic-focus camera. From the designated "photo spots" in theme parks to the bogus backdrops of his own studio, the whole search for prettiness was an exercise in lifeless, mechanical reproduction, the pursuit of an inauthentic ideal. It was exactly what he had come to France to escape.

True art, in contrast, had its own vitality, which Richard imagined as rising through a sort of spontaneous generation from the primal slime of man's grossest instincts and most mundane acts. Since art was life, and life, at least by Richard's definition, was not pretty, it followed that pretty pictures were not art. Therefore he was financing his search for artistic integrity by producing a work of anti-art.

Unable to resolve this paradox, he had decided to get the calendar over with as fast as possible. By Tuesday, he had already photographed the farmhouse from every conceivable angle. As Vivian had suspected when he gave her the keys to the new car, he was planning to hit the road.

Stalking the Picturesque

THAT NIGHT, Richard plotted his route. After some browsing through the guidebooks, he settled on two locations, chosen because they suggested the highest clichés of sentimental tourism. In the damning words of the guidebook, both were very picturesque.

Tomorrow he would go to Les Baux-de-Provence, an ancient hilltop fortress that had become a tourist center after the local bauxite mines had stopped bringing in a profit. Thursday he would set out in the opposite direction for Roussillon, another mountain citadel whose fortifications had been breached by tourist barbarians. Friday he would get the film developed and see how much longer he had to pollute himself with this garbage.

Richard liked to eat a big breakfast on days he was going out in the field. That way he could miss lunch if necessary — a fate that had never yet befallen him but for which he liked to be prepared. Now that he was in France, he also felt he should start the day like other workmen, with a shot of brandy at the truck stop bar. It was midmorning before he reached Les Baux-de-Provence and found a space amid the tour buses in the parking lot at the bottom of the hill.

Once he had climbed to the village proper, Richard quickly realized that Les Baux was as much a ghost town as St-Etang, although considerably more crowded. From the priest's house to the pigpen, every enclosure of the original village had been vacated to make way for boutiques where modern-day worshipers of the picturesque could purchase plastic-wrapped reminders of rural occupations they themselves had driven out of business. At every crumbling door stood a true citizen of Provence, selling burlap bags stuffed with dried rosemary or glass rolling pins filled with lavender and wrapped with colorful ribbons. Cotton place mats and tablecloths, printed from the original eighteenth-century wood blocks of the Souleiado company and therefore priced slightly higher than cloth of gold, spilled from shelves mounted in what appeared to be a former horse stall. Traffic on the narrow pedestrian walkway, the only thoroughfare, could be stopped entirely by a single disagreement over the correct change.

Jammed into a corner by a slow-moving group of Japanese shoppers, Richard picked up a plastic "camera" from a tray of souvenirs a child was hawking. By holding the toy up to his eye, he could see a different local scene every time he clicked the "shutter." Six in all, each prettier than the last. He considered buying it, smashing the case to get at the transparencies inside, and sending them directly to Extended Vistas for their calendar. Shaking off the thought, he decided to get on with the job and get out of town as quickly as he could.

Sidestepping a stout German couple in matching shirts advertising an Italian bicycle company, Richard leaned over a stone parapet to photograph a ginger cat sunning itself on a blue-painted windowsill. Then he shot a roll of close-ups of the door-way just beyond his elbow, its splintering wood held together with massive, rusting iron bolts. That accomplished, he ducked down a relatively empty path that led to the old church grave-yard. There were supposed to be some Saracen tombs there. Maybe they would be pretty.

Just outside the stone wall of the churchyard was a small store. Judging from the window display, it apparently served the few remaining residents of the area, selling the humdrum necessities of life. Instead of postcards and calico packets of herbs, the window displayed six rolls of toilet paper, several pairs of faded cotton socks, a cardboard rack of disposable lighters, a book of blank receipt forms, and a strangely familiar pink box.

"It's Barbie," Richard exclaimed in a tone of pleased surprise, as though recognizing an old friend. "It's Barbie, right here in Provence." Feeling better than he had all morning, he stepped inside and bought the doll for Lily, then matched it with a dusty but functioning remote control race car for Justin. He even remembered to ask for batteries. Cupping his hand to receive his change, he felt cleansed of the burden of tourist perspective. Newly optimistic, he walked over to the cemetery to get the pictures he had come for.

First, however, he had to check out the doll. Three years ago, when Lily made her first trip to the dentist, he had bought her a toy to console her for the terrible experience of letting some brute stranger pick her tiny, perfect teeth. "Here's a special Barbie just for my brave little girl," he had told Lily. "Barbie goes to the dentist, too." So of course she tore open the box to see her eleven-inch plastic alter ego, and, first thing, its head fell off. It took him months to appreciate how funny it had been when Lily went flying out of the room screaming, "She's demented! She's demented." Justin must have taught her that word. Since then, he inspected every purchase.

Sliding his thumb under the pink cardboard latch, Richard pulled out the molded plastic tray and undid the twist ties that anchored the doll to her perch. This one was wearing a pink leotard and some kind of frilly skirt with sparkles. "Ma Première Barbie," it said on the box. My first Barbie. For Lily it would be maybe her thirty-first, but that was okay. Everything seemed to be in working order.

Arranging the doll's arms over its head and its legs in a gymnast's split, Richard perched it on a stone tablet carved with somebody's coat of arms. Barbie could be his muse. Under the doll's blue, unblinking stare he photographed the churchyard, the town, the sky, the road, and everything in between. He even took several pictures of Barbie before trudging back uphill for more "pretty" views of the village. Five rolls, he thought with satisfaction. That should help keep the sentimental bastards happy.

Because Art Is a Lonely Calling

THE NEXT DAY Richard drove north to Roussillon, his second candidate for Provence's most insipidly pretty hilltop village. Where Les Baux was a study in gray and white, an austere backdrop that made a window box of geraniums look like an explosion of color, everything in Roussillon had the ruddy glow of a perpetual sunset. According to one of the two guidebooks Vivian had managed not to lose, the hills took their deep red color from the blood of the Lady Seramonde, who had leaped to her death from the castle tower after being tricked into eating her murdered lover's heart. This had happened sometime in the Middle Ages, as far as Richard could tell. What a mopey dame, he thought.

The other, less romantic book heralded the area as a smaller version of the American Grand Canyon. Much smaller, Richard decided, peering over the railing that rimmed the municipal parking lot. It would take maybe five minutes to hike to the bottom.

The one thing both books agreed on was that Roussillon hadn't always been as dramatically perched as it was today. Once upon a time, back in the days of Seramonde and her complicated love life, the village sat at the summit of a normal hill. Starting in the seventeenth century, though, the residents had mined the hillside to sell its seventeen shades of ocher clay. For two centuries they had literally cut away the ground beneath their feet.

After the Second World War, Roussillon fell on hard times when chemists figured out a cheaper way to manufacture dyes. Finally, like Les Baux, the town converted to a tourist economy.

Richard hoped his photographs would vibrate with the ironic awareness that these fairy-tale villages with their romantic winding alleys were built on a hard rock of mineral exploitation — somewhat undermined, but still cold and solid. Not that it mattered. As long as he included plenty of blue sky peeping between russet arches and ocher roofs, the calendar people would be satisfied. Irony was a dish only a few knew how to savor.

And while he was thinking of dishes, Richard began to notice the doors closing on the four restaurants that occupied the town square. He had been busy since noon capturing their various charms — earnest waiters threading their way through crowded sidewalk tables, a menu displayed in a lace-covered frame, sprigs of lavender and thyme decorating a bright orange platter of pork cutlets and steamed potatoes. Now, after two hours of crouching and clicking his way around these extremely attractive country restaurants (food being one of the few areas where Richard thought good looks were a virtue), he couldn't believe they weren't open to serve him some of that great-looking stuff he had been putting on film. The proprietors were adamant, however. Closed was closed.

Nursing the beer and the slice of pizza that a grudging café waitress had finally provided, Richard was surprised to see Didier Renard coming out of an elegant looking gift shop across the way. Without thinking, Richard hailed him and invited him to share a beer. In truth, he was lonely.

The Fellowship of Men

R ENARD, ON THE OTHER hand, was wary of any personal relation with his temporary neighbor. In the twenty years since
he had returned to St-Etang, he had never considered his isolation as anything but an advantage. Both customers and suppliers
came to his door, providing a regular pattern of human contact
without staying around long enough to grow irritating. His
brother Antoine had developed a real talent for renting the house
across the road, but the tenants were almost always pompous
professors who wanted to discuss wine without actually buying
any or, even worse, aspiring painters who expected Renard to
slake their thirst on credit.

When Richard waved him over to the café in Roussillon, Renard feared he was stuck with a pest who would follow him
everywhere and expect him to drop everything whenever the toilet overflowed. But instead of demanding repairs or even complaining about the rent, which would have been completely
appropriate, Richard bought him a beer and let him drink it the
proper way, in silence. Only on the second round did the American offer some conversation, and then on the always interesting
subject of the Tour de France.

The bicycle race had started the week before, but Renard had
not expected his tenant to know that. An American who understood something about sports beyond stuffing a ball in a hoop.
Remarkable, Renard thought. Also, good for business. Richard
should come to the truck stop in the evening, he suggested. They
had a television in the bar with a satellite link for the stations that
rebroadcast the highlights of the race each day. And now he must

leave, to continue his travels. Thursday, you will recall, was Renard's day to distribute his artistic efforts to the boutiques of Provence.

Lonelier than ever after Renard's departure, Richard decided he had enough pictures of Roussillon. As he pulled off the road to take a final long shot of the village and reached into the wooden backseat for his camera stand, he noticed the doll he had forgotten to give to Lily. If he got the angle right, could he make it look like the doll was falling from the summit? Cheered by the idea of a modern Seramonde, he rigged Barbie to a tree with the nylon fishline he always kept in his camera bag and spent twenty minutes adjusting for distance. First Barbie stood on the parapets. Then she mounted to the tower. Then, with the fishline wrapped around her left foot, she plunged off toward the rocks below, her arms splayed behind her like a child holding up a make-believe cape. Reluctantly, Richard then cut the doll down and took the traditional shots he had stopped for.

On Friday, Richard brought his film to a lab in Cavaillon, the nearest town of any size. It took less than two hours to realize that he had succeeded beyond his worst fears of artistic self-betrayal. No matter how carelessly he chose a subject, everything he did was pretty. The skies were blue, the stones were mellow gold, the flowers glowed with color, and the very air between the objects seemed to give off sparks of vitality. Instead of developing his own style in France, he was being co-opted into the cult of mindless scenic beauty. His work was banal. It was ordinary. Worse, it was commercial. So far the only distinctive thing he had accomplished in France was to start growing a beard, and even that was turning out a distressing shade of gray.

Resolving the Conflicts of Family and Work

WHILE RICHARD STRUGGLED with the oppressive hegemony of prettiness, Vivian was having her own quarrels with her muse. She had been very proud of the research arrangements she had made before she left New York, but that pride had only lasted until Wednesday morning. Not long after Richard set off for Les Baux, Vivian began calling her various contacts in Provence. The results were daunting. The agricultural archives she had expected to find in Marseilles had all been sent to Paris for the new, expanded Bibliothèque Nationale. The curator of the Cézanne Studio in Aix-en-Provence, during a businesslike exchange of telephone calls that had included the precise dates of Vivian's arrival, had failed to mention that the library was going to be closed for renovations and he himself was leaving town. The asylum where van Gogh had painted many of his landscapes was now a private conference center, booked solid until a year from September, and even the vast and ageless mountains, so endlessly open to Cézanne's transforming gaze, were now spotted with high-security military zones rumored to hold missile silos.

Fine, thought Vivian angrily, after she had run through her list of telephone numbers and come up with an unbroken string of disappointments. Forget site research. I'll write about what I feel and what I know by instinct. That's what I'm best at, after all. That's why people pay to hear me talk. And then she went outside to argue with the so-called groundskeeper, who lived twenty kilometers away but drove over every day to make sure her family was not trespassing on his fields. He had already tried to attack Richard for setting up a tripod next to one of his precious lavender bushes, and Vivian was afraid to think what would happen if he ever threatened Lily. The girl was afraid of her own shadow as it was. To keep the children on the premises, Vivian went out in the midday heat and scrubbed and strained the swimming pool to an acceptable level of sanitation.

Wednesday afternoon was spent moving furniture and cursing Richard for vanishing just when she could have used another set of hands. The goal was to find a place to write. Vivian felt claustrophobic in the bedroom, grimy in the kitchen, and reduced to torpor by the hypnotic rows of lavender if she went outdoors. Justin and Lily had rearranged the bunk beds to make a fort, so the second floor was out.

Even after she settled at the big table in the front room, Vivian was far from happy. There was no light, she complained. The table wobbled. The children shrieked. Listening for the vital pulse of the earth, she heard nothing but the steady roar of trucks. The gushing observations about the French landscape which used to spring to mind so effortlessly during her tedious commute to New Jersey dried up in the actual sun and wind on which she had staked so many of her fine ideas. When Richard came back at seven and stood around clicking his disapproval that she had done nothing about dinner, Vivian was ready to pack up right then and return home. Except that home was now occupied by a German lawyer who was doubtless enjoying her well-lighted desk and ergonomically superior chair.

"There's a drought," she told herself sternly. "It hasn't rained here in five years. The whole area is shriveling, and my brain with it. I need to get away." That night, with some trepidation, she arranged for Renard's daughter to stay with the children while she left to seek her inspiration elsewhere.

In Search of the Goddess

O N THE FLIGHT from New York to Paris, Vivian had studied the Air France magazine, trying to read the articles in French without peeking too often at the English translations on the facing pages. She had pored over ads and articles alike, diligently studying unfamiliar words and phrases. Even the long feature on Catherine Deneuve's beauty secrets provided some useful new vocabulary.

What had really caught her attention, though, was an article on ancient cults of goddess worship and their relevance to modern life. Vivian had stared at the illustration, a faceless stone statue with gigantic hips and grotesquely engorged genitals. Now, as she tried to decide where to go in her escape from the farm, she remembered the piece. Pulling the magazine from the pile on the floor, she noted the statue had been found not far from Aix-en-Provence.

Cheered, she determined to go there the next morning. Aix was the modern incarnation of an ancient Roman trading post. Before the Romans, warrior tribes had lived there, decapitating their enemies and making human sacrifices to their pagan gods. Somewhere in Aix was a museum where you could see a stone doorway with carved niches to hold the severed heads. Somewhere else in Aix was the Cézanne Studio, with its archives that had to be open sooner or later and that doubtless held documents full of damning statements of masculine oppression. And behind them all was the dangerous, tempting female goddess, image of fertility and sister to the earth itself, the goddess the male establishment was forever struggling to suppress.

The pieces were starting to fall into place. For two thousand years men had worked to destroy the natural synergy of woman, goddess, and nature. They had used the terror of force and the rigor of faith, and finally, most deviously, the seductive charm of art. If Vivian wanted to show how Mother Gaia had been denatured by modern painters, there could be no better place to start than Aix-en-Provence. In Aix, surely, she would be able to write.

The Departure

CLOTILDE RENARD WAS a broad-shouldered, slow-moving redhead with a perpetual scowl and an ominous spike hairdo. She met none of Vivian's usual requirements for a child-care provider, but in St-Etang one's choices were somewhat limited. It was either Clotilde or the two whores from Toulouse who worked in shifts behind the truck stop. Clotilde had been hired.

Thursday morning, while Richard was on his way to Roussillon and Didier Renard was packing his watercolors for delivery, Vivian spent the hour from nine to ten instructing her new nanny. Lily was not to go out without her sunblock, her hat, and her bee-sting medicine. Justin was to practice French conversation with Clotilde for at least a half hour before lunch and an hour after. Then the children should swim (though not before checking the pool for scorpions), and then Clotilde could do the laundry. Convinced at last that her children would be well tended in her absence, Vivian set out for Aix-en-Provence to amass conclusive evidence that the subjugation of women was related to the triumph of Impressionist art.

The Children

THE CHILDREN HAD the worst of it, and then the best. Seven and eleven, Lily and Justin were too old not to notice their abandonment but too young to do anything about it. Their parents had assured them they would find playmates in St-Etang, but that had been back in New York, when they all still thought St-Etang was a real place. If work went well, their parents said now, they would take the weekend off to play with them and show them the sights. In the meantime, Justin and Lily were to develop their own resources. And then, just four days after arriving in France, their parents drove away in opposite directions, leaving them stranded in the care of the terrifying Clotilde.

At first they whined a great deal. Next they spent the better part of an hour testing their initial, correct impression that Clotilde was too impassive to bother tormenting. Finally, bored with fighting, they decided to explore the countryside.

Clotilde was happy to send them off, since that left her free to entertain her boyfriend, the forest ranger, on the one decent bed in the dump these stupid Americans had rented. Ignoring all of Vivian's instructions, she put lunches in their backpacks and presented them each with a hiking stick, snatched from the litter of branches an overnight windstorm had torn from the tree in the courtyard. She even suggested several routes, ones that would take them far away with little chance of an early return.

"Chase insects in the meadow," she urged. "Go look for the Roman road to Arles — it's around here somewhere. See who can climb the highest tree without breaking his neck. Then stay there!" Grinning wickedly, she shooed them out of the kitchen and telephoned the ranger station, her powerful thighs already damp with anticipation.

Standing on the back terrace, the children debated where to go. To the north were the Luberon Mountains, with acres of forest preserved as a national park. To the south were the gentler slopes of the Trevasse. To the west were the Alpilles, the "little Alps," whose strange chalky outcroppings had inspired settlers to carve their houses out of the rocks. To the east was a complex and fascinating system of canals.

Within walking distance, however, there was nothing. In front of the house was the highway, an uninviting destination. On the other three sides were fields of purple stuff their mother explained was used to make perfume. Yesterday, she had worked out a deal with the farmer; they were allowed to walk through the fields as long as they didn't touch any of the bushes. Then their mother had insisted they come with her for a walk, to demonstrate their rights. The farmer had followed behind them, twirling a dangerous looking scythe. Justin and Lily understood that playing in the lavender was out.

Still, they had to go somewhere. They set out through the forbidden purple flowers, walking sideways like ancient Egyptians, careful not to touch a single blossom of Monsieur Maudit's smelly old plants. After a breathless twenty minutes, they crossed a narrow irrigation ditch into a field of melons and felt a little more relaxed.

Not that the melons were much of an improvement. The sun beat on their heads, the leaves scratched, and the tangled vines threatened to trip them with every step. Besides, watching melons grow is not the sort of entertainment to excite a child. For another half hour they trudged forward. Soon even the melons ended, leaving them to make their way through a weedy expanse of dry and prickly vegetation.

Lily was tired and Justin was bored. They were about to give up entirely when they found themselves at a shrunken, overgrown pond. Years ago, back when there was still a village, the villagers of St-Etang had watered their cattle here. A tangle of old trees, growing by the water's edge, provided shade. It was either stay here or go back to Clotilde. They decided to stay.

Some time in the distant past, someone had set a circle of flat stones around the pond, but decades of drought and diversion of streams into irrigation canals had lowered the water table, leaving a wide band of mud within the stones. This, at least, looked safe. Even Lily didn't think anyone would blame them for stopping here.

Squatting on the edge, they ate their lunches and then settled into the serious business of play. First they built a channel in the mud and tortured the water bugs that had the poor judgment to float down it. Next they built a dam. When Lily started making mud pies, Justin pulled out a book and told her to watch for the pond monster. He figured that would keep her from wading out to the middle and drowning.

Justin knew all of Lily's secret fears and was an expert in using them to keep her in line. The farmer would cut off their noses if they tried to smell his flowers, he told her. Lion Man lived in the drainage ditch in front of the house. The pond was full of dead bodies, and he would bring up a skeleton to haunt her if she didn't quit bugging him when he was trying to read.

As it happened, however, it was Lily who found the skeleton. If it hadn't been for Justin's teasing, she probably wouldn't even have recognized the rocky lump as a skull. First she thought it was a big fish sleeping underwater. She threw a crust of bread to wake it up, and then, when it didn't move, she decided it was just an old rotten melon, grown slimy. When she threw a rock at it, though, it made a noise that didn't sound like melon, so she poked it with her walking stick. And then she started to scream.

Justin Takes Command

R OUSED FROM HIS book, Justin came running over to see
what his sister had found. He seized her stick and, wiggling
the point through the eye socket, pried the crusted lump from
the shallow water and swung it, dripping with pond grass, over
the flat stones that ringed the pond. Something else was also
caught on the stick — a thin, bumpy circle the size of a child's toy
crown. Where the surface muck was scratched away, Justin could
see the glint of golden metal. Holding the stick carefully with
both hands now, he moved to higher ground, searching for a
comfortable place to examine this double prize.

Where Lily saw a skull, Justin recognized a story. Most of the
books he read featured child detectives, so he understood how
these things went. He knew, for example, that the mystery would
seem to be supernatural — ghosts, eerie lights, unseen bells, and
so on — but would turn out to be about greed. Maybe someone
was trying to scare them away from an oil well, or keep them
from finding the place where robbers had stashed their loot.
Those kinds of things happened all the time in books. At the end
there would be an explanation for the secret treasure, and usually
a fat reward, too, but first the kids had to solve the mystery.

Most important, they had to do it all by themselves. In the
books the children who solved the mystery were usually orphans
or else their parents had gone on some long trip or something,
but Justin figured he and Lily qualified. Their parents were about
as absent as you could ask for, as long as you didn't count the
time they were sleeping. It all fit. It was their destiny. Lily had

found the evidence, but it was up to him, the clever older brother, to solve the crime.

It took Justin some time to explain this to Lily. At first she wanted to show off her discovery, but Justin convinced her that if they told their parents they would have to stay in France forever. That ended that.

Grabbing his own stick, Justin walked back out onto the mud to reach deeper water. he felt some things he hoped were rocks, and something that was shaped like a manhole cover but was too heavy to pry up. Sliding the stick through the mud, he pulled up two more circles, smaller than the first.

Lily watched him, then looked under the trees until she found another stick with some branches still on it. Nervously, she drew the stick toward her through the water like a rake. As she had feared, she dragged up several long knobby things that her imagination assured her were bones. Following Justin out onto the mud, she thrust her stick forward again. This time she got a lot of leaves and a twisted piece of metal that looked like a skinny barrette with a dented knob on the end. That was better, but not so wonderful that she wanted to wade back into the muck. Instead, she sat on the grass for a long time watching the pond, until Justin asked her what she was looking for.

"I'm waiting to see if a monster comes out of the water now."

Justin watched, too, but the water stayed as it had been all afternoon, and after a while it was time to go back to the farmhouse. Neither of them wanted to touch the skull, so they poked it back into the pond for safekeeping and arranged three stones on the bank to mark the spot. They did, however, take the rest of the loot, stuffed into Lily's backpack. They didn't know what they had found, but whatever it was, it seemed too interesting to leave behind.

Examining the Treasure

Excited by their discovery, Justin and Lily quickly made their way back through the fields they had traveled so listlessly that morning. As they reached the farmhouse, a tall young man in a dark green uniform mounted a motorbike and headed up the dirt road back to the highway. Clotilde was in a much better mood than she had been that morning, and she didn't object when they passed through the kitchen with their dirty shoes and headed for their parents' bathroom, which had a lock. Closing the door and locking it behind them, they dug their find out of Lily's backpack. Justin took the first piece Lily had found and held it under the showerhead. The other pieces went in the sink to soak in hot water and shampoo. Lily pawed through their mother's makeup bag to find something they could use to scrape away what wouldn't wash off.

They began with the big golden circle, using a nail clipper and a tweezers, trading turns as their fingers grew tired. Under the hardened slime was some sort of crown, or maybe a collar. Impatient at first, they worked more slowly as a design began to emerge. The metal gleamed where Lily rubbed it with the corner of her father's shaving towel.

"Sweet-ola," whispered Justin, looking at the images that began to appear beneath the crust. There were strange animals, and wavy lines, and shooting stars. One panel, slightly larger than the others, was about the coolest thing that he had ever seen. Definitely the coolest if you didn't count stuff on video. It was a full-length portrait of a lady with spiked hair and glaring eyes. Rubbing harder to get in the cracks, Justin stopped to admire the bolts of lightning that shot from her fingertips and the snakes that twined up her legs. Across her brow she wore a duplicate of the metal circle on which she appeared. And that was all she was wearing.

Justin showed Lily what he had uncovered, then grabbed the circle back when she tried to ram it on her head.

"Let me hold it," he ordered. "You'll break it."

"I will not!"

Justin was always saying stuff like that, Lily thought, but he was the one who couldn't walk through a room without dropping a glass or kicking over a table.

"She's naked," observed Justin.

"She's awesome," countered Lily.

"You don't know anything, poop face," answered her brother.

"I found it," the little girl reminded him. "It's mine! I'm Xena, the warrior princess. Admit it or I'll tell."

They would have started fighting and spoiled the secret then and there, but Clotilde was pounding on the door for them to get out of the bathroom. Their mother was due back soon, and Clotilde wanted the brats waiting outside the front door so she could leave at once.

Drinking Deeply at the Source

O N ARRIVING IN Aix-en-Provence, Vivian's first imperative was to drink strong coffee and marshal her thoughts. From the municipal car lot, she walked directly to the Cours Mirabeau, the most fashionable street in town, surveyed the line-up of sidewalk cafés, and settled at a table at Café des Deux Garçons.

She knew she should be roaming the countryside for examples of agricultural oppression and scouring the library for texts that would illuminate the masculine warrior mentality of nineteenth-century painting, but the appeal of the Cours Mirabeau was irresistible. The stores, the banks, the taxis, and most of all the glorious, magnetic, intoxicating presence of other people, all kept her in her metal chair. One cup of coffee led to another, and then a sandwich, and then more coffee. After the second coffee, she had crossed the street to buy three more guidebooks, two paperback novels, a blank notebook with an attractive sky blue cover, and a felt-tipped pen with a particularly inspiring rubber grip. Then she returned to the café for lunch. It was well into the afternoon before she noticed the fountain.

At first she took it for a broken stepping-stone, a moss-covered mistake in the middle of the Baroque town houses. Flipping through her newly purchased Michelin green guide to see if she still had time to get to the art museum, Vivian was jolted to see a sketch of the same uninteresting rock right in the middle of the page. The caption claimed that this dull lump was in fact a fountain, built to contain a hot spring prized since Roman times.

So informed, Vivian gave the fountain her full attention. Sure enough, it began to signify many things. The moss, pubic hair around the hidden female genitalia of the water, was an emblem of nature's irrepressible lushness, an eternal spring of creativity welling up even in the middle of the severe old commercial center. How typical of the city fathers to channel the natural spring into a controlled stream, a masculine pisser, instead of the welling lake of moistness that nature so clearly intended for the site. She looked at the copy of *Jean de Florette* she meant to start reading as soon as she finished her coffee. Wasn't that about water, too? The jacket blurb was all about Gérard Depardieu, who had starred in the movie, but she was fairly certain water figured somewhere in the plot.

Before they went home, Vivian decided, she would steal a cutting from the fountain. Wouldn't it be fabulous to have a stone on their windowsill back home on West Eighty-Sixth Street, covered with real moss from Provence? Already she could imagine herself explaining the sexual implications of cutting through the springy green turf to reach the sweet flow of warmth that welled up from the ground below. Gratified and inspired by her own inventive genius, Vivian opened her new notebook and wrote three pages on the sexual implications of piped-in water before it was time to head home. Tomorrow she would find her way to the Cézanne Studio to ask if the curator had returned from Greece.

Fieldwork

A LL FRIDAY, Justin and Lily worked intently at their own private archaeological dig. Clotilde suspected they were up to something, so busy and happy and full of secrets, but that was no concern of hers as long as they stayed out of the house. Monsieur Maudit, normally vigilant against any intruders on his tidy crop of lavender, had just won five thousand francs in the national lottery and was stuck at home receiving visitors who came to inspect his new color television. And so Justin and Lily were left in peace to explore the hidden treasures of the pond, pulling out whatever loot they could reach with stray branches and a rusty pruning hook they had found outside the house.

Even with these imperfect tools, they amassed a good-size pile. The pieces they suspected were bones they left under an oak tree, covered with a loose arrangement of leaves and branches. The other stuff they set out to clean.

The process of scraping centuries of scum off fragile antique metalwork leaves a good deal of time for conversation. By the end of the afternoon, brother and sister had come to an agreement. The stuff they were finding in the pond was too cool not to be worth something, and the life they were leading was too dismal to be endured. Therefore, they should sell their treasure. Once they had money, they would find a way of escaping from the farm.

They would be like the brave children whose stories their parents had made them read at the Ellis Island Immigration Museum, children who had crossed the ocean alone with nothing but a sack of stale rolls and an address torn from an envelope.

Whatever risks they had to take, they were determined to better their lives. Pinning their hopes on the only commercial center to which they had any access, they would wait for the Saturday flea market at Oppède-le-Percée. Marcel, they had decided, would help them sell their find.

The Most Authentic
Farmers' Market in Provence

O N SATURDAY MORNINGS Oppède-le-Percée roused itself from its usual hostile isolation to host what was possibly the most authentic farmers' market in Provence. No herbal soaps or nostalgic peasant clothing here. Contained within the low stone walls of the old sheepfold, this was a place where men and women who worked with their hands came to sell what they didn't need and buy what they didn't have. Most of the market was food and wine, with a smaller area for trading farm tools and machinery. Between the two sections was a narrow row of stalls where you could buy coffee, bread, wake-up shots of marc, the local brandy, and hot sausages stuffed in steaming rolls. Outside the market proper, optimistic scroungers set up a scruffy flea market of junk and bric-a-brac. After a week of disappointments, the Saturday morning scene lived up to every one of Richard and Vivian's preconceptions about unspoiled country life.

While their parents surveyed the stalls, trotting back and forth with little cries of greedy rapture, Justin and Lily bided their time. They were there to sell, not buy.

The children had been up early, consulting their traveler's phrase book to prepare for the complicated transaction they had in mind. Lily had hidden several pieces of their find in her backpack so they could start the business right away. Justin had wanted to bring it all, but Lily was afraid their parents would notice if her pack was too lumpy. Besides, she was determined to hold on to the strange crown with the cool pictures, whatever Justin thought.

They had no doubts about finding Marcel. The Saturday morning market was one of his chief topics of conversation as he enjoyed the sunshine at the village fountain. He had explained in great detail how he came there every week to sell whatever he found on his daily walks. On Wednesday, the last morning their mother had driven them to Oppède-le-Percée, he had shown them two hubcaps, a thermos bottle, and a paperback novel (only slightly water-damaged) that would be part of this week's inventory.

The only difficulty they foresaw was escaping from their parents. The moment came while Vivian was in ecstasy over a frightening quantity of zucchini she was apparently planning to buy. Richard was staring longingly at the wine merchant's truck, where a solemn cluster of farmers were knocking down the free samples.

"Can we go over there?" Justin waved urgently toward the other side of the low stone wall, where the junk vendors had gathered. They would look for picture books, he added earnestly. They would stay together. They would not take any food or drink from strangers. Lily stood beside him, a picture of sisterly devotion and obedience. As soon as Vivian nodded, they were off.

"Marcel," Lily called joyfully as they approached his table. "Stay there, you little snot!" she added. Young and quick, she had already picked up several new French phrases from Clotilde. She was never entirely sure of what she was saying, but it seemed to get people's attention. For emergencies they also had the phrase book, which Justin carried in his backpack.

"You think he'll do it?" Justin asked tensely.

"Of course he will," Lily answered. "Marcel sells things at the market. You have to help me explain, though. You promised."

"Sure," Justin agreed, going to greet Marcel. "As long as I get half the money."

The children had already learned that Marcel would not begin a conversation until everybody had shaken hands. Their mother said this was what people did in France, but so far the only person they had met who observed this particular courtesy was Marcel. After that was over and Lily had taken a turn jumping with Marcel's rope, they got down to business.

"Are you selling your treasures?" Lily asked in her baby French. That was what Marcel called the things he found on his walks.

Nodding seriously, Marcel gestured to his table. Only a single empty wine bottle remained.

"Will you sell a treasure for us?"

Marcel shrugged. If it was a nice treasure, he would sell it.

"Oh, it's a nice treasure," Lily assured him, drawing from her backpack the skinny barrette, now revealed as a four-inch-long brass pin with a roughly chiseled owl on the end. The piece was small, but it had polished up nicely. "Clean as a nun's tit," Lily added proudly. That was something Clotilde had said only yesterday. After some hesitation, she added three bulky armbands and a large but dented brooch to the pile.

"Sell these, and we'll bring more the next time we come to town," she said.

Now Justin chimed in, using sentences he had worked out from studying his book. "You have to give us the money," he said. "You can keep ten francs for yourself."

He glanced over at Lily. They hadn't discussed this, and he was afraid she might balk, but she seemed untroubled by the arrangement. Justin himself was rather proud of it. He had a friend back home whose mother sold real estate, and he knew that people who sold stuff for other people worked harder when they got commissions. Not that he could have explained this to Marcel, of course. Or at least not in French. So he had just settled on ten francs as a payment.

Marcel nodded. He came to his cousin's truck stop every week on the fourth day after the fair, just after lunch. He would visit them then to give them the money, and they would give him more treasure. Shaking hands again to seal the deal, they returned to their mother just in time to help lug what seemed like a lifetime supply of garlic and smelly cheese to the car.

The Young Man

W EARY OF WINTER and thwarted in love, Peter Wall had arrived in the South of France from New Haven, Connecticut, eighteen months before, leaving the Yale School of Architecture after his first semester to recover from a sudden seizure of misanthropy. Since then he had supported himself by doing odd jobs as caretaker, carpenter, and plasterer while conducting what he liked to think of as an independent study of classical architecture in Provence.

On this particular morning, he was trying to ram his ancient gray Fiat through the Saturday morning traffic of central Cavaillon, in his opinion the least attractive Roman city of Provence.

As far as Peter was concerned, Cavaillon's glory days had ended as soon as Julius Caesar pulled out of town. Since then its greatest claim to fame was the sweetness of its melons and the occasional violence of its outbreaks of anti-Semitism. It was not as desolate as his hometown of Castroville, California, self-proclaimed Artichoke Capital of the World, but it was certainly not a shining example of urbanity. Peter was beginning to formulate grim theories about municipalities that tried to build civic reputations on the reflected glory of fruits and vegetables.

Perhaps it was that same Southern California childhood that made him so conscious of false reputations. Perhaps it was his own rather mortifying appearance. Tall but not hulking, slender but not gaunt, attractive but not in any way threatening, Peter was uncomfortably aware that he resembled the youthful movie stars admired by preteen girls and elderly women. With his short

blond hair and beardless pink cheeks, he projected a general aura
of cleanliness that he dearly hoped, someday, to outgrow.

It had been a mistake to bring a car here on market day. Diesel
trucks loaded with wooden crates of melons blocked the entry to
every street. Smaller vans and wagons clogged the alleyways. Al-
gerian peddlers sold plastic housewares from tables jammed into
the narrow sidewalks of the old Jewish quarter. School was starting, the last Saturday half day before the summer holiday. Children swarmed through the traffic, banging their palms on the
hood of his car as they passed. After three weeks of lonely work
restoring a Renaissance fountain in an overgrown garden of a vacant house, Peter had been so happy to finish that he had jumped
in his car without thinking about traffic. Now he was paying for
that childish exuberance. At this rate, he would barely make it out
of town before sunset, much less get to Gordes in time for a swim
before dinner.

Through his rearview mirror, Peter could see the top of the
Roman arch, sole remnant of the city's imperial past. The gathering heat made the Fiat's plastic seat cushions soft and slightly
sticky, creating a moist seal with the bare part of his thigh. A fine
sensation, but only if you happened to be a suction cup. Before
him was a crowded traffic circle presided over by a looming bill-
board advertising the wares of Monsieur Bricollage, the discount
hardware king. Looking at the avenue of auto-body repair shops
beyond, Peter decided he could not stand one more kilometer of
urban decay. He would take a detour along the Durance River,
taking the old departmental roads that had once been the only
way to travel.

To Market Once Again

AFTER FORTY-FIVE minutes of back roads, Peter's good humor was restored. Billboards had given way to the dappled shade of plane trees that lined the narrow pavement. The smells of the city were forgotten in the scent of lavender, thyme, and ripening apricots that wafted from the passing fields. He was going only half as fast as he could have, but in each town there was a church to admire, a canal to cross, or an ancient fountain to note for future reference. Peter's principal employer was a local real estate agent who hired him to repair fountains, paint walls, and cover cracks in aging plaster, and counted on him to do so without destroying the sense of antiquity that gave the property its value.

Maquillage, the agent called it. Makeup. For houses that needed major surgery she had to go to a real builder, but for *maquillage* Peter was perfectly competent, and good with the growing number of English-speaking clients. When he was working, Peter slept on the site. Between times, he stayed in a tiny outbuilding of a very grand country house belonging to a client of his father's. It was, he knew, an aimless life, and he had every intention of giving it up soon. He was now twenty-six, still young enough to believe in good intentions.

It was only eleven o'clock when Peter passed the old stone sheep pen that marked the outskirts of Oppède-le-Percée, but his day had started at dawn, and he was famished. Willing to follow any road that might lead to lunch, he turned in and soon found himself at the tail end of the farmers' market. The farmers were already packing up, but the café owner was still frying sausages and filling glasses with strong red wine.

Satisfied, Peter wandered over to the other side of the wall to check out the bric-a-brac, stopping to examine three massive, lumpy-looking bracelets set out on a card table next to an empty bottle. Early-twentieth-century primitives, he guessed. Mirielle, the real estate agent, had a friend in Paris who sold antique jewelry at prices so high that even Peter got a decent commission for anything he sent her.

The placid, moonfaced young man behind the table named a price so low Peter agreed at once, without even trying to bargain. Shaking hands, the seller put Peter's money in a side pocket of his overalls, placed the bracelets in a crumpled plastic bag he pulled from another pocket, and returned to playing with a dirty piece of rope. Fifteen minutes after he had turned off the road, Peter was back at the stone sheep pen, ready to resume his back-road jaunt.

The bracelets had been out on the market for even less time than that. Justin and Lily had barely left Marcel's side when Peter arrived. When the children looked back, their friend was still standing by his table, but they were too far away to see that the bracelets were already gone. A minute later, the brooch went for twenty-five francs, less than five dollars, to the wife of a tomato farmer who knew a storekeeper in Cavaillon who would happily pay her a hundred when she brought it in. The pin with the owl head went to the postmaster's son in exchange for six batteries, still in their plastic shrink wrap. Ten minutes later the batteries were sold for twenty francs, exactly half what they would have cost in the store from which they had been stolen. Carefully, Marcel counted out the children's money and put it in a separate pocket from his own.

In fact, the children's arrangement with Marcel, which seemed to Justin and Lily an extraordinary proposal, was a natural extension of his usual routine. Everyone who lived in Oppède-le-Percée knew Marcel's routes for his daily walks, and people often gave him things to sell at his booth on Saturday. Sometimes they were gifts and sometimes he was told to bring back the profits the following week. All of this was perfectly normal.

It was also normal that Marcel sold out his stock every Saturday, usually as soon as he put it on display. No one exactly stole from Marcel, but taking advantage of his innocence was considered entirely legitimate. The only unusual part of Justin and Lily's arrangement was the ten-franc commission. Most people were not so generous.

A Family Outing: First Attempt

A FTER THE MARKET, Vivian had planned an afternoon of scenic touring. They would see pocket-size vineyards still cultivated by hand. They would see geese in the road and pigs in the pen. They would pass through hill towns, each with its own castle on the summit. They would have a picnic by the side of the road, with food bought at the market that very morning. For one day, at least, they would explore the primal romance of agricultural Provence.

They had taken the lime green car, the one with a real backseat, which was now piled with extraordinary quantities of produce. Strangely agreeable, the children had climbed in without a word of complaint. Lily, swathed in greens like a goddess in a vegetarian allegory, pulled a doll from her backpack and entered the world of imagination. Fueled by the benevolent warmth of many free samples of the local vintage, Richard agreed to let Vivian drive. They were off for a day in the country, the first real family outing since they had arrived.

Almost at once, they stopped. The instant they passed through the ancient northern gate of Oppède-le-Percée, they found themselves in the midst of a traffic jam worthy of Manhattan on a rainy Friday afternoon. A break in the line of vehicles had enabled Vivian, in her ignorance, to pull onto the road. Once on, however, they were stuck in a bumper-to-bumper crawl. Stone walls, protecting the fields on either side, barred any exit.

It wasn't just the traffic that was surprising. It was its nature. Six days of living next to a major truck route had given them all a fast education in the long-distance carriers of Europe. They had become familiar with the roar of the Volvo engine, the distinctive whine of the Renault diesel, and the absence of mufflers on trucks originating in eastern Europe. Now, it appeared, they were about to enrich their knowledge of smaller commercial vehicles. Minivans of every description, many of them embellished with radio antennae and even satellite dishes, snaked before and behind them. Sleek conveyances with futuristic headlights and tinted windows followed close behind flatbed trucks, grocers' vans, and rustic contraptions probably still littered with a few unsold melons. As far as they could see, theirs was the only ordinary passenger car in the line.

For a quarter of an hour they inched along, unwilling participants in some mysterious cortege. Vivian, the self-appointed navigator, felt somehow responsible for the traffic. As the pace slowed from a crawl to a halt, she turned to face the children and assured them, in a voice throaty with groundless optimism, that the road would open soon and they would proceed to the unspoiled rural vistas she had planned. Justin said nothing. Lily, dozing, jerked awake. Richard started making clicking noises. After another ten minutes he threw the car door open, jumped out, and started running down the road.

A Wife's Worst Fear

WITHOUT KNOWING IT, Richard was enacting Vivian's most secret fear, that she would be an abandoned wife. The panic would strike her almost anywhere, a sudden premonition of domestic disaster gripping her chest like an attack of angina. Crossing the George Washington Bridge, waiting for Justin at the orthodontist's, washing lettuce for dinner, she would be visited by a searing vision of her husband's departure. Sometimes it would be a drunken argument that ended in an irrevocable slam of the apartment door. At other moments she imagined a heartbreaking note on the kitchen counter, or a cowardly vacancy in the closet. Whatever the original image, it was always followed by a vivid depiction of her own lurching fall into the diminished circumstances of single motherhood.

Even at her most self-pitying moments, however, Vivian had never imagined Richard would abandon his family in the middle of a French traffic jam on a Saturday afternoon. She thought she had left this nightmare in New York, a bad dream tucked into the car visor next to the road map of Long Island.

It was outrageous, really. How could he desert her? How could he leave her in a foreign car, with the children in the backseat? Clutching the steering wheel, she stared at the license plate of the van in front of her. The number indicated it was registered in Paris. A sticker on the rear door said RADIO FRANCE. Jammed against the back window was a shopping bag from Fauchon. How comforting to know her life was being destroyed among vehicles that traveled to the best addresses.

Behind her, the children were stirring.

"Where's Dad going?" Justin asked.

"I don't know."

"Is he coming back?"

Vivian caught her breath. Just to ask the question suggested that Justin, too, had imagined the possibility of Richard's desertion. The boy was growing up. Maybe it was time to start taking him into her confidence. After all, he would have to be the strong male figure of Lily's adolescence.

Vivian stopped herself. The loss of their father would be cruel enough. She must not rob the children of their youth as well. If Richard was acting like a child, that did not mean Justin should be treated like an adult. She had read enough advice columns to know that, at least.

"Coming back?" she repeated brightly, after a pause that had lasted much too long. "Of course he's coming back."

And then he did, reappearing suddenly at the driver's side window.

"It's the Tour de France," he reported, leaning in Vivian's open window to talk over her head to the children. "It's a big bicycle race, like the Olympics for bicycles. It goes on for weeks. Everyone from all over Europe watches it on television, so these are all the newspeople who come along to report on the race." Turning to Vivian, he added, "I saw a camera van that said ABC Sports, so I went over to ask them what was going on. Why are you crying?"

"Richard, you're wonderful," Vivian sobbed, rummaging in her purse for something to wipe her nose. What she meant was, You're back. She didn't have to be a single mother. She didn't have to think about dating. She didn't have to change her hair or find a new apartment. She hadn't said anything incriminating. She could explain away the tears. And now, to cap a suddenly glorious moment, the traffic was starting to move.

"Get in," she said lovingly, groping for the gearshift. "Get in before I get rammed from behind."

Life in the Slow Lane

CRAWLING ALONG was better than standing still, but not by much. While Vivian stared at the bumper before her, Richard expounded on the Tour de France, with particular emphasis on its system of cumulative scoring. In American sports, each game was a fresh start, just as each day was the chance for a new beginning. In the Tour the France, each racer was the sum total of all that he had done, whether it was on the easy flats outside Paris or the grueling hills of the French Alps. According to Richard, it was emblematic of the European mentality, where you could never escape from your past.

He pulled out a brochure that explained the route for this year's race, something he had mooched from the guys in the truck. Tomorrow the racers would pass through the ancient Roman city of Orange, only forty-five minutes away. Apparently everyone had been talking about it for weeks. And there were also lots of local races that were getting unusual coverage because the television crews were here anyway. There was a hot racer from Venasque who was something of a local hero — he had been a parachute firefighter, trained to jump into the middle of a blazing forest and extinguish the flames.

Even Richard, the world's greatest authority on practically everything, was unclear on how that qualified him as a long-distance bicycle racer, but at least it caught the children's attention. Justin wanted to know how old you had to be to jump out of an airplane. Lily, predictably, was worried that the farmhouse would catch fire while they were out.

Meanwhile, the line of trucks and minivans continued to inch forward. Up ahead the road widened and a good number turned off to a field that had become a makeshift parking lot. Beyond the field, traffic seemed to be moving at something close to a normal pace. Just as Vivian was beginning to feel that the day might be salvaged, Richard jumped out of the car again.

"The ABC guys said I could hang out with them for a while. They'll be meeting up with the photographers from *Sports Illustrated* and the Associated Press. People I should know. Anyway, I've seen the countryside. I'll get back somehow. Have fun."

And with that he was gone, lumbering off toward the growing cluster of vans. Muttering furious curses, Vivian swung abruptly into a narrow road that had opened on her right. It had to lead somewhere. Anywhere was better than here.

The Shoelace

B UT IN REALITY the road led nowhere. The first five minutes took them through a tidy lane that passed between two orchards of ripening pears. After that the pavement twisted upward through a heavy growth of evergreens, shutting out all views. The heat and smell of the traffic jam seemed a distant memory, the very existence of other people an illusion. There were no signs to suggest where they were going, or where they had been. At wide intervals trees displayed a plastic triangle that signified the possibility of hiking. The only other notice they saw was a dented metal post emblazoned with the single word LACET. At Vivian's insistence, Justin searched for *lacet,* first on the road map and then in his phrase book.

"It means shoelace, Mom," he said at last. "Can there be a town called Shoelace?" Vivian didn't think so. After pawing through the phrase book for several minutes, Justin announced that *lacet* also meant winding road.

By then, this was no revelation. While Justin had been searching, the shoelace had twisted ever upward. Occasional gaps in the trees offered magnificent vistas just beyond an extremely sheer drop. The children, always prone to motion sickness, had closed their eyes — what they missed in scenic wonder they also avoided in acrophobic terror.

When it seemed impossible to climb any farther, they arrived at a tall radio tower with a bit of a paved surface at its base. Grateful for the chance to loosen her death grip on the steering wheel, Vivian turned in.

"Where are we?" Justin asked. It had been his constant question from the moment they arrived in France.

"A very pretty place for a picnic," Vivian answered brightly.

"But where?"

"I don't know. Somewhere. Anyway, we can eat lunch." She thought of the bread she had bought at the farmers' market, and the pâté that had been so cool and tempting in the thin sunlight of early morning. Richard, of course, had the pocketknife.

"I feel sick," Justin moaned, leaning his head against Lily's shoulder. Around them rose the increasingly pungent odors of melons, green onions, strawberries, and cheese. A slab of fresh honey in the comb, wrapped in a grape leaf and tied with twine, had been crushed by a bottle of olive oil as they rounded one of the mountain's many hairpin turns. Moving her leg, Lily stepped in the mess, then held up her sandal to show Vivian the damage.

"I'm scared," she cried. "The bees will sting me. Do I have to get out?"

"No," Vivian answered, restarting the engine. And that was the last word anyone said for the rest of the afternoon.

Three more hours of winding road took them steeply down and then steeply up again, never with the slightest hint of where they were or how they might get off this shoelace from hell. On and on they drove. The first and only time Vivian dared go faster than a crawl she immediately swerved off the pavement, crashing through the underbrush for several panic-stricken seconds before regaining the road.

As the light took on that golden effulgence that lends radiance to every leaf and blade of grass on summer afternoons, she abandoned hope of ever finding her way back to the farmhouse. Time had lost all meaning. They were in some vehicular limbo where they were doomed to drive an endless mountain road, never arriving, always encountering one more hairpin curve, and then another, and then again one more. In five hours they had not seen a single person or another car. The sun moved overhead, but never far enough toward sunset to provide a sense of direction. The only sign of progress was the gas gauge, which had registered empty for quite some time. Looking off to the side of the road, searching for some sort of shelter, Vivian was startled to see an ancient wooden sign, badly faded but still entirely legible. ST-ETANG, it said, 6 KILOMETERS.

Perhaps they really had entered a time warp. Maybe the long-destroyed village would reappear at the end of this mysterious road. Terrified, Vivian steered around yet another blind curve and suddenly found herself on a dirt lane that ended in a stand of tall grass behind Renard's garage. As the car bounced to a stop in front of the gas pump, she saw that the road had once connected to the still-intact route they had taken to Oppède-le-Percée that morning. She had been traveling, very slowly, in a circle.

After several minutes, Clotilde sauntered out to fill the tank.

"Slow day," the girl remarked. "I guess everyone is at home watching the Tour de France."

The car smelled like a garbage dump, she noted with disgust. Her father should demand an extra payment for damages when it came time to reclaim it from these American savages.

Vivian had nothing to say about the Tour de France. In silence she paid for the gas. Then she revved the engine, looped around the figure eight, bounced over the ditch, and pulled up on the stones of their own courtyard. At fourteen minutes after 6:00 P.M., seven hours after leaving the farmers' market, Vivian roused the children long enough for the three of them to stagger inside.

Quite a bit after midnight, Richard returned to find the car doors still open and the backseat piled with plastic bags of decaying food. Justin and Lily were asleep in their clothes on the living room futon, Vivian sprawled diagonally across the big brass bed. Using the pillow as a pivot, he drunkenly pulled her around by her feet until there was room for him to crawl in beside her. Soon he, too, was asleep. They had been in France a week, and they had all earned a rest.

PART II

Crossroads

A Triumph of Decay

Now that the Harts are actually in France, as settled as can be expected of such skittish people, the time has come to visit their neighbors. Not the residents of the Truck Stop St-Etang but the Harts' spiritual neighbors, fellow travelers on the expatriate high road of cultural enlightenment.

Where to begin? We could look for Ariel Stern, who will be waking soon to catch the Sunday morning bus from Nice to the hilltop village of Gordes. We could find out more about Peter Wall, dreaming of catapults in his tiny room above that same Provençal village. We could spend some time with his hosts, Hugo and Rosalie Bartello, each of them charming but both, at the moment, sound asleep. We will start instead with the least attractive of our various Americans abroad, since he is the only one who is currently awake.

Francis Xavier O'Connor had not meant to become a derelict. His present state of physical and moral decay was impressive but unintentional, the by-product of other efforts. The question was not what he wanted to be but what he wanted to avoid.

The answer was, almost everything. Although no one was pursuing him, Francis was a man in flight. He had fled his ancestral home, which for four generations had been a Brooklyn neighborhood more provincial than any Irish village. He had fled his family vocation, which for those same four generations had been either motherhood or the New York City Fire Department, depending on gender. And then, like a man discovering his destiny, he had fled the twentieth century altogether, devoting himself body and soul to the recovery of Celtic Gaul.

The process had taken several years. It began with a short burst of conspicuous madness, a psychic version of clearing the decks. Francis was still living at home, in Brooklyn, when his widowed mother prevailed on him to go with her on a parish-sponsored pilgrimage to Italy, highlighted by three days in Rome and an audience with the Pope himself. With the desperate logic reserved for mothers of thirty-year-old bachelors, Mrs. O'Connor was hoping the world's foremost exponent of celibacy would inspire her son to marry and start a family.

Francis never made it past the Medici Chapel and the Church of San Lorenzo in Florence. To his mother's deep embarrassment and everyone else's horror, he interrupted their guided tour to announce, in a very loud voice, his true identity as Jesus Christ. After this he quickly mounted and dismounted the high altar, ran down the nave, and tried to ram his head into an early Renaissance font (splashing a good deal of holy water in the attempt), before falling into a merciful swoon. The whole event took under five minutes, during which time nobody in the tour group could remember drawing a breath.

The doctors at the psychiatric hospital in Fiesole said he was suffering from nervous prostration induced by the overwhelming presence of so much superlative art. It was called the Stendhal syndrome, they explained, named after the popular French novelist of the previous century who had first described the symptoms. This uniquely local malady, a kind of spiritual vertigo that affected the more sensitive tourists, was one they were well qualified to handle. Mrs. O'Connor should complete her travels, and in a few weeks they would have her son ready to rejoin her in Brooklyn. The austerity of their clinic would restore him to himself, they were sure.

The doctors were wrong. It took only a few days for their patient to realize that he was not Jesus (who was always depicted as a slender brunette, after all, while he himself was a barrel-chested redhead). He remained equally sure, however, that he was not

Francis Xavier O'Connor. With a degree of cunning that had never before been evident in his character, he kept this last conviction from the doctors and so was able to arrange an early release from the psychiatric hospital, complete with complimentary ride to the train station to make his connection in Milan. There he shook hands with his doctors, walked to the end of the platform, and stared at the clock on the terminal tower until his train had departed. He then retraced his steps, exiting the way he had come in, and started walking west. Passing a policeman, he felt a moment of panic and decided to change his name. The firefighter formerly named O'Connor was hereafter known, to himself at least, as Flic-Flac.

Flic-Flac was in no hurry. He had no destination. He turned west because that was the direction he faced when he emerged from the train station. He kept to the coast, once he found it, to avoid walking in circles, but circles would have been all right. He ignored his hair and beard, which grew until his face was wreathed in a mane of tangled reddish curls like that of a dirty, freckled lion. Nor did he bother with bathing or changing his clothes, except to add or remove a shirt depending on the weather.

It took him five weeks to walk through Italy and into France. Still keeping to the coastline, he continued walking around Monaco, past Nice, past Antibes and Cannes and St-Tropez, until he arrived at the ancient Mediterranean port of Marseilles.

Something about the landscape awoke in Flic-Flac a distant memory of Brooklyn. Perhaps it was the seedy waterfront, or the large number of seafood restaurants that catered to obvious gangsters. Perhaps it was the uneasy cohabitation of different ethnic populations, each so palpably despising the others that the very air of the Vieux Port smelled of looming violence. Whatever it was, it made our demented wanderer pause in his travels. Stealing an envelope from a distracted tobacconist in the tourist district, Flic-Flac stuck his passport inside, along with a postcard view of the Château d'If, the legendary prison built on a rocky isle in the middle of the Marseilles harbor. On the back of the card he wrote, "Don't worry. I'm not here." Then he mailed it off to his mother, who enlivened her final years with frequent, futile trips to Europe in search of her errant son.

From the Harbor to the Hills

SOME DAYS LATER, as Flic-Flac was lounging around the Vieux Port of Marseilles, staring out at the prison where, as already noted, he was not incarcerated, he was approached by a builder looking for someone strong to haul rocks. The builder asked no questions, paid cash, let him sleep on the premises, and gave him a liter of wine at quitting time every day. It was the best job Flic-Flac ever had.

That was nine years ago. After the Marseilles job Flic-Flac had accompanied the builder inland to the Luberon district of Provence, where there were numerous newly fashionable hill towns full of stones needing to be lugged from one location to another. Flic-Flac liked the hills even better than the harbor, but he was just as happy when the building season ended in October and he was allowed to drift off on his own. He had not left Brooklyn, after all, to go into construction.

Since then Flic-Flac had acquired a deep knowledge of the villages and forests of northern Provence, a fluent acquaintance with gutter French, and a rusty Deux Cheveaux he had found abandoned in a ravine. During the summer he slept in the open next to his car. In the colder months he broke into vacation houses, leaving squalid messes to greet the owners when they returned the following season. When he needed money he dug ditches, broke stones, fought forest fires, or gathered grapes. Mostly, he stole. Secondhand dealers throughout Provence became familiar with the mangy bum who always had something to sell but only grunted if you asked him where he got it. Not that the dealers Flic-Flac frequented were the sorts to ask.

And so he lived: dirty, crazy, usually drunk, a man who had pulled a loose thread in the fabric of civilization and stepped right through the resulting hole. Yet he still didn't know who he was. If art had knocked Flic-Flac out of himself, it was only fitting that art should bring him back. Specifically, the grand exhibition, Provence Before Caesar, at the Museum of Pagan Art in Arles.

The Awakening

F LIC-FLAC LIKED Arles. The women were pretty, the tourists were easy to rob, the Roman Arena had many shady nooks where a bum could sleep in peace, and there were several store-keepers along the banks of the Rhône who were happy to buy whatever he brought them. On this particular morning, however, Flic-Flac was short of things to sell. He had spent the hours between midnight and 3:00 A.M. attending to various expensive pleasures that had emptied his pockets of everything of value. Now he was wandering through the city, enjoying the dim coolness of the early morning and waiting for fortune to drop something in his path.

Eight o'clock found him at the Place de la République, where it was sometimes possible to steal cameras and other valuables from people using the cash machines. Even here, however, a Sunday morning torpor prevailed. In any case, Flic-Flac soon forgot his mission, distracted by the color posters advertising the current exhibition at the Museum of Pagan Art.

The museum, located in a former church, had stored away its regular collection of Roman statues and mosaics to make room for a temporary show depicting life in pre-Roman Gaul. Flanking the entryway, a pair of columns displayed notices advertising the exhibit within. The poster on the left showed several pieces of early jewelry, greatly enlarged to reveal the complex detail of twisted gold and chased enamel that had been the fashion some two thousand years before. Scattered on a drape of blood red satin were intricately crafted clasps and pins, some in abstract patterns of twining wires, some in the shapes of birds or animals.

An array of armbands was arranged in overlapping circles at the bottom of the poster. At the center was a large gold torque, the open-clasped necklace favored by Celts from Ireland to Turkey. Its end finials were in the shapes of rearing horses, their hooves still showing traces of the original lapis blue overlay. The effect was at once luxurious and brutal.

Flic-Flac studied the many circles of twisted gold, bending forward so close to the poster that his nose touched the glass. He stared at the horses until their hooves seemed to beat in time with his pulse. It was the longest he had looked at any form of art since his unfortunate experience in Florence — not that he had any memory of that or any other time before his arrival in France.

After several minutes of concentration, Flic-Flac turned to the poster on the other side of the entry. It showed an enlarged detail of an Italian sarcophagus carved with a relief of Romans battling Gauls. You could tell the Romans by their short curls, firm jaws, pleated tunics, and elegant metal helmets. The Gauls were ragged and hairy and displayed gaping wounds that lost little of their horror for being depicted in cold, white stone. At the center of the melee, a Roman centurion brandished a sword above the fallen figure of a stout, bearded Gaul whose nakedness was emphasized by the heavy bands of jewelry that encircled his arms and throat.

The sarcophagus itself, on loan from the Capitoline Museum in Rome, was on display in the open courtyard just beyond. Mesmerized, Flic-Flac moved toward it. He circled the sarcophagus several times, studying it from all angles but always returning to the prostrate Gaul, whose face, magnified almost to life size, had caught his eye in the poster.

Even a child would have noticed the resemblance. Especially a child, not yet trained to relegate the past to a comfortable island of over-and-done that could have no significant connection to the present. Flic-Flac considered his own body, comparing it with the vibrant carving on the sarcophagus. The same broad chest and thick neck. The same muscular arms. The same anguished eyes. The same wild hair and beard. For a last, long moment he squatted before the carving, staring intently at his double, glowing in the radiant certainty that he had at last discovered who he was.

Rising from his reverie, Flic-Flac spent a long time studying the first poster, making a precise mental inventory of the jewelry it portrayed. He then headed straight for a pawn shop on the Avenue Victor-Hugo, swerving for only a moment to make his way through a crowd of tourists getting off a bus. He remembered having seen something there that he now realized he would need.

Hunting Treasure

S EVERAL YEARS AGO metal detectors had been all the rage in the South of France. Men who would never deign to hold a broom spent hours sweeping long-handled magnetic sensors over the surface of their garden plots, hoping for gold coins or diamond rings and turning up an impressive number of old keys and broken corkscrews. But fashions pass in the byways of Provence almost as quickly as they do on the boulevards of Paris, and the shop owner was willing to listen when Flic-Flac offered to trade a pair of tickets to tomorrow's bullfight in the arena for this useless device. The tickets, for those who are keeping track of such things, had just been acquired from a tourist who had not been watching his backpack as carefully as ordinary prudence required.

In his period of study outside the museum, Flic-Flac had taken full note of the necklaces and pins and great gleaming platters of chased and beaten gold. They were his, the treasures had whispered. And he was theirs, his muddled heart had replied. When he thought of the metal detector, it had been like the confirmation of a long-held plan. From now on he would devote himself to unearthing the sacred treasures of ancient Gaul. He would travel the remote countryside of Provence, sweeping the fields and forests for the sacred objects his people had left there two millennia ago. Since the French, in his experience, stayed at home at all opportunities, Flic-Flac felt he had a good chance of finding areas that had not been disturbed since his glorious naked brother warriors had been overcome by those hairless invaders in their ridiculous skirts.

First, however, he had to learn how to operate the metal detector. Even a madman is only as good as his tools. Draping the machine over his shoulder, Flic-Flac walked back to where he had left his car and prepared to study the instruction book somebody had thoughtfully taped to the handle of his new acquisition.

He was resigned to a long morning. Leaning against the curb of the outdoor parking area beside the Roman Arena, his legs stretched comfortably out into the street, he skimmed the descriptions of VLF circuitry, ferrous/nonferrous controls, shaft extensions, and special adaptations for highly mineralized ground. It was all an exercise in stalling. The first page had contained the crucial information, and it was bad news. The metal detector ran on nine-volt batteries. Three of them. One thing Flic-Flac really disliked was stealing from children. Frowning, he stood up and retreated to the shadows to await his prey.

A Family Outing: Second Attempt

IN A RATIONAL universe, the Hart family would have spent their second Sunday in France lounging around the pool, nibbling from platters of chilled fruit and admiring the shadows of clouds upon the lavender that stretched in rows out to the distant hills. Under the system of chaotic influences that dominates our current habitation, where the flutter of a butterfly's wings in Asia can bring devastation to the capitals of Europe, the pool was already claimed by mosquitoes and scorpions, and the lavender made Vivian sneeze. When the children woke the morning after their long drive to nowhere, rested and starving and thrilled to find themselves already dressed, their mother amazed them by proposing that they all get back into the car and drive to some distant place called Arles.

It was a famous city, she said, with a giant arena where gladiators used to fight each other, and lots of ancient statues and stuff. If they left at once, she said, they could see the Roman ruins in the morning light and still have time to locate the house of some painter whose name sounded like a cough. They would eat breakfast in the car. The important thing was to get going before something happened to interrupt the plan. It was absolutely essential that they get *some*where and do *some*thing as a family before the day was over.

Barely sober after three hours' sleep, Richard nonetheless recognized the hysteria seeping into Vivian's voice. He had heard that tone before, most notably after an ill-considered fling with a really petite shoe model just after Justin was born. They had agreed to put the incident behind them, but that didn't mean Richard had forgotten the way his wife sounded just before she fell apart. Leaping out of bed with surprising agility, he pushed the children into the kitchen, wiped their faces with a wet dish towel, slapped together some sandwiches to eat on the road, and had them all in the car in seven minutes. And that included scraping the honey from the backseat.

While Richard drove, Vivian read aloud from her historical guidebook, the one that skipped existing attractions to linger over vanished archaeological wonders. It offended Vivian that the author concentrated so exclusively on the monuments of masculine imperialist conquest, but it was a good book to read in the car. You were going too fast to see anything anyway, so it didn't matter that most of the marvels mentioned were long since gone.

She had just been reading the section on Arles, where the arena was built to seat 25,000, with special sections for the followers of the Roman forest god Silvanus and the Egyptian goddess Isis, protector of sailors. Looking up, she was astonished to see a road sign with the same name as the next entry in her guidebook. On this site, she said firmly, one can still see the marks of ancient centuriation. On that site. The one they had just passed.

"Whazzat?" Justin asked, spraying bits of cheese sandwich around the backseat. "Whazzat?" was his second most favorite phrase, after "where are we?"

"Centuriation," Vivian repeated, reading from her book. "The boundaries of the plots of land given to retired centurions from the Sixth Legion."

Centurions were like majors or lieutenants, she added. When the Roman armies conquered a region, the land was divided up and given to the officers as a reward for service. The soldiers got more than they could ever have bought with money, and Rome was sure to have its territories populated with people friendly to the home force.

"Forty acres and a mule," Richard muttered.

"I don't see any mules," Lily complained from the backseat. "I don't see anything!"

"Well, you could if we were going more slowly," Vivian said. "Not mules, I mean, but the marks of the Roman land. See, after the army conquered here, they gave the land away to the soldiers, so they could build houses and live here."

"What about the people who lived here already?" Apparently Justin was developing a social conscience.

"I guess here was lots of empty land," Vivian offered lamely. "Anyway, the people who lived here already were defeated, and that meant they didn't have much choice."

"I thought after you lost a war you got foreign aid," Justin objected. His fifth-grade class had just spent a year studying the Second World War and its aftermath. For weeks his favorite game had been Firebombing Dresden, played with flying Ninja Turtles and toppling Lego buildings.

Vivian took a deep breath, ready to launch into a brief analysis of the Marshall Plan, but Richard beat her to it.

"That, pal, is a very modern concept."

"Whatever."

"Whatever" was Justin's third most favorite expression.

Flic-Flac is Recognized, After a Fashion

FLIC-FLAC NOTICED THE Harts' car as soon as it pulled into the municipal parking area. Obviously tourists, and not very clean ones, judging from the strange pieces of grass and branches that were stuck in the car's fenders. The driver, a paunchy papa who needed a shave, was of no interest. The woman, a scrawny, freckled blond dressed in shorts and an unbecoming beige T-shirt, was equally dull. Flic-Flac watched as she walked between cars to study the shuttered grocery store across the way. The mama hen was seeking provisions for her chicks. Fine. Well-fed children carried toys, and toys carried batteries. Flic-Flac needed batteries. He concentrated on making himself invisible while the children squirmed out of the backseat.

A pink backpack. A blue backpack. The little girl sat down on the curb while her brother, older and more awake, unzipped his bag and took out a dirty yellow tennis ball. Soon he was bouncing it off the wall of the arena, trying to hit the matador in the bullfight posters. Timing his steps to the noise of the ball, Flic-Flac moved toward the curb and the blue bag abandoned there. He almost had it in his grasp when Lily turned around and started screaming.

And why not? Lily was no stranger to crazy bums. There were several who made their home right on her block in Manhattan. Even by her sophisticated standards, however, Flic-Flac was a terrifying figure. His broad chest straining against a torn and filthy shirt, his matted red hair reaching well past his shoulders, his blackened toenails curling like weapons out of his rubber sandals, he looked like a nightmare and smelled considerably worse.

Plus he had his hand out for her brother's backpack, which was lying on the curb not six inches from her own pale and tender bottom. Screaming was what you were supposed to do when you needed help. That's what all the grown-ups told her. Yell, run, scream, get help. So now she did, and her father got angry.

To do him justice, Lily's screams were not what Richard needed right then. What he needed was a cold beer. Back in New York, when he had dreamed of coming to Arles, his vision hadn't included lack of sleep, a crazed wife, hungry children, or confusing street signs. Thinking back to the photography festival, he had imagined himself leaning against the zinc counter of a nice, cool bar, talking shop with an international array of colleagues. Now he was standing in a shadeless parking lot waiting for some poor excuse of a breakfast, his head splitting from the noise his son was making with that stupid ball. When Lily broke down for no reason on earth and started shrieking about a lion man about to attack her, Richard lost his cherished paternal cool.

Needless to say, there was no man of any sort in the area. Flic-Flac had vanished with the first turn of Lily's little head. By the time Vivian returned, empty-handed, Lily was at the hiccup stage of recovery and Justin was expressing an urgent need to find a toilet. Smiling grimly, Richard announced that he was about to introduce his son to the French way of paying respect to the walls of public buildings. After that, he added, they would see the sights.

In the Footsteps of van Gogh

THE ATTRACTIONS OF ARLES divide into two types: omnipresent and underrated remnants of antiquity, and absent but cherished icons of modernity. In a city where every sewer project uncovers another Roman shrine, atrium, or wine cellar buried since the first century, reminders of the classical past are a part of the civic infrastructure too available to demand much commemorative effort beyond the necessary erection of a gate from which to charge admission.

The recent past, however, has proven more in need of resurrection. Vincent van Gogh, for example, who was derided, imprisoned, and eventually driven out of town during the brief period when he lived in Arles, is now a patron saint and presiding genius of the local souvenir trade. From the multistoried McDonald's serving Big Macs beneath elegant tile murals reproducing Van Gogh's landscapes to the actual Café de Nuit, which has its limestone facade painted yellow to match the artist's moonlit vision, every effort had been made to remind visitors that they were now in the adopted city of the divinely deranged master. Little of van Gogh's Arles actually remains, however; the closest the modern pilgrim can come is to follow the set of ceramic footprints that have been embedded in the sidewalk to mark places where he almost certainly, at some time or other, must have walked.

Somehow this fact had escaped Vivian, who insisted they begin their sightseeing with a fruitless search for the yellow house that she eventually conceded was gone. As the sun rose higher and the early morning blue of the sky gave way to an oppressive dusty bronze, Justin and Lily complained loudly about having to walk through stupid streets looking for places that weren't there, following some dead guy's clay footprints.

Bribery was the temporary solution. The only stores open on Sunday morning were the souvenir kiosks, but those seemed ready to meet all the children's needs. First they demanded Cokes to keep them from dying of thirst. Next they wanted straw hats so they could walk around without getting sunstroke. Then it was time for more Cokes, and postcards, and water pistols that the salesman assured them they could have filled at any fountain if the current drought hadn't left the fountains dry. At Richard's suggestion, they filled the guns with Coke and practiced squirting them in each other's mouths.

By 11:00 A.M. Vivian was defeated. They would stop for an early lunch, then see the sights. The real ones, the ones that were still there. The Roman ruins. The only restaurant open at that hour was an outdoor café with a menu printed in five languages. Justin and Lily were delighted. They did not want authenticity. They wanted pizza. Orders placed (including, of course, another round of Cokes), the children sank back in relief and counted how many Campari ads they could read on the umbrellas.

Picking at her *salade à la grecque,* which had sounded promising but turned out to be wilted, Vivian kept up a running commentary on the weather. "It wouldn't be this hot if it weren't for the Roman conquest," she told Justin, trying to explain away his complaints. "Before the conquest, all of Provence was a vast forest. Two thousand years ago, you could walk through pinewoods all the way from St. Etang to the Mediterranean Sea."

Justin was staring at his pizza, not his mother, but Vivian continued. They had come to France to expand their horizons. She couldn't waste this opportunity to talk about Important Things.

"When the Romans settled Provence," she went on brightly, "they treated the Rhône river like a conveyor belt, chopping down the trees all along the banks and sending them to the shipyards here in Arles. They cut down the trees in the cities, too, because you can't put up an arena or even a warehouse in the middle of a forest. From an eco-feminist perspective," she added, "all the Roman construction was also natural destruction. Those guys were out to get Mother Nature."

"I can't stand it," Justin said suddenly, a catch in his voice.

"Deforestation?" Vivian was pleased he had been listening, but she wasn't used to such an emotional response to her lectures on ecological history.

"This pizza," he answered. There was a definite quiver in his voice. "It's gross. It has ham in it. I hate ham. I want to go home."

"But we haven't even seen the arena yet, or the Roman baths. It's too early to go home."

"Not back to the stupid farmhouse!" Justin shouted. "Home! New York!" He was talking loud so he wouldn't burst into tears.

Now Lily was crying. "I want to go home, too," she sobbed. "I hate France. I hate this pizza. I want to play Barbie."

"Barbie!" Richard exclaimed, looking up from his beer as though he had just parachuted into the conversation. "Let's show Barbie the arena!" Rummaging in his camera bag until he found the doll he had still not remembered to give Lily, he swept the children up and away.

Instead of gratitude for the way Richard had solved the crisis, Vivian felt deserted. That's just like him, she thought spitefully. Run off on an adventure and leave me here to pay the bill. Leave Vivian to deal with everything while you go search for your art, or your cronies, or your next drink! Run off to see the arena without me! What about *my* art? she wondered, hot with resentment. What about *my* feelings?

The waiter was staring at her. Vivian slapped on her sunglasses so he couldn't see her teary eyes. She was being unfair, she knew, yet she couldn't shake the conviction that her discontent was Richard's fault. Instead of rekindling romance in passionate Provence, they had barely spoken to each other since the plane landed. He rose at daybreak, claiming to need the early light for his calendar pictures but stopping, she was sure, for a wake-up snort with the truckers on the other side of the highway. Then he came back in time for dinner, drank several glasses of wine, and was sound asleep before Justin had brushed his teeth. In the past, they had always patched up quarrels with great, sloppy sessions of lovemaking, but here there was no quarrel and no sex, either. Between packing and flying and getting over jet lag, it had been almost two weeks . . .

Then, squaring her skinny shoulders, Vivian confronted the real problem. Stale marriage, cranky children, uncertain future — all of these were true enough. But they were merely symptoms of the larger problem, which lay within herself. With every passing moment, Vivian felt she was losing her foothold on the cutting edge of cultural commentary. Everything she did and said, everything she stood for and everything she wanted was becoming trite.

Even her crises were commonplace. How unoriginal to be torn between ambition and family obligation, to worry about losing her husband and losing her youth. She had already lost her job, after all. Now that she was really in Provence, she suspected that it, too, had become passé. Probably this year all the really smart people were in Burgundy. Certainly having a breakdown in a café was the essence of banality. Pawing through her bag, she found the credit card that had fallen to the bottom. When the waiter demanded payment in cash she pretended not to understand any of his five languages, including English.

Young, Healthy, and Full of Opinions

A RIEL STERN, YOUNG, healthy and full of opinions, prized detachment above all other qualities of intellect. As far as Ariel was concerned, actual knowledge of one's subject was a source of aesthetic corruption. The purpose of art was not to hold a mirror up to nature, as Shakespeare had supposed, but to create an alternate and entirely different world. As a literary style, realism was hopelessly out-of-date.

Thus Ariel was particularly annoyed, early in July, to find herself preparing for a six-week sojourn in Provence. This was a part of France that she had heretofore regarded as only a rumor, a legend, a whiff of atmosphere, and, of course, the setting for the historical novel she was writing. To go to Provence would restrict her imagination, distracting her with images of what was instead of more important dreams of what might be.

Left to her own devices, she would have stayed in Paris. She had gone there straight from her graduation from Berkeley, to be in a place where intellectuals still commanded some respect. She had spent her undergraduate career reading incomprehensible translations of feminist, post-deconstructionist literary theory. It was time to read the incomprehensible originals, and to meet, or at least share a telephone exchange with, the authors. If she hadn't made a name for herself by the time she was twenty-five, she intended to move back to California and go into public relations with all the other English majors from her class.

When Ariel had announced this plan a year ago, her mother had sighed twice, reminded her that it was as easy to get AIDS in Paris as in San Francisco, and given her a ride to the airport. Ariel's father was living in Denver with his third wife and their two despicable children, so she hadn't bothered to ask his opinion.

Getting to Paris had been easy. Staying there required a job. Fortunately, Ariel had a plan. The editor of *Huit Jours* had spent the previous semester as a visiting lecturer at Berkeley, and she had been the star of his seminar on comparative journalism. In a drunken moment at his farewell party, he had told her to visit him at the magazine offices in Paris. Dropping her bags at the apartment of the friend of a friend who had agreed to put her up for one week, max, she changed into the severe black outfit she thought made her look particularly intellectual and went to take him up on the invitation.

Like most men, Henri Fort remembered Ariel's large breasts and small, even teeth, the nimbus of implausibly curly, dark brown hair that bounced on her shoulders when she walked, and the delightful crooked bump in her nose. To his credit, he also remembered her ability, unusual for an American, to talk about ideas instead of things.

None of these charms, however, was enough to justify an editorial post at France's second most popular weekly magazine. Expressing infinite regret, he pointed out that Ariel's French was not quite sufficient for the position to which she aspired, even had union regulations permitted such a plan. As an afterthought, he added that he and his wife were in urgent need of an au pair for their two young daughters. Their English nanny had just resigned, and Henri was most eager to find a replacement before his mother-in-law decided to move to Paris to help.

Further Notes on the Exploitation of Women

EVEN AS A twelve-year-old, Ariel had scorned baby-sitting. It was stifling, ludicrously underpaid, and nothing less than a covert program to socialize young girls into their roles as exploited servants of the male power structure. She knew this was true because it had been the topic of many campfire discussions at Woman Warriors, the camp she had attended every summer between the ages of eight and fifteen.

"I am an intellectual," she replied, "not a nursemaid." Leaving her résumé, she nodded coldly and bounced out to find her destiny elsewhere.

Five days of increasingly humiliating job searches changed her mind. Faced with the imminent prospect of being homeless in Paris, Ariel swallowed her principles and made another call to the office of *Huit Jours*. If the position of nanny was still open, she would be happy to discuss her qualifications.

In fact, it was an ideal situation. Henri, the publisher, rose every morning to have breakfast with his daughters before going to his office. His wife, Marie-Hélène, a stunning blond who starred in an extremely popular soap opera directed by a disciple of Eric Rohmer, dropped the girls at school on her way to the television studio. Ariel's job was to meet the girls at school in the afternoon, escort them home, supervise their after-school activities, teach them English over dinner, get them ready for bed, and make sure nothing evil happened until their parents returned, generally quite late. For her efforts she received the equivalent of a thousand dollars a month and a small but pleasant room of her own three floors above the elegant apartment of her employers.

That was how she thought of them: "her employers" when in the plural; "the publisher" when it was Henri alone; "the actress" when it was Marie-Hélène. Her ego demanded this degree of depersonalization. The children, who were six and eight years old, she thought of as Agathe and Hortense. Her employers were bright, rich, talented, and very busy, which made them extremely grateful for this instant replacement for that irresponsible girl who had so abruptly decamped to marry her childhood sweetheart. The publisher was rather nicer to her than the actress, but Ariel was sane enough to know that an affair with him would be an extremely bad idea.

As her French improved, she was encouraged to attend the Thursday morning press screenings of American films, during which she would provide the publisher with whispered translations for the more difficult aspects of American slang. *Wayne's World,* only now released in Europe and laced with many obscure synonyms for *vomit,* had proved particularly incomprehensible to the European ear. *Aladdin* had been another challenge, with its many visual and verbal wisecracks by the shape-shifting genie, but with Ariel's help Henri had goaded his leading commentator to a full-page exegesis on the body as prison in American film. Circulation had risen on the strength of the piece, which was cited on three different talk shows the day it came out. Ariel was presented with a very chic headband from Chanel in recognition of her contribution.

Apart from housing, money, and the dubious thrill of having her knee fondled by two editors, one on each side, during movie screenings, the central virtue of Ariel's new life was that it left her plenty of time for literary pursuits. After some consideration, she decided to write the great modern novel.

At first, this was an enterprise defined by what it would not be. Four years of study at a first-rate university had given Ariel a clear sense of what to avoid. She scorned the clumsy apparatus of

the coming-of-age novel, full of callow crises of sexual and professional identity. She had no patience for the lurid accounts of
drugs and violence that had made names for other writers her
age, or for the tales of desperate lives in trailer parks that came so
regularly from the graduates of academic writing programs.

However much others might pander to the crowd, she, Ariel,
had standards. She would not insert real people among her fic-
tional characters. She would not dwell on her traumatic childhood, and believed she would not have done so even if she had
had one. She would not write in dialect. She would not include
recipes. Beyond these negatives, however, she had no idea what
she intended to write. Her subject was something she expected to
discover in Paris.

And so she had. At the actress's suggestion, Ariel had obtained
a student visa by enrolling at the Sorbonne, where it was possible
to take an open-ended number of classes without approaching
anything so definitive as a degree. The curriculum that best fit
her schedule was a series of lectures called Deconstructing the
Giant: Julius Caesar and Gaul. It had changed her life.

According to the lecturer, a celebrated literary theoretician and
writer of popular detective novels, all previous attempts to understand the history of France had been tainted by an unsavory
yearning after facts. Since most of the past was a mystery and
would forever stay so, the professor pointed out, the only authentic history was that created by the imagination. This was particularly true of ancient Gaul, since the tribes that lived there had left
no written records. The sole statement about the Gallic Wars the
professor would accept as true was that Julius Caesar lied.

As he spoke about the early Gauls, Ariel was enchanted by the
possibilities. Her novel would be set during the first century B.C.,
she decided, a time about which she and most of her readers
knew next to nothing. Her heroine would be a Druid priestess —
a role she was not at all sure had ever been available to women.
She would learn only enough about her subject to recognize how
little she knew, so that her own ignorance would become, subtly

but inevitably, the true subject of her work. To guarantee that her readers would never succumb to any suspension of disbelief, willing or accidental, she would tell her story backward, starting with the heroine's death.

Every morning she wrote for an hour, directly after waking. Classes, meals, and errands occupied the rest of her day until it was time to meet Agathe and Hortense at school. In time, Ariel hoped, she would make some friends her own age, but in the meantime she kept busy. She even put together a short list of texts on Druid life that she should try to read, once she realized there was no threat of overfamiliarity with received opinion. The documents she sought were housed at the Bibliothèque Nationale, the great national library where, on rare occasions, with the proper credentials, it was possible to see a book.

Banished

IN THIS WAY a year had passed. Agathe and Hortense were learning excellent English and seemed genuinely fond of their funny American au pair. With help from the publisher, Ariel sold an article on goddess worship to Air France, for their in-flight magazine. In time, the publisher said, there might even be an opening for her on the staff of *Huit Jours*. But first she must finish her novel. He would never forgive himself if he kept her from her art. Or, of course, from her job taking care of his children.

By her second June in Paris, Ariel was deemed sufficiently trustworthy to transport the girls to the actress's mother in Nice. After depositing Hortense and Agathe with their grandmother, Ariel was to proceed to her employers' newly acquired vacation house in Gordes, prepare it for their own arrival later in the season, and fetch the children to meet them there in the middle of August.

Thinking with regret of the Parisian routines it had taken her so long to establish, of the books that she had still not managed to read at the Bibliothèque Nationale, and not least of the extremely handsome young librarian whose job it was to inspect her credentials, Ariel reluctantly packed her clothes, her laptop computer, and her unread copy of the *Goddess Guide to Europe*. It was only after she left Agathe and Hortense with the rather austere old lady they called Meemee that she realized she was, for the first time since her arrival in France, completely alone.

It took four bone-shaking hours for the local bus to wind its way from the palm-lined promenades of Nice to the stone-shadowed streets of Gordes. Although she had a window seat for the passage from seaside to mountain, Ariel did not look at any of the celebrated scenery along the route. Instead, she spent the whole trip scrawling illegible notes on a pad clenched between her knees. It was important to write something every day.

When the bus pulled up at the central square of Gordes, Ariel capped her pen and got out. Following the actress's written directions, she crossed the square, passed the church, bore to the right down a narrow stone passage, and unlocked the faded green door of the seventeenth-century town house that had been gutted and rehabbed during the previous winter. In recent years Gordes had become the summer playground of the French media elite, and neither the publisher nor the actress could afford not to be there during the better part of August. In the meantime, Ariel could have the place to herself.

The first order of business was finding a place to work. The dining room, oddly located on the highest of four floors, was the largest and brightest space. If they had banished her from Paris and then trapped her in this hillside prison, she would at least take possession of the tower room. Unplugging a flashing neon sculpture that would have been a charming conversation piece if she had known anybody in the area with whom to converse, Ariel connected her computer and sat down to work. Brecca, her heroine, was calling to her. Ariel began describing the eclipse that had (working backward) already sealed her priestess's doom.

Through History with Asterix

B ACK IN ARLES, a cool breeze cleared the air and, with it, everyone's mood. By the time Vivian reached the arena, Justin was playing with his remote-control car. Lily had posed her new Barbie on a crumbling stone, with the tiers of seats rising behind her, and Richard was showing her how to use the light meter.

"We're starting an album," he explained, deadpan. "Barbie in Provence. Maybe it will be a photo novel. Keep your thumb off the lens!" he bellowed suddenly at Lily.

Justin came running, always eager to see his sister get into trouble. Then they had to discuss whether to walk through the shadowy arcades on the lower level of the arena or start by climbing to the top and circling the upper tier. By the time Justin remembered his new toy car, it was gone. Flic-Flac had seen to that.

"Easy come, easy go," Richard announced, so Justin would know there was no point in begging for a replacement. "Anyway, it eats nine-volt batteries, and they're hard to get around here. Let's go act like gladiators."

After climbing over the arena, they headed back to the center of town, where the guidebook said there was a tourist office. Vivian wanted directions to the Hôtel Dieu, the lunatic asylum where van Gogh had been an inmate. Richard wanted to see if he could get any information on the photography expo, due to open with a gala ceremony the following night but currently invisible, at least to him. Lily wanted a Coke. They had almost passed the Museum of Pagan Art when something caught Justin's eye.

"Lily, look at this," he hissed, moving back a step so his sister could see the poster. Then he turned to his parents.

"Can we go in? Please?"

Richard and Vivian hesitated, bewildered. Justin hated museums. Two minutes ago he had been threatening to walk back to
the farmhouse if they made him look at any more of their stupid
historic junk. Now he wanted to see a museum show about
Provence before Caesar. What was going on?

"*Please?*" Justin begged. "This looks *very* educational."

Even Lily was staring at him now. Then she, too, looked at the
poster.

"Oh, dope!" she exclaimed. "Let's go in."

Well, of course, they had to, after that. Richard and Vivian were
hardly the sorts of parents who would refuse to take their children to an art exhibition.

Passing through a small courtyard crammed with stone heads,
metal cisterns, and a huge marble thing that looked like an over-
wrought bathtub, they entered the museum proper and watched
the introductory slide show.

It was a cartoon history of Provence narrated by Asterix,
everybody's favorite early Gallic warrior. The first part was about
killing, with lots of grunts and whacks to demonstrate the local
resistance to the Roman invaders. The second part was about
finding the remains of those battles, which was more complicated. First Asterix dug in his garden and discovered the founda-
tions of an early Celtic settlement. Then his fat friend Obelix
threw a few centimes in a wishing well, which was apparently a
distant echo of an ancient Celtic custom of throwing treasures
into sacred ponds to please the gods. Then they both attended
some kind of sunrise prayer service, after which they grabbed the
main priest and threw him into the pond. Other cartoon figures
filed after him, throwing bowls and platters into the water. At the
end of the cartoon, Asterix was shown snorkeling through a
marsh where glittering tiaras hung on the underwater reeds, invisible to the modern family fishing from a boat above.

To Justin and Lily, the slide show was nothing short of an
enlightenment. They absorbed each frame with rapt attention,

treating Asterix with a respect they would never have thought to give their human teachers. In school, all they ever heard was useless, irrelevant information. Asterix had just provided a highly pertinent explanation of their own recent adventures.

As they moved out of the dark into the exhibit proper, Justin and Lily dashed ahead to the room where the goldwork was displayed. Vivian stopped to study a large table covered with a relief map of Provence as it had looked in the first century B.C. From where she was standing, it looked like a voluptuous female figure lying on her side. Mount Ventoux was the head, the Luberon Mountains the shoulders and arms, the area of Marseilles the dip of waist and belly, and then the coastal mountains were a great, protective haunch.

This was a gift, Vivian realized. A chance angle of vision showed her how to approach her subject. Everything she had been struggling to say was laid out before her in fiberglass and felt. She pulled out a notebook and began to scribble. "The Landscape as Body," she wrote at the top of the page. "Earth is a woman," she continued, "ready to nurture those who settle into her curves and hollows, but in modern times she has been ravaged by invaders. They violate her waters, eviscerate her forests, brutally penetrate her mountains, and drag the quarried stones to cover over the softness of her level ground."

Squinting at the scale model of Provence, with its tiny toothpick trees and acrylic blue waters, Vivian thought of a photograph she had seen of a woman's torso after a mastectomy. That was what the Romans had done to Gaul, she thought. All later agriculture was just a reenactment of that first brutality, all landscape art a record of the mutilated carcass. Viewed in this way, van Gogh's fields were like diagrams of different kinds of sutures.

"Sutures," she wrote. "Mastectomy. Roman rape." She wasn't quite certain how this would relate to the lush vineyards that blanketed the current landscape, or how she would bring it to the Impressionist painters who were, in theory, her subject. Once she started writing, though, she was sure it would all make sense.

Justin and Lily in the Museum

THERE WAS ONLY one other room in the small museum, and it held the heart of the exhibition. When Vivian rejoined them, Justin and Lily were staring into the cases of gold jewelry.

On the wall were life-size black-and-white drawings of ancient inhabitants of France — not the idealized sculptures of the Roman period but something closer to what historians thought the Gauls had really looked like. Superimposed on the drawings were color photographs of the artifacts in the cases. A sketch of a Celtic princess featured a photograph of the elaborate necklace she wore beneath her cloak. A group of well-dressed revelers, each wearing torques and cloak pins matched to those on display, watched while a naked man in a wooden cage was set on fire. Two solemn men in fur tunics carried a large oval bowl. Looking at the real bowl, in the case before them, Justin and Lily started whispering in excitement when they saw its sides were engraved with emblems that looked a lot like the stuff they had found in the pond.

The children were swiveling their heads back and forth from the case to the walls, nudging each other and whispering furiously. Lily tried to borrow her father's camera, but the guard said photographs were *interdit. Interdit* was a big word in France, she had already noticed. As far as she could tell, it meant, "No way."

"You are an imbecile cow," Lily answered sweetly, in French. That was another of Clotilde's phrases, the one she always used when giving in to any of the children's wishes. Head turned, Lily failed to see the guard's outraged expression. Justin continued running from case to case, stopping only to moan out things like "awesome," "dope," and "wicked cool!" Vivian drifted back to the fiberglass landscape to commune with Gaia. This went on for over half an hour.

Alone of his family, Richard was bored. Jewelry was definitely not his thing. Neither were grainy photographs of archaeological digs or statues without noses. He turned to the guard, meaning to ask about restaurants close to the photography expo, but the man walked away. For some reason he acted as though he had been offended.

Eventually they left, though not before Barbie had been immortalized standing in front of a particularly beefy "Dying Gaul" out in the courtyard, where cameras were allowed. By then, nobody had any energy for the Roman baths, or anything else except another round of Cokes. While he was paying, Richard let the children choose something from the array of toys strung up around the drink seller's wagon. When Lily asked for a plastic beach set, he bought it without even wondering what she planned to do with a shovel, rake, and sieve on the concrete margins of their swimming pool.

The Seeker

L OADED WITH JUSTIN's batteries, the metal detector began a steady click. Flic-Flac made a trial run though the south arcade of the arena, gathering enough loose change to buy some gas. Then he drove north, into the foothills, to pursue his real quarry. Somewhere lurked an ancient treasure destined for him. Flic-Flac's mission on earth was to bring it to the surface. Of this, the born-again Celtic warrior was sure.

The Limitations of Pure Idea

ARIEL LOOKED OVER yesterday's pages with disgust. Her intention was to write a narrative of pure idea, one that would reveal the workings of her own superior intellect while avoiding the encumbrances of race, class, and gender that kept so many other writers from the true fluidity of nontransgressive expression. What she had achieved was a heavy-breathing imitation of airport-rack romance, an embarrassingly incoherent sequence of stilted episodes peopled by dull-witted, muscular characters whose actions made no sense of any kind. Scenes of sexual confrontation, of clan brutality and physical intimidation, of ethical crises and spiritual ecstasy — all these came easily. The mundane but essential business of getting her characters from situation A to situation B seemed to be beyond her creative capacity.

For a time she had hoped this wouldn't matter. Since her theme was the unknowability of knowledge, surely she didn't have to bother with anything so pedestrian as plot. She would be admired for her highly elliptical narrative structure, she told herself. Her book would be one of those short novels with lots of dots that were always described as "suggestive" and "profound."

Back in Paris, wearing black and reading Derrida in snatches as she rode the Métro, that had seemed a reasonable plan. Under the brilliant sun of Provence, where anyone insane enough to wear dark colors soon found them faded into mottled shades of brown and gray, she was starting to realize her scheme would never work. Historical novels had to have heft, or at least transitions. Only characters of the twentieth century or later were allowed to live their lives with ellipses. Perhaps they were required to do so.

Her own life, for example, was becoming nothing but a series of dots, omissions with no substance in between. For the first few days, Gordes had been interesting. She had visited the castle, now a museum displaying an incongruous collection of modern paintings, had recognized it as the perfect example of the present imposing its interpretive vision on the past, and had found the exhibits so boring she could not imagine ever going back. She had studied the menus of the restaurants whose prices she could not afford, memorized the wares of the handful of shops that catered to the tourists, and made a pilgrimage of her daily trip to the only grocery store in town. It had been exciting to start each morning with no responsibilities except to her art, and wonderful to turn each afternoon to a new route for her daily walk. But then she had run out of both art and routes, and was left with a dry well of creativity and the dusty prospect of another empty day. There in the midst of the open country, with a vast house at her sole disposal, she was trapped as thoroughly as any medieval princess in her tower.

And as lonely. Sartre said that hell was the others, but what did he know? Since arriving in Gordes she had spoken to no one but shopkeepers, and not much even to them. She missed her student café, her few hard-won friends in Paris, and even Agathe and Hortense. She thought with increasing wistfulness of the clerk at the Bibliothèque Nationale, of a lawyer who had been transferred to Brussels after their second date, of comrades from Berkeley, and even of her first boyfriend, who had dropped her most cruelly their sophomore year at Santa Rosa County Consolidated High School. She tried to keep to her routine, mornings spent working on her novel, afternoons given over to domestic chores and aimless wandering, but she found herself increasingly dissatisfied — with her book, with her schedule, with her life. Restless and edgy, she went out for yet another walk.

The Perfect Hosts

T HE FRENCH LOVE WALLS, and they build them well. The golden stones that sheltered Rosalie Bartello's garden in Gordes had lasted over two hundred years. They had been used as barricades during the local sieges of the Revolution, rebuilt according to the principles of scientific farming during the nineteenth century, and pockmarked by German bullets during World War II, when Gordes had been a center for the French Resistance. They had withstood the aggressive renovation of her first husband, Bernard de La Fontaine, when he had transformed a rough farmhouse into an elegant summer retreat for his young American bride, and they had given up a few of their number to form the monument when he died twenty-five years later. And now they reflected the soft candles lighting the private dinner Rosalie was enjoying with her new husband, Hugo Bartello.

If middle-aged people are allowed to have fairy-tale romances, as they certainly ought to be, then the marriage of Rosalie and Hugo clearly deserved the title. She was beautiful and rich, he was clever and charming, and both were intelligent enough to know there was no percentage in not being kind. Everyone winked when the newly appointed director of the Metropolitan Museum married the long-retired but still famous fashion model of the 1960s, widow of the founder of one of Paris's most influential fashion magazines, but nobody who saw them together thought it was anything but a love match. They kept his apartment on Fifth Avenue and her houses in Paris and Gordes, and they were setting out together to enjoy what promised to be a charmed life.

Charmed in its prospects, at least. The first weeks had been far too harried for any real pleasure. A private wedding, attended only by Rosalie's two grown daughters and Hugo's mother, had been followed by a staggering number of official parties associated with the opening of the largest show of Impressionist paintings ever assembled (the show that had assured Hugo's rise to the director's office). Rosalie sometimes felt their marriage license had been mistakenly exchanged for an entry ticket in a marathon dance.

Two months later Hugo and Rosalie had finally arrived in Gordes for a welcome respite and a belated honeymoon. It seemed the greatest luxury in the world to be sitting barefoot at a table set on the grass, eating small amounts of simple food and not having to sparkle. In the fall Hugo would have to find some marvelous new exhibition, something to fill the museum calendar up and prove that his appointment had not been a mistake. In the fall Rosalie would have to make some hard decisions about her future role in the La Fontaine publishing empire. In the fall the social season would begin in earnest. But now it was the beginning of July, and for the moment, at least, they had escaped.

In theory, they were resting. It was essential, they agreed, to escape the clamor of city life, the pressures of work, and the intrusions of the press. Their sanity depended on it, to say nothing of their health and, of course, their marriage. Obviously, then, the first order of business was to host a party. Only after their respective circles of friends had had their chance to gawk at each other would the newlyweds be allowed to start getting away from it all. It wasn't cynicism that made them think this way. It was practical knowledge of the world.

But it wasn't any fun. Seizing the pen and paper she had put down beside her plate, Rosalie started going over a list of names Hugo's secretary had prepared. Every day since her marriage, it seemed, Rosalie had attended a donor's dinner, a director's lunch, an opening gala, or a benefit tea. She and Bernard, her first husband, had entertained often and well, but it had never been as grueling as this.

"Let's invite only people we like," she said suddenly.

"Dream on, dear," Hugo responded.

"Well, at least let's not invite anybody we hate."

"What about that nasty Claude person?" Hugo asked. "The one who writes for *L'Express* and bares his nicotine-stained fangs at me every time we meet. Does that mean we don't invite him?"

"What are you thinking?" Rosalie objected. "We can't not invite Claude. He's my neighbor. Our waterline goes through his land."

"Exactly," Hugo agreed, pleased to have made his point. "We entertain because we must."

Rosalie went back to the list.

"Why do we know so many people?" she asked. "Why didn't I become a Sister of Charity? That's what I meant to do in second grade."

Even a much duller man than Hugo would have known not to answer such a question. He reached across the table and touched Rosalie's arm, a gesture of sympathy that changed into a laugh as she seized his wrist, pulled him from his seat, and raised her arm, still clutching his.

"We are champions!" she whispered, defying the hills and stars to deny her claim. She always spoke low, to keep the servants from overhearing. "We are champions, and we will prevail!" And then she dropped her arm, gave Hugo an exaggerated curtsy, and turned to smile at the distant moon. Or was it a distant electric light? The village council had recently voted to install hideous Second Empire streetlamps, to make it easier for the tourists to arrive at night. Without her glasses Rosalie could not be sure.

Ariel, passing on the secondary road she had chosen for her walk, had just reached the single place where a quirk of geography allowed a glimpse into Rosalie's secret garden. Looking down over the hedges, she saw an elegant couple performing some sort of antique quadrille in the moonlight. The steps involved bowing and pacing and sudden raising of arms. Entranced, she stopped to admire the scene. At that moment the woman looked right at her and smiled.

Startled and vaguely ashamed, Ariel hurried on, not stopping until she barked her shin on a huge hollow block of stone, the remains of an ancient olive press. By then it was really dark. Taking the main road back into town, she hurried inside her employers' summer house and opened a dusty can of sardines for her solitary dinner.

The Theory of the Fourth Artist

RICHARD HAD A THEORY about how to become a famous photographer. Actually he had a number of theories, any of which he was happy to expound. You have to wear leather or you won't be respected was one. You have to be invited to the right parties was another. You have to be gay was a third. Those were conspiracy theories, the loser's whine. His latest theory at least relied less on superstition and more on his own energies. The ticket to fame, he had decided, was to be the fourth person on the next bandwagon, wherever it might be going.

According to Richard's calculations, timing was more important that content. The way he saw it, the first person to do something was never recognized until the thirty-year retrospectives, and Richard had no desire to achieve fame when he was too old to enjoy it. The second person to do something was dismissed as marginal. The third was the one who convinced the critics that they had to develop a vocabulary to deal with this stuff, whatever it might be. The fourth, though, was the real winner. He was the lucky stiff who got the reviews, the appreciation, the media coverage, and the gallery sales. Like the radio shows that give a prize to the seventh caller, the gods of fame bestowed their favors according to where you were in the line. The really great artists were the ones who knew how to jockey for position.

That was why Richard was back in Arles on Monday afternoon. The International Exposition of Photography was about to open. If his theory of the fourth artist was correct, this was the place to find out what the first three innovators were up to, so he could hitch a ride on their ideas.

He had spent the morning in aimless driving, pulling off the road to shoot anything he saw that looked like it might keep the calendar people off his back. At noon he had come upon a field of early sunflowers, huge green stalks whose orange flowers cast purple shadows on the sun-baked ground. Even Richard was pleased with the effect, especially when he realized the sunflowers were next to a restaurant with a promising number of local trucks parked on the grass in front. Another of Richard's theories was that plumbers and electricians knew all the best places to eat.

Two hours later, contentedly running his tongue behind his teeth to pick up stray fragments of oxtail stew, Richard returned to the parking lot behind the arena to get down to the business of the day. After he had paid for his three-day pass, however, it turned out that the opening gala, with its sneak preview of the works of seventy-five contemporary photographers of international renown, was by invitation only. Richard was not invited.

Neither were most of the other festival participants, who were expected to be satisfied with less stellar exhibits displayed in scattered venues around the city. Those more interested in self-promotion could hang their own works at an outlying soccer field that had been cleared for the display. Like everyone else, Richard leaped at the chance to show the world his art.

As he stood in the soccer field crowd, Richard could see a good many of the other portfolios on display. This was unnerving. Everywhere he looked was someone who seemed to have set up his tripod in front of the same field of sunflowers Richard had wasted a roll of film on that very day. "It was disgusting," he proclaimed, waking Vivian at four in the morning to report on the expo. "It was putrid. I don't care how much money they offer. I will never ever shoot another thing in bloom."

He was having trouble holding on to his tone of righteous indignation, partly because he was drunk but also because the day had improved greatly after he abandoned the embarrassment of the soccer field for the solace of a cold beer. Standing at the bar, he had met a trio of photojournalists who invited him to join them on a tour of the drinking establishments of Arles. None of the real pros went to the official shows, they explained. If Richard wanted to know what was going on, he should just listen to them.

Rubbing her nose in an effort to stay awake, Vivian asked who they were. Richard was going to tell her anyway, but it seemed more polite to ask.

"They're photojournalists," Richard repeated grandly, "which means they don't cut themselves off from the world around them. In fact, they're very influenced by the cultural climate of the day. And in France today the cultural climate is dominated by the Tour de France."

"What are you talking about?" Vivian objected sleepily. "The Tour de France is a bicycle race. You told me that yourself."

"If you have to know, they work for *World Sports Illustrated.*" For some reason, Richard felt a need to defend his new friends in their careers. "They're very talented, though. Real visionaries."

Which they were, though each had his own peculiar line of sight. In addition to the stuff they provided for the sports tabloid, each was pursuing another theme for the Tour de France. Greg, a whiz kid who had started selling his work when he was still an undergraduate in Iowa, was shooting nothing but the overflowing trash bins that marked each town through which the bicycle race had passed. Vanko, a Slav who couldn't even guess to what country his hometown was at this moment attached, was shooting the rear ends of cyclists in their spandex shorts, planning to go back and print them as diptychs alongside appropriated images of Edward Weston's famous photos of pears. Mac, whose real specialty was boxing and who was only there to cover particularly gory accidents and fights, refused to take any pictures of the bicycle race, claiming that the very act of opening his aperture in Provence would give his camera "V.C."

"What's V.C.?" Vivian asked.

"Visual clap," Richard explained. A dose of sentimental stupidity that no amount of penicillin would ever cure. Victims of V.C. were the ones out at dawn, shooting the mist as it cut through the hilltop villages and hung over the grape fields. Neither of them mentioned that those were the very shots Richard had been chasing for the past week.

By the end of the evening, Richard's fourth-on-the-bandwagon theory had been completely discredited. Vanko dismissed it as typical materialistic self-delusion. Greg and Mac just laughed.

"There *is* no way to conquer the market," Richard explained to Vivian, in a voice that was kind but firm. "To even make such an attempt is to subjugate your art to capitalistic oppression. If the market finds you, you are doubtless doing something wrong."

A Formative Encounter

Vivian, who was not so tired that she couldn't smell how much Richard had been drinking, avoided pointing out that the three financial purists who had taught her husband this lesson all had steady jobs. Instead she sat up in bed, clanging the wobbly brass headboard against the wall, and asked, "Are you going back to the expo tomorrow?"

"It's already tomorrow," Richard answered. "I'm going to get some sleep, then go back for the awards tonight. Probably a waste of time, but I already paid for the ticket. Maybe I'll get hit on the head by some new ideas."

Unlike most of Richard's predictions, this last one was fulfilled. Walking away from a shuttered café at two the next morning, trying to remember where he had parked the heap, he showed that slight lack of self-command which is so dangerous in the modern city. As soon as he stepped beyond the reach of the café lights, he was shoved into the street by a scrawny drug addict who stole his shoes and his camera bag and ran off before Richard could gather his senses to yell.

Driving home from Arles, his bare feet cold in the night air coming up through the broken flooring, Richard realized it could have been much worse. He hadn't been seriously beaten. He hadn't been shot. He hadn't even lost his camera, which was in his fanny pack. In fact, he had profited from the encounter. The mugger could keep the fifteen rolls of film, the aerosol lens cleaner, and the package of Callard & Bowser chocolate caramels. Richard had found the subject that would make him famous.

He was going to do portraits of the outlaw derelicts of Provence. As they tried to steal from him, he would steal back from them, appropriating their essence into his photographs. He would work at dawn, the hour of transition and transformation, when the flop drunks and druggies were sprawled in the gutters in defenseless stupor. *A Season in Hell in Provence,* he thought, playing with titles for his new series. *Down and Out in Nice and Monte Carlo. Country French Derelicts.*

The fear and outrage of an hour before had given way to the exhilaration of a breakthrough idea. From now on, Richard announced to the night sky, he was ignoring the demands and dictates of the marketplace. He would follow his genius, and if it led in directions the world was not ready to explore, then he would blaze the trail. Let others jostle for the fourth seat on the bandwagon. He would be in the lead.

Richard stayed home the next morning, strutting around the patio massaging his growing stubble and getting in Clotilde's way. Then, as Vivian had feared, he decided he would have to spend more time in the local bars, immersing himself in his subject. He began by crossing the highway. Monsieur Renard was very sympathetic to his project, though he had few true derelicts among his clientele. The highway screened them out, he noted complacently. You can't be a long-distance driver and a real *clochard* at the same time. *Clochard,* Richard learned, was the French name for the kind of guy he was seeking. According to Renard, Richard's scruffy beard was an excellent way to infiltrate their ranks.

The Treasure Trove

A RMED WITH THE PLASTIC rake and shovel, Justin and Lily made faster work of dredging the pond. While their father was seeking inspiration in Arles and their mother was ruining her digestion drinking coffee in Aix-en-Provence, they methodically cleaned and sorted their swag. By the following Wednesday, they had filled both backpacks with ancient Celtic gold they had decided to entrust to Marcel.

They hadn't seen their business partner since the Saturday market, and they were relieved to spot his distinctive egg-shaped figure passing through the parking lot of the Truck Stop St-Etang at 2:00 P.M., just as he had promised. Then he vanished for a few minutes, only to reappear walking along the drainage canal on their side of the highway. Justin wanted to ask how he had gotten there, but Lily was focused completely on the project at hand.

"Marcel-e," she shouted, giving the name an extra Provençal syllable in the accent she was learning from Clotilde. "Come here. I am waiting for you, you little goose shit! You are making me late!" Those were the words Clotilde always used when they were straggling home in the afternoon.

Marcel kept to his steady pace, scanning the margins of the ditch for attractive junk. When he reached the children, he shook their hands and waited patiently for whatever they had to say.

"Did you sell the treasure for us?" Justin asked, using the sentences he had cobbled together from his phrase book models.

"Yes," answered Marcel, smiling his usual vague smile.

"Did you bring the money back to us?"

"Yes," answered Marcel again, reaching into his pocket and taking out two twenty-franc notes and a ten-franc coin. "But ten francs I keep."

"Oui, okay," Justin agreed, pleased with the ease of the transaction. Marcel was not as slow as his mother thought.

Lily reached into her backpack. "Here's more treasure," she said. "Sell this, too."

First she took out a heavy necklace of braided gold, a kind of slip-on collar that she had learned at the museum was called a torque. Two more torques followed, along with a broken fragment of something they couldn't identify but still thought was cool enough to sell. To the pile she added a large cloak pin and a small hammered bowl whose purpose neither Lily nor Justin had been able to guess.

After a moment's hesitation, she pulled out four armbands, each different but all more intricately patterned than the ones they had sold the week before. Lily and Justin had argued since Sunday about whether to hold things back to give to a better salesman than Marcel, now that they knew what they were finding. But there wasn't anybody better, and so they had stayed with their original plan. Nervously, Lily handed over all ten pieces.

"They're very nice," she said, looking at Marcel to make sure he was listening. "They're worth a lot. They're *very* old," she added, her voice rising. "You should ask for a lot more money. At least a million francs!"

Marcel was not a man to be flustered. He took the bracelets, tried to fit one over his own fat wrist, then carefully put them with the other items in his bag.

"I will take them to the market on Saturday," he said slowly, as though repeating instructions. "I will bring you the money on Wednesday. I will put it in this pocket," he added, patting his shirt. "This is your money. My money goes here." He patted his pants.

He looked over to the house, where Clotilde was backing noisily out the door, dragging a plastic hamper full of wet clothes to dry on a line that stretched over the dusty car park. Before she could turn around, Marcel had vanished back into the shadows of the ditch. For a fat man, Marcel could move fairly quickly, especially to avoid people he did not like.

An Ancient and Honorable
Form of Commerce

A S IT TURNED OUT, the children's treasures made it to market even before Saturday, though not entirely as planned.
On Marcel's route back to Oppède-le-Percée, he passed through
a grove of unripe olives in which Flic-Flac was dozing away the
afternoon. As soon as he saw the young man's blank, round face,
Flic-Flac recognized a person worth knowing.

"Anything to trade?" he called, stumbling up from behind a
tree.

Barter is an ancient and honorable form of commerce. Similar
exchanges had taken place in this very field two thousand years
before, when it had been a regular stopping place on the tin route
from Manchester to Marseilles. But even twenty centuries ago,
when few people were as picky about dress and hygiene as they
are today, many would have been put off by Flic-Flac. It wasn't
just a question of matted hair and warped toenails, after all.
There were also the unpredictable shrieks and moans that punctuated his conversation, and his unsettling way of standing too
close and twisting his head sideways, as though trying to look up
your nose.

None of this bothered Marcel. Having lost out on that neural
arrangement by which the child learns to apply prior lessons to
new experiences, Marcel lived in a state of fairly constant astonishment, which he had accepted as normal. He noticed Flic-Flac's
appearance, of course, and was surprised that his grandmother
didn't make him bathe more often, but Flic-Flac was no more be-

wildering than most of the people Marcel encountered, and certainly no less worthy of his attention when it came to a trade.

When Marcel shrugged in a way that suggested he was open to an offer, Flic-Flac pulled a brightly painted metal chicken out of his pocket and set it on the ground. At first nothing happened, but after Flic-Flac smacked the toy on its tin head it began to hop up and down, pecking the dirt and making funny noises that sounded nothing like a real chicken but were amusing all the same.

Marcel wanted the chicken. Reaching into his bag, he offered a paperback novel in the original Swedish. Flic-Flac threw the book on the ground. When Marcel pulled out a gold armband, however, Flic-Flac's blue eyes grew wide and his black pupils dilated to deep pools of darkest lust. Making a loud, snorting noise, he grabbed the band, thrust it on his left arm, and pushed it up as high as the elbow. Then he ran to his car to gather whatever else he could find to trade.

In the next few minutes, Flic-Flac acquired seven more pieces of antique jewelry, in return for which Marcel received a pair of designer sunglasses, a clipboard with built-in solar-powered calculator, a carton of antidiarrhea tablets, and three pairs of extra-cushioned hiking socks still in their original packages. When he sold these things, Marcel reasoned, he would give the Americans their money. Also the profits from the two armbands that were still in the left-side pocket of his pants. The wad of money in the right side was his. It had not occurred to him to offer it in exchange for any of the valuable goods Flic-Flac brought to barter. It had not occurred to Flic-Flac to ask.

Can the Artist Ever Be Truly Invisible?

L IKE MANY PHOTOGRAPHERS, Richard behaved as though his physical presence ceased to exist when he got behind a camera. He felt he could enter and exit at whim, like the stage-hand in a Noh drama whose black clothes signify that he is to be regarded as invisible. What mattered was the image captured on film. What went into creating that image was immaterial.

This opinion was not shared by the demimonde of Provence. It is difficult to take a dozen pictures of a derelict scratching his armpit and not have your subject, however drunk, wonder what you're up to. By 8:00 A.M. of his first day of shooting, which had started at dawn outside the bus station in Orange, vagrants were telling Richard exactly what he should do with his camera, a host of suggestions as colorful as they were anatomically impossible. By the fourth day, word of the hairy American idiot who ran around taking people's pictures without so much as a please or thank you had spread throughout the Luberon. As Richard ducked under the river causeway at Avignon, where he hoped to find some subjects sleeping in the dappled shadows of early morning light, he was met instead by a trio of ugly brutes posing with their flies open and their fists clenched.

Moving at a speed he hadn't achieved in years, Richard climbed to the safer, more public vantage of the park overlooking the famous bridge. No need to stay in Avignon, he decided. He would drive to Salon-de-Provence, a barracks town where Renard had said he might find a few amateur drunks in uniform. Surrounded by military police, Richard felt secure that anyone who tried to jump him would be exiled to Devil's Island.

The Aesthetics of Barbie

DESPITE HIS EAGERNESS TO LEAVE Avignon, Richard hadn't forgotten to take a picture of Barbie. Lily had given him a doll to keep in his camera bag, and he had become superstitious about the effort. Every shoot now ended with Barbie. Even the disasters.

Standing in the park overlooking the Rhône River, recovering from his recent fright, Richard searched for the best vantage in which to portray his eleven-inch goddess. The next minute he was down on the grass, jamming one of the doll's pronglike plastic feet into the soil and twisting the other into what he hoped was a festive, prancing sort of kick. From this angle, it would look like the doll was standing on the bridge. His own life might end at any minute, but at least Barbie could dance. On the bridge. In Avignon. As his heart dropped back to its normal beat, Richard paused to regret not capturing an image of the guys under the bridge, but he soon forgot them in the puzzle of deciding how to backlight Dynel hair.

Richard and Vivian had been surprised at how easy it was in rural France to find the same toys they bought in America. Since they arrived, Lily had acquired four new Barbies, the first one Richard's gift from Les Baux and three others the result of extended begging outside the distant supermarket Vivian had finally discovered. To Richard, it had been astonishing that this plastic figurine had so large a place in the childhood games of chauvinistic France. It was disturbing in a way he couldn't quite define.

Vivian, always quick on the theoretical draw, came up with a fast judgment of the dolls. They were part of a steamroller of cultural hegemony, she proclaimed, under which children around the world were forced to play with toys that embodied a standard of blond California beauty that was not only impossible to achieve but also completely alien to anything they had ever seen. She could have made a whole lecture of it, if she had still been teaching at Malcolm College of Knowledge. But since she was stuck in the country and temporarily deprived of her usual audience, she gave an abbreviated version, really just an outline, to Richard.

In a surprising move never attempted by her students, he had disagreed. Richard maintained that the dolls they bought in France were slightly darker, more Mediterranean looking, than the ones they got in New York. They were different, he insisted. Maybe you had to have strong visual training to catch it, but the difference was there.

What he meant was, they were sexier. Vivian had seen him finger one of Lily's recent acquisitions, the one with a blond streak in her otherwise brunette mane, and had resisted the impulse to have her own blond hair streaked black. If she had seen him in Avignon, running his thumbnail idly over Barbie's impossibly perky, eternally firm, always symmetrical bosom, she would have been deeply disturbed.

Even a Madman Must Eat

FLIC-FLAC LOVED THE TREASURE he had acquired from Marcel. He loved its look, and the taste of metal in his mouth, and the way the gold turned warm when he wore it against his naked flesh. But that same flesh had other needs, as well. Like everyone else, Flic-Flac required food and drink and shelter. He craved companionship, he needed gasoline, and he understood, at least dimly, that these things all cost money. He chose an armband for his own adornment and somehow managed to anchor a broken fragment of braided gold to the tangle of hair on his chest. The rest he was forced to sell.

In the summer in the South of France, when every truck becomes a boutique on wheels and every strip of grass a market, it was easy for Flic-Flac to find vendors of bric-a-brac and jewelry who would buy his wares and usually resell them before the day was over. An intricately enameled armband left his pocket in the picturesque village of Lourmarin, sold to a university student who had set up his gypsy wagon in the shadow of the old château. A large cloak pin changed hands in a garage in Avignon. A small basin of hammered silver found its way to a pawnshop on a back street in Arles, where it sits to this day. Two torques were sold to a woman who planned to put them out with her other costume jewelry at the Sunday flea market at L'Isle-sur-la-Sorgue. And so the treasure spread out across the hills and valleys of Provence.

Stalking Cézanne

DURING HER SECOND WEEK in France, Vivian wrote seven postcards and a letter to her agent, bought five boxes of macaroni (currently the only food her children would eat), and continued her efforts to penetrate the archives of the Cézanne Studio.

The promises of access she had received while still in New York had been a cruel fiction. Whenever she called the studio, she was informed that the director was away and the collection closed. This was a problem, since she had already appointed Cézanne to a pivotal role in her central (though as yet unwritten) discussion of the commodification of nature. Hiding in the archives, she was sure, were letters, journals, and account books that would validate her portrait of the artist as a man of strictest double-entry mentality. Each day that she was turned away increased her certainty of the treasures that lay inside. Vague hopes had hardened into concrete delusions. She could see the ink faded to a brownish violet on the ledger page. She could feel the crumbling green morocco leather of the letter portfolio, and she had almost memorized the diary entries she had first imagined, then anticipated, and now fully expected to quote.

By Friday it had become an obsession. Plotting a new strategy, Vivian decided to forgo the telephone and simply drop in unannounced. She would do this every day, for as long as it took for her to get inside.

Cézanne had spent part of his childhood on the Cours Mirabeau, which was still Vivian's favorite place to drink coffee and look over the notes that would soon blossom, she was sure, into a full-fledged book. His studio, however, was on the outskirts of Aix-en-Provence, high on the plateau. Only after she had made three complete tours of a traffic circle where the exits were very inadequately marked did Vivian reach the windswept summit from which Cézanne had looked out over the valley to his beloved Mont Ste-Victoire.

What had once been a remote, unsettled district had long since become a typical suburban warren of low-income apartments, the blight of every city in France. Laundry in strange shades of saffron and turmeric hung from crumbling cement balconies. Swarthy children with hardened faces eyed her resentfully as she drove through their games. Women wearing head scarves hurried children into courtyards, as though Vivian would contaminate them with her presence. Parking hurriedly, before she penetrated too completely into this labyrinth, Vivian flagged down a postal driver who gave her directions to the Cézanne Studio, two blocks away.

Naturally, the place was closed. Repeated pounding on the gate finally roused a woman who looked like one of the crones who sit outside the public toilets in Paris but who claimed she was the building manager.

Was this the woman who answered telephone calls? Certainly she showed the same indifference to Vivian's letter of introduction, and the same bored insistence that there was no possible way to see the studio or the archives.

You're being too businesslike, Vivian told herself. What's needed here is an appeal to the nurturing female instinct. Trying to suggest that the director's absence might be a perfect opportunity for her to explore the archives, she stumbled through a labored translation of the expression "when life hands you a lemon, make lemonade."

Vivian had forgotten that in French "lemonade" was a carbonated soft drink. In her version, the proverb seemed to suggest that if life presents you with fresh fruit, you should reject it for a can of 7UP. Since this fit rather well with the manager's prior observations of American dietary patterns, she suggested that Vivian try the market around the corner.

Hail the Conquering Curator

FOLLOWING THE DIRECTION OF the woman's pointing finger, Vivian was startled to see a large, florid, strangely familiar figure coming into view. It was the man on the back of the Impressionist catalog at the Metropolitan Museum, and on the videotapes, and over the Acoustiguide rental booth. It was the man who had inspired this whole wild goose chase.

If she hadn't been feeling so extremely dislocated, she would never have recognized him. As it was, however, Vivian's mind was so free of the images of people she actually knew that his name sprang to her lips before she was even aware of how loud she was calling.

"Hugo," she announced firmly, as though answering a question on a quiz show. "Hugo Bartello."

Hugo was used to being addressed in loud, firm tones. He tended to shout himself, a quality much appreciated by the elderly donors he courted on the museum's behalf, most of whom were hard of hearing. This must be another museum person, he thought.

"Hugo Bartello!" Vivian cried again as he drew closer. Lost in a vast, uncharted sea, she had recognized something she could name. "Vivian Hart," she added. "I loved your Impressionist show at the Metropolitan."

Who on earth was Vivian Hart? Hugo wondered. Where had he met this drab little outcast, turned away from the gate behind which, he knew, the director was eagerly awaiting his own arrival? Hugo's conscience was tweaked by the realization that he had no memory of who she was, and he was touched to see how calmly she anticipated that possibility.

"But of course, my dear," he answered. "Was I looking vague? The Cézanne Studio is closed? How very difficult for you." He glanced back to see if the director had come out to greet him. All clear.

"At least we can walk together to the corner," he boomed, steering her away from potentially embarrassing encounters at the entryway. "What are you up to these days?" That should bring a clue. Surely he would recognize even a junior curator. Maybe someone from his apprentice days in Chicago? Hugo prided himself on having an excellent memory for names and faces.

"I'm finishing a book," Vivian offered. No use burdening this refreshingly friendly stranger with the history of her inglorious past career at Malcolm College of Knowledge. "We have a house at St-Etang."

"Well, then," Hugo answered, wracking his memory for some image of where St-Etang might be, "you must come see us in Gordes." To his horror, her face brightened at the thought. Were they neighbors? What on earth had he said? Might as well get it over with.

"Did you know I've gotten married?" he asked, stepping back to give her room for the exaggerated gestures that usually followed this announcement. "Yes, really," he continued, although Vivian had taken the news far more calmly than most. "Rosalie de La Fontaine, who used to be Rosalie D'Albo." Again, Vivian failed to show any of the usual gleeful recognition. "We're throwing ourselves a reception in Gordes," Hugo added. "Tomorrow, in fact. Perhaps you can join us. Any time after eight. Rather a crowd, I fear, but perhaps it will be a chance for you to see some of your old comrades."

Again he peered down at her, hoping for at least a clue to her field. Nothing came. "Here's the number," Hugo said in despair, pulling a card from his suit pocket. "It will be delightful to see you." And then he shook her hand with a spin that sent her off around the corner, and he returned in the direction he had come. Making a strong mental note to tell Rosalie about the invitation, he rapped twice on the gate of the studio, which opened instantly.

As soon as she was safely out of sight, Vivian stopped to consult her map. Eager as she was to bring home Hugo's invitation and lay it at her husband's feet, it was imperative first to figure out how to get back to the car.

A Summer Party

The Guests

A S HUGO HAD PROMISED and Rosalie feared, the final guest list for their belated wedding reception reflected all the usual obligations. From Rosalie's side, most of the editors from Bernard de La Fontaine's publishing house would be there, and the fashion people she kept up with from her modeling days, and the television people who had discovered, en masse, that Gordes was the chic place to get away from it all. The editor of the *International Herald Tribune* was coming with his wife, a rising star in the European home exercise video world. So were the hosts of the two rival talk shows that each claimed to be the absolute intellectual center of contemporary France. The former prime minister would arrive from his rustic retreat two hilltops away, bringing several members of the interim Czech cabinet who were *his* houseguests at the moment. He knew the delightful Rosalie would not mind.

For his part, Hugo had invited al the directors of the Louvre and of every provincial museum he had ever so much as entered, and also the international contingent in town for the Op Art painting conservation seminar being held right down the road at the castle in Gordes. Several rich American collectors were expected, a carefully chosen group Hugo calculated would be titillated by the sophisticated chatter of the French cultural establishment but not lured into donations to a rival institution.

Then they had invited people to whom they owed favors or for whom they held affections. In the first category were the more notable journalists and academics summering in Provence, who had to be hosted so they would remember to be kind to the museum in their future writings. Among the latter were the local plumber, his brother the postmaster (who was also a long-distance bicycle racer), an extremely old Russian countess whose society Rosalie had inherited along with the property, and Marie, the retired schoolteacher who had helped nurse Bernard de La Fontaine when he became so very sick so suddenly, two years ago.

Naturally, Peter Wall was also expected. Rosalie had known him since his father had brought the family along while he installed the farm's irrigation system, twenty years before. Older now, though still not quite grown up, he was staying in her guest-house while deciding what to do with the rest of his life. She was counting on him to run errands, keep peace among the musicians, and listen patiently to any particularly boring guests.

All in all, they would be entertaining close to two hundred people. They had rolled up the good rugs, cleared the tabletops of breakables, and hired half the waiters in Gordes to pass hors d'oeuvres. Marie's sister had come a week ago to supervise the cooking. Wine was chilling in the great stone trough where the original farmer had watered his sheep. The grass was too parched to risk fireworks, but there would be music, and dancing for anyone who felt the urge. The front lawn would serve for parking, with the grocer's two assistants hired to watch the cars.

Saturday morning Rosalie was out at daybreak, cutting flowers for that evening's bouquets. Nervously, she allowed herself to admit the party preparations were shaping up. Then she rushed inside, before the sun could open the flowers too soon, and combed her hair before meeting Hugo for breakfast. The honeymoon, after all, was not quite over.

Three's A Crowd

P ETER WALL WAS NOT happy. After finishing the Cavaillon
job the previous Saturday, he had been out of work all week,
with no way to escape the many menial chores involved in getting
ready for this stupid wedding reception. Rosalie had made him
mow lawns and move furniture, and had volunteered him as a
taxi service for an annoying number of dear friends who needed
to get from various airports to various summer homes. Now, in
the heat and crush of another Saturday afternoon, she had sent
him off to Apt to pick up hundreds of disgusting almond candies
that she said were essential to a French wedding party. Essential if
you want your guests to die of food poisoning, Peter supposed.

No, that was not fair. The candy would be fine. It was the occa-
sion that was nauseating. Why did Rosalie need to marry anybody, much less that know-it-all monument of pomposity she
had brought back from New York? As a child, he had accepted
Bernard de La Fontaine as a necessary ogre of his summers in
Provence, but now that he had grown to manhood he had assumed Rosalie was past the age of such inconvenient liaisons. Peter disapproved of the whole arrangement, and having to run yet
another string of errands didn't improve his mood.

The more he thought about it, the angrier he grew. Veering
sharply to get to the candy factory, he cut off a farm truck piled
high with melons. Let them screech to a halt for a change, he
thought vindictively. Let the fruit bounce all over the road. Let
the candy be forgotten. Let Rosalie and Hugo start their stupid
party without him. Then Peter checked his watch. It was important to get back before the musicians arrived.

A Family Outing: Third Attempt

VIVIAN WAS ALREADY FLUSTERED when they turned off the main road for the long, steep ascent to Gordes. Clotilde had agreed to baby-sit, but then changed her mind when she received a last-minute invitation to a carnival on the other side of the mountains. Struck by a vivid image of all the mischief two active and quarrelsome children could do in an isolated farmhouse in a country where they didn't speak the language, Vivian was afraid to leave the children alone but equally reluctant to stay home herself. Justin and Lily would come, too, she decided. So then she had to find them decent clothes, which of course delayed her own preparations.

Richard put on a clean black turtleneck and stood around complaining all afternoon about how they would never get there on time, which was hardly fair. After all, he didn't have to decide between the blue chiffon outfit, which was really more appropriate for a garden wedding, or the Indian harem pants, which were fine in concept but rather grubby in fact. By the time Vivian chose the harem pants, pressed the matching shirt with its embroidery that kept snagging on the iron, sent Justin back to wash his face, and made a snack for Lily, her mind was awash in calculations of what, if anything, she could see of Gordes before the party. In the guidebooks, it was reputed to be very scenic. She hoped she had time to find out.

But first, of course, they had to get there. The canal attendants were on strike, meaning even more trucks than usual on both the highway and the secondary roads. Farmers were returning from the various Saturday morning markets. The tide of vacationers, drawn to the South of France by some gravitational attraction as irresistible as the moon, was rising steadily in anticipation. The Tour de France had inspired all the local amateurs, until it seemed every cyclist in Provence was out on the road. And then, to add to all the ordinary confusion, a truck had spilled its load of melons at a crucial intersection. Judging from the haze of flies, it must have happened several hours ago, but the road was still littered with broken fruit and traffic was down to a single lane for both directions.

As the bicycle racers threaded their way through the pulpy debris, spectators mounted the roofs of the immobile cars to cheer their favorites. Bottles of wine appeared and were passed from hand to hand. Fights broke out, and Justin watched in fascination as a pair of boys who looked about his age began gathering melons and smashing them on the pavement. His parents would never allow him to do that.

By the time they passed the cantaloupe bottleneck, the damage was done. The engine was already overheating as they approached the long, steady slope to Gordes. Richard, stuck between two enormous trucks that were crawling up the steep grade, tried to pass where the road widened for a scenic turnout but only ended by stalling at a point where he was able to paralyze traffic in both directions.

Justin looked out the rear window and counted as far as he could see. Twenty-three cars before the road curved out of sight, and probably at least that many up ahead. This was a family record, beating the memorable incident last week when his mother had gotten confused in the traffic circle at L'Isle-sur-la-Sorgue and gone in the wrong direction over a one-way bridge. That had only been eighteen cars, though it had lasted longer. He said nothing, already on his good behavior in preparation for the party that he and Lily hadn't really been invited to attend.

His dad really really really wanted to go to this party. He kept on talking about how this was his breakthrough moment and his chance to meet the important art dealers. *Dealers* was a word his father used when he was trying to sound important. Otherwise he said bloodsuckers, or assholes, or capitalist shits.

Mom was like that, too. When they had company, she would start talking about the cinema. When it was just family they saw movies, or sometimes, as his mother said, went out to "catch a flick." She would say it, and then hear herself, and then laugh and try to pretend that she had meant to sound dated and funny.

It was very interesting, Justin thought, watching your own parents trying to look good in front of their children. He remembered when stupid Lily had been studying endangered species at that Saturday nature class Mom made them take, and she thought a flick was some kind of bird their parents were going out to trap. Lily started screaming about how it wasn't fair, it was cruel. So of course Mom thought her precious little sweetheart was suffering from separation anxiety, and she promised Lily a Barbie doll the next day if she would just be quiet and stay with the sitter. After they were gone, Justin explained it to her. Catch a flick was some stupid expression old people used. It meant movies, not birds. They were going out to the movies. Then he had to explain about movies, about how you could watch them in big theaters as well as on the VCR. It had been very boring. The next time something like that happened, he just let his sister figure it out.

Justin was shaken back to the present by a sudden shadow across the backseat. They hadn't been moving for quite some time. Looking up, he saw the car was surrounded by large, hostile men with vivid tattoos on their bare and hairy arms. All of them were at least giants. Justin was impressed when his father got out to talk to them, but instead of solving the problem, his dad tried to take their picture, which made them even angrier. Mom got out and started talking, and the men started pointing across the road, and then, without warning, they stooped down, out of sight. As they vanished, the car began to move. The two abandoned children were being lifted up and carried away.

Lily, next to him in the backseat, cringed and clutched Justin's arm. It was the kidnappers she always feared. Two minutes later they bounced down in the scenic turnoff on the side of the road. Justin and Lily just sat there, too terrified to move. Finally, their parents appeared, ordered them out of the car, and force-marched them up the hill to a castle that was also a museum of weird pictures that made your eyes hurt. They stayed there until closing, then hung around the town square until it was time to go to the party. Nobody said anything about the men with the big hairy arms. Not even Lily.

An Architecture of
Simple Geometric Forms

PETER HAD PICKED UP the candies in Apt, the flowers in Ménerbes, the special bread Rosalie had ordered from the baker at Cabrières-d'Avignons, and his good pants from the cleaners in Cavaillon. Since there is satisfaction in the successful completion of even the most mindless tasks, he was now in a much better mood. He didn't complain when the traffic inexplicably began to slow on the incline that led to the hilltop center of Gordes. Ignoring the sheer drop on either side of the road, he allowed his mind to wander.

Seen from below, the famous honey-colored stone houses of Gordes looked a lot like the milk-carton villages he had made during his first year in architecture school. All structure could be reduced to simple geometric form, his professor had insisted. Cube and hemisphere, log and brick. Especially brick, the three-dimensional rectangle that could be combined in so many different ways to meet practically every building need. Rectangles could be stacked into a high-rise, placed at right angles to form courtyards and loggias, or cantilevered out over imaginary streams, just like Frank Lloyd Wright's famous Fallingwater, that house he designed in Pennsylvania. Traditionalists preferred heavy cardboard for their architectural models, but Peter liked the way the waxed milk cartons held their shape, and he enjoyed cutting them out with his X-Acto knife.

The experience had stood him in good stead when he was looking for a way to make some extra money in France. For the past year he had constructed models for a publisher who produced a series of ready-to-assemble greeting cards depicting the houses of famous artists. Folded flat, with a blank space under the roof for messages, they were popular souvenirs of whatever town the tourist was visiting. Peter's job was to engineer the image so that, once tab A and slot B had been brought together, the cards would stand up on a tabletop, three-dimensional paper images of the buildings in which immortal art was made.

His first attempt, Monet's house at Giverny, he now regarded as much too fussy. He had included separate pieces for chimneys and verandas, with all the extra slots and tabs, and even a cutout of Monet himself to stand at the front door. The publisher sold thousands of the cards, but Peter was much prouder of his later works. He particularly liked the austere simplicity with which he had re-created van Gogh's house at Arles, an ocher-colored cube with little more than a punch-out set of shutters to spoil the line. It was, in his opinion, a brilliant piece of paper engineering.

Looking beyond the smoking engine of the car in front of him, Peter regarded the looming prospect of Gordes. Perhaps he could make a card showing the entire hillside, the houses all springing up at once when you pulled a single tab. That would be an interesting piece of work, he thought. And easy, too, with all those flat facades and shallow roofs sloping in the same direction.

A half mile up ahead, the traffic seemed to be moving at last. Putting aside his vision of pop-up architecture, Peter shifted gears for the trip up the hill, through the village, and around to the farm. He would still have time to change before the party. He dearly hoped Rosalie had invited plenty of pretty girls.

The Morality of Isolation

B Y WEDNESDAY, ARIEL HAD given up working in the dining
room and had moved her papers to the side of the swimming
pool, a long, narrow basin that had been most ingeniously inserted into the steep hillside at the back of the house. Instead of
staring out the window, daydreaming, she now stared into the
water. It was a small but potentially inspiring distinction. Thursday she had written three paragraphs about drowning before re-
verting to imaginary reunions with men she had known casually
in the past. Yesterday she had returned to her tiny chlorinated oasis, determined to explore the sexual implications of human sacrifice in a nonlinear way. The effort had been interrupted by a
strange, shrill noise that seemed to be coming from the filtration
system.

It was the first time the telephone had rung since her arrival.
Fumbling with the receiver, cleverly hidden in a rustic basket, she
heard an obviously American voice asking in French if he had
reached the Fort household. "Yes," she answered in English. "You
have the right number."

"Marvelous!" boomed the unknown man on the other end.
"Rosalie speaks so very highly of you, I'm delighted to have
found you at home. Didn't realize you were a Yank like me. This
is Hugo Bartello, and we are so hoping you will both join us at a
festive gathering we're having tomorrow night. Something of a
belated wedding reception, you know. Rosalie had thought you
were not arriving until August, but then she saw your lights so
she asked me to call. You will, I hope, accept our apologies for the
lateness of the invitation."

"Certainly," Ariel answered, referring to the apologies, too swept up by surge of the stranger's cordiality to correct his obvious error.

"Marvelous!" the voice shouted again. "Eight o'clock. The second gate past the olive press. But of course you know that. I look forward to meeting you at last!" And then he hung up.

Ariel lost a good deal of sleep wondering what to do. Friday night and Saturday morning passed in a fog of moral indecision. On the one hand, it was obvious that the invitation had not been meant for her at all. On the other hand, it was also obvious that this was going to be a kind of party to which she, Ariel, would never receive an invitation. The temptation to crash was enormous, compounded by what she realized was a loneliness so great that it seemed to be making her physically sick.

To clear her mind, she walked into the town center for a glass of lemonade, but even in the crush of the holiday weekend she felt her isolation. The only café she could afford was the Foyer d'Agricole, a dusty bar filled with hard-eyed farmers who treated her like an unattractive prostitute. Fortunately, there was a tiny balcony to the rear of the bar. The waiter never bothered to go there, but if she got her own drink she could sit in the sun and watch the traffic coming up the hillside. It was no less desolate than the house she had left, but at least it was a different view.

From this new vantage point, she could look down on the neighbors whose house was perched above her on the hillside. They were an unpleasant couple who left their dogs out in the garden, yapping furiously, until well past midnight every night; Ariel took some satisfaction, from her perch, in watching one of the beasts lift a hairy leg to pee into their swimming pool.

Forcing herself to look in another direction, Ariel studied the traffic coming up the hill. It was the predictable Saturday afternoon assortment: tour buses, family cars, delivery vans making a final visit to restock the markets that depended on their summer profits to survive the rest of the year.

Actually, traffic was moving even more slowly than usual.

Some sort of tie-up twenty yards below the crest. As she watched, the line slowed even further, then stopped altogether. Up and down the hill, drivers were jumping from their cars and opening the hoods to keep the engines from overheating. A large blue van from a popular Paris moving company slipped several yards backward before the driver reasserted the emergency brakes — fast enough to avert a catastrophe but not to prevent frantic honking of horns.

The problem seemed to be a Peugeot sedan painted a very peculiar shade of green that had somehow gotten stalled diagonally across the road. She could hear the horns getting louder and louder, until they were coming from the town square right behind her. More and more people were getting out of their cars. Drivers were standing on the pavement next to the stalled car, fanning themselves and venting their frustration in furious conversation. Suddenly six large men detached themselves from the gathering crowd and encircled the stalled car. After a brief exchange with the driver, they stooped in unison, lifted the car, and carried it out of the roadway. With a series of stalls and backfires that sounded like an orchestra tuning up, traffic resumed its normal pace. It was an inspiring example of what people could achieve, if they acted together.

Leaving her glass for the lazy waiter to clear, Ariel hurried back through the bar and down the cobbled street to her employers' house. If she had reached the point of envying the sociability of people stuck in traffic, it was definitely time to crash a party.

Citizens of the World of Ideas

THREE HOURS AFTER their humiliating entry into Gordes, the Harts had recovered their poise. The children were stuffed with pizza and ice cream, the only food available between two and seven in the afternoon. Richard had run into a fashion photographer he knew from New York, here to shoot a Christmas catalog for Saks, who regaled him with a long, obscene anecdote about diverting a spotlight from some famous religious shrine to better display a model and her virtually transparent bathing suit. Just listening on the outskirts of their conversation, Vivian could feel her mind coming awake, her thoughts stretching as though after a long, stiff sleep.

It was as she had suspected. She needed to be around other intellectuals. She wouldn't know anyone at the party tonight, but she was confident she would be with her own sort of people. Expounders of theories. Entrepreneurs of insight. They would be citizens of the world of ideas, and she would pass among them. Maybe she would run into an editor with better connections than the one in New York. Unless, of course, she went directly to television. Anything was possible, she told herself. Nothing ventured, nothing gained. You can't win if you don't enter. He who hesitates is lost. And then, having momentarily run out of inspirational truisms, she gathered the children and got ready to introduce them to her wonderful new friend, Hugo Bartello.

Even with the delay in restarting their car and persuading the children to get in it, they were the first guests to arrive. After they'd waited an embarrassingly long time under the suspicious gaze of an elderly housemaid, Hugo arrived at the door, straightening the lapels of his gorgeously tailored blue linen jacket. The children, after his first surprise at seeing them, were deployed to the kitchen, where he assured Vivian they would be given something to eat, then sent to the barn to search for kittens. By the time that was settled, other people had started to appear.

Hugo had greeted Vivian like his best friend and had roared with laughter at her first story, but before she could begin another, he was off across the room, welcoming a Parisian director and congratulating him on his television series about post-deconstructionist architecture. Richard had vanished. And then more and more guests were arriving, all of whom seemed to know each other and none of whom had the slightest interest in meeting Vivian Hart.

The problem was that there were too few Americans present. The French, she soon noticed, did not find it at all amusing that she was staying in a house with ugly Formica cabinets, and they looked horrified when she said she gave lectures on French painting. They were not interested in learning anything about her, in fact, or in answering any questions about themselves — a double assault on her social arsenal which effectively shut down her powers of conversation.

Looming above the other guests were a number of very tall and strikingly beautiful young women. Each of them seemed to have an escort, generally an older, shorter man — but the men would drift from group to group, fetching drinks and exchanging greetings, while the tall women stood motionless for extraordinarily long periods. Intrigued, Vivian tried to talk to a few of them but soon discovered they were all fashion models from countries like Byelorussia or Burkina Faso and spoke no English beyond the few phrases needed to indicate they spoke no English. Somewhere outside, she could hear music and laughter. Vivian hoped Lily had not taken it into her head to show off her ballet steps or her Pocahontas underpants, but she lacked the courage to find out.

Unsure of herself though she was in so many things, Vivian at least felt she knew how to behave at a party full of strangers. She would follow the example of the models. Instead of circulating, she would pick a vantage spot and stay there. If she stood still long enough, someone would approach her. Probably it would be someone using her as an excuse to get out of a boring or otherwise undesirable conversation, but what other choice did she have?

And so Vivian picked a spot in the middle of the room and assumed an expression of ironic observation. She was Athena, goddess of wisdom, standing in judgment over this nocturnal assembly of paltry humans. She was Dorothy Parker, ready with a brilliant quip for the first lucky person to come her way. She was the woman of mystery whom no party should be without. She was hungry and bored, and she would walk right up to that ring of men in the corner if someone didn't approach her soon.

And then someone did, though it was the last person she would have expected. A bosomy young woman wearing elaborate earrings but no makeup, her fair skin set off by a great mass of curly black hair that matched the black of her clinging slip of a dress. Vivian had seen her enter the room and instantly dismissed her as the thinking man's midlife crisis, a bimbo cultivating the intellectual look. Then she realized with astonishment that the girl was seeking her out.

Ariel Makes Her Introduction

I'M DELIGHTED TO HAVE the opportunity to make your acquaintance," Ariel said stiffly. "The Forts were so kind as to invite me to occupy their house. They regret very much that they cannot be here tonight."

The words fell out of her mouth in ugly chunks, like the toads and lizards that afflict the wicked sisters of fairy tales. She had walked from Gordes practicing the speech she would make to her hostess, jumping every time a car swerved around her in the deepening twilight. She had thought it would be better to admit she had been invited by mistake than to risk exposure. Since her mysterious host had spoken English, she decided to use it now, but she was so nervous that it was hard to speak at all.

The anxious woman in the harem pants and embroidered tunic looked at her quizzically. "Well, at least you made it," she replied. "Since you're here, you might as well stay.'

"Yes," agreed Ariel, not knowing what else to say. It wasn't the warmest of welcomes, but she didn't seem in danger of being evicted. Could she stop now, or did she have to find the owner of the terrifyingly hearty voice that had called her in the first place?

The silence grew. Vivian wondered if this was another of the Russian models, maybe some kind of cleavage stand-in for her taller, less endowed colleagues. Perhaps the woman had used up all her English on those three sentences. An odd formula to memorize, but one never knew.

"I am here to complete my novel about historical ambiguity," Ariel heard herself saying. "It takes place in the first century B.C., during the Celtic resistance to Roman conquest. Logically, it should not matter, but I find it amusing to be here amid the very hills and forests of which I write."

In French, you get extra credit for any sentence beginning *Logiquement*. In English, you sound like an idiot.

"Logically," Vivian echoed, instinctively slipping into that tone of apprehensive agreement that people adopt when dealing with the truly mad. She would have backed away, except a waiter appeared with a tray of glasses and Vivian was feeling in need of a drink. It was a strategic error of some consequence. While she was taking her first sip, Ariel decided to explain her work.

The point, Ariel insisted, was not to construct an illusory reality of early Gallo-Celtic life but to deconstruct the eighteenth-century exaltation of the classical era. Glaring defiantly at Vivian, who was showing no signs of protest (in fact, she was barely listening), Ariel railed against the political complicity of words and the harmony of socially constructed values. Since the Celts had left no literary records of their world, she continued, the writer must draw the landscape of narrative from inner terrain.

Vivian forced herself to concentrate. As the girl rattled on, however, using terms that were as incomprehensible as they were polysyllabic, Vivian realized that the only piece of true literary creation here was the willful transfer of various parts of speech, so that nouns became verbs and verbs became nouns. Or maybe adjectives. It was hard to tell. What did it mean to "signify the erasure"? How could she "triangulate the binary"? The binary what?

Giving up, Vivian tried to eavesdrop on other conversations. Behind her, a woman with a strong French accent was describing the enormous profits she was making publishing fan magazines devoted to the cartoon stories inspired by the characters on *Baywatch*. To her left, another woman was giving an appallingly detailed description of her recent liposuction. To her right, a man who sounded like Henry Kissinger was analyzing the profit potential of Balkan real estate. Turning to see if it really was Kissinger, she met the gaze of a very fat man with bushy eyebrows who slowly and seductively licked his lips, then blew her a kiss.

Vivian Learns More Than She Wants to Know

STARTLED AND A BIT afraid, Vivian turned back to the demented young woman who seemed to be her dreadful destiny this evening. Ariel was now explaining that her novel was going to recontextualize the hermeneutic ambiguity of the present within the sexual ambiguity of the past. Vivian shifted her shoulders, a small shrug meant to indicate she followed what Ariel was saying without endorsing it. What with all the new diseases she kept reading about, she wasn't sure the world was ready for more contexts for sexual ambiguity.

Vivian's tunic had come from India, where children who work for five rupees an hour had plied their needles across every square inch of its thin cotton surface. Scattered among the embroidered flowers were tiny mirrors stitched in place with lilac-colored floss — too few to be vulgar, Vivian felt, but just enough to catch the light from time to time. In the aftermath of her shrug, one of the threads that anchored the mirrors to the cotton had caught on the strap of her brassiere. She twitched her shoulders again, this time trying to undo the snag. Failing, she reached inside her neckline in what she hoped would be interpreted as a harmless bit of autoerotic massage.

Not to worry. Ariel was now on automatic pilot, giving a fervent but stilted lecture on the impact of eco-feminism on narratology. Vivian straightened her shoulders as soon as she heard the term "eco-feminism," breaking the tangled thread and dropping a tiny mirror on the stone floor. Here was a chance to wring something of value from this insane, one-sided conversation. She needed some eco-feminist catchphrases to bolster her rather skimpy discussion of the mythos and topos of haystacks in early modern art.

Unfortunately, Ariel chose this moment to move on to an account of her relations to the Forts, which Vivian thought were military installations until the context made it clear that Fort was someone's name. First, Ariel expressed her deep admiration for Monsieur Fort's political commentaries, which Vivian took as confirmation of her original assumption that the girl was somebody's mistress. Then she attested almost hysterically to Madame Fort's kindness to children. Vivian wondered if her tormentor was one of these blessed infants. Certainly she must have been somebody's favorite child. Had no one ever taught her it was not polite to monopolize the conversation? Only brutal measures would stop the torrent of words.

"I wonder where they hide the toilet," Vivian said abruptly.

"Excuse me?" Ariel answered.

"The toilet," Vivian repeated. "The john. The WC. They must have a toilet here somewhere."

"But . . . isn't this your house?"

"My house?" Vivian echoed, with exaggerated astonishment. "Certainly not!"

Vivian turned a disdainful eye to the terra-cotta walls, the arched alcoves for the Greek statues of undisputed authenticity, the sofas covered in midnight blue Scalamandré silk, and the doors that opened to the terrace overlooking the mountains. She would have killed to live here.

"It's marvelous in its own way, I suppose," she said, "but I prefer something a bit more . . . authentic. Gordes is becoming very superficial, don't you think?"

Without waiting for an answer, Vivian swept away, almost as if she knew where she was going.

The Hostess

ARIEL FELT GREAT FLASHES of embarrassment course through her body. She had always thought that was just a figure of speech, but here they were, electric currents of remorse prickling her back and raising ugly pink splotches on her arms and neck. When she had seen a solitary woman standing in the middle of the room, alert and anxious, scanning the crowd, she had assumed she was the hostess. Whoever that woman was, she must think Ariel was out of her mind. At least no one else had heard her.

That was the problem, of course. Ariel hadn't spoken to anyone in so long, she had almost forgotten how, and then when she started, she hadn't known how to stop. She was preparing to slink away when a tall, gray-haired woman with melting brown eyes and enviable cheekbones appeared at her elbow, offering a glass of champagne. Ariel knew she had seen her before but couldn't remember where. Then it came to her. This was the woman she had watched in the garden, the first night she arrived in Gordes. The woman who had smiled at her in the moonlight.

"I'm Rosalie Bartello," the woman was saying. "So glad you could come."

"I'm Ariel Stern, and I don't know what I'm doing here." And then, to complete her humiliation, Ariel started to cry.

Flic-Flac

USUALLY, FLIC-FLAC DRIFTED to the bigger towns on the weekends. In Marseilles or Arles, or even in smaller cities like Orange or Cavaillon, there were shops that bought and sold anything and bars that served big meals and didn't care what you looked like as long as you had money. There were places where you could get a girl and a bed together for a good price. Sometimes the girls made him wash before they would undress, but they never made him talk. Flic-Flac appreciated that.

But now he was on his hunt, so everything was different. He stayed in the country, roaming the fields and forests in the small hours of the night, listening to the changing voice of the metal detector. He found many coins this way, and once a gold watch whose insides had long since rusted back to brittle orange shards, but not yet the treasure he was seeking. Each night he went farther into the hills, taking the old paths that the charcoal burners had first cut through the forests centuries before, following the beds of rivers that had been dry for generations. At dawn he would find a farmer's shed or the shell of an abandoned building where he could curl into a corner and drink himself into a stupor.

On Thursday and Friday he had prowled the valley of abandoned gristmills north of Gordes. On Saturday afternoon he was roused by a boisterous group of German hikers. Saturday night he was roaming the apricot orchard behind Hugo and Rosalie's house. In the past, he would have tried to break into the cars parked in front for the party. Now he was busy. Treasure was near. He could sense it. Treasure was near.

Vivian Recovers Her Poise

How could I let that girl drive me off, Vivian scolded herself. You should always stand your ground at a party.

But she had run away, fleeing the large and gorgeous salon for a dark corridor that showed no signs of leading anywhere of interest. She had already peered into a vacant bedroom and an equally deserted study, and feared she would get arrested as a cat burglar if she weren't careful. At the end of the hallway was a stone arch and a set of wooden doors. Since they were already open, Vivian felt she could safely step through.

She found herself on a sheltered patio built into the angle of the house. At least she was not alone. Off in the corner, a clean-looking young man was trying to steal an enormous stone planter.

"Not to worry," he called, without looking up. "I'm just looking for signs of ancient habitation."

The people here tonight have very strange ideas of small talk, Vivian thought. She waited to see what would happen next.

Wedging a shard of flagstone under the base, Peter managed to turn the planter about six inches from where it had first stood. With a grunt and a smile of satisfaction, he pointed to a trio of handprints in the cement. Vivian came closer and peered at the spot. They didn't look very old, but she was taking no chances on revealing her ignorance.

"Is that a cult inscription?" she asked brightly. "I met a woman inside who claims to be writing a book about a Druid princess in ancient Gaul. She kept talking about runes and dolmens and inscrutable relics of the unreadable past. Do you think those marks are related?"

"Not too likely," Peter answered, still studying the handprints he had uncovered. One of them was his, put in when his father had finished laying the pipes beneath the cement. "Dolmens. Those slab things. Like Stonehenge, right? Not exactly my period."

Then he straightened up and gave Vivian the self-deprecating smile he had perfected for dealing with fussy renovation clients. "I'm interested in classical architecture, myself. Order, symmetry, the golden ratio, all that sort of stuff. Do you think I should meet this lady and find out what I'm missing?"

"Oh, no," Vivian objected hurriedly. Then she would be stranded again. "She's a rich man's mistress, and I'm sure he wouldn't like it at all. The French are possessive about their kept women, you know."

What an absurd thing to say.

"Besides," Vivian continued, "I want you to tell me all about the classical presence in Provence. I'm interested in the primal landscape, but I can't seem to get past the Roman interventions. Great earth movers, weren't they? Should I start with that aqueduct in Avignon?"

"I'm afraid it's closer to Nîmes," interrupted Rosalie. Passing through the kitchen, she had seen Vivian from the window and recognized her as that peculiar woman who had abandoned her children at the door and then stood by herself for twenty minutes, glaring at everybody. If she was somebody important, Rosalie had to rescue her from Peter. If she wasn't, she had to rescue Peter. Rosalie was an experienced hostess, and she knew the dangers of letting a couple cannons roll around together on the patio.

"Avignon is the famous bridge and the Palace of the Popes," Rosalie continued. "Just the place for children." Then, realizing this might be taken as a reflection on their entirely unsuitable presence here tonight, Rosalie cast about for some brief intimate gesture that would placate the stranger. For all Rosalie knew, she could be a rich contributor or foundation officer being romanced in hopes of future grants. The cheap third-world outfit made it seem unlikely, but with art types you could never tell.

"Let me show you our renovations," Rosalie said. "Peter is bored with the subject, having been here every summer during the work, so I'm going to send him out to distract a guest who seems to be having some sort of breakdown in the salon." She turned to Peter. "You'll recognize her as the one who's crying." Then back to Vivian. "I think he should take her out to the musicians and stir up some dancing. Were you at the Metropolitan for the Costume Institute benefit in May? They had dancing in the Great Hall. Such a warm, welcoming building, don't you agree?"

Fortunately, Rosalie was not expecting any reply to this barrage of nonsense. Instead, she steered Vivian back to the large salon, handed her a glass of wine, and introduced her to a conservation expert from Chicago who was eager to explain the effects of air pollution on acrylic paint.

A New Perspective on Nature

MANY HOURS PASSED, and many strangers. By midnight Vivian had received unsolicited reviews of several Thai restaurants in her own Manhattan neighborhood, defended the National Endowment for the Arts to a florid man in a Stetson hat who insisted culture should be reserved for those who could afford to own it, and received instructions on the proper way to dust a chandelier from an extremely well-dressed woman who seemed to take her for a housemaid. She had also discussed nineteenth-century English poetry with the shoe editor of *Marie Claire* and infuriated a young television producer by praising a PBS special on Cézanne that turned out to be the work of a hated rival.

Retreating in the face of his sudden silence, Vivian wandered toward the great stone fireplace, decorated for the summer with copper caldrons full of fragrant lavender. The lavender matched the tight cotton T-shirt and denim pants of a remarkably handsome man who was standing on the hearthstone, holding forth to an appreciative group. His pale, almost feminine clothes accentuated his deep tan, dark curls, and excellent muscle definition. It was some time before Vivian tore her eyes from the fascinating pulse at the base of his throat and listened to his actual words.

"It is our most powerful symbol," he was asserting, using the low, rapid monotone favored by French television intellectuals and almost incomprehensible to nonnative speakers. Straining, Vivian forced herself to understand.

"It is thought itself, which flows like a river, lies as a deep pool in our primal consciousness, quenches our thirst for knowledge, washes away our sins. It is the source of creation, that from which our ancestors sprang. It is the force of dissolution, able to destroy the very mountains of the earth."

Was this a game? Vivian wondered. It sounded like a pretentious form of twenty questions. She waited for a pause in his discourse to see if anyone volunteered a name for the object that was inspiring his passion, but there was no pause. There was only the same low-pitched flow of words.

"In our region," he continued fiercely, "all around us, you see the power, the divinity of water."

So that was the answer.

"There are the aqueducts," he continued, "but that is water harnessed for use, subdued by the conquering Romans just as Gaul itself was, for a time, subdued."

He paused for a moment so they could all mourn that ancient but temporary setback, then went on.

"Like Gaul, the water defeats the invader in the end. It hides itself. The rivers dry. The fields grow brittle. You see it happening all about us, in this so terrifying drought. Yet there remain the secret sources, the forest springs known to the ancients. Only the wisest among us can find them, but they are there, even in the driest summer. Somewhere lies the hidden source of the Sorgue, the river which flows from nowhere. From somewhere comes the water that surges up to fill the basin at Fontaine-de-Vaucluse. If we do not understand these mysteries today, does that mean that none have ever known?"

Vivian tried to anticipate the answer, yes or no, but apparently it was a rhetorical question. More followed.

"Was it cowardice that led our pagan ancestors to the shaded grove to perform their most sacred rituals?" the handsome speaker hissed. "Of course not! Was it avarice that taught them to toss their charms and amulets into the well, like a farmer burying his gold beneath the hearthstone? I spit on such a theory!"

Vivian noted with relief that the spit, too, was only rhetorical. With a toss of his curls, the speaker continued.

"When I pursue my explorations, why is it, so often, that I turn up gold? Why do I discover ancient coins, and modern, too? How can it be that I find a golden louis along a ditch line dug in our grandfather's time?"

He glared fiercely around the circle. No one answered. Flaring his nostrils in Vivian's direction, he answered himself.

"It is the water, calling to the gold. I tell you, the attraction of the liquid element is a power that is beyond doubt. It is beyond denial! It is a force of nature before which we can only bow!"

He stopped, giving them all the benefit of another searing gaze before he turned to the fireplace, the better to display his profile. There followed a long, rapt silence, during which Vivian considered several ways of introducing her own theories about the organic magnetism of the landscape. Start with flattery, she decided.

"This must be a fascinating region in which to pursue such archaeological researches," she offered. "Do you have an active dig in the area?"

Why was everyone looking at her that way? What terrible breach of etiquette had she committed? Finally, the man in lavender spoke.

"If Madame wishes a pipeline to be installed, she can call my office on Monday morning," he answered coldly.

A pipeline? Clearly Vivian had missed some crucial information, though she had no idea what. Chastened but curious, she waited for illumination. After a long pause, and a new version of the glacial stare with which Vivian was becoming all too familiar, the conversation was rescued by an anorexic woman wearing a dress fashioned from credit cards held together with bits of silver chain.

"It's quite true, Monsieur Casteron. When you replaced our water pipes last summer, we were so thrilled by the ancient coins you uncovered."

With a sinking feeling, Vivian realized she had been listening to the local plumber. Slowly her embarrassment faded, as others began describing their own plumbing adventures. Soon the talk turned to legends of ancient wells and near-miraculous discoveries of water that had saved this village or that in the bygone time before the canals had been constructed and agriculture had moved so thoroughly to the valley. Folding his muscular arms across his chest and again tossing back his beautiful dark curls, Monsieur Casteron managed to imply that he, personally, was still able to find these hidden bodies of water.

Vivian thought of all the *résidences secondaire* advertised in the windows of the real estate offices in Gordes, and the difficulties of installing running water in houses built to the standards of the rural peasants of previous centuries. Naturally, everyone around here would be on good terms with the plumber. After spending the better part of a million dollars on a vacation cottage, people would want to be able to take a bath. She recalled with satisfaction the truly excellent water pressure in the farmhouse at St-Etang but decided not to make it a subject of general comment. St-Etang was not, she suspected, part of Monsieur Casteron's accepted territory.

Looking around at the thinning number of guests, Vivian realized it was growing late. Richard, she saw, was hovering close to a large refectory table spread with the remains of an impressive buffet. He was drinking vodka now, gesturing widely with his glass, and indignantly seizing another morsel from the table every time his companion seemed to contradict. Moving closer, Vivian overheard enough to realize they were arguing about the care of AIDS patients in eastern Europe. It was Richard's favorite kind of conversation, on a gritty topic that seemed realer to him than anything in his actual experience. Perhaps he'll get a Benetton contract out of it, she thought. That would be art.

As she watched, she saw Richard's companion pull out a tiny leather notebook, scribble something with a grotesquely fat fountain pen, tear out the page, and hand it to Richard. At least he was making some of the contacts he had hoped for. Behind the music, she could hear cars starting off down the road. For the first time in several hours, she wondered about Justin and Lily. Perhaps it was time to go home.

First In, Last Out

LOCATING THE CHILDREN WAS no easy project, Vivian discovered. Told they were outside, she wandered about for an
inordinately long time, snagging her clothes on a field of bram-
bles behind the garage and making an extended detour around
the swimming pool, to no avail. It was well past 1:00 A.M. when
she finally found them blubbering outside some smelly shed that
was swarming with cats. Justin, desperate for sleep, had gone beyond cranky to vicious and was dangling a kitten by its hind legs.
Lily shrieked that they couldn't leave until she woke the fairy
lady, but Vivian just pulled her back along the path to the front
lawn and lifted her into the backseat, locking both of them in the
car while she trudged back to pry Richard away from the bar.
Everyone else had left by then, so he was easy to spot.

"So glad you could come," Hugo said, politely ignoring Lily's
sobs. Sound travels so clearly through the still night air. Richard,
drunk and sentimental, gave Hugo a great hug before stumbling
out toward the noise. Stunned into silence, Vivian gathered her
car keys and her dignity and followed.

Peter's Bracelets Are Identified

PETER WALL HAD INDEED gone to look for the tearful young woman, as Rosalie suggested, but he hadn't found her. Instead, he had been captured by a vehement couple from Pound Ridge, New York, who wanted to know what the younger generation was doing to improve the arts. Then he had tried to hit on a Dutch fashion model whose long legs were matched by her short attention span, after which he was dragged into conversation with a chubby American photographer who seemed to be living in the area and had some strange, drunken theories about how only ugly things were beautiful.

Peter had been roused at sunrise by the first delivery truck honking at the gate. The lightweight sports coat he had donned in Rosalie's honor was chafing the sunburn on the back of his neck. The longer the party lasted, the more he wanted to escape into his own little guest house. He was about to slip away when he felt a bulge in his jacket pocket and remembered the bracelets he had bought on the road the week before.

He should show them to Hugo before he sent them to the dealer in Paris. Dealers, Peter had discovered, were not trustworthy. Peter wasn't sure he trusted Hugo, either, but he felt Rosalie wouldn't have married anybody who was actually dishonest, and he was confident Hugo would know if the bracelets had any great value. Even in their brief acquaintance, Peter had come to the grudging realization that Hugo knew a great deal about the buying and selling of art. And so he hung around the edges of Hugo's circle, freshening drinks and making conversation until the last of the guests had finally left, the wails of their children fading into blessed silence as they drove away.

"I never did find out who they were," Hugo muttered to himself. Then he turned to Peter. "What's on your mind?" he asked. "You've been hovering at my elbow for the last half hour, so you must be waiting for something."

"Well, yes," Peter admitted, feeling awkward and obvious. "I'd like to get your opinion on something." He pulled out the crumpled plastic bag in which Marcel had wrapped his purchases and removed the three circles of hammered metal.

In the dim light of Rosalie's scented candles, the bracelets looked both cruder and older than they had in the market. On the clasp of the largest one were two red stones that glittered like eyes, something Peter hadn't even noticed before.

"I thought perhaps nineteen twenties Afro-Cubist," he suggested nervously. "Or even Russian primitive, sort of a jeweler's counterpart to the Ballet Russe. I have a dealer in Paris who buys things like this, but I like to know what I'm selling."

Hugo turned the bracelets over and over, pulled them up to eye level, hefted them on his palm, then put them down on the table and drew a candle closer.

"Where did you find these?" he asked. There was a surprising urgency to his voice.

"At a flea market," Peter answered. "I was driving by and thought I'd see what they had. These caught my eye."

The bracelets seemed to be absorbing the light, giving off a rich gleam that was less reflection than inner glow. Hugo moved closer, his finger tracing the circles of twisted metal on the table before him.

"Caught your eye!" he repeated. "I should hope so!" He reached for the electric light switch. Suddenly the room sprang back into its everyday grandeur, a huge, luxurious space littered with dirty glasses, soiled napkins, and awkward clusters of chairs. Near the fireplace, the cook and the maid were piling dirty glasses onto a large wicker tray. Rosalie was outside, checking that the last of the musicians had indeed left.

"Absolutely marvelous," Hugo muttered. "Very similar to what we've got, but complementary. We'll have to check with INFAR, make sure they're not stolen." Seeing Peter's blank expression, Hugo elaborated. "International Network for Art Recovery. IN-FAR." By now he was clearly excited.

"I can't be positive," he continued, "but I think these are remarkable. We need to trace the source, see if there's a trove some amateur has uncovered. If you find any more like this, well, the boys at the Louvre will turn absolutely pea green with envy!"

"I didn't know you were so interested in jewelry," Peter said, still uncertain of what was going on. "Rosalie was telling me you have a clothing department, but I didn't realize it was such a big deal."

"Clothing Department? You mean the Costume Institute? What are you talking about? No wonder you get fleeced by the dealers!"

Hugo picked up the largest bracelet and slowly ran his finger along the braided edge. "This is not jewelry, my boy. This is ancient civilization. This is a golden footprint that can lead us back to the glories of the past!"

The Artifact Is Meaningless
Without the Explanation

PUTTING THE BRACELET back on the table, Hugo circled it, hands clasped behind his back. He had once done a lecture series at the Cloisters, "Precious Goldwork of the European Past." It was all coming back to him.

"Look at this patina," he said, his voice loud enough to reach the far corners of some imaginary auditorium. "Look at the shaping of these stones. Admire the combination of force and delicacy, the enormous skill used to shape the stylized owl that forms the closure. Typical Celtic emblem, especially when joined with this braided work around the edge."

Then he went back to his normal voice. "They had something like this at the big show at the Louvre last year. 'Les Romains et les Celtes.' It's in Rome now. Perhaps you saw it? No? You would have remembered. The catalog was so heavy they sold it in a charioteer shopping bag with plastic wheels. Brilliant from a merchandising point of view.

"Now let me consider . . ." Hugo ordered, as though there had been a danger of interruption. His face took on the motionless impassivity of rapid thought. It was like watching a lion, waking to the presence of its prey, grow suddenly still while planning the attack.

"It's a very interesting problem," he murmured. Another minute passed before he turned back to Peter, all animation once again.

"Here's the story," he said cheerfully. "You've found something marvelous. Maybe it was a singular piece of luck. But maybe, just maybe, there's more where this came from. We are in Celtic country here, you know. People think it's only Normandy, or Ireland, of course, but there were lots of Celts right here."

Peter thought of that jittery little woman who'd found him out on the patio searching for the last trace of Bernard's presence. She had been talking about Celts.

"These sorts of pieces usually surface as part of a trove, not singly," Hugo observed. "What we need to do is find the rest of it, and the site it came from. Most important, we have to construct a context for the work."

"What if I don't find the rest?"

Hugo drew closer and gave Peter the warm smile of an adopted uncle. "Then you'll have to wait a bit longer for your lucky break. And so will I, I suppose. Now that I'm in charge at the Met, a good part of my job is to keep coming up with new marvels to bring in the crowds. If I can identify a lost treasure, and explain it, I'll be earning my keep."

"I get it," Peter said, trying to sound wiser than he felt. "You want me to find more of this stuff so you can buy it for the museum and keep a bunch of curators busy researching where it came from and what it means."

"Oh, no," Hugo answered. "Quite the opposite. What we must do first is decide what it means, so we'll be in the right position to establish our interpretive claims as soon as the rest of the treasure turns up. What's essential here is to preempt all rival theories. Then we have a reason for making acquisitions."

Running his fingertips one more time around the edge of the armbands, Hugo crossed the room in search of a comfortable chair. Peter followed, struggling to suppress yet another yawn. He had asked for a quick appraisal, not a lecture on current trends in art history. He was perfectly happy to sell the bracelets to Hugo, but he hoped they wouldn't take too long deciding on a price.

"I've thought this through, you know," Hugo began, ignoring Peter's obvious impatience. "In my business, you have to wonder why people collect precious objects, and why they give their collections away. Because it happens all the time. As soon as people get rich enough they start buying art, but it doesn't take them long to realize they've got a cluttered house and a very large insurance bill for their troubles. So they start lending it out to museums, which leads to invitations to every charity ball there ever was. Fun for a while, of course, but ultimately not satisfying. The next step used to be to build your own museum, a big marble warehouse with your name over the door. The Morgan. The Frick. The Gardner. The Getty. Ever wonder why they do it?"

Peter had no idea. He had never thought about it. He didn't want to think about it now.

"It's not just yearning after fame that makes them give their art away," Hugo announced. "If it were simply the thrill of having their names chiseled on a wall, they could buy a hotel, or a casino, or even a hospital if they were feeling high-minded. No, my boy, what they are after is power — the power of authority, the indisputable voice of the arbiter of taste.

"In the past, you know, it was physical control that mattered. That's why the Romans paraded their prisoners in chains through the city. The object was to demonstrate possession of the body. But times have changed. Now it's intellectual control that matters. Ownership is merely an accident of money. Authority is what counts. If you have the power of interpretation, you will possess that thing, much more than if you had it in your pocket."

"I do have it in my pocket," Peter objected. "Or at least I did. All evening." Hugo's talk of power and authority was making him uncomfortable. And who was this "we" he kept citing?

"So you did," Hugo agreed dismissively. "In your pocket. As I said, physical possession is no longer sufficient. Intellectual possession is the goal. And speed is the key to intellectual possession. Whoever mounts the first show and publishes the first book will have staked a claim to possess that art. But of course you will be paid properly for your pieces. On that I will insist."

Peter wondered if Hugo would mention a price now. The answer was no. He yawned.

"Wake up to what you've got, boy!" Hugo commanded. "If you

get busy and find the rest of that treasure, it could be the making of you. I'll get you some pictures, so you know what to look for."

Beaming still, Hugo drifted off to the bedroom, where Peter was uncomfortably aware he was phoning New York, where it was only 7:00 P.M. He would still have time to catch his assistant before she went out for the evening. As ever, Hugo's timing was perfect.

PART III

Convergence

Ariel's Dream

MORNING CAME, SETTING off a great chatter of birds. Ariel was sleeping very badly. She was deep in a dream in which the buffoonish heroes of *Wayne's World* were driving through Paris. Wayne and Garth were lost and kept stopping for directions, but nobody could understand their peculiar version of English. "Way?" Garth kept asking at every intersection. "No way," Wayne would answer in growing despair.

With the absolute certainty possible only in dreams, Ariel knew she and she alone could get them safely through the traffic circle at the Place de la Concorde. Somehow, though, she had become one of the great stone statues that mark the eight-sided intersection. As she struggled to come down from her pedestal, her foot caught in a snare of fine-mesh, gunmetal gray, all-weather nylon strapping. Jerked awake by actual pain, Ariel rubbed her toe and realized she had spent the night asleep on a chaise at the side of Hugo and Rosalie Bartello's swimming pool. It was very early, and she was extremely cold.

Worse, she was not alone. Her hostess, wearing a white terry-cloth robe and a pair of yellow rubber clogs, was seated beside her, holding a steaming bowl of café au lait.

"We were playing a game," Ariel explained groggily, wriggling about in an effort to get her skirt down lower on her thighs. "They were supposed to find me."

"They didn't," Rosalie observed, not unkindly. She was relieved that the girl hadn't burst into tears again at the sight of her face. "It gave me quite a turn," she added, "seeing a body out by the pool. Come in and have some breakfast. I'm sure you'll feel better."

Rosalie believed in a cosmic balance of good deeds and assumed that at this very moment someone was performing an act
of kindness for one of her own daughters. Smiling, she ushered
her unexpected guest inside.

Dazed and embarrassed, and unaware of her role in her hostess's system of moral bookkeeping, Ariel gratefully followed her
into the blue-tiled breakfast room, accepted both a large cup of
coffee and the loan of a cotton shirt, and tried to reconstruct the
events of the night before. After she started crying she had
dashed out the front door, intending to march straight back to
Gordes, three kilometers away. In the darkness, however, she had
trouble finding the road. Cars were parked at odd angles on every
inch of open ground. Feeling her way from hood to bumper,
wishing she had a sleeve on which to wipe her nose, Ariel was
consoling herself that the evening could not possibly get worse
when she stepped on something small and soft. Something that
let out a surprisingly loud wail of outrage.

A little girl, about the same age as Agathe, had been hunched
down next to one of the cars. Now she stood up, clutching a pink
backpack to her chest.

"You stepped on my hand!" the girl shrieked. "I hate you! I hate
everybody! I want to go home."

American, of course, Ariel thought, her own tears drying up in
the face of younger sorrows. The French would never bring children to a party like this. As her eyes adjusted to the gloom, she inspected the injured hand. No permanent damage, she decided,
giving it the automatic kiss and pat which marked her as an experienced baby-sitter.

It hadn't seemed right to leave the girl there in the dark,
crouching between the automobiles. Ariel remembered walking
her to a cluster of buildings behind the house and then agreeing
to sit on the chaise and hide her eyes while the little girl went to
get some surprise she wanted to show her.

"The kittens, I suppose," Rosalie interjected, trying to bring some
logic to the story. "They had gone to the barn to see the kittens."

"Something like that," Ariel agreed. "But then I must have fallen asleep."

"Well, good morning!" Rosalie said loudly. It was an odd greeting, after they had been talking for the better part of twenty minutes. Then Ariel realized someone new must have come into the room. Turning toward the door, she saw a fair young man with the kind of well-scrubbed good looks her Berkeley friends had always dismissed as "preppy." They stared at each other in surprise. Peter was amazed at seeing Rosalie sitting in her bathrobe drinking coffee with a disheveled stranger in a low-cut black dress. Ariel was seized by a terrifying suspicion that this was the mysterious Hugo she had never managed to meet the night before. Rich women often did marry much younger men, after all.

But apparently not in this case. "This is my dear friend Peter Wall," Rosalie announced. "Peter, this is Ariel Stern, who never quite made it home last night. Take her out to pick some raspberries, won't you please?"

Without saying a word, Peter took a basket from the counter and headed for the door. Not knowing what else to do, Ariel followed. They walked in silence across the patio, around the old stone facade of the original farmhouse, behind the former goat shed, past the long fronds of a patch of asparagus gone to seed, until they came to a sloping hill covered in briars.

"Are you visiting Rosalie for the weekend?" Ariel asked, to break the silence.

"I live here," Peter answered.

Another silence followed.

"What do you do?"

Peter considered. What should he say? Graduate school dropout? House sitter for Rosalie? Handyman restorer for Mirielle, the real estate agent? Junk-shop scrounger for Annette, his jewelry dealer in Paris?

"I suppose you could say I live off the generosity of older women," he answered finally, with what he hoped was the right ironic note. "Rosalie keeps me around for her own amusement."

A gigolo. A real-live American gigolo, just like in that movie with Richard Gere. Ariel was shocked, then disappointed, then annoyed. She had finally met someone her own age, and he was in it strictly for cash.

"And you?" Peter asked, after another awkward pause. He had been expecting a few more questions, but none were forthcoming. Maybe he had been too flip.

"I'm writing a novel," Ariel said grandly.

"What's it about?"

"A Celtic princess. But, really, it's not about plot. It's about power and transgression and the limits of knowledge. At base, my subject is the unnarratability of narrative, but of course that goes without saying."

If the narrative couldn't be narrated, why was she bothering? Peter wondered. Then he remembered the woman who'd surprised him on the patio last night and her description of the young writer and her rich, possessive protector. Could this be the same girl? Dumping a handful of berries into the shallow basket he had brought from the kitchen, Peter tried to work out a way to ask.

"Do you, um, have any other, um, job?" he asked, paying close attention to an unripe cluster of raspberries that were resisting his awkward pull.

She should have known better, Ariel told herself. Why would a stud-muffin care about literature? Not wanting to admit she was a lowly baby-sitter, she searched for a more honorific title.

"I work for a publisher in Paris."

"A secretary?"

Lots of girls Peter knew worked as secretaries. Or waitresses. Some even cleaned houses. Those were jobs you did with a degree in liberal arts. Those were acceptable occupations.

"More like a slave," Ariel responded. "I have to be there every night, and of course Wednesday afternoons. My employer counts on having me there then. The worst of it is, it absolutely keeps me from having any other social life."

This was uncharted territory. Peter didn't have any friends from college who were working as sex slaves.

"I suppose your, um, employer gives you your own little apartment?" he asked. He was working from the dim memory of old movies, sex farces he had barely understood when he saw them on television as a child. Ariel was the first real live kept woman he had ever encountered.

"Oh, of course," Ariel agreed. "I never would have lasted, otherwise. It's really too much if you live with the family. There has to be some separation."

"Of course," Peter echoed, cheeks flaming. "Does the wife know you're here?"

Ariel had been nervously plucking raspberries with her left hand and putting them in her right palm. Now she dumped them in Peter's basket.

"She's the reason I had to leave Paris. With the girls gone, there's not much use for English instruction, so she wants to make sure I earn my keep. No fun allowed. Only suffering."

English instruction. Wasn't that a code name for bondage? Who were these "girls" Peter wondered. Was Ariel part of a harem? And who was this wife? Some Parisian version of the Mayflower Madam?

Oblivious to the misunderstanding she was fostering, Ariel continued. It wasn't that often she had a chance to complain about her job. She relished every moment.

"I'd much rather be in Paris," she announced, frowning at the idyllic vista stretched before her. "But what do my preferences matter? Ten days ago, they told me to pack my bags for Gordes. I have to stay here until the middle of August."

"Just like that?"

"Just like that. Pack your bags and go. The job isn't as easy as you might think."

"I guess not," Peter agreed, more titillated than he wanted to admit.

Conversation, American Style

IF THEY HADN'T BOTH been Americans, this confusion would never have occurred. Only an American would think it appropriate to start a conversation by asking what you do for a living. Only an American would jump to such absurd conclusions. Far from home, both Peter and Ariel were still swathed in the cultural assumptions of their native land. And since they were both young and winsome and unattached, the news, or what they took as the news, of their mutual unavailability, made them each very grumpy.

Having exhausted the topic of jobs, they moved on to hometowns (competing agricultural centers tapping into the same inadequate aquifer), schools (competing branches of the same state university system), and college majors (literature and engineering, eternal antagonists in the intellectual sphere). Faced with rivalries so deep, they naturally began to argue about things that didn't matter at all. It started in a heated dispute about the merits of clay-tile roofs, which became a heated debate over the merits of classical architecture and, from there, a caustic attack from Ariel on the oppressive cultural hegemony of ancient Rome.

Peter could not understand why anyone would criticize the past in terms of current political theories. Ariel could not imagine how anyone could refuse to accept that all history is socially constructed and has no existence outside of current political thought. Enflamed by an incendiary combination of conflicting ideologies, mistaken occupations, and suppressed attractions, they both plunged into the raspberry patch without paying attention to where they were going and received an inordinate number of scratches for their efforts.

The Kitchen Inquisitor

B Y THE TIME PETER and Ariel got back to the kitchen, the real Hugo, still damp from his morning swim, already knew they had a guest for breakfast, so Ariel never did have to make her speech about being a representative for her employers. Instead she ate raspberries and toast, fresh goat cheese, and delicious salmon tarts left over from the party, all seasoned with Hugo's amused probing of where she came from, what she was writing, and what she wanted out of life. He wondered why she was staying in Gordes, but his first question had been answered with an anguished expression and a urgent request that they not talk about her job. Since Hugo had never met the Forts and wasn't interested in their domestic arrangements, he dropped the topic.

It was strange, Ariel thought, fielding questions from a distinguished older man wearing a blue-and-white-striped robe. She felt as though she had arrived for a job interview with one of Pharaoh's overseers, if not the man himself. Hugo snorted a bit when she told him about her novel, but he was surprisingly well-informed about recent literary theory and even suggested a few books she might want to read. Peter, sitting on the opposite end of the table and doodling on a piece of paper, seemed to pay no attention to the conversation. He also ignored Hugo's hints that he should "get to work," whatever that meant. Ariel was relieved to see some friction between the two men. It would have been too weird otherwise. It was too weird in any case.

While they talked, Rosalie drifted in and out of the kitchen, entering with another pot of coffee, leaving to confer with an invisible cook, returning to arrange flowers in large majolica jugs.

Somewhere in the distance, Ariel could hear a vacuum cleaner sucking up the debris of last night's party. Then the telephone began ringing, a series of calls from the outside world.

"I have to go," Ariel said, trying not to sound as reluctant as she felt. She could have stayed there forever, nibbling toast and watching her first-ever close-up view of an operating ménage à trois. Rosalie was all for having Peter walk with her back into Gordes, but Ariel insisted she would much rather go alone. Babbling apologies and thanks, she scrambled out the door, then returned a moment later to return the borrowed shirt. As she left the second time, Peter joined her, walking with her as far as the gate and the olive press that marked the entrance to the main road. As she turned toward Gordes, he handed her the paper on which he had been doodling.

It was a drawing, a surprisingly finished architectural rendering of a Roman arch topped with a chariot drawn by four prancing horses. The woman driving the chariot was clearly herself. Beneath a Roman helmet her hair frizzed out in what Ariel feared was realistic disorder. Her arms, extended to grasp the reins, were covered to the elbow with leather gauntlets, but her dress was the one she was actually wearing, revealing an embarrassingly accurate depiction of her body.

Blushing, Ariel handed the paper back.

"Don't you want it?" Peter asked in a mocking voice. "I thought you'd enjoy the role. The costume isn't right, historically speaking, but I understand that doesn't matter. Something about how we all recast the past to suit our own purposes. Isn't that how it goes?"

"Tape it up on your locker," Ariel snapped, wishing she could walk faster in high-heeled sandals. She hurried along but then couldn't resist glancing back at the turn in the road. What was she to make of this drawing, with its strange erotic echo of her dream? More important, what was she to make of the artist? Through the trees, she could see Peter walking back to the house, a tall young man in faded jeans and pale blue denim shirt. Why was he living with these middle-aged newlyweds? Was that really what he wanted in life, to be the in-house pet of a rich older woman?

He thinks he's so good-looking, she told herself. Well, he can think again. And with that feeble denial she minced back to town, turned on her laptop computer, and wrote for two hours. It was the chapter of her novel where the hero, abandoned by his Druid princess, defiles himself with a slave girl he finds cowering before the fire.

More Treasure

PETER WALL WOULD HAVE been perfectly happy to defile himself with Ariel before the fire, by the swimming pool, in the backseat of a Buick, or anyplace else she would have him. A wide range of similar possibilities had been racing through his mind all morning, but he had been raised in an age and culture that discouraged putting such ideas to action without the clear agreement of the other party. Judging from their brief acquaintance, Peter doubted he could ever get Ariel to agree with him about the time or the weather, much less a more intimate collaboration.

Instead, he decided to follow Hugo's urgings and search for further treasure. Hugo had found a book titled *Barbarian Gold* in Rosalie's library and insisted Peter look at the illustrations, managing in the process to be so offensively smug that the younger man felt he had no option but to take up the challenge. Choking on a thin breakfast of raspberries and resentment, Peter left to see if he could locate the placid vendor who had sold him the bracelets the week before.

He couldn't. He barely found Oppède-le-Percée, now sunk back to the near invisibility that was its usual state, and when he decided that this really was the town, the only people in sight were three old crones sitting by the village fountain. It was noon, and Marcel was eating dinner with his tante Felice, as he did every Sunday. If Peter had come two hours later, he would have found Marcel standing in his grandmother's doorway, blissfully unoccupied and happy to chat.

But of course Peter had no way of knowing that. Operating on the reasonable, though incorrect, assumption that the man he sought made the rounds of the local markets, as most vendors did, he drove another forty minutes to L'Isle-sur-la-Sorgue, the undisputed center of secondhand selling in Provence. Held every Sunday, spreading over the entire center of the town, the outdoor market there was the darling of travel writers and the salvation of decorators, who came religiously to check the new arrivals at the umbrella-shaded stalls. Ordinarily, it was a place Peter avoided as overpriced, overcrowded, and generally depressing, but today he felt he had no choice.

When he got to L'Isle-sur-la-Sorgue, it was even worse than he had imagined. Watching the avid masses moving through the crowded streets, Peter felt like a solitary mourner in a gathering of grave robbers. He stared in sorrow at the clotheslines hung with old nightshirts, bleached and starched and priced at approximately the annual incomes of the original wearers. He sank into melancholy contemplating the racks of LP albums he remembered from his childhood, already considered quaint enough to sell as antiques, and the cartons of faded views of Italy brought back as souvenirs by tourists of a century ago and now resold to their grandchildren. He tasted the black futility of irrecoverable time as he studied the booths devoted to collections of old railroad timetables and expired telephone cards.

Most of all, he despaired of the people who flocked there to finger all this junk. If they wanted to surround themselves with reminders of the past, why didn't they at least find better examples? They could have been out admiring the Roman Theater at Orange. They could have been strolling along the alley of tombs outside St-Rémy, where they might well have run into a wedding party drinking champagne among the ruins. They could have been exploring L'Isle-sur-la-Sorgue, for that matter, with its wonderful web of canals and moss-covered mill wheels that had once made the town's economy turn. Instead, they were greedily turning over yesterday's trash under the mistaken notion that it was treasure.

Nobody cares about infrastructure, he thought sorrowfully. Nothing has value unless it's fleeting. Great surges of misanthropy, as pure and undiluted as when he had first arrived in Provence, propelled him through the sea of tables in search of two-thousand-year-old sacred jewelry.

To his astonishment, he found something almost at once. There, right in front of him, tangled in a pile of Indian ankle bracelets and cheap silver rings imported from the Philippines, were three necklaces that looked very much like the pictures Hugo had insisted he study before he set out. Two were thin circlets of twisted wire with bulbous finials on the ends. The third was a flat crescent incised with geometric designs. All had the open-collar design of the Celtic torque. Astonished at his luck, Peter gingerly picked one up. It was heavy, which Hugo said was important. A discreet scratch with his thumbnail penetrated the surface patina to reveal the yellow-green luster Hugo said was characteristic of very old gold. The vendor was a woman in her forties, and her manner was as different from that of the seller of the week before as the rest of her merchandise. The jewelry, however, seemed to match.

"For you, Monsieur, a special price. Five hundred francs for the three."

"Two hundred," Peter countered, knowing they would settle on three. Three hundred francs was sixty dollars — steep for a sidewalk sale, but cheap for a trophy to keep Hugo happy. Then Peter inflated the market for battered jewelry even further by asking the vendor if she knew where to get any more like them.

That depended, the woman answered, running her finger along the sharp edge of the golden crescent. These were not her usual stock. She had bought them from a *clochard* who had disappeared as soon as he had her money, no doubt to go off to the fields and get drunk. If he ever sobered up and came back with more to sell, she would hold it for the gentleman. The gentleman should always come back to her table, she added, pocketing the scribbled telephone number Peter handed her folded in a fifty-franc note. She had the highest quality merchandise of anyone in Provence.

So there it was. A drunken derelict, cunning enough to dig the hoard out of its hiding place but too ignorant to realize what he had found. Now all Peter had to do was locate the bum and follow him back to the site of the treasure. Finding the site was of paramount importance, Hugo had said. Absolutely paramount. Peter wondered when in Hugo's career he had started talking that way, but he didn't suppose he would ever find out. Easier to find the drunken bum.

The Museum of Pagan Art

To HUGO BARTELLO, PETER'S discoveries were an intriguing new entertainment he had been unexpectedly invited to attend. On Saturday night he had encouraged the young man to hunt down more ancient goldwork as a matter of course — a friendly piece of professional advice. When Peter astonished him by turning up with three new necklaces on Sunday afternoon, pieces that seemed very much like ancient Celtic torques, Hugo realized it was time to get serious about authentication. To this end, he rose particularly early Monday morning and set out for Arles. He wanted to be at the Museum of Pagan Art as soon as it opened.

Nadine Morel, director of the museum, was flattered by Hugo's interest in her very small collection, and she gave her distinguished colleague a complete tour of the premises.

Hugo endured as much as he could. For forty minutes he slathered her with buttery praise, as though she were a toasted muffin that he intended to devour at any moment. Only after they had toured the last case of Celto-Ligurian crockery and corroded belt buckles did he reveal the executive powers that had, after all, gotten him where he was in life.

"Ma chère madame," he bellowed suddenly, halting Nadine's description of the special mixture of plastic used for the dioramas. A pair of elderly ladies scurried for the nearest exit.

"This is all very lovely," Hugo continued, just as loud, "but now I must consult your expertise." Then he looked carefully around, a portly parody of stealth. Apart from the guard, they were alone. "Perhaps we can go somewhere private?"

Baffled, Madame Morel ushered him into her office and closed the door. Hugo drew a lumpy package from his briefcase. With a flourish, he untied the string holding the tissue paper closed.

"I have here a set of armbands recently bought on the open market," he announced, sounding more like an auctioneer than an art historian, "and a trio of necklaces that are almost identical to ones you have on display outside. I want you to examine them."

From a cabinet behind her desk, the director quickly extracted a black velvet cloth and a jeweler's loupe. Turning her halogen desk lamp to shine full strength on the velvet, she examined each of Hugo's pieces with the magnifying lens.

"I have to run chemical tests to be sure," she said at last. "They could be forged. But they look good. They also look as though they're fresh out of the ground. Where did you acquire these, Monsieur Bartello?"

"I'm afraid I can't tell you that," Hugo answered. "I've come to you because I know you are the leading authority in this field, and because time is something of an issue, but the owner desires to remain anonymous until he knows the value of his acquisition."

"But how can I tell you the value if I don't know the provenance?" Madame Morel objected. "I don't even know if these have been sold through legal channels. Were these bought in the United States?"

"Can't say. The owner is certainly American, I can tell you that. As for where he got them, well, I really don't know. Now, how soon do you think you can do the laboratory tests?"

Hugo's Interpretation

USING ALL OF HIS considerable charm, combined with a promise of future loans of Roman cameos from the Metropolitan collection and an immediate invitation to a splendid lunch, Hugo persuaded Madame Morel to examine Peter's flea market acquisitions that same day, and without any further information on their source. Satisfied with his morning's efforts, he then returned to Gordes to persuade Peter to hang on to his finds. If they were authentic, they would sell for a decent sum, but not nearly as much as they might be worth if Peter had the sense to build up some interest in their discovery. Stretching his imagination even further, Hugo allowed himself to speculate on what a pleasant show he could arrange if Peter had indeed stumbled on a new and major hoard of ancient gold. What a joy, he thought, to organize an exhibition with complete confidence that the artist and even his most remote descendants were long past demanding royalties on the museum reproductions. For, to tell the truth, Hugo had become entirely too well-acquainted with the heirs of Impressionist painters while arranging his most recent exhibition.

He didn't really know this young houseguest who seemed to come as an attachment to his wife's property, and he wasn't at all thrilled at having him along on what was supposed to be a honeymoon retreat. Still, it was part of Hugo's job to manage a large staff of people with diverse and often prickly personalities, cajoling them to creative heights while working to suppress their less attractive traits. Surely he could manage one young and rather sulky underachiever. But how?

He could not appeal to Peter's ambition, Hugo decided, because the young man seemed to have so little. Nor did he have high hopes of calling on a sense of duty, since Peter felt no particularly allegiance to either the Metropolitan Museum or the larger cause of connoisseurship. He couldn't promise enormous profits, because there might not be any, and he couldn't even offer celebrity, beyond the momentary flash of interest in anybody who found anything new hidden beneath the surface of the earth. What might work was his sense of curiosity. There was a historical mystery here. If he presented it right, Hugo might persuade Peter to try to solve it.

Turning in the driveway by the old olive press, still happily digesting the truffled veal that had been the centerpiece of his lunch, Hugo was pleased to see Peter washing his car on the gravel apron in front of the house.

"Delighted to find you!" Hugo shouted, before he had even come to a stop. "Must talk! Join me in the library!"

What had he done wrong? Peter wondered. He always washed his car on the gravel. He was keeping up on the repairs. He had run all of Rosalie's stupid party errands and talked to all of Hugo's boring guests. He had even let Hugo take those necklaces with him this morning. That was probably it, Peter decided. There was something wrong with the necklaces. He hadn't really believed all that stuff about precious objects from the ancient past.

Hugo was already in the library, ensconced in a large, red leather wing chair.

"Come in, come in," he called. "Have a beer! I brought some out from the kitchen!"

"No thanks," Peter said.

"Well, at least have a seat! I won't bite, you know!"

Cautious, confused, and uncomfortably aware of the damp spot where he had tucked the car rag into the waistband of his shorts, Peter sat down.

"We need to talk about this jewelry of yours," Hugo began.

So Peter had been right.

"I've gotten a preliminary analysis, and I think you may have turned up something of real interest. No, no, don't thank me yet," he added, forestalling a burst of gratitude Peter hadn't even thought to offer. "I haven't gotten the final report, and we always have to be ready for disappointment. And besides, I have a stake in this."

"You do?"

"Well, I certainly expect you to let me display your find," Hugo said, pouring his beer into a tall crystal flute. "And publish the book, if we get to that point. But let me tell you what I'm thinking."

Did he have a choice? Peter wondered, reaching for a glass. If he was going to have to sit here and listen to this windbag, he would have that beer after all.

"We need authentication," Hugo was saying, "but I don't want to get bogged down in formal analysis. We could spend a year studying the workmanship of the individual pieces you've turned up so far, and the best we could hope for would be to come up with some hypothetical 'master of the Provençal torques.'"

Peter tried to find an expression that would show his disgust at such a prospect. Failing, he took a swig of his beer.

"We don't want to go the other way, though," Hugo continued. "No sense in entering the swamp of Celtic cosmology. The last thing I want is a museum full of neo-pagans, clogging the corridors with Druid rituals and complaining about inauthentic crystals in the gift shop!"

Peter stared, trying to imagine what horrors Hugo envisioned.

"What I do like is trade routes," Hugo said, pulling out a large aerial photograph of Provence he had borrowed from the Museum of Pagan Art. Hugo was very used to making presentations, and he knew the importance of graphics in driving home your point.

"What we have to do," he explained, pointing to the photograph, "is take this lump of earth and imagine it covered with traffic. What airport do you know best?"

Peter was getting used to the quick transitions. "Los Angeles," he said, without even asking why Hugo wanted to know.

"Fine. Los Angeles. Think about the view when you fly into LAX during daylight. You see the smog first, and then the ocean, and then miles and miles of tract houses and strip malls and office plazas stretching out all around you until you can't imagine why anyone would want to live in this place."

Hugo raised his hand to forestall Peter's defense of his native California. "I'm talking about first impressions," he continued. "But compare that with the view when you fly in at night. The terrifying black vacancy of the ocean against the thrilling network of highways, throbbing with the flow of moving headlights, alternately red and white. That's why they call them arteries, you realize — they look like the circulation of the blood. And then you see the squares and crescents of the residential areas, and the overwhelming sodium-vapor brightness of the retail centers and the office buildings, and the spotlights that always seem to be crossing the sky in one part of the city or another. When you come in at night, you see the real metropolis exposed beneath you."

Excited, Hugo extended his analogy. "It's not just Los Angeles. Fly into Chicago after dark and you feel like a hero, all those roads conquering the flatness of the prairie. Think about Paris. I don't know if you've ever arrived by night, but when you see the illumination of Paris from the sky, it's like entering L'Enfant's dream of the imperial city. And that," he concluded with a flourish, "is what we have to do for the ancients."

"Fly in at night?"

"Don't be absurd." Hugo peered at Peter to see if he was serious, then went on. "Get the overhead view. See the bones and sinews of their settlements, light up their traffic lines like the throbbing lifeblood of ancient trade, red going north, white going south. If we could do that, what would we find?"

Peter was not about to venture another stupid comment.

"A gold route, that's what," Hugo concluded proudly. "A vast set of shipping lanes, from mines to mercantile exchanges, with way stations that were crucial not as shrines (though of course they were used for that) but for restocking the wagons, weighing the goods, collecting taxes, and whatever else these very mysterious people did. Are we really to believe the Druids built Stonehenge to use just twice a year at some sort of solstice ceremony? Or was it occupied at other times as a magnificent holy outdoor marketplace? If we searched right, we could locate the markets of the ancients up and down the Rhône, mercantile centers from England to Egypt. It's there for the looking, I'm sure. You're interested in architecture! Go out and find it!"

Art News in the Information Age

IN THE WAVES OF gossip that washed across the fashionable summer enclaves of Provence over the next few days, the most glittering item was the rumor of a new discovery of ancient art. By Monday night, everyone had heard there were some striking pieces of Celtic goldwork that Hugo Bartello, that lucky bastard, had somehow gotten his hands on. By Tuesday, it was a well-known fact that Hugo had acquired a virgin hoard, never before on exhibit, and was mounting a major show. By Wednesday, it was agreed that early European antiquities would be a top attraction for the start of the new millennium. Thursday saw a number of people rising from the Bastille Day celebration with a sudden urge to spend August in a remote village in the South of France. Any remote village would do, but if the rental agent knew of any recent excavations in the area, they had always wanted to observe such a process and would consider that a great added attraction. Price was no object.

The fact that they had nothing to go on was little impediment to the nimble minds and well-tuned fax machines of the art community. Was it true that a major hoard of ancient jewelry had been uncovered? Was it true that an itinerant mason had unearthed an ancient ceremonial site on the grounds of an old villa in Cavaillon? Did they need a photographer? A cultural historian? An archaeologist? A bodyguard? A witch? Had they sold the movie rights?

The marketplace of ideas was crowded with eager vendors, some traveling from distant lands to hawk their expertise and promote their role as indispensable sources of information. Every specialist in Celtic arts from Helsinki to Houston was trying to reach Hugo, seeking either to preempt the show it was assumed he was mounting or to get cut in on the deal.

Since this was France, the gossip was soon colored by issues of national pride. French cultural sovereignty must be protected from the crass influences of American commerce. First, it was necessary to celebrate this latest demonstration of France's native genius, whatever it might be. Second, it was equally necessary to make sure this celebration was directed by and for La Belle France. To this end, the cultural affairs editor of *L'Express* hurriedly inserted a feature on Provence in the next week's issue, using recent photos from the Cannes Film Festival to demonstrate that the South of France had always been a hotbed of creativity. The Socialist minister of the arts dusted off his favorite legislative initiative for the protection of national treasures as an instrument of job creation. The Conservative premier commissioned a position paper on the economic value of ancient treasure in stabilization of the European currency. Representatives of the ultranationalistic Popular Front claimed the Celts as the only true progenitors of Gaul, while their Communist counterparts readied charts showing the transnational unity of these early migrants. The leading authority on prehistoric cave paintings rushed into print with a polemical essay, *"Graphique/Plastique,"* reasserting the intellectual primacy of drawing over metalwork in understanding the ancient past but reminding his readers that both forms of expression had reached their highest development in France.

After two thousand years of submersion, Celtic jewelry was fresh. It was sexy. It was useful. Best of all, it was different. In accordance with the natural cycles that govern the ebb and flow of artistic fashion, everyone in the business was ready to start caring about something new. Celtic metalwork was about to become the latest discovery.

Is it any wonder, then, that the telephone lines were humming?

Starting Over Yet Again

NONE OF THOSE calls was for Vivian Hart. In gossip, as in so much else, she was entirely out of the loop. On Monday, while Richard drove around searching for derelicts to photograph and the children continued their excavations under Clotilde's neglectful care, Vivian drove to St-Rémy, where she spent a full twenty minutes soaking in the view of the asylum where van Gogh had been housed in his final, hectic days. Then, as usual, she retired to a café. She was determined to draft at least an outline of her great work.

Pulling out the exercise book she had brought for this purpose, its pages ruled into squares to encourage better penmanship, she began to write. She would have three sections, she decided: Earth, Water, and Stone. Earth would be van Gogh and the need to valorize the regimented, agricultural landscape. Water would be Monet and the appropriation of the primal fecundity of wetness. Stone would be Cézanne and the masculine compulsion to build monuments. As for Renoir, Pissarro, and all the other Impressionist painters who didn't fit her scheme, they would be mentioned in passing. After all, depth of insight was more important than breadth of coverage, and passion more important than either. The introduction, a brief history of the suppression of women, she would call "Void." The conclusion, an invocation of the goddess, would of course be "Gaia."

Exhausted by the effort of composing this outline, Vivian took a break to observe the scene around her. At the next table were two young men who had seemed to be almost asleep, until joined by a radiantly pretty girl in her early twenties. Her well-washed jeans and plain white T-shirt were the epitome of casual elegance. Her long brown hair swung before her face as she bent to kiss each of her companions. Taking her seat, she reached into her dark green leather shoulder bag and pulled out a portfolio and a handful of colored pencils.

Entranced, Vivian watched as the girl gathered her hair into a bun and secured it with two of the pencils before opening the portfolio and spreading its contents on the table. Reaching avidly for their own pencils, her companions began to make quick additions to her works. They were artists, Vivian realized with an ecstatic shiver. She was sitting next to a trio of real live artists. If she eavesdropped, she could pick up some art vocabulary.

But what was the beautiful girl saying? "Le product launch" did not sound like a phrase an artist would use, or at least not in conjunction with "Le teamwork." Craning her neck more than was strictly polite, Vivian realized the papers were spreadsheets, not sketches. Business Franglais, she realized with a sigh. One of the problems with France was that nobody dressed clearly. The restaurant owner looked like a banker, the manicurist like a motorcycle moll, the baby-sitter like a woman warrior, and the sales manager like an artist with pencils in her hair.

Chastened, Vivian reopened her notebook. On the top of the first page she had written two words. "Runaway Best-seller." Below was an array of doodles. With great deliberation, she uncapped her felt-tipped pen and crossed out the word *Runaway,* inserting in its place the word *Surprise.* "Surprise Best-seller." That seemed more realistic. She would settle for surprise.

Vivian's Awakening

A T NIGHT, WHEN THE children were asleep and Richard was still across the road in Renard's bar, Vivian transcribed her day's notes on her computer. First she wrote an account of whatever she had visited or discovered or, more commonly, made up during her travels. It was rarely more than three pages, but it usually took her an hour or two to flesh out her scribbles and enter them on the keyboard, and it was always a painful and frustrating business.

Then, to clear her mind, she turned to a separate file she had labeled "My Secret Life." This was a far more energetic, often fantastic account of what she had not accomplished, with special attention to the hellish tribulations that kept her work from progressing faster.

In this secret journal, Vivian allowed herself the fullest range of wicked exaggeration. Richard was a bumbling sot, Clotilde a monument of sullen selfishness, Monsieur Renard an avaricious schemer, the children ungrateful parasites. Even the landscape, which should have been her solace and her inspiration, was always rising up to thwart her attempts at understanding, communion, or simple transit. She cast herself as a sort of modern Candide, the optimistic simpleton whose generous expectations could be proven wrong day after day and still spring up fresh the following morning, as green and innocent as grass.

To keep things from being too negative, she also included a number of scorching sexual fantasies. From the debonair waiter who ran his tongue across her ear as he delivered her café au lait in the morning to the brooding, earthy guard who had his own reasons for admitting her after hours to the antique monuments at Entremont, her journal recounted imaginary gratification that balanced out her far too real physical and intellectual frustrations. Sometimes one led to the other. Thinking about water, she had struggled to transcribe as much as she could remember of the plumber's discourse from the Bartellos' party. Unable to separate the teacher from the lesson, she had included a long description of the plumber himself, which had somehow led to a juicy fantasy in which he invited her to investigate his fixtures. This she transferred right away into her secret journal, which was getting longer every evening.

On Monday night, she was deep into a delicious description of what might have happened if the trio at the next table had been artists after all when she was startled by the ring of the telephone. It was Kirstin, the literary agent from New York.

Kirstin was twenty-four years old, weighed ninety-six pounds without her nose ring, and had a wispy voice that forced listeners to guess at half her words. In the darkness of the quiet house, Vivian felt she was getting a secret message. Did she know who had the buried treasure? Was she writing about it? Was she far enough along to make it an instant book?

"I don't know what you're talking about."

This, for Vivian, was a very difficult admission. It went against her deepest principles to concede ignorance. Usually she could pick up the information from the context, but with Kirstin you needed to know the context to fill in the inaudible gaps.

"Everybody was . . . the Hamptons," Kirstin whispered. ". . . a fax about it . . . the book fair . . . Düsseldorf." Then her voice rose in indignation. "I can't believe you haven't heard."

"Well, I have heard something," Vivian lied. "Who could escape it? But tell me what you have in mind."

According to Kirstin's highly garbled account, treasure hunters from all over the world were converging on Provence, where pagan gold was springing to light practically in everybody's backyard.

Not in mine, Vivian thought glumly, imagining the reaction of the hot-tempered Monsieur Maudit if she tried to dig around his precious lavender bushes. But she had already made one embarrassing admission and was not about to repeat that mistake. Desperate for a piece of the action, she assured Kirstin that all the rumors were true and that it would be a simple thing to reorient her book toward goddess worship and Druid rituals.

Since her subject, as recently as that morning, had been Impressionist painting, this might seem an impossible boast. Given the fluidity of Vivian's ideas, however, and the extremely sketchy nature of her draft, it turned out to be surprisingly easy. When Richard came in at midnight, he found Vivian busily editing her notes, pumping up Gaia and pulling back on van Gogh. It was always energizing, Vivian found, to have some positive encouragement from an authoritative source.

Collaboration

RICHARD WAS ALSO FEELING more optimistic about his work. The hostility and even threats he had encountered when he began shooting portraits of the local derelicts had turned out to be nothing more than opening positions in a fairly simple series of salary negotiations. Once he agreed that even a *clochard* deserved to be paid for his time, he had no trouble at all finding subjects. Over the last two days he had taken pictures of tall bums and small bums, fat bums and gaunt bums, bums who wore fur caps and padded overcoats in the heat of July and bums who were willing — nay, eager — to pose in the nude. He had bums harvesting grapes and selling newspapers, bums sleeping in gutters and rummaging in trash cans, and even one extraordinarily hairy specimen with disgusting toenails who seemed to have some sort of antique medallion pinned directly into his chest. Provence might be short of rain, affordable houses, and authentic bouillabaisse, but it had plenty of bums.

On Monday afternoon Richard had gone to Carpentras. He was looking for photogenic derelicts to pose against the buntings already installed for the Bastille Day celebration. Instead, he discovered an NBC crew doing advance work for a news feature on the remaining artifacts of pagan Provence. They had been winding up their coverage of the Tour de France when the news manager called from New York and told them to cancel their return and get moving on the new story. Who knew why? Neat way to get a vacation.

"It blew me away," he reported to Vivian that night, his vocabulary already infected by an afternoon spent trailing the twenty-five-year-old producer. "Tucked right into the corner of this ugly church there's a wall of crumbling stone, and on it is the most amazing monument to some Roman victory over the Gauls. It's a carving of a tree, with a prisoner chained to the trunk on either side, but the far-out part is, this whole monument was made right there. I mean, get this scene: the Romans come in and capture the leaders and drag them back to Rome in chains, and meanwhile they leave some centurion behind to command the natives to carve a tribute to their own defeat. The research guy says the tree represents the Roman empire, and the naked captives have knock-knees to symbolize submission. Talk about eating shit!"

Ever sensitive to the documents of marginalization, Richard had decided to pose his models against this backdrop of earlier victimization. He had worked until dark, driving potential subjects from the bus station, their favorite hangout, to the side of the church, where he photographed them next to the carved images of their ancestors in chains. It took so long because Richard was afraid to travel with more than one bum in the car at a time. One of those lessons they don't teach you in art school.

If the Carpentras shots worked out, Richard planned to move on to Aix-en-Provence, where he hoped to bribe several of the city's rankest citizens to accompany him to the Granet Museum and pose among the headless torsos of Celtic warriors displayed there.

"How did you know about that?" Vivian asked.

"You told me," Richard answered. "Don't you even listen to your own stories?"

"It's a good idea," Vivian responded, without answering Richard's embarrassing question. "If we're both in Aix-en-Provence, maybe we can get Clotilde to stay late while we go out to dinner." One of Richard's frequent gripes was that they had been in France for over two weeks and hadn't yet managed to eat a proper dinner in a restaurant.

And so they made their plans, poring over the road maps and

guides to antiquities together long after the children had gone to bed. They finished a second bottle of wine and made love with great energy in the rattling brass bed that was designed for precisely that sort of exercise. It was the most pleasant night they had passed since they arrived.

Violent Dreams

P ETER WONDERED WHAT THE penalties would be if he murdered Hugo. He suspected his chances for acquittal would be
good, especially after the judges heard of the way he had been
pushed aside in the hunt for the ancient gold. It would be a crime
of passion, brought on by insufferable smugness. The French pe-
nal code was famously tolerant of crimes of passion.

The chief deterrent was Rosalie, who was not only Peter's first
love and current provider of the free housing that allowed him to
remain in France but also a woman who would raise the sympathies of any courtroom. In her youth, when she had graced every
magazine cover in Europe, Rosalie had been dubbed the Mod
Madonna for her long brown hair and expression of otherwordly
serenity. Grayer now, her youthful glow replaced by a burnished
elegance, the serenity had matured into an air of calm, unshak-
able understanding. She looked like everyone's personal vision of
justice. No, Peter decided, better not risk standing trial as the
murderer of Rosalie's husband.

But this did not mean he would endure any more of Hugo's
condescending instructions. After the authentication report had
come back, proving that the pieces Peter had bought dated from
the first century B.C. and were almost certainly of local design,
Hugo had become insufferable. He wanted to hire diggers. He
wanted to publish a teaser article, with photographs but no attri-
bution for the new discoveries. He wanted to smuggle the treasure back to New York. Which is to say, he wanted to take charge.

A week ago, Peter had bought a few old bracelets at a country
market, and on Saturday night he had shown them to Hugo

Bartello. Now, it appeared, Mr. Bartello had big plans for Peter's discovery — plans that did not include the discoverer himself. Peter knew he couldn't stop Hugo's efforts, but he was determined not to cooperate. He, Peter Wall, would find the treasure. He would find it by himself, and he would sell it to the highest bidder, intellectual significance and all. Just as he had been the first discoverer of twisted gold, he would uncover its source. If Hugo had to look elsewhere for a show to dazzle his board of directors, that was his problem, not Peter's.

July in Provence

M EANWHILE, THE REST OF Provence continued pursuing its own affairs. Bastille Day had come and gone, creating all the usual noise and leaving a residue of belief that the country would last another year. The striking canal workers returned to their locks. The truck drivers continued to transport melons north and plastic sandals south. Vacationers in Marseilles developed a nasty rash from swimming in polluted waters. The rose harvest ended in the perfume fields outside Grasse, and the workers piled into the trucks that would take them inland for the lavender harvest about to begin.

Closer to home, Peter Wall continued to comb the flea markets for new examples of Celtic gold, though with little of his earlier success. Hugo Bartello, staring up at the many military planes that jetted across the Provençal skies, wondered what it would cost to sponsor a reconnaissance mission to hunt for secret excavations. Didier Renard continued to paint his little "postcards," and his wife, Marianne, continued to mount them under elegantly understated squares of inexpensive glass. Clotilde continued to entertain her lover, the fire ranger for the national forest, when she was baby-sitting for the Harts. Glad to be left alone, Justin and Lily continued to dredge treasure out of the pond, polishing it as best they could with an old undershirt before hiding it in the growing pile of goods they would soon be presenting to Marcel.

And Richard and Vivian Hart traveled ever farther afield in their search for fame and fortune. Whether the focus of attention was derelicts or dolls, prehistoric troves or phallocentric painters, the ultimate goal was always the same. Richard wanted to be known as a serious photographer. Vivian wanted to be known as a commentator on art and culture. But, most of all, they both simply wanted to be known.

They could have saved themselves a great deal of trouble if they had paid more attention to what their children did all day, but that never crossed their minds. Despite their largely accurate sense of themselves as loving and caring parents, both Richard and Vivian shared the widespread delusion that their children entered a sort of suspended animation when they, the parents, stepped out the door. Obviously irrational, never articulated, never even rising to the level of conscious thought, it was nonetheless one of the things on which they most completely agreed. To think about how the children passed their time would create a paralyzing sense of guilt and inadequacy. Not to think about the children was to eliminate those dismaying emotions. In fact, it was to eliminate the children entirely. *Non cogito de liberis, ergo liberi non sunt.* I don't think about the children, therefore the children do not exist. The briefest extension of logic will show that nonexistent children do not find treasures.

Nobody had explained this to Justin and Lily, just as nobody had bothered to tell them that the contents of their pond were poised to become the focus of an international art revival. Left every morning to the gruff ministrations of Clotilde, who was always eager to get them out of the house and completely indifferent to what they did while gone, Justin and Lily might as well have been marooned on another planet. No events, global or local, penetrated their isolation.

They did know that their efforts to buy their way out of this stupid foreign country weren't bringing in nearly the cash they had hoped. They had been sadly disappointed when Marcel presented them with twenty francs and a wind-up chicken as the total profits of their second week of sales, but at least they had established that there was a market for the stuff. Somehow, someday, they would find the money to get home.

Ariel

HIGH IN THE TOWER of her employer's summer house, Ariel was working on her novel. She had moved back into the dining room, where she had the table stacked with as rich a library of fourth-generation deconstructionist ideology as her budget could afford. By staying inside, she reasoned, she would not be misled into false sympathies with nature or meaningless exposure to actual historical sites.

When she first learned she was going to Gordes, she had consoled herself with the surety that she would not fall prey to the virus of false authenticity. As in so many other convictions, she had been wrong. In a process she was helpless to explain, the volumes of literary theory were sinking to the bottom of her stacks, and the maps and guidebooks she found herself buying were rising to the top. For several days she lost herself in an illustrated history of the Luberon, full of warring tribes and religious massacres. She felt the presence of an ancient Provence, a place where men went into battle naked, their hair bleached with lime and molded into savage spikes, and where worshipers gathered around forest pools to conduct their rituals of blood and penance. No matter how firmly she turned her chair away from the window, Ariel found herself weaving specific bits of local detail into her text. It revolted her, but it was happening. Her story was sending out the first frail lines that would soon find her tangled in recognizable settings and historic fact.

Peter

IT IS NOT EASY to feel gloomy at eleven thirty on a July morning in Provence, but a childhood in Southern California had steeled Peter to the therapeutic charms of blue skies and bountiful fields. Goaded into action by Hugo's insufferable winks and smirks, Peter had left every morning to search for the source of the ancient gold, but eight days combing every available antique store and flea market from Apt to Nice had turned up nothing. When he followed his instincts, he ended up spending too much for cheap reproductions or original junk. When he tried to play detective, his search went even worse. Most dealers laughed when Peter asked them if they had bought anything recently from a drunken bum. Drunken bums were among their principal suppliers, second only to impoverished grandmothers. Apart from using up a lot of gas, his quest had gotten him nowhere.

Peter's understandable frustration at his failure to find anything was increased by the tantalizing evidence of other people's success. You would think that the stuff was falling from heaven, straight down into the lap of everybody but Peter Wall, who deserved to find it because he was the one who had made it famous, after all. If he hadn't shown those bracelets to Hugo, there would have been no knowledge, no rumors, no steady stream of visitors seeking confidential appointments with the experts at the Museum of Pagan Art.

But there was all of that and more. Most of the people who thought they had stumbled on an ancient treasure were wrong, of course, and it was easy to laugh at the stubborn fools who brought in a rusty medal in memory of somebody's first communion and insisted it was twenty centuries old, but enough was real to show that somewhere, somehow, something big had been uncovered. The story was always the same: bought at a flea market, or a fair, or by the side of the road, usually from a vendor several removes from the original merchant. The price was always low, the transactions always too vague to trace.

Hugo's theory was that the discoverer was afraid the government would seize his treasure if he announced the find or tried to sell it all at once. The way he talked about it, you could tell he was already making mental drafts for the catalog, and probably hard copy for his memoirs. Even if they never found any more pieces and never discovered the source, Hugo would have a story to peddle, the story of the hunt.

That was not very comforting for Peter. When he bought those first three bracelets, he had been happy with the prospect of a quick resale and some extra cash. Then he had gotten notions of establishing his name as the brilliant discoverer of an ancient Celtic hoard. Lying awake in his tiny room, Peter had imagined himself as a younger, Europe-centered Indiana Jones, combining his background in architecture with his uncanny instinct for treasure to leap from adventure to adventure. For almost two weeks, it had seemed the whole world was waiting for his next discovery, confident that it would soon arrive. Then reality set in. Three armbands and three necklaces did not a major exhibition make, or a major art trend, or a major anything at all. The journalists and art historians returned to whatever it was they had been doing before Peter's dramatic discovery, the politicians pushed their proposals back in the drawer, and the collectively bated breath of the international art market turned into a cool whistle of disinterest. Even Hugo had hinted that he might do better if he went back to his restoration work, making some condescending, platitudinous remark about finding success when you least expect it. Stung, Peter had left early the next morning to comb the local markets. The only faintly promising object he had found was a badly tarnished metal bowl. It wasn't jewelry and it wasn't beautiful, but he bought it anyway. And probably paid too much.

As he turned up the hill toward Rosalie's villa, back to another afternoon of tactful silence about his fruitless searches, Peter glimpsed a possible distraction. Ariel Stern, wearing a green-and-gold Oakland A's baseball cap, snug cut-off jeans, and a gray Alcatraz T-shirt, was walking slowly down the long slope from Gordes. She was carrying a camera and studying a folded piece of paper. Pulling the Fiat over to the side of the road, Peter leaned out the window to renew their brief acquaintance.

A New Quest

ARIEL PEERED INTO THE car. It was that offensive jerk from the party, the one who sponged off older women. He was offering her a ride.

"You're not going my way," she said, noting the obvious fact that Peter's car was heading uphill, not down.

"Where are you going?"

"I'm looked for a dolmen. The map says it's somewhere between Lacoste and Ménerbes. I'm trying to figure it out."

"You were planning to *walk* from Gordes to Ménerbes?" Peter couldn't hide his amazement.

"Not everybody has a car," Ariel said sharply.

"It's a good fifteen kilometers. Lacoste isn't much closer. And I'm not sure there's any dolmen around there. I've never heard of one."

Fifteen kilometers. It had taken her an hour to get where she was, and now she discovered it was nowhere near where she wanted to be. Her feet were already sore, and her nose felt hot in a way that signaled tomorrow's sunburn. Hating to admit her miscalculation, she turned on Peter. It was a natural response, though hardly fair.

How could it be, she wondered, that a person who claimed to cherish the purity of antique architecture had not yet seen this local treasure? Leaning halfway into the open window so he could hear her over the noise of the passing cars, Ariel described a dolmen in terms appropriate to a very simple intellect. He was to think of big rocks, she started. Really big, flat rocks. Then he was to think of them set on end, like giant building blocks, each block of stone forming a wall. On the top, another flat stone made a roof. It was like Stonehenge. Surely he had heard of that. He would like it, she assured him. It was even older than his lady friends.

Peter knew he was being insulted, though the precise meaning was rather obscure. But after a long and frustrating morning chasing elusive circles of twisted gold, he was in no mood to ask. "Are you sure you read the map right?" he countered. "If there's a Stonehenge around here, I would have seen it."

"Well, not necessarily Stonehenge," Ariel admitted. "Some dolmens are pretty small. It might have been a shrine, or a place for rituals of sexual initiation. Not that it matters what it was built for," she added defiantly. "My object is to explore the transgressive area where the symbols on the map intrude upon the words of my narrative. The physical overlay does not signify."

"Rituals of sexual initiation?" Peter repeated, ignoring the last part of Ariel's speech. "Sounds like a must-see."

And so, without actually accepting his company, Ariel found herself in Peter's car, in joint pursuit of one obscure remnant of megalithic architecture.

Roman Stones

WHILE PETER DROVE, ARIEL kept up a rapid-fire description of Druid rites. For someone who insisted that historical knowledge was a snare and a delusion, she seemed intent on
showing Peter how many facts she knew about the past. He found
himself wondering about her mysterious "employer." Maybe the
lit-crit theory jargon went with the "English instruction." Giving
way to an impulse, he pulled off into the weeds by the side of the
road.

"Why are we stopping?" Ariel asked, trying to keep the nervous-
ness out of her voice. She was perfectly comfortable discussing
rape as a vehicle of political awakening, but it was something else
to experience it.

"I want to show you something."

"The dolmen? Are we near the dolmen?"

"Oh, no," Peter answered. "Much better."

Ariel peered through the windshield, wishing she had worn
her contacts instead of these prescription sunglasses. Everything
was so dark.

Peter was already out of the car and walking away. "Come on,"
he yelled back. "I'm not going to attack you."

Mortified that he had read her mind, Ariel waited for a lime
green Citroën to rattle by before she crossed the road and
climbed down the grassy slope to the side of a narrow river. She
stared after the car for a moment, trying to remember where she
had seen that color before.

"I wanted to show you my side of the world," Peter said. "This
is the Pont Julien. The bridge of the Consul Julien. A perfect ex-

ample of Roman stonework, third century B.C. Still carrying traffic, of course. Because they may have been conquerors and they may have been brutes, but they were also very good at what they did."

What followed was a long and surprisingly heartfelt description of the Roman genius for military engineering. You couldn't win the battle if you didn't have the troops, he explained, and you couldn't get the troops there if you didn't know how to build a very strong bridge, very fast. President Eisenhower, she remembered, had funded the interstate highway system in the 1950s so he would be ready to move troops if the Communists invaded America. That was the kind of topic her mother talked about at dinner, her voice quivering with outrage at the evils of the military-industrial complex. To her mother, it had been all about injustice and the brutality of power. To Peter, she realized, it was about making things that would last for centuries, even if you needed them for only a few weeks. Before she realized it, she was climbing farther down the bank to admire the fitting of the keystone arch.

"It's holding up well," Ariel admitted, not sure where the conversation was going.

"So maybe some kinds of knowledge are real?" Peter asked. "Maybe a touch of engineering here and there keeps the world together?"

A trap. She was being made fun of by a kept man. Probably he had just heard about this bridge from somebody at Rosalie's house. Maybe her husband.

"Okay," Ariel agreed curtly. "They were great military engineers, if you value military engineering. Now can we go?"

Yes, Peter decided, the offensive rudeness must be a carryover from her work. Dominatrix stuff. All this intellectual research was just a cover. He could tell.

Celtic Rocks

B ACK IN THE CAR, speeding along in angry silence, Peter and Ariel climbed the hill to the village of Lacoste. At the summit were the ruined remains of the castle where the marquis de Sade had tried, without success, to lead a quiet life during the French Revolution. Ariel said the dolmen was somewhere between Lacoste and Ménerbes, but she wasn't at all sure where. Time to find out.

Pulling into the dry dirt field behind the castle, Peter stopped to consult the map. First he studied the page Ariel had been following, traced from a book on prehistoric Celtic migrations that was long on speculation but very short on useful landmarks or guideposts. According to this map, Provence consisted of two rivers, a wide port, and a broad swath of forest dotted with little stick figures who were supposed to represent Celts. The dolmen, shown here as a sort of stone shed ringed by particularly substantial stick Celts, seemed to be next door to Gordes. Looking at the way the landmarks were bunched together, Peter could understand how Ariel had gotten the notion that she could reach it on foot.

"Are you memorizing that?" Ariel asked at last. "It's not a treasure map, you know. You can get your own copy if you like."

"No thanks," Peter replied. "It's not that helpful." Reaching under his seat, he pulled out his Michelin map. It was short on stick figure settlements but useful for locating actual pavement. To his astonishment, a small emblem on the map indicated a *monument megalithique* not far down the road. If it had made it onto the

Michelin, this thing must actually exist. Peter pointed the car toward Ménerbes.

However clearly marked on the map, the dolmen was invisible from the road. After driving back and forth between Lacoste and Ménerbes three times, Peter parked on a bit of gravel next to a field of vines, determined to search on foot.

On the other side of the road was a narrow ditch and, beyond it, a solidly built woman of about sixty who sat on a large wicker basket reading a magazine. She appeared to be waiting for a ride.

Two small dogs with bows in their hair peeped out of a window in the basket and set up a frantic yap as Peter and Ariel approached.

"Tais toi, Marius!" the woman instructed. *"Soi sage, Fanny!"* She rolled her magazine in a menacing way, then laid it on the seat and went to meet these road-worn strangers at the end of her property.

"Good day, madam," Peter began in his rather courtly French. "I wonder if you would do us the great good favor of instructing us as to where we might find the ruins of the Druid people, indicated on this Michelin map?" Ariel held out the map, conveniently folded open to the right section, but the woman seemed to understand without consultation.

"That way," she answered, pointing down the road. "You have to look where the road passes over the irrigation ditch. There are some rocks. Leave your car here."

Brushing aside their profuse thanks, she returned to her dogs and her magazine.

Ariel and Peter walked another fifty yards, until, indeed, the road went over a small ditch that passed beneath the asphalt to the grape fields below.

Ariel adjusted her camera strap over her neck and slapped her baseball cap back on her head. Peter looked around. No dolmen that he could see. No water, for that matter. A dry ditch, sheltering nothing.

Leaning next to the edge of the pavement was a broken board.

Picking it up, Ariel saw the word DOLMEN painted on the other side, with a wobbly arrow pointing straight to the ground. Looking down beneath the road, they at last discovered the dolmen.

Or at least they assumed that was what it was.

Was this all? Peter wondered. He had seen only pictures of Stonehenge, but he had the distinct impression that it was big. Awesome. Overwhelming. This was a squat stone box, less than six feet in any direction. Three large slabs of rock had been set upright for walls, then topped with another slab for a roof. Where the fourth wall would have been, there was an open space. Evidently this was a provincial dolmen, a satellite shrine, like the drive-through teller at a branch bank in California.

If Ariel shared his disappointment, she kept it to herself. Scrambling down the slope by the side of the road, she studied the upper surface of the rock, then stooped and vanished inside.

At One with the Past

ARIEL WAITED FOR HER eyes to adjust to the gloom. The top of her head grazed the stone ceiling. As she savored the cool simplicity of her chamber, she strained to erase the distracting reminder of the present age. It was like a yoga exercise, she told herself. She must clear her mind. First she erased the ditch, then the road, then the woman, the dogs, and the last two millennia. Finally, making a special effort, she abandoned all thoughts of Peter Wall.

Long ago, people had somehow brought these enormous stone slabs to just this spot, to mark a site. But of what? Was it a sacred grove? An altar? A holy way station? Shaking her head slightly, Ariel reminded herself that what mattered was not authorial intentionality but reader response. What did it signify to her? That was the important question.

Crouching slightly, she patted the rough surface of the rock, then stooped to study the single boulder that formed the back wall. Was it her imagination, or was there a head etched into the stone? She ran her hand over the surface, surprised at how cold it was, but couldn't tell it if was a genuine image or an irregularity of the rock. She took a photograph, but the light from the flash was too brief for her to see what she had recorded.

After several more moments of silent, crouching communion, Ariel straightened up, banging her head on the ceiling. Apparently the rock was shorter here in back.

"Having a good time?" Peter called from outside. "Like some company?"

"No. Thanks."

Ariel tried to retrieve her mood of solitary enlightenment. Just when she thought she had it, she heard the scrabble of feet on the stones outside. To ward off the intruder, she ducked out.

In the sunlight, she felt suddenly dizzy. She hadn't eaten anything since breakfast, and the long walk, followed by the backtracking car ride and the mounting heat, had done her in. Plus, of course, the anxiety of wondering what impression she was making on Peter, though Ariel was not inclined to factor that into her calculations.

"Can you wait a minute while I take some notes?"

"No problem," Peter answered.

"Can you wait up there?" She pointed back to the level of the road.

"Sorry, Your Highness."

Several minutes later, when Ariel climbed up to join him, she was still pale and had trouble finding her footing.

"You feeling all right?" Peter asked. "Eat anything strange this morning? You look like you're about to lose your cookies."

Was this the gallantry that won over all those older women? Ariel sat down and tried to put her head between her knees without exactly showing what she was doing. It wasn't indigestion that was affecting her, she wanted to explain, but the inescapable and horrifying significance of the place.

"Without question," Ariel announced faintly, "this dolmen is a metaphor for the profanity of modern life, a holy site desecrated by a drainage ditch."

This struck Peter as completely unfair. If not for the ditch, no one would have uncovered the dolmen, buried under twenty centuries of dead leaves. Ariel's nauseous communion with the past had been made possible by the nineteenth-century revolution of scientific agriculture. Besides, who was she to talk about desecration? But, then, she really did look green. Better not argue.

After another minute, Ariel raised herself, walked to the car, and climbed inside, wincing when the hot vinyl of the seat cushion touched the back of her thigh. Peter followed. She hadn't even thanked him for taking her there. Pulling onto the pavement faster than he should have, he was glad to see her wince again as her shoulder bumped against a new zone of inflammatory plastic.

They drove back past the dolmen, past the stout woman still waiting with her dogs and her magazine, past the vast stone quarry carved into the backside of the Luberon mountains. When they got to Goult, Peter parked next to a restaurant and announced it was time for his Saturday afternoon aperitif. This was a ritual he had invented only a moment before, but it seemed time to remind his grumpy passenger of how much of his day he was devoting to driving her around.

I should have known he had a drinking problem, Ariel said to herself. Who ever heard of a gigolo who didn't?

The Village of the Boring

SATURDAY AFTERNOON, VIVIAN had an inspiration. Richard
was off finding derelicts, but she and the children could visit
the Village des Bories, a gathering of primitive stone huts on the
outskirts of Gordes that had become a tourist attraction. Maybe
she could use them as part of her new early Gallo-Celtic orienta-
tion.

There was nothing particularly rare about a borie. Hundreds
of the small, round structures were scattered over the plateau of
the Vaucluse like rocky beehives. There was something thrilling,
though, about the mass of them together, something that made it
possible to imagine that they had indeed once been inhabited.
Any day of halfway decent weather would find the paths of the
Village des Bories crowded with families and school excursions,
clucking gleefully over the immense discomfort that must have
reigned in the cold stone dwellings all about them. It ennobled
their own lives to see how miserable their ancestors must have
been. For all their Neolithic appearance, none of the bories dated
from before the sixteenth century, and many were little more
than a hundred years old.

Distracted by the complaints of her carsick children, as well as
her persistent problem finding third gear, Vivian almost drove
past the site. Suddenly she realized that those dark piles of rubble
were what she was looking for. Pulling to a stop at the end of a
low wall, she grabbed her bag, her sunhat, her notebook, helped
Lily find her Goofy hat, checked to make sure the trunk of the car
was locked, and then realized that Justin was still inside.

"Come on, Justin," she called. "Let's have an adventure!"

Justin wasn't interested. He was not getting out of the car to look at what he insisted on calling the village of the boring. If she made him, he would kick over their stupid rocks. He would run away. He would scream and break things and hate her forever.

Vivian gave up.

"Have it your way," she told him. "Ignore everything we came here to see. Lily and I will be on the other side of that wall. If you change your mind, remember to close the windows and lock the car. And don't talk to any strangers."

Pulling Lily away before she could ask to stay with her brother, Vivian lifted her over the wall and then clambered over herself. Justin would be all right, she told herself. He had his Game Boy. They wouldn't be long.

On the other side of the wall, a well-worn path wound between groups of black stone huts. Somewhat ahead of them were two silent, self-possessed little boys led by a stout grandmother. When they caught up, Vivian could hear her murmuring about the poor, poor people who lived here. Off to the left she could see a parking lot and a ticket seller's kiosk. With a thrill of achievement, Vivian realized she had gotten in for free.

She peered around, searching for fresh ideas for her book. She thought of the hogans of the Plains Indians, and the circular houses of mud and straw that showed up in different parts of Africa. Perhaps she could argue that current buildings, with their straight walls and right-angle corners, had erased the female circle that had once dominated Provençal architecture. She would try it out in her notes tonight —

Her musings were interrupted by Lily, tugging on her arm. She wanted Justin to climb with her on the buildings. Other children were running on the low stone walls that ringed some of the individual structures. Hoping to get Justin out of his sulk, Vivian happily lifted Lily back over the wall and climbed after her. She reached the car just in time to see her son sliding off his seat in a dead faint.

Motivated by equal parts of fear and hay fever, Justin had

locked the doors and rolled up all the windows as soon as Vivian was out of sight. Inside the car, the temperature had quickly risen to over a hundred degrees. Lost in the world of Super Mario, Justin hadn't noticed until it was too late.

Terrified, Vivian unlocked the car door and pulled Justin onto the grass. His sweaty face was an alarming shade of cherry red, but he was still breathing. "Stay with your brother," she shouted at Lily. Then she scrambled into the car and drove to the main entry to get help.

Flic-Flac at Home

MOST PEOPLE WHO VISITED the Village des Bories wondered how anybody had ever lived in their cold stone darkness. Flic-Flac wondered why people lived anywhere else. Here he was undisturbed by campers, lovers, poachers, or any of the other frightening intruders who sometimes crossed his path when he slept out in the national forest. His mind was soothed by the bleakness of the bories' interiors, mercifully free from sharp corners or reflecting surfaces. When the mood was on him, Flic-Flac could be driven to a frenzy by the glint of sunlight on a brass doorknob, his fragile imagination pierced with an ecstasy that was more extreme than any passion, and more frightening.

Curled up in a stolen sleeping bag on the dirt floor of a dry stone hut, Flic-Flac felt safe. He liked to sleep in the first hours of the evening, waking after midnight to sweep the forest for its treasure, then returning for another few hours of rest before he left for the day. He entered only after hours, when he had the village to himself, but closing could be delayed if the gatekeeper thought he might find a few last paying customers. Thus it happened, from time to time, that Flic-Flac arrived at the Village des Bories while a few stragglers were still on the site. Hiding his Deux Cheveaux behind a dense stand of bushes, he would sit in a dark corner of the wall and wait.

Today he had arrived even earlier than usual, tormented by the heat and seeking refuge in the cool and ancient stones. It was barely five o'clock when he pulled his car behind the trees at the far end of the reconstructed village. Justin was lying in the grass, taking shallow, panting breaths. Lily was sitting in the shadow of the wall, far away from any watching eyes. Or so she thought.

She felt like she had been there a long time. She had chewed the long rayon ears of her Goofy hat into a slimy pulp and had given her Barbie a full narration of the village and its round houses. She had taken a stick and written her name in the dirt, and still their mother hadn't returned. Justin had fallen asleep. Lily was bored. She decided to take everything out of her backpack and lay it out on the ground. She would pretend she was selling things at the market, like Marcel.

Flic-Flac watched the little girl. With the sun behind her, the elongated brim and droopy earflaps of her hat merged with her head, making a strange new creature with the body of a human but the ears and muzzle of a hound. There was something familiar about her, something connected with Arles, but Flic-Flac could go no further in his memory. Tired, waiting for the day to end, he simply watched, wondering if the backpack might contain good things to steal.

Working methodically, Lily took out her blond Barbie, her curly blond Barbie, and her Barbie that had only one leg. She laid out the plastic Hamburgler toy that had come with a McDonald's Happy Meal, and the educational activity book her mother had bought for the plane. Next came a cheap plastic camera the same shade of pink as her backpack, a pad of games and puzzles the flight attendant had given her when they were still on the runway in New York, and a cartoon book about going through customs that even Lily had trouble pretending anyone would buy from her store. Digging deeper, she came up with a box of crayons, a pencil sharpener in the shape of a yellow plastic heart, an eraser in the shape of a pink parrot, a tiny memo pad, most of a pack of Juicy Fruit gum, and an Archie Double Digest comic book.

Tearing a sheet from the memo pad, Lily started to trace the picture of Veronica on the comic book cover. Then she looked around, stood up for a moment to see if she could spot her mother, and reached into the backpack one more time. Flic-Flac watched as Lily removed the Goofy hat. The sun, hanging in the west, turned her hair red-gold, and the circle she placed on her head shone like a crown of fire. Flic-Flac's heart began to pound with desire. He was moving now, crawling on his belly over the parched grass, moving carefully to make no noise.

"Lily! Lily, I'm here! I brought water for Justin! Is he all right?"

Lily jammed the sacred circle into her backpack, swept the toys over it, and ran to meet the car. Flic-Flac shuddered and lay where he was. He would find her again, the dog-girl with the golden crown. Then he rose and turned back to the stone city that would be his shelter for the night. A wind was starting to blow. It was time to get inside.

The Bicycle Race

Richard arrived home at the precise moment when Vivian, at the Village des Bories, was splashing Justin's face with Evian water provided by a sympathetic fellow tourist. Finding the house empty, he crossed the highway for a quick beer at Renard's. By the time he finished, the wind had started to blow for real. It was a true mistral, the legendary dry storm of Provence.

In such weather, Renard claimed, the truckers didn't want to pull into his oasis. If they went fast enough, they thought, they would avoid the stones that stuck in the underchassis and the uprooted shrubs that liked to lodge beneath the windshield wipers. Also, a lot of the newer trucks had mini-TVs mounted in the cabs, and Renard knew for a fact that most of the drivers were following the final heat of the Tour de France while they pretended to watch the road. So it was just the two of them, with Clotilde and Marianne washing up in back, the eternal bickering of mother and daughter softened by the sound of the broom and the rhythmic clank of dishes in the basin.

For some fabulous amount of money, the owners of Disneyland Paris had arranged for the finish line to be at the entrance to the amusement park. In anticipation of their victory, several of the racers were wearing Mickey Mouse ears taped flat against their racing caps.

"They look like idiots," Richard observed after his second beer.

Didier Renard grunted his agreement and added his opinion that the entire Tour de France had been corrupted by this infusion of tawdry American culture. That settled, they watched the race in silence for another quarter hour as the wind rattled the windows in their frames.

"What would you wear?" Renard asked idly.

"If I had a team?"

"Of course a team," Renard responded. "Be logical. You would not race alone."

Richard looked down at his plump, hairy legs, which did not show to their best advantage in the safari shorts he was wearing. He tried to remember the last time he had been on a bicycle. Not since he was married, anyway. In Manhattan, the only people suicidal enough to get on bicycles worked for messenger services.

"Gold and green," Richard said decisively. "Gold for the fortune you make when you win. Green for the fields that have swallowed your town. And on the back, a portrait of your daughter brandishing a bicycle pump!"

"Ah," Renard laughed. "She will be our patron saint, eh?"

"With all respect," Richard hastened to add. Clotilde terrified him, and he didn't want her father to get the wrong idea. But Renard seemed charmed by Richard's suggestion. He poured him a glass of brandy, and then another, and by the time the wind died down they were both singing old Motown hits and making plans to race in an amateur competition on August first. That was only a week away, but Renard insisted they would train every day. They would restore the glory of St-Etang. He would provide the bicycles. They would start tomorrow. It was, he said, the dawn of a new life.

Blown Together

THE RESTAURANT TERRACE in Ménerbes turned out to be a decent place to wait out the heat of the afternoon. Lunch was over and dinner wouldn't start for hours, but Peter managed to talk the waitress into a carafe of white wine and a basket of bread. They sat at a table overlooking the valley and sipped their wine.

"Do you like being a gigolo?" Ariel asked, trying to sound blasé. Peter choked on his wine.

"A gigolo!"

"Excuse me," Ariel corrected herself. "Do you like living off the generosity of older women?"

"I don't know why you put it that way," Peter protested. Then he remembered. He had used that description himself. "Rosalie lets me stay because I act as caretaker," he explained. "Besides, I've known her since the beginning of time. My father worked for her before I was even born."

Ariel stared in amazement. A second-generation kept man. Peter continued, creating more confusion with every word.

"Mirielle pays me by the day," he noted proudly. "She's my main customer, really. I earn my keep. Besides, it's only until I finish my independent study. I'm learning all about Provençal masonry."

"What's to learn?"

Where had that come from? At moments like this, Ariel thought she ought to be a channeler, one of those women who go into a trance while dead people speak through them. She had a talent for it. There was no other explanation for the way her mother's voice took possession of her body, or maybe the voice of her Jewish grandmother she had never met.

Peter, unaware that Ariel was having an astral experience, was merely insulted.

"There's a lot of good vernacular architecture in this region," he answered stiffly. "Lots to study." He pointed to a crumbling stucco shed that was somehow sticking out of the hillside just below the level of the terrace. "The way they build things around here hasn't changed in centuries. See those three rows of tiles there, under the roof? They're for clearing rainwater. It's a technique that predates gutters by about two hundred years. I learn a lot, patching these old houses together."

Ariel watched the muscles on Peter's arm as he pointed out the various features of the local buildings. Why was he lecturing her on roof tiles when he should be crushing her to his chest in a powerful embrace like the ones featured on the covers of romance novels?

"Wouldn't it be more useful to study building codes and structural steel?" she asked.

Peter's annoyance grew. Ariel had inadvertently named two of the three courses required for second-year architecture students. All that was missing was Concrete. What right did she have to be lecturing him on useful knowledge? What would happen if he casually rested his hand on her thigh, under the table?

"Architecture," he announced, "is the structuring of purposeful space to meet the physical and metaphysical needs of humanity." He was quoting his professor at Yale, Intro to Architecture, who started every lecture that way. Back in New Haven, it had been like an incantation. On a restaurant terrace in Provence, it sounded incredibly pompous. Peter soldiered on.

"This is a great place to study classical construction," he continued. "There's a long tradition of it, too. Thomas Jefferson used the Maison Carrée in Nîmes as the model for the Virginia State Capitol. Maybe I'll end up an architectural historian. Or do restoration. If I go back to California, I can use a lot of these ideas for high-end houses there. Build Roman villas in Laguna Beach. Stuff like that."

Ariel didn't blink at this rapid segue from high art to crass commerce. She admired the way he was keeping his options open, and hoped she was being as flexible herself. Right now she could see herself pursuing any of a number of intellectual fields, some of which actually paid decent wages, but she hoped she wasn't ruining her chances for the future by working as an au pair.

As though reading her mind, Peter asked if she ever thought of leaving her "employer."

"I can't," Ariel answered, wondering why he said "employer" with such a grimace.

"Why not?"

"I signed a contract. I signed myself over, body and soul, until the middle of August, with rights for renewal for the following twelve months. What was I supposed to do? I was practically homeless."

Peter had no idea the business was that formal. Only in France did you make your mistress sign a contract. Even Southern California hadn't gotten to that.

"Do they stamp it on your visa? Is this your profession for life?" Peter couldn't help asking. It was like picking at a scab.

Ariel had never thought of that. Was she entered under "babysitter" on some international database, a permanent source of future humiliation? Horrified by the prospect, she launched into a defense of spiritual compartmentalization as a necessary and desirable aspect of modern intellectual life.

As Ariel liked to see it, physical existence, and the compromises it entailed, was separated from the realm of analytic imagination by walls more solid and more lasting than the masonry Peter spent so much time patching back together. Derrida's transformative analysis of the indeterminacy of language did not stop him from telling his taxi driver where he wanted to go, after all. What she, Ariel Stern, did to earn money had nothing to do with her intellectual life.

While Ariel floundered around in this rhetorical swamp, Peter studied her nose. Unlike the button features of his high school dream girls or the thin, patrician profile of the girl who had broken his heart in New Haven, Ariel's face had more character than symmetry. Her nose, for example, had a funny bump in the middle. The bump was pink with sunburn, like a mountain peak that holds the light for a last few precious moments after darkness has fallen over the lower ground. Peter knew he must have read that somewhere. Probably some survey course in nineteenth-century poetry. He didn't pretend to have as literary an education as Ariel, but he thought he could hold his own in whatever this crazy conversation was about.

Now she was saying that nothing existed outside the literal text. *"Il n'y a pas de hors-texte,"* she insisted, quoting Derrida. Making an effort, Peter mentally acknowledged the autonomy of the text, ALCATRAZ, from the heaving but irrelevant materiality of Ariel's T-shirt.

He could have followed her argument more closely if he had not been distracted by the pounding in the background. The town was holding its summer festival next week, an event advertised on every wall and lamppost for miles around. Arts and crafts. A bicycle race. Carnival rides. A rock concert. In preparation, a pair of workmen was putting up a bandstand in the parking lot next to the restaurant. Ariel was explaining something about "the Gaze," which sounded like a leer with political overtones. Behind her back, one of the carpenters hammered his thumb instead of a nail. Peter let out an involuntary groan of sympathy.

"What's the matter?" Ariel snapped. "Am I getting a little too close to home? Or do you think you escape commodification because you're a man?"

She glared at Peter. But he had endured a long and unsatisfying day himself. If they weren't going to have sex, he would settle for violence.

"You think I don't know I'm a commodity?" he demanded angrily. "You think it's wonderful getting a letter from my parents every week, asking when I'm going to grow up and get a real job? A man today is just a money machine or an errand boy. Women have it much easier. Your friends from college probably think what you're doing is romantic and exciting. My friends keep me posted on how rich they're getting. But that's not the point."

"And what is?" Ariel asked. Out in front of her, the fields and vineyards showed the same unnatural neatness as the fields and vineyards she saw from her window in Gordes. The furrows were always straight, the corners square. The trees that shaded the roadways were planted in even pairs, mated for all agricultural eternity.

Peter, facing the other direction, watched two boys play on the scaffolding under the bandstand. As they swung from pipe to pipe, the smaller of the two kicked out the extension cord that had been powering the carpenter's drill. The carpenter tried to reach below and capture his saboteur, but the boys darted out the other side and went screeching back up the hill. Standing, the carpenter accidentally upset the bucket that had been holding his tools, and dozens of metal bolts and couplings rolled down into the dirt. It would take him twenty minutes to gather them back.

"The point is . . . I don't know what the point is," Peter admitted, his burst of anger over. "Maybe that life is messy. That's all I'm trying to say. Life is messy, and if you're going to write a novel, you have to show that. You think all that matters is some neat system of philosophy, but nobody really lives by a system. The way you describe them, your characters are nothing more than a series of strange gestures. If you can't write about real life, stick to your other line of business."

Peter thought Ariel would be insulted by that dig, but instead she smiled for the first time all day. "Strange gestures," she repeated. "I like that. I can use that."

Mistral

A WIND had started up from nowhere, flapping the canvas umbrellas over the restaurant tables. Soon clouds of dust were swirling around Peter and Ariel, pelting their bare skin with bits of chalky grit. They ran to the car, then sat there waiting for the storm to blow over.

Watching the summer afternoon turn into a blustery premonition of autumn, Ariel looked ahead to her return to Paris. Perhaps her life wasn't as neatly compartmentalized as she liked to think. Could she really spend another year being a Left Bank intellectual in the morning and a surrogate mother in the afternoon? What did it mean that she devoted so much of her time to picking up somebody else's children after school, correcting their table manners and their pronunciation, supervising their baths, and packing them off to bed? What had Peter called it? Her other line of business?

"I wonder how Hortense and Agathe are doing," she murmured.

"Who are Hortense and Agathe?"

"Oh, nobody," Ariel stammered. She wasn't ready to tell everything about her life in Paris. Let Peter think she worked in the publisher's office. "I was thinking out loud. They're the girls I stay with, in Paris."

"You don't live alone?" Peter's knowledge of kept women was extremely limited, but he had assumed the arrangement involved a separate living space, available for impromptu visits, paid for by the protector. Roommates did not seem to be a viable part of the deal.

"Well, of course I have my own room. But I spend the evenings with Agathe and Hortense."

"What do you do?"

"Live. Eat. They practice English, take baths. I'm teaching them poker. Nothing much."

"Don't you get bored?"

"No," Ariel confessed. "I kind of like it. Besides," she added grandly, "I have my novel. What do you do when not waiting on Mrs. Bartello?" It gave Ariel great pleasure to refer to Rosalie with the respect due a member of a much older generation.

"Move over," Peter ordered. Ariel stared in surprise. Was he ordering her out of the car? Outside, the wind showed no sign of letting up.

"What?"

"Move over. I want to get something from the backseat. I need some room."

Confused, Ariel pushed herself against the door of the car. Peter moved out from behind the steering wheel, pressing his hip against her hip, his thigh against her thigh. Then he twisted his body around so he could pull a package from the narrow trough that passed as the backseat of the car. As his head fell, his legs rose, grazing the side of Ariel's face.

"Got it!" he exclaimed, twisting forward and sliding back behind the wheel. "Tell me what you think of this."

Inside a plastic grocery bag was the hammered bowl Peter had picked up that morning.

"What's this?" Ariel asked.

"I'm not sure," Peter answered. "It might be junk. But I think it might be buried treasure. That's the other thing I do right now, besides running errands for Rosalie, as you like to put it. I hunt for buried treasure."

Joining Forces

IN THE LONG sessions of emotional haggling that are known as courtship, possession of arcane knowledge is a valuable part of negotiations. Taking a potential partner to a moonlit beach is often effective. Taking a potential partner to a moonlit beach and explaining celestial navigation is infallible. Unable to preen and dance like other creatures, humans must find alternate forms of self-display. Which may explain why Peter told Ariel about his recent triumphs as a discoverer of ancient Celtic gold.

As the wind blew and the daylight faded over the hills, he described his lucky find and confided his determination to discover the rest of the lost hoard. Maybe if he borrowed her books about ancient settlements, they would help him in his search. If she wanted to come along, he added hesitantly, they could visit places for her novel.

Abandoning all prior beliefs in the purity of the uninformed imagination, Ariel accepted without even a moment's regret.

"That would be helpful," she agreed, trying not to show her eagerness. "It's been hard for me to go places without a car. Not that it matters for my novel," she finally thought to add, "but I should see something of Provence. I mean, I'm here."

"You should," Peter echoed idiotically. "It would be a shame not to."

"A shame," Ariel repeated.

Outside, the wind was still blowing furiously. The carpenter had abandoned his scaffolding. The waitress had closed the umbrellas on the terrace and stacked the plastic chairs so they wouldn't blow away. Inside the car, the air was growing hot and the windows steamy. Staring straight ahead, clutching the steering wheel to keep his hands out of trouble, Peter managed to ask the burning question that was on his mind.

"So," he croaked, by way of preface. "Being in Gordes and all, that relaxes the rules, doesn't it? I mean, you can go out and stuff, right?"

Ariel thought about the house with all its tasteful furnishings, its modern paintings and antique photographs, its silver place settings it was her job to guard until her employers' arrival at the beginning of August.

"Well, sure, I can go out," she answered, "but I can't be away from the house for too long, and I can't have any guests. It's stupid, I know, but that's the deal. If I don't live up to the contract, they'd find out."

"I guess it matters that you keep your job."

"Absolutely. I have to live, you know. Total fidelity is part of the package. I mean, it's like I'm sold into bondage or something, but that's the deal. They hold all the cards."

Never, ever, ever would Peter understand women. How could they be so promiscuous and so obedient, both at the same time? He should forget this girl and go right back to repairing masonry.

"It's okay for us to drive around together," Ariel ventured, breaking the silence. "Nobody could object to that."

The Team St-Etang

THE MORNING AFTER the mistral, Richard was astonished to find Renard rapping at his bedroom window at daybreak. Vivian, groaning, pulled the sheet over her head. Richard peered outside. Leaning against the side of the farmhouse were two surprisingly sleek bicycles. Too groggy to quarrel, he stumbled into his clothes and joined Renard. The first day's workout had begun.

As they labored up the slope of the old road that ran behind the truck stop, Renard began shouting that St-Etang would rise again. Richard thought his breakfast would rise before it, except he hadn't had any. He hadn't worked this hard in years.

The second hill was steeper, and when they got to the top, Renard stopped to relieve himself. Richard, thankful for the break, joined him. Two men at daybreak, pissing against a tree. When they were finished, Renard laughed and declared they were like cousins. Richard nodded, grinning. Relatives in France. The farthest his family had ever extended before was an uncle who retired to Florida.

That first morning, as they coasted down the long shallow slope into Oppède-le-Percée, Renard began shouting instructions on how they would enter the bicycle race, Le Tour de Luberon, as the official team of St-Etang. They would lose, of course, but it would be for the honor of their village. Until then, they would practice an hour every morning.

"Not long enough," Renard admitted, in what Richard took as a classic piece of Gallic understatement. "But we are both businessmen! We must be about our affairs!"

The Explorers

THE NEXT WEEK involved a great deal of driving around in circles. Richard continued his camera safari, stalking the indigenous derelicts of Provence. Vivian was making a survey of the fountains of Provence, trying to tie them to her theories of sacred springs and matriarchal traditions. Hugo Bartello, who found it amusing to visit obscure local establishments like the Museum of Bread Making or the Museum of Corkscrews, ran into Vivian repeatedly without ever solving the mystery of where they had met. Rosalie, ignoring the hubbub, spent her days visiting friends, tending her garden, and admiring the different views from her villa. Flic-Flac continued to drink and steal and use his metal detector, always keeping one eye open for the dog-goddess with the golden halo.

The most active, though not by any means the most successful, of these explorers were Peter and Ariel. Every morning at eight, Peter would be waiting in the square before the castle at Gordes, where Ariel would join him for another day's search. Every afternoon they would stop at a café to work out the next day's plan of attack. Neither felt comfortable inviting the other into his or her borrowed home. To hide their social embarrassment, they treated their days on the road like military expeditions.

If they'd had more time, they would have mounted their maps on corkboard and used different-colored pins and bits of wool to mark the routes. As it was, they tried to pick a likely itinerary, set out early in the morning, and hit as many flea markets and obscure antiquarians as they could before it was time to head back for the night. After a particularly hot and boring visit to the ruins of the Celtic settlement on the plains above Aix-en-Provence, Ariel had reasserted the need to clear her mind of distracting history. After that, they simply poked around looking for treasure. None ever turned up.

And still they traveled on. It was random, exhausting, tedious, and unrewarding, at least in terms of finding the source of the Celtic hoard. Above all, it was extremely intimate, this botched approximation of a treasure hunt they were conducting. Five days of chasing elusive treasure under the hot July sun brought them to the kind of familiarity that some couples don't achieve for decades. Peter knew that Ariel preferred hot chocolate to coffee in the morning and understood that she would dart across any street without notice if she saw a stack of used books to rummage through. Ariel knew that Peter liked to strike up conversations with the parish priest (remarkably often an amateur archaeologist), and she was resigned to the fact that he would stop at every bridge and underpass to inform her yet again of the historical importance of the keystone arch. They had noted all the obvious similarities and differences between California and Provence, and had played who-do-you-know long enough to realize that they did not, in fact, have any friends in common.

What they did not discuss was anything having to do with their personal lives. Ariel had seen how flustered Peter was by her few references to Hortense and Agathe, and had concluded, wrongly, that he didn't like children. Peter had tried to explain his long acquaintance with Rosalie but had noticed that Ariel resolutely changed the subject whenever the older woman's name came up. Tormented by opposing forces of curiosity and shyness, both avoided any mention of romantic or sexual experiences.

Instead, every day they found something new about which to quarrel. In Nîmes they argued about the safety of municipal water systems. In Salon-de-Provence they argued about the astrological prophecies of Nostradamus. In Apt they argued about candy, of all things, and in Orange about the economics of having homeless people sell newspapers.

On Saturday it was the possibility of transcendent space. Peter maintained that the greatest architectural creations rose as expressions of religious faith and lived on as inspirations to all ages. The cathedrals of the Middle Ages were awesome to anybody, Catholic or not. The temples of Angkor Wat convinced all beholders that they were in the presence of mystery. The Parthenon inspired every onlooker to rapture, and always would. It inspired rapture in him, and he had never even seen it, except in slides and photographs.

To Ariel, this was nonsense. "Great art" was nothing more than a culturally determined habit devised by a hegemonic elite. If Peter was impressed by the ruins of some crumbling enclosure constructed for the ceremonies of a false ideology, it just showed that he was still under the influence of the slave-dependent Roman cultural construct.

"So you think that art takes its intrinsic value from its role as symbolic construct?" Peter was proud of the way he was learning Ariel's lingo.

"Of course not," Ariel replied. "Besides, there is no intrinsic value. It's all culturally imposed." Ariel wondered how Peter could be so dense. Having spent the better part of a week in her company, he had apparently failed to pick up any understanding of her intellectual position. Indeterminacy. Relativism. Subjectivity. History as social construct. If he had been a member of the Flat Earth Society, Ariel could have dealt with it. But to be an unreflective Realist was way beyond what she considered the bounds of acceptability.

"Okay, let me get this straight," Peter said. "The worship of Athena was a hoax, the cathedral of Chartres was built to keep the rabble busy, and even that precious dolmen of yours is nothing more than a stone shoe box that some poor jerks were conned into putting up to suit the sinister ends of the dominant Druid culture. There is no such thing as spiritual content in architecture. According to you, I guess there's no such thing as spiritual content in anything."

"No, no, no. the dolmen *was* spiritual," Ariel explained, trying to sound less irritated than she felt. "It *was* religious. But the religion was influenced by cultural pressures of race, class, and sex, just like everything else. *Everything* is culturally determined."

"So the work you do in Paris, that's something that's determined by race, class, and sex, right? At least, definitely sex."

Since when were they talking about what she did in Paris? Ariel considered the female ghetto of child care, and the consequent low pay and low status of her work.

"Yes," she agreed, reluctantly.

"But you tell yourself some story to make it a spiritual thing, right? Just like the Druids."

"What I do in Paris is purely physical labor," Ariel answered stiffly. "I told you that before. It has nothing to do with my spiritual nature."

"You can say that again." Peter snorted, making a sharp left. He had decided to show Ariel the old ghetto synagogue in Cavaillon.

A Baroque Confection

ARIEL'S UPBRINGING had been completely secular. Her parents had never belonged to any church or synagogue, though she was pretty sure that one of her grandmothers had been Jewish and another Catholic. Her clearest memory of her father, before he left for Colorado, was the year he burned all the Christmas cards that came in the mail, without even opening them. Her mother, who devoted her weekends to protest marches and rallies, considered political activism religion enough for anyone.

Nonetheless, Ariel was not entirely uninformed. She had been to at least a dozen bar mitzvahs in her California adolescence, and she knew the fundamental precepts of Jewish architecture. Clean lines. Nonrepresentational art. Natural wood. Framed reproductions of the works of Ben Shahn and Marc Chagall. A few large, rough stones included as a reference to Jerusalem.

The synagogue at Cavaillon was a revelation. In some ways, it was the proof of her argument, a structure influenced more by its time than by its faith. A Baroque confection of blue and silver, built in the eighteenth century, during one of those occasional episodes of Papal tolerance that had deluded European Jews for centuries, it had survived the Second World War only because the German troops occupying Provence were under the mistaken impression that the building was a tearoom. It was also one of Peter's favorite places, an exception to his rule that classicism was the highest form of architecture. He loved its lightness and its grace. It was the first sanctuary he had been in, in fact, that suggested that worship could be a joy as well as an obligation.

But still there was about the place an inescapable reminder of sorrow. The people who had worshiped there had not shared their sanctuary's talent for disguise; the Jewish community of Cavaillon, long on the wane, had been wiped out entirely during the Holocaust. Noting Ariel's dark hair and vaguely Semitic profile, the guide who showed them the building asked if she was Jewish. Before she could decide, he observed that perhaps her ancestors had worshiped in this very building. With great flourish, he showed the oven, carefully hidden from the occupiers, where those same possible ancestors had baked their matzoh and pointed to the curtained balcony where the women had sat.

He's right, Ariel thought, startled by the possibility. Some great-great-grandfather could have been a rabbi here. If my parents had kept any track of their families, I might know where I came from. The sky blue panels and silver-gilt moldings which had seemed so fussy and ornate when she first saw them were now illuminated by a radiance of personal significance. If only she could know for sure. How unbearable to build on empty speculation, constructing a story of her family that might not be true. If only there had been records, and survivors, witnesses left to tell the tale. A disturbing thought entered her mind. Perhaps there was, after all, a place for factual knowledge in the scheme of historical understanding.

To Peter's great discomfort, Ariel spent the remaining minutes of the tour berating their guide for living in a country that preserved the building while happily exterminating its occupants. And why, she wondered, was he even open on the Sabbath?

The Team St-Etang Takes to the Road

THAT SAME SATURDAY was the day of the Tour de Luberon. Richard rose before dawn, dressing in the kitchen so he wouldn't wake Vivian. Grateful for the darkness, he pulled on the embarrassingly tight black racing shorts and the gold and green jersey Renard had brought over the night before.

"These are the colors of St-Etang," Renard had declared. "Gold for our fortune, green for our future! You said so yourself! We must uphold the honor of our village!" Ever since they had started training together in the early mornings, Renard had begun talking like this. He was a new man.

Richard, unfortunately, remained as he had always been — overweight, unathletic, subject to alternating attacks of bravado and panic that made it impossible to maintain the focus needed for any successful competitor. To help his father prepare, Justin had insisted on reading aloud the section in his phrase book on medical emergencies, with special emphasis on "it hurts a lot," and "I have a pain in my testicles." Richard consoled himself that at least no one he knew would see him make a fool of himself.

The Team St-Etang had few followers. Madame Renard had watched the Tour de France on television and thought it a fair description of the way most people spent their lives: working their legs off to give their ass a ride. If her husband chose to amuse himself in such a wasteful and exhausting way, that was his business. It went without saying that she would remain at home.

Vivian was of much the same opinion but felt an obligation to cheer Richard on. In any case, it seemed a good day to be out of the house. As she was leaving the night before, Clotilde had mentioned that the lavender cutters were coming in the morning. From her description, the dust and noise would make the farm uninhabitable.

"Leave at sunrise," Clotilde had advised. "Close the shutters before you go. Take the children. I'll be busy feeding the cutters."

And so they had left, though not quite at sunrise. The trucks, three of them, had come rattling up the drive while Lily was still searching for her other sandal and had parked in such a way that Vivian had no way to get out. It took her forty minutes to locate the foreman and persuade him to move at least one of his vehicles, and that was only accomplished when Vivian planted herself directly in the path of his scythe. Even before they set out, Vivian sensed that it would be a horrible day.

A Family Outing: Final Attempt

THE TOUR DE LUBERON, Richard's bicycle race, began and finished in the picturesque but inconvenient village of Venasque, accessible only by a torturous single-lane road that wound over the spine of the Vaucluse Plateau before entering the town square. This was adequate for the permanent residents, who numbered fewer than a thousand, but when traffic was swelled by several hundred cyclists and their followers, access became more difficult. By the time Vivian had extricated her car, shooed the children into the backseat, waited while Lily went back for her Goofy hat, and stopped for breakfast in Cavaillon, the road to Venasque was closed to further traffic. For that matter, so was the road from Venasque. Anyone who wanted to watch was advised to try to find a spot along the road by the hospital in St-Didier, where the cyclists should be passing on the final stretch. How appropriate, Vivian thought. She wondered if Richard would be peddling by or checking in.

It was hopeless to try to find him. Instead, she would show the children some of the other villages of the area. It was about time they learned to savor the fields and fountains that reconnect the modern spirit with Mother Earth. They should start to appreciate her work.

What Vivian had failed to grasp was the extent of local athletic enthusiasm. The Tour de Luberon was designed to wind through a number of hill towns before completing its course. Vivian visited them all. No matter where she went, it seemed, there was a bicycle race in progress. They sprang up like the briar hedges of a fairy tale, instantly and completely blocking what had only the day before been a perfectly usable road. It wasn't simply that they were shut out of Venasque. They were also barred from Le Beaucet, detoured around Gordes, red-flagged from Goult, and forced into endless zigzags along farm roads in the hills behind Lacoste. Time after time she would chug up the winding road to the town center, only to realize after a final turn that she was once again about to be stopped by an unsmiling official waving a red flag. After a delay just long enough to stall her engine and throw all the drivers behind her onto their horns, the flag waver would point the way to a side alley barely wide enough for a pregnant goat, down which she was supposed to detour.

Through all this, Justin and Lily didn't even look up from their toys. There was no place they needed to go and nothing they wanted to see. Back in Oppède-le-Percée, they were sure, Marcel was selling the latest installment of their trove. At the farm, Monsieur Maudit was out with his hired thugs, killing all the purple flowers. By now they were convinced that wrong turns and engine problems were the normal mode of travel in Provence. Nothing that would happen for the rest of the day would shake that impression.

Le Menu

IN THE ROILING sea of Vivian's regret over missing Richard's bicycle race was an island of separate worry that concerned her menu for the following day. Running into Hugo Bartello for the third time in a week, this time in the multi-fountained but otherwise rather empty town of Pernes-les-Fontaines, Vivian had impulsively invited him and Rosalie to Sunday lunch. She had been shocked to learn that Richard had done the same for his three photographer buddies from *Sports Illustrated,* who were coming down from Paris for the weekend. To round out the party, they would be joined by Monsieur and Madame Renard. Vivian had extended a vague invitation at the beginning of their stay and then forgotten all about it until Marianne Renard called Friday afternoon to say that they would like to join the Harts for the midday meal this Sunday, when the café would be closed for fumigation. Unable to imagine any way this disparate group would get along, Vivian was channeling all her anxiety into the question of what to serve.

Her usual fallback, the French country picnic, was obviously inappropriate. In New York, where goat cheese retailed at eleven dollars a pound, it was considered extremely chic to eat like peasants. A crusty loaf, a tangy cheese, an exquisite apple in the fall or a peach in the summer, and you had a lunch fit for anyone you cared to entertain.

In France, however, it was not so simple. When she spoke brightly of picnics in the country to people she met in her travels, they looked at her as though she had expressed a bizarre enthusiasm it would be most polite to ignore. Germans ate picnics all the time, wurst and beer on the hood of the car, a scene Vivian saw enacted on the side of the highway every day. The English packed cans of beans when they went hiking, and Americans were always enraging Renard by pulling into his restaurant and asking for a meal "to go." The French, however, sat at a table, preferably for several hours at a stretch. Furthermore, they expected a meal of at least three courses, not including the cheese, which came after the salad. For reasons that Vivian could not comprehend, nobody seemed to gain weight. If she spent the entire day crashing into private gardens and blazing unauthorized trails in her retreat from the races, where and when would she buy food to prepare this feast?

By 2:00 P.M. she had decided to treat catastrophe as karma. The car was stalled anyway, the latest man with the inevitable red flag was gesturing impatiently to the left, and so it was only prudent that she follow his hint and turn down the sloping driveway into the municipal parking lot. At least there she could drift to a halt without having to try to restart the engine.

"We're here!" she announced brightly, then bit her tongue at what she knew would be the response.

"Where's here?" asked Justin.

"Well, I'm not quite sure. Let's find out!"

"I have to go to the bathroom," Lily whispered.

"That's fine!" Vivian exclaimed, scaring both children with her heartiness. "I'm sure there's a public toilet here!"

"Where's here?" Justin repeated.

Vivian snapped.

"*I don't know*," she shouted. "Now roll up the windows, take your stuff, and *get out of the car!*"

Two men who had been leaning on a nearby Saab stopped their conversation to stare at her.

"These Americans," one remarked to the other, after Vivian had passed, "they are so emotional about their automobiles."

The Village Fair

A SERIES OF inquiries revealed that the toilet was at the top of the hill, housed in a former stable wedged between a sixth-century church and the outer walls of an even older château. When Vivian and Lily got inside, Lily said at once that they were in the wrong place. With a heavy heart, Vivian noted the absence of a modern toilet and the presence of a primitive grate in the floor, flanked by two rusty metal footprints. To add to the day's struggles, she was going to have to explain to her sheltered daughter the primitive simplicity of municipal plumbing in the older districts of France.

Back in the days when all women wore voluminous skirts and few bothered with anything underneath, it was no big deal to place your feet on the metal shoes and pee into the grate below. For a small girl in shorts and Tinkerbell underpants, it was a major trauma. Removing her clothes entirely would have offended Lily's delicate sense of decency, even if the floor hadn't been so wet that it wasn't a practical idea. Lowering her pants merely hobbled her in a way that made it impossible to use the grate. After a few minutes of experimentation, they decided on a method of foot bracing and wrist grabbing which worked well enough for the moment but not so well that Lily wasn't newly reminded that she really, really, really wanted to go back to New York. Making rash promises for the delivery of consoling treats, Vivian helped her daughter reassemble her clothes and took her off to find Justin, who was waiting outside.

Justin had been putting his time to profitable use. With the help of his phrase book and a passing student eager to practice his English, Justin had made out the gist of a notice posted on the doorway of the church, and also on the telephone poles around it. Today was the town fair. A dance would be held tonight, and there were rides and games of chance beforehand. It was all supposed to begin at three, which he thought was probably right this minute.

"A fair!" Lily exclaimed. "I want to go to the fair. I *need* to go to the fair. I want to play games and go on rides! And, and . . . and I want a Coke!"

"Yeah!" Justin agreed. "Me, too. I want a Coke!"

Back down the hill, past the parking lot, on the large, level terrace that housed the post office and the village school, the carnival had indeed arrived. There was a booth where a stern young woman sold fritters, several tables for the purchase of beer, wine, cider, and sausages, and a dozen stalls where one could pay to hurl objects at targets on the slender chance of winning a stuffed doll. In the school yard, workers were still decorating the dance floor, unraveling vast, tangled piles of extension cords and colored lights. Nowhere that Vivian could see was anything her children would deign to drink.

In front of the post office was a smaller set of attractions for little children. A balloon seller stood chatting with a woman who offered face painting, and a patient-looking goat was available for petting, but the main event was a circular contraption of midget airplanes that twirled around a central engine. Forgetting their thirst, Lily and Justin both agreed at once that a turn on this ride was the thing they had wanted all day, all week, perhaps the one thing they had wanted most their entire lives.

"But you don't feel well," Vivian protested. "You're carsick, remember?"

"No," the children shrieked in unison. "We're fine! We're fine!"

"I think you're too big," she warned Justin, eyeing the toddlers who were lining up for seats. "This is built for little children."

"Ask them," he pleaded. "Just ask. I really, really want to go on the ride."

Shrugging, Vivian went to negotiate for tickets. The seller had a Provençal accent so rich that at first she thought he was doing a curious French imitation of Chico Marx.

"Bon-a jour-a madam-a," he sang out, adding an extra syllable to the end of every word. "How-a many-a tickets-a, please-a?"

Before Vivian could answer, he rattled off a series of options. As far as she could tell, the price changed if she bought ten tickets for 600 francs (which seemed expensive) or maybe he said sixteen (which seemed cheap), or else it was a special price for children under six years, or before six at night. Or perhaps he was offering a bulk rate for groups of six. Glancing back at the line of customers, full of earnest country children wearing T-shirts proclaiming the glory of the Boston Red Sox and the Chicago Bulls, Vivian dismissed all notions of sophisticated marketing.

"Two tickets," she said firmly, making no attempt to match this accent. "One time for each of my two children."

"Of course, madame-ey," the seller responded, giving her change from her twenty-franc note. Hurrying back to the children, she herded them into the newly forming line. The stout wife of the ticket seller was shocked to see a big boy like Justin and swore he would break the mechanism, but Vivian decided to pretend she didn't understand. The children stuffed themselves into a bright green metal biplane with yellow stars painted on the wings.

Around and around they circled, serious as pilots on a dangerous mission. Soon the crowd of parents started whispering, then pointing to Justin and Lily. All the other airplanes were going up and down as well as around and around, but Vivian's children just hovered stolidly a few inches above the ground.

"*Tirez le bâton!*" one of the other mothers shouted. Justin grinned, oblivious.

"*Tirez le bâton!*" repeated a father. Bewildered, Justin and Lily realized people were shouting at them.

"They don't speak French?" the first woman asked Vivian.

"Not much," she confessed.

"*Alors!*" the woman answered, and launched into an emphatic pantomime that even Justin could understand. Reaching in front of his sister (who was by then feeling as queasy as she had claimed to be before), he pulled the bright yellow lever that caused the plane to rise and fall along with the rest of the squadron. All the parents in the circle clapped, and Justin took a funny half bow, grinning with a joy Vivian saw too seldom on his sardonic little face.

While Justin and Lily continued their flight, Vivian wondered how Richard was faring. She knew they should try again to drive to Venasque, but it was hard to imagine how.

When the children finished their ride, Justin seemed strangely subdued. Maybe he thought he had been uncool to take that bow. Maybe he had decided he really was too big for kiddie rides. Whatever the reason, he stopped teasing Lily and become the ideal older brother. He held her hand as they watched the band set up, waited patiently outside the door while she visited the toilet a second time, let her choose the two games of chance that Vivian allotted, and even shared a drink without his usual elaborate disgust at the possibility of germs. Vivian could only assume he was on his best behavior because he wanted to stay. Justin had seen a poster announcing the rock concert that evening, preceded by mask making, juggling lessons, and a circus performance at 6:00 P.M. It was Saturday, he reminded his mother. Dad was off at his bicycle race. They could eat dinner in a restaurant. It would be fun.

It would, Vivian agreed. While Lily and Justin made masks, she could walk down the narrow streets, poking into all the interesting looking shops that her family always complained about entering. She could find food for her guests tomorrow morning. Smiling, indulgent, more relaxed than she had felt in weeks, Vivian agreed to stay at least until dinner. Which shows what can happen when you let down your guard.

The Tour de Luberon

RICHARD'S BICYCLE RACE had not gone well. The first half hour had been fun, drinking brandy-laced coffee from a thermos while Renard drove through the dark with the bicycles on the back of the truck. As soon as they turned off the highway, though, Richard started getting nervous. The route to the starting line was crowded with competitors, each car bristling with bicycles mounted on its roof. Richard thought of bull elk brandishing their antlers as they battled for dominance of the herd. He remembered a nature movie he had seen where the loser elk was left to die at the edge of the forest clearing.

When they pulled into Venasque, the town lot was already full, and Renard had to persuade an official to let them through. The road was being closed to all traffic, he was told. So many racers had entered this year, there would barely be room for the participants, much less onlookers.

There were two hundred and fifty-six entrants, representing sixty-two bicycle clubs — sixty-one of them larger than the newly formed Team St-Etang. For the past week, Renard had been lecturing Richard on the importance of riding together as a team. Now, confronted by the extent of the competition, he abandoned all plans. "I'll wait for you at the finish line," he called, a moment before the starting gun was fired. And then he disappeared with the rest of the pack.

By the time Richard reached the narrow causeway that ran over the spine of the mountain just outside Venasque, he was already falling behind. That's okay, he told himself. He was in this to have fun. It was a beautiful morning and he was biking through Provence. To complete the experience, he decided to sing every old rock song he could remember.

Several kilometers later, he could not even see the other racers. As the sun rose higher and the road stretched up before him without so much as a water station or a timekeeper, Richard began to consider the possibility that he had missed the route. Probably that downhill stretch a while back when he had closed his eyes and coasted, singing "Twist and Shout" at the top of his lungs. He could have missed a sign there and never known.

No problem. He would turn around and go back until he found the right road. As he rose off his seat, ready to brake and dismount, he was struck by a leg cramp of a severity he had never experienced in his life. Great jolts of pain shot through his left calf, doubling him over the handlebars and sending both bicycle and rider off the road. When his wheel hit a rock and the bicycle pitched suddenly down the side of the mountain, Richard realized he was going to die.

Flying helplessly through the air, he relived in excruciatingly slow motion his hasty decision to use toe clips. Because of that instant of meaningless bravado, it was impossible for him to jump off the falling bike. He would never see his children grow up. He would never be famous in his own lifetime. Richard was still composing the list of things he would now not live to accomplish when he landed against a tree with a tremendous bump that knocked him unconscious but saved him from tumbling farther downhill.

The Vineyard in the Middle of Nowhere

WHEN PETER and Ariel left the synagogue, it was close to noon. Without really being hungry, they sat down in a café near the center of Cavaillon and ordered the cheapest dish on the tourist menu. That was what they were, Ariel thought grimly. Tourists. Transients. Disposable people who left no footprints upon the sands of time. Fiddling with the wine bottle, she started reading the tag that hung from the neck.

"Come to the enchanted castle of precious wines," she read, translating as she went along. "Slumbering in our limestone cave, carved from the living rock, are bottles of the finest vintage, waiting for the intrepid explorer who can search them out. Go east of the mountain, west of the river, south of the sun, and north of nowhere. Find us if you can . . ." Ariel fiddled with the tag, wondering how a Frenchman had ever succumbed to so much whimsy. "These are the stupidest directions I've ever heard," she muttered.

"Actually, they're not bad," Peter said, grabbing the tag to look at the map sketched on the back. "I think I know where this is," he added. "Never been there, but I know the road. I wonder what they mean by carved from the living rock. Maybe they know the guy who made your dolmen. They don't say how ancient their château is, do they?"

"I think we can assume it's postmegalithic," Ariel answered wearily. Why did Peter have to disagree with everything she said? Did he find her that boring? Sent into social exile in the remotest region of Provence, she had managed to hook up with the one fellow American with whom she had not a single interest in common. Statistically, it seemed almost impossible, but there it was. She should return to Gordes as soon as possible and get back to work. She had wasted enough time on this stupid idea of research.

"We might as well find this winery," Peter was saying. "No sense in going back to Gordes."

The Finish Line

By four o'clock, the bicycle race was almost over. The winners had long since crossed the finish line and collected their trophies. The rest of the pack was still coming in. Tired cyclists were swigging from bottles of water, peeling off their sweaty shirts, examining the chalkboard where the judges were still entering official times and scores, accepting congratulations from families and teammates.

It was the older racers who were finishing now, men in their thirties whose families cut into their training time and whose legs weren't quite as strong as they had been ten years before. Just past the finish line, little boys proudly held their papas' handlebars while their sisters poured water over their papas' heads. Wives uncorked the bottles of wine they had tucked in their bags for this moment of triumphant completion. Looking at these family groups, Renard wondered where Madame Hart was with her ill-mannered children. Perhaps they had left when they saw Richard was not among the winners. There was nothing Americans could do that would surprise him. He himself would wait for his comrade to arrive, however long it took. And next year he would suggest to his brother Antoine that he seek a tenant who was in better shape.

Losing Lily

Vivian was standing by the town hall of a village named Goult. As usual, she was looking for her children. Justin and Lily had persuaded her to give them fifty francs and let them play the carnival games. They would meet her by the fountain at four, they had promised. They would stay together and speak to no strangers, except of course when paying for their games. They would count their change. They would be polite. Then, astonishingly, they had both kissed her and run off. And now it was quarter to five, and the children had not returned.

Angrily, she flipped through the stack of prints for sale outside the souvenir shop next door. Most of the pictures evidently came from some sort of military manual from the First World War. There were illustrated instructions on how to assemble a rifle, how to raise a tent, and even where to attach embroidered decorations to one's uniform.

The best was a water-stained page which seemed intended to teach the reader how to swim. In six separate vignettes, a solemn man in full uniform demonstrated different strokes while bending over a camp stool, the name of each stroke thoughtfully provided under his high-booted feet. Distracted as she was, Vivian stared at the final image, a picture of the same soldier, still in uniform, diving into a swimming pool that did not seem to contain any water. She pitied the poor recruit studying this manual as the boat took him to Morocco or Algiers. Stuffing the picture back in its folder on the rack, she turned to face the town hall clock as it chimed five. At that moment Justin appeared.

"Where have you been?" Vivian demanded, not waiting for an

answer. "And tell your sister to come out of hiding, because it won't do her any good. You guys are in *big* trouble."

"Is Lily hiding?" Justin asked, suddenly looking hopeful.

A lizard of panic slithered down Vivian's spine. "What do you mean?" she asked. "Isn't she with you?"

Justin shook his head.

"We were watching people trying to knock down bottles," he said. "To win prizes, like. Then Lily screeched, 'There's the Lion Man.' Then she ran off into this alley, and then she was gone. I waited and waited, but she didn't come back. You always say to wait where you are when somebody gets lost. You say that."

Sweaty and scared, Justin stared at her, waiting for directions. Waiting for forgiveness. After all, he was only eleven.

"Go back to the carnival games and look for Lily," Vivian ordered. "I'll wait here in case she comes this way, and if she doesn't turn up in fifteen minutes, I'll come find you. Go find her, Justin! Go!"

For a few minutes, Vivian scanned the crowd milling through the square, but it made her too nervous. Lily would find her, she told herself. She would see her mother looking in the windows in the souvenir store. Lily would turn up before she had finished taking in the display.

Scattered around the window were watercolor sketches of local scenes, pale washes of blue and beige that somehow represented vineyards and courtyards and ocher hills in spaces the size of postage stamps. Postcards, in beautiful full-color photography, showed those same mounds of foliage converging on those same slope-roofed terra-cotta farms. Vivian wished they had never left their own farmhouse this morning. Why had they fled the lavender harvest? It would have been so novel, so picturesque. When else could they see such a sight? Swept by regret, Vivian forced herself to study the pictures. She was starting to feel dizzy from all the lines of convergence, but she was afraid to look away. If she turned around and Lily was not there, she would have to admit that something bad had happened.

"When I look up," she told herself, "Justin and Lily will be coming around the corner." She stared at a color postcard on which a brother and sister in full peasant regalia, the kind no one had worn for the better part of a century, simpered at each other across the back of an overdressed donkey. The boy was the same age as Justin. The girl looked a lot like Lily, if you substituted a lace bonnet for the Goofy baseball cap. Vivian turned around. Lily was still nowhere to be seen.

Carved from the Living Rock

A CCORDING TO PETER'S calculations, the winery was located in a quadrant of the map no more than ten kilometers on any side. Furthermore, most of the land in that quadrant was flat, so that any rock, and certainly one large enough to give rise to a château, should be clearly visible from above. Driving east from Cavaillon, he took the back road that led to Oppède-le-Percée.

Ariel didn't even notice when he mumbled something about having to check out the market. Slumped in the passenger seat that seemed both prison and second home, she was sunk in depression. Her writing was stalled, and she was losing confidence in the whole enterprise. If history was not, in fact, socially constructed, she would have to do a whole lot more research. If she did research, she would have to spend even more time in Provence, where she knew no one but this dropout architect.

That was another problem. Even though they were together ten hours a day, Peter hadn't made the smallest sort of approach. Not that she cared, Ariel told herself, but was she so terribly unattractive? Shuddering, she realized that he must really be in love with Rosalie Bartello. That must be the answer. Peter adored Rosalie. He had even said so, several times, and Ariel forced herself to accept it as true. Her loneliness was beyond remedy, it seemed.

When they arrived at Oppède-le-Percée, Ariel said she would stay in the car. Surveying the end of the Saturday market, Peter was almost relieved to see Marcel's empty table. He was in no mood to bargain over antique junk. He was worried about Ariel. She seemed so quiet. Was she angry about the synagogue? Was she angry at him? Then a much worse thought crossed his mind.

Did she miss her employer? Rushing back to the car, he was relieved to see she hadn't vanished. Not knowing what else to do, he drove on until he reached a rise in the road where they could see most of the valley to the north.

Sure enough, there was a conspicuous whitish lump in the distance. The château in the middle of nowhere. Shifting gears, Peter drove down one narrow lane after another, until he saw a sign with an arrow pointing to the left.

ENCHANTED CASTLE, it said, in English. Both sides of the driveway were planted with vines, the stumpy central branches already bearing the grapes that would form next year's "rare and admirable" vintage. At the end of the drive, they saw a large stone outcropping honeycombed with natural caves. This formed the base of the château, which was really nothing more than a large country house that appeared to date from the early nineteenth century.

Their arrival was announced by a trio of snarling mastiffs who had been sleeping in the partial shade of the wrought-iron lawn furniture. Like the rock and the château, the dogs were a pale mushroom gray. The only spot of color was a set of wooden doors fitted into one of the holes of the rock. The doors were bright red. Over them, painted on the rock itself, red letters spelled the English word TASTING.

After several minutes of canine hysterics, a man in black trousers and a blue polo shirt appeared and shouted at the dogs to shut up. When it seemed the beasts were finally taking his advice, Peter got out of the car. After a few moments more, Ariel joined them. Maintaining the smooth backward motion the park rangers at Yosemite had recommended as the best way to escape a bear, she kept her eye on the mastiffs while edging toward the red doors that sheltered the tasting room.

Two hours later they had drunk eight glasses of wine, the vintner matching them glass for glass. He was English, it turned out, retired from the advertising business to fulfill a long-cherished dream of living in the South of France. Yes, he agreed, the tag was stupid, but then, it had brought them there — which suggested at least that he knew something about writing copy. After the first two glasses, an acidic chardonnay and an insipid sauvignon blanc, he had started in on the negative impact of the European Union. Over a decent fumé blanc he described his efforts to get his vineyard certified by the regional authorities. The simple words "Cote du Luberon" would allow him to boost his prices ten francs a bottle, he said.

When they moved from white wine to red, their host grew more confidential. He admitted they were his first customers in three days, and his retirement bonus was shrinking rapidly. What did they think of his making the château into a small hotel? Maybe a special place to have weddings? Leering drunkenly over his glass of merlot, he suggested they should try out his matrimonial-size mattress and give him a report. Drunk herself, Ariel tried to get out a protest but managed only an incoherent mumble.

"We're not together," Peter explained in a melancholy tone.

The vintner looked puzzled.

"I mean, not together that way. She has . . . she has a job."

"My God, man!" the vintner exclaimed as Ariel staggered out the wine cellar door. "This is the twenty-first century! You're allowed to screw a working woman!"

Down and Dirty

THIS SELF-EVIDENT truth hit Peter's wine-soaked brain like a message from Delphi. Why was he being so scrupulous? It wasn't as though Ariel had taken a vow of chastity. Quite the opposite, in fact. What a wimp she must think he was. Stumbling in his eagerness to act on this insight, Peter tossed his wine-smudged glass to his host and rushed out in pursuit of the only interesting woman he had met in two years in France.

The wine had advanced Ariel's mood from depressed to maudlin, and the reference to the honeymoon suite had sent her fleeing for a spot where she could sob in privacy. One of the many tragedies weighing on her heart was her tendency to keep bursting into tears.

She had forgotten the dogs. They appeared as soon as Ariel emerged from the red-painted doors, leaping and snarling and obviously not interested in her welfare. Paralyzed by fear, Ariel stood so absolutely still that the dogs lost interest and ambled back to the shady side of the château. As soon as they were out of sight she ran in the opposite direction, which happened to be into the waist-high rows of vines. When she stumbled across a root, she didn't even try to get up.

Peter found her there, face down on the hard-packed dirt, crying in long, unattractive, gulping sobs. Not knowing what else to do, he sat beside her and patted her shoulder. Then he patted her hair, and then her shoulder again, and then started on slow sweeps from the back of her neck to the base of her spine. Ariel's sobs lessened, then stopped. Peter kept stroking her back in long, slow strokes. Now he was moving lower down her spine, over her buttocks, down the backs of her bare legs.

This was getting interesting. Wiping the grit from her face, Ariel turned her head toward Peter. You can kiss me now, she thought.

Sliding down beside her, Peter did just that, for a long time. Then he made a very stupid mistake. He mentioned the other woman.

"Rosalie keeps telling me we should fall in love," Peter whispered.

"What!"

Ariel twisted away from Peter's embrace. Her face was smudged with dirt, her hair was strewn with twigs, and her brown eyes were cold with fury.

"Rosalie talks to you about me?"

"Rosalie runs my entire life," Peter said dreamily. "I depend on her for everything." He draped his arm over the curve of Ariel's waist and moved his hand upward to her breast.

Ariel gave him a sharp elbow in the stomach, rolled over, and sat up.

"Get up," she ordered. "We're leaving. Now."

The Gypsy Girl

F LIC-FLAC HADN'T meant to visit the carnival at Goult. The
music and the colored lights strung over the road stirred up
troubling memories of parish fairs in Brooklyn. He had only entered town at all because he was following the circus.

Nobody else would have even called it that. It was only a gypsy
family traveling the countryside doing tricks. The father, dressed
in a sagging one-shouldered leotard, claimed he would lift a Fiat,
all by himself. He was the strong man. The contortionist mother
sold tickets outside the tent before going in to lie on her stomach
and smoke a cigarette held between her toes. There was a boy
of twelve or thirteen, his upper lip just beginning to show the
shadow of a mustache, who made a sow dressed in a tulle skirt
dance on its hind legs — a trick that seemed to bore them both.

The real star was the daughter, a compact brunette who did
stunts on the back of a dappled pony. She had the most interesting tufts of hair that showed whenever she raised her arms to
snap her fingers at the horse. Flic-Flac was so entranced when he
saw her passing down the road that he followed her into the village. He lost sight of her for a time in the confusion of a crowd of
children lining up for an airplane ride but then found the family
setting up for their performance next to a row of games of
chance. Waiting for the pony girl to have her turn, he joined the
group watching two men compete at knocking down bottles with
a hard rubber ball.

He hadn't even noticed Lily until she walked past him,
shrieked, and started to run, but the flash of a dog-faced hat going down the alley caught his attention. There was something the

child had that he wanted. Without bothering to remember what, Flic-Flac set off after.

Lily was clever, but she was only seven and hadn't yet learned that the best place to hide is in a crowd. Instinct made her bolt away from Flic-Flac, and by the time she thought about where she was going, she was halfway out of town, on a deserted stretch of pavement, with no idea of where to turn.

What should she do? She was afraid to turn around, because the Lion Man was right behind her. If she left the road, she might be lost in the forest forever. And so she went forward, trotting breathlessly downhill until she reached a fork with a signpost. One arrow pointed to Lacoste, the other to Bonnieux. Neither name meant anything to her. Crouching in the bushes, she tried to hide, and might have succeeded if it hadn't been for the reflector strips on her sneakers. Some time later, when Flic-Flac was returning to his Deux Cheveaux, he noticed the flash of fluorescent yellow created by the headlights of a passing car. Parting the underbrush, he found Lily.

Lily

A CHILD IN PERIL. It's a terrible thought, but a common event. Children, even little children, are agents of their own destiny, and if that destiny includes putting themselves in harm's way, there is really only so much we can do to stop them.

Lily hadn't liked the woods at all. She had been there for a long time, too far from town to hear more than the occasional blast when someone set off fireworks, too tearful and tired to think she could ever find her way back. When Flic-Flac had found her in the bushes, she had had to choose between two terrors: getting in the car driven by a lion man, or staying alone in the dark.

Flic-Flac didn't want the girl, but he didn't seem to be able to get rid of her. When he grabbed her backpack, she ran along and jumped in the car behind him. Flic-Flac did not notice, because by then he had fallen into what was for him a familiar trance. He had forgotten Lily. He had forgotten the circus girl. He sat in the car and looked back toward Goult to see the fireworks blossoming in the sky above the trees. When the fireworks stopped, he drank from a bottle of red wine. Then and only then did he drive ten kilometers to Lacoste, where he parked on the level space of cleared grass behind the château.

When the car stopped, Lily waited to see what the Lion Man would do. Eventually she realized he had fallen asleep. It was her turn to act. Without even trying to recover her backpack, she threw open the car door and rolled out, the way she had seen many kidnap victims do on television.

On television, the rolling escape was always followed by the kidnap car screeching to a halt so bad people with guns could jump out in pursuit. To Lily, the opposite happened. Startled by the noise of the opening door, Flic-Flac woke, restarted the engine, and drove off into the night, leaving her behind.

Confused, Lily looked around. It was very dark. A few trees loomed up out of the night, but not nearly as many as in that frightening woods. Off in the distance, she could see the lights of a village perched on top of a neighboring hill. From here it looked like one of the tourist boats she had watched go on evening cruises up the Hudson River. If she turned in a circle she should see other villages, clusters of light against the gloom, with ribbons of headlights showing the roads between the towns. Unable to see anything close at hand, she found a tree and leaned up against the trunk. She would wait there, she thought, until somebody found her. Before long she was asleep.

Searching

VIVIAN HAD FOUND Justin hours ago. They had gone back to
the toilet, the car, the airplane ride, and the row of stalls
where new customers were still trying to knock down bottles.
Finally, she forced herself to admit that the situation was serious.
It was time to call the police.

She found two young gendarmes lounging, hands in pockets,
outside a makeshift caravan painted with silver stars. After several attempts, she pulled their attention away from a grimy young
woman in a sweaty leotard who was rubbing down a horse with
lascivious gestures.

They listened gravely to her account of Lily's disappearance.
Then one went to search the crowd and the other to unlock the
police station, a square stone building that was also the post office. While the second officer was telephoning his superior, Vivian could hear the music from the circus ending and the rock
band starting to play. Yes, the gendarmes assured her, they had
searched the gypsy tent and trailer, which even Vivian could see
were simple structures with few places of concealment. They had
alerted all the hotel keepers, and the café owners, and the gas station manager. She should not despair. Very likely, all was well. She
should not be too desolate. Perhaps Madame's daughter had simply fallen asleep somewhere. Perhaps she was trying to telephone
her mother even now.

Vivian remembered the card of emergency information she
made Lily carry in her backpack, and the ten-franc piece Lily
tucked in her sock every morning for just such a crisis. What if
Lily was trying to call her? She had to get back to the farm right

away! The officers would continue to search the town, and parties would start looking in the woods at first daylight. They would call her every hour to report. They promised that.

Justin had cried himself out and was asleep in a stiff wooden chair, his head lolling against a green metal file cabinet. Gently stroking his forehead until he awoke (a tender gesture she never would have dared in ordinary times), Vivian told him they were going home to wait for Lily's call.

"Back to New York?" Justin asked sleepily.

"No," Vivian answered sorrowfully, "back to the farm."

If they had stayed in New York, this never would have happened. Now that it was too late, Vivian understood Lily's sense of Provence as a place of dark and menacing danger. Why had they ever left the security of Manhattan? Why had she taken her precious children to this dangerous hellhole?

As the night spread over the hills of the Luberon and covered the valley of the Durance and the Rhône, Vivian drove quickly back to St-Etang. For once, there was no traffic. The younger of the two police officers followed, insisting that Madame Hart should not be driving alone in so distracted a state. Besides, he thought proudly, this way he would be there if any ransom calls came through.

Dancing in the Dark

B Y THE TIME Ariel and Peter had found their way out of the vineyard, located a restaurant, spent ten minutes each brushing the bits of vines and grape leaves out of their hair, and wolfed down two baskets of bread, they were running out of topics to talk about. Too scared to broach the topics on their mind — love, hygiene, their past romances, their misconceptions of each other's present entanglements — they were too distracted to talk of anything else. Usually they argued, but now they veered away from any sort of disagreement.

Even food, normally a reliable subject for neutral conversation, betrayed them tonight. The first course was bright green nettle soup, too suggestive of penance to provide any comfortable conversational fodder. The trout with spinach raised no better topic than fly fishing, which neither of them had ever done. Over salad they turned in desperation to disjointed compliments of each other's work. Not the work they each still thought the other was doing, the taboo topic of sex for sale, but the work they planned to be starting soon. There was nothing more noble than architectural restoration, Ariel insisted. Oh, no, Peter protested. The only worthy life was one devoted to literature. Since neither could offer any evidence to support these opinions, silence followed.

By the cheese course they had reached the worst awkwardness of the worst first date either of them had ever had. Dessert (three small and exquisite balls of hand-cranked ice cream flavored with honey and lavender) was consumed in silence, punctuated by occasional panic-stricken smiles. When a rustic master of ceremonies jumped on the bandstand and invited everybody to dance, Peter and Ariel almost overturned the table in their eagerness to stand up.

The lead singer, a young girl wearing an iridescent plastic minidress, had apparently memorized the entire repertoire of Tina Turner. As she moaned suggestively about her "good job down in the city," Peter held Ariel at an absurdly respectful distance and wondered when her employer was arriving from Paris. Ariel, swaying to the music, helplessly savoring the warmth of Peter's hands on her back, plotted various ways of eliminating Rosalie Bartello.

Above them, colored lights blazed on the wires strung across the square, and above the lights the harder brightness of the stars. It was too dark to see the orderly squares of vineyards, or the wine cellars of the château carved out of the living rock. It was too dark to recognize the strange and memorable green color of Vivian's car speeding toward the highway, trailed by the police. It was much too dark to see Flic-Flac sputtering toward Lacoste with Lily in the rear hatch alongside his precious metal detector. Wrapped in panic over what their future might be, oblivious to the many crises unfolding around them, unable to think of anything else to do, the two young people danced on.

Richard Revives

W HEN RICHARD CAME to, it was pitch black and he was thirsty. His first thought was to get the water bottle from its special rack on his bicycle frame. Then he remembered the fall. Somehow, finally, he had gotten off the bicycle, which was no-where to be seen. Neither was the water bottle. He wondered why his feet were so cold, until he realized the nylon uppers of his rac-ing shoes were torn away, probably still attached to the toe clips.

Shifting slightly, Richard assessed his injuries. He winced whenever his fingers touched a raw scrape but was happy not to discover anything that felt like blood. His shoulder ached, but it wasn't unbearable. Waiting a few more minutes for his eyes to ad-just to the dark, he set his sight on two craggy rocks close to the summit and started to climb.

After only a few minutes, Richard gave up. His head ached, his shoulder throbbed, and a scrape on his leg had started to bleed. Clutching a board that was lodged against a rock, he decided to rest against it and wait for daylight. In a few seconds he was asleep.

He dreamed he was an actor in a movie about World War II. Over and over they strapped him into a dummy cockpit to film the scene where he was shot down over France. He told the direc-tor the union would lodge a protest if they didn't let him take a break, but nobody on the set could hear him over the sound ef-fects of fighter planes. When he woke at dawn, he found he had been leaning against a sign announcing he was in a high-security military area where trespassers would be shot. Overhead flew a formation of the military planes he had been hearing in his sleep all night.

Lily Rescues Herself

W HEN LILY WOKE at daybreak, she found herself outside a crumbling castle that looked exactly like one of the scarier illustrations in her book of fairy tales. Ignoring the rotting sign for a long-closed art exhibition and the small yellow earthmover parked next to a shattered wall, Lily walked cautiously to the other side of the ruin. She hoped to make her escape before an ogre or a witch showed up to complete the picture.

As she had expected, a winding set of overgrown stone stairs clung to the side of the old château. Climbing down, shrinking past the narrow slits from which the Lion Man might reach out and snatch her, Lily was surprised to find herself abruptly transported from a fairy-tale nightmare of roofless castles and evil monsters to what even she recognized as an old but ordinary French hill town.

It was still early in the morning, but a pleasant-looking woman in a blue jogging suit had set up an easel in the middle of the street. Moving closer, Lily saw she was painting a picture of a narrow archway that curved overhead. Being a grandmother as well as a student in the Cleveland Institute of the Fine Arts Summer Session Abroad, Mrs. Shirley Lewis knew all the right answers to Lily's halting questions. Yes, she assured the child, she would help her find her mother. She would make sure the Lion Man (whoever he might be) didn't get her. While she was at it, she thought to herself, she would get the child some breakfast. Maybe after she had eaten her story would make more sense.

Flic-Flac

A FTER THE NOISE of the car door startled him awake, Flic-Flac's first thought had been to drive to his most recent hiding place, a secret stone room he had discovered hidden next to a dry immigration ditch. Inside, he had already stashed two cooked chickens and a liter of wine stolen from the supermarket cart of a woman who made the mistake of putting her baby in the car before unloading her groceries. After he had eaten, Flic-Flac wiped his fingers on his pants and turned his attention to Lily's backpack. He had already forgotten the frightening dog-child who had brought him this treasure.

The contents stopped his heart. Not the toys or the camera, though in ordinary times he would have taken both for easy resale. But the gold! The gold! Strapped in a dirty cloth were three golden torques. One was a spiral of twisted gold, with half-moon finials curved to lie flat against the back of the neck. One was a rope of golden braid. The third was a large hollow tube made from thin sheets of beaten gold, tapered at the ends like a cow's horn. And then, at the bottom of the pack, hidden inside a pink tulle nest, was Lily's first great find, her most precious treasure, the mysterious necklace with no opening.

Like everyone else, Flic-Flac puzzled over how to wear it. It was too large to fit comfortably on his arm, too small to go over his head, and too wonderful to put aside. The other torques he had already clasped around his neck, rejoicing as always in the feel of metal against his flesh. But what was this? He ran his fingers over the pictures, puzzling them out in the dim starlight that pene-

trated between the dolmen and the bridge. All night he sat upright, legs crossed, torque held in both hands. When morning
cast some sunlight on the entrance to the dolmen, he replaced the
mysterious circle in the backpack and put the pack aside. Then he
squatted in the irrigation ditch to move his bowels.

The Dolmen at Dawn

FLIC-FLAC WAS IN a vulnerable position, ragged pants around his ankles, when Ariel found him. The band had played until two in the morning, and she and Peter had clung together on the dance floor all that time. Then the restaurant owner had come out with pitchers of beer and platters of pizza, and they had joined the band in an impromptu party. At daybreak, having postponed the inevitable for as long as possible, they were on their way back to Gordes for clean clothes and a serious conversation. Suddenly Ariel insisted they visit the dolmen. Who knew what she would find if she stood there at daybreak? It was important to her work.

Peter stayed at road level, staring at the distant hills and wondering whether this was going to turn into anything more than an incomplete roll among the vines. At Ariel's shriek, he turned just in time to see a really dirty bum clutching a filthy pair of trousers scramble up to the road. The bum ran to a tiny car so rusted Peter hadn't even noticed it against the trees, and drove away. Ariel came into view a second later, a child's backpack pressed tight against her chest.

"Follow him!" she demanded grimly.

"Did he hurt you?" In daylight and in disarray, Flic-Flac did not look very threatening.

"Follow him," Ariel repeated more shrilly. "He stole her backpack. Something is wrong. I know it."

Peter had no idea what Ariel was talking about, but he obeyed. The bum had driven off to the east. Piling into the car, Peter set off in pursuit, with Ariel beside him urging speed and moaning incoherently about some poor little girl. When they got to the fork in the road, a cloud of chalky dust showed the car had turned toward Lacoste. Peter turned, too, and soon saw the rusty car on the open grass by the ruined château. Stopping next to it, he was relieved to see the owner had already jumped out.

"Find him!" Ariel ordered. "We have to find him!"

Trying to look braver than he felt, Peter ran across the grass to see where his quarry could have gone. On one side was a sheer drop to the valley where he and Ariel had dallied amid the grapevines not twelve hours before. The other side was the way they had arrived. The only other option was a steep descent down an ancient set of stone stairs. With Ariel right behind him, he scrambled down, pushed past an artist who had placed her easel smack in the middle of the narrow street, and rushed onward in pursuit of he knew not what.

Flic-Flac had vanished. After several minutes circling madly and pointlessly through narrow passageways, Peter arrived back at the stone stairs. Here he found Ariel, who seemed, most incredibly, to have halted her chase to take part in an artistic conversation. Since she was the one in charge of this mysterious pursuit, Peter stopped running, too.

Of course Ariel wasn't really discussing art. She had recognized Lily, sitting beside Mrs. Shirley Lewis's easel, crying in the same steady, hopeless way she had been when Ariel first stumbled on her on the Bartello's lawn. Wordlessly, Ariel held out the backpack. Surely, this was the rightful owner. Pink Barbie backpacks did not belong under a Druid dolmen, or in the possession of a half-naked derelict. Blinking and snuffling, Lily took the bag and clutched it with both arms. At that moment, the shadow of her earlier doubt crossed Ariel's mind. Perhaps there was, after all, some order in the universe.

By the time they had roused the café owner and persuaded him to sell them fresh coffee and yesterday's stale rolls, they were beginning to understand the events of the night before. Lily had gotten lost, and a yucky man had taken her backpack and then abandoned her to sleep outside all night. No, he hadn't hurt her. He hadn't touched her at all. He had taken her backpack, but now she had it back. And that was all that Lily would say.

Mrs. Lewis sensed there were some holes in this story, but she was relieved to discover someone who actually knew who this child was and where she belonged. If possible, she would like to get back to her easel while there was still a hint of sunrise on the stones. Otherwise she would have to get up again at dawn tomorrow, and she was really getting too old for that. Some of her classmates cheated and painted at twilight, but she herself felt their work never conveyed the same sense of promise.

Scorched Earth

ONCE SHE RECOGNIZED Ariel as the fairy lady who had rescued her when she had been locked out of the car at that
very long party, Lily perked up. Inside the front compartment of
her backpack was a card with the address and telephone number
of the farmhouse. The rest of the bag was empty, except for the
magic circle. Lily didn't say a word about what was missing. She
hoped the Lion Man wasn't hurting her Barbies, but she didn't
say a word about that, either. The fairy lady could take her back
to her mother. The new man could drive. That was enough.

They tried to telephone the farm from the public booth in Lacoste, but the line was busy, and so they decided simply to drive
Lily home. From Lacoste to St-Etang would take about ninety
minutes, Peter estimated. He had never been there, but he'd seen
the sign on the highway.

As they moved through the tree-covered hills of the national
forest in the stillness of the Sunday morning, Peter ran a mental
calculation of his recent adventures. Ariel had cut short their
vineyard tryst, but not in so brutal a way that he wasn't highly
optimistic about the future. Plus he had danced until dawn, rescued a terrified child from a mysterious kidnapper, and was now
about to reunite her with what he assumed would be her over-
joyed parents. Compared with his frustrating search for antique
gold, these were all major triumphs. Not bad at all, Peter told
himself. Not bad at all.

To entertain Lily, he began singing every television theme song
he could remember, supplemented with advertising jingles. Ariel

joined him, and then Lily started smiling and sang a few that they had never heard.

It made him feel old and out of touch. The exaltation of a minute before gave way to a sudden pang of dissatisfaction. Why was he living in France? Peter wondered. Why was he hanging on to his own childhood, instead of making way for the real kids like Lily? Embarrassed, he realized his eyes were welling up with tears. He glanced at Ariel to see if she had noticed and found that she was crying, too. After a few seconds of furious blinking, he realized the problem was physical, not sentimental. There was something wrong with the air.

Rolling down the window, he coughed at the rush of smoky air that entered the car. A strange gray cloud covered half the sky. The left half. The forest was on fire.

Five years of drought had left the hills ready for conflagration, as everybody knew, but it was one thing to hear official warnings about forest fires and quite another to realize you were driving through one.

Lily, turning to look out the back window, was the first to see the planes. Back toward Lacoste, the air was full of big-bellied airplanes, their holds full of water, specially designed to fly over forest fires and dump their liquid cargo on the flames. The air force had imported them from Canada when the drought began. The investment was now paying off.

The worst of it seemed to be behind them. Peter had hiked these forests. He remembered the old charcoal burners' huts and the faint remnants of the indigenous pine forests that had once covered the region. Pine burns fast and hot, he remembered. He was glad they were driving away from the trees.

Flic-Flac Finds Peace

DEEP IN THE FOREST, Flic-Flac came to a stop. When the woman with the snake hair surprised him, he had run to his car and driven back to Lacoste, where he knew many hiding places in the old castle. But that did not feel safe any longer. After he was sure the snake-haired woman was gone, he had set off on foot down a rocky path that led directly from the castle cellar to the edge of the forest. His destination was a cluster of abandoned buildings perched on the margin of the section of national park known as the Forest of Cedars. There, at last, he could be alone with his treasure.

The rocky path grew narrower, then turned into a trail. Soon enough, the trail became nothing more than a thin line forged by hunters searching for the wild game that had vanished from all but the deepest woods. Abandoning even that thin line, Flic-Flac plunged off into the trees. There was a pond he knew, next to an abandoned borie. All his consciousness was wrapped up in the gold twisting its magic circles about his neck and his arms. He wanted to be quiet and enjoy them, far from chasing eyes. Everything else was forgotten.

At last he reached his destination. Stripping off his clothes, Flic-Flac walked into the water, icy cold and as high as his neck. When he emerged on the other side, he rearranged the torques and armbands, fastened the cloak pins in his hair, and sat on the ground with his back to the water. For the first time in many years, perhaps for the first time in his life, he was fully at peace.

Overhead, he heard the airplanes, flying slowly and strangely close to the trees, but they were nothing to do with him. He continued to sit on the ground, not feeling at all cold despite his wet and naked state. He felt as though he were sitting before the great fire of the ancient clan, warm and exalted and ready to fulfill his destiny. It was a wonderful feeling.

Flic-Flac heard the plane coming closer and wondered what the new noise could be. He was still wondering when the doors in the belly of the plane opened and seven tons of water fell to the forest floor. In time the fire would reach as far as his body, melt away his golden ornaments, and burn his bones beyond recognition. By then he had been dead for hours. No one missed him. No one at all.

A Month of Sundays

A T TEN O'CLOCK Sunday morning, there was still no sign of Lily. Richard's whereabouts were also unknown. According to Renard, he had vanished almost as soon as the race had started, over twenty-four hours ago. Unlike Madame Hart, he, Renard, had stood at the finish line for hours, waiting in vain for a glimpse of his comrade. Only when he called his wife and learned that the police were across the road had he returned to his home.

This was true. Renard had been hanging around Venasque all the previous day, helping himself to free Gatorade and enjoying the chance to show off his new team uniform. It was close to midnight when he called Marianne. He was planning to stay even longer, but at the first word that the *gendarmerie* were in St-Etang, he had rushed back. Without stopping to change from his racing clothes, he had roared across the highway to share his information with the police. He also woke Clotilde and instructed her to come along and stay the night. Madame Hart would no doubt need assistance with the children. And it was important to have a representative of St-Etang present during any inquiries.

By daybreak Vivian had stopped thinking of the police as her allies. A fine cloud of lavender chaff, left from the harvest, had seeped into the house, coating everything. A dusty trail marked where she had spent the night pacing back and forth. She wanted to go back to Goult and search for Lily, but the young officer told her they had to wait for his commander. He said that trained searchers were combing the area, but she didn't believe that for a minute. Not with all the other questions he asked.

"Were there problems in your marriage?" he wanted to know. "Had Monsieur Hart taken the little girl's passport?" He asked the same questions over and over, stopping only for an occasional shot from the bottle of cognac Clotilde had plunked on the long table when she arrived. He seemed to think Vivian was lying to him.

Vivian shook her head for the thousandth time. No, she insisted. Every marriage had problems, but Richard would never kidnap Lily. She explained this repeatedly and even dug Lily's passport out from her own bag to show him that Richard had not planned to remove their daughter to another country.

Then she got angry, which was better than being afraid. She was standing at the open doorway, pointing dramatically across the fields and screaming at the officer (who was only nineteen and not trained for this) that he should be out searching for the lost girl, not harassing a grief-stricken mother. At this moment a navy blue Mercedes drove up in a great cloud of lavender dust. Hugo and Rosalie Bartello had arrived for lunch.

"Who is this?" the police officer asked, eyeing Hugo as he emerged from the car. An older man. A rich older man. Rapidly he revised his suspicions. Perhaps the woman had done something to get rid of an inconvenient child. Then he noticed a woman also exiting the car. The case was becoming even more complex.

Vivian, still by the door, remembered her hopeful schemes of getting a job from Hugo, realized her humiliations were now complete, and gathered strength from the totality of her loss. She drew herself up, smoothed her rumpled clothes, and addressed the officer with a dignified simplicity worthy of classical tragedy.

"These are my guests," she said. "They know nothing of what has passed. They have come for lunch. I will have to send them away."

But Hugo Bartello was not a man to be dismissed in an emergency. He hadn't been excited by the prospect of spending the hot hours of the day with silly Vivian Hart and her opinionated, inebriated husband. He had accepted her invitation during an uncharacteristic moment of distraction brought on by his continued inability to remember where or when they had met, and he had been berating himself ever since. As soon as he understood what was going on, however, Hugo came into his own. The mask of courteous attention gave way to genuine competence. Silly or not, Vivian Hart was in trouble and needed someone to take command.

The detective, for his part, was relieved to find himself dealing with someone who spoke with proper regard for the rules of French grammar and moreover showed no signs of hysteria. Soon Hugo was going over the story with Vivian, relaying it yet again to the officer and simultaneously making calls to the chief of detectives at Apt and the American consul in Marseilles. They would put blockades at all the borders. They would check all trains and airplanes. The mountain-climbing clubs would assemble to comb the hills. Lily would be found.

Rosalie Takes Charge

WHILE HUGO WAS organizing the search along more diligent lines than the gendarmes at Goult had thought necessary, Rosalie found her way to the kitchen. A muscular young woman with an unfortunate punk haircut was slowly washing the floor. From the looks of the patch she was scrubbing, three shades paler than the rest of the room, she had not moved in quite a while. Eavesdropping, obviously. The timeless function of the servant. Ignoring Clotilde, Rosalie continued out the back door. She was not surprised to find the sullen boy she had sent off to hunt for kittens in her barn. Three weeks had passed since then, but Rosalie remembered.

Justin was sitting on the concrete patio, jabbing a plastic rake into the lavender dust on the surface of the swimming pool. His mother was still inside quarreling in French with the police. Clotilde had come over late last night and insisted he go to bed. She had been there in the morning, too, making eyes at the policeman while she served Justin a steaming mug of hot chocolate and two thin slices of bread. Since then she had been hanging around the kitchen, cleaning things she hadn't touched all summer, even though it was her day off. She was being nosy, Justin thought, but he was still grateful. He hadn't eaten anything since the carnival yesterday, and probably wouldn't have had anything today, either, if Clotilde hadn't come.

When Rosalie sat down beside him, Justin barely glanced at her. He was trying to think what had happened to Lily. If she had gotten lost in the town, she would have found help by now, but if she was in the woods they might never find her. Lily had a lousy sense of direction. He pictured her wandering in circles, sleeping on the ground, trying to eat leaves and berries, and ending by poisoning herself, because what did his dumb little sister know about living off the land?

What if she never came back? Maybe she had been found by some other family, and they would raise her. He stirred the pool, trying to imagine Lily in her new life, forgetting her old name or that she had ever had an older brother. But it was all a lie, and he knew it. Lily hadn't gotten lost. She had run away from the Lion Man.

Justin was the only one who knew the Lion Man was real and not simply another of Lily's nightmares. He had seen him three times: once at the market with Marcel, and twice again at the fair, first by the airplane ride and then outside the circus tent. That was one thing Justin knew that nobody else did.

The other thing he knew was that the Lion Man was wearing some of their treasure. He had seen it poking out from underneath his clothes while they were on the airplane ride. Every time the airplane ride went past a certain place, there was a dirty arm wrapped around the pillar, one of Lily's armbands showing through the hole in the sleeve. Probably no one else would have noticed, but Justin did. When the ride stopped he looked back at the place and saw the Lion Man.

He should have told Lily. He hadn't because he didn't want her to get frightened and make him leave the carnival, and now she was gone and he might never see her again. He should have let Lily tell their parents about the treasure. Somehow, he was sure, she would still be here if they had told.

Justin had been thinking this since last night, going over in his mind all the ways he had failed to be a good big brother, but he hadn't had anyone to tell. His dad was off somewhere riding his bicycle. His mom had spent the whole night crying or talking to the police, or both. If he couldn't talk to his parents, he wanted to be left alone, but that wasn't happening, either. Clotilde came out with a big wad of wet laundry to hang on the line. And who was this lady sitting on the lawn chair? She looked familiar. If she didn't go away soon, Justin was afraid he would start to cry in front of her.

At least she didn't try to talk. It was the lady from the party, Justin realized. He remembered teasing the kittens in her barn. He remembered how he had locked Lily out of the car to be mean, and how Lily claimed she had found a fairy lady to rescue her. Then he couldn't help it — he was going to cry after all. He ducked his head and watched the tears make fat circles as they hit the pool, and pretty soon he was able to catch his breath.

What is it about me, Rosalie wondered, that makes people burst into tears? Leaning forward, she handed Justin a clean handkerchief from her purse. When he was through wiping his nose on the first cloth handkerchief he had ever seen, he told her everything. He told her about the Lion Man, and about the necklace in Lily's backpack, about Marcel, and about the treasure in the pond. Like most true stories, it came out backwards, but Rosalie listened patiently until he was really finished, way back at the first day Clotilde had sent them out to play in the fields. She didn't interrupt, and she even waited awhile to be sure there wasn't more. Then she said they should go inside and tell the others.

"I'll do the talking," Rosalie offered. "But you have to listen and tell me if I'm getting it right. Can you do that?"

Snuffling, Justin nodded yes. His eyes hurt and his nose was damp, but he felt better than he had since Lily had vanished. Stepping over the pile of laundry Clotilde had left by the back door, he squared his shoulders and went in to face his guilt.

Spreading the News

A LMOST AN HOUR passed before everyone had heard Justin's story. Most of that time was spent trying to get their attention. Didier Renard had gone back to Venasque to search for Richard and was telephoning every half hour with fresh reports. First there was the confirmation that Richard had never finished the race, then that they were searching the route, then that there was signs of a terrible accident and Madame Hart should prepare herself for the worst. Rosalie was trying to speak to Hugo in private when the telephone rang again. Vivian gasped, and everyone stopped talking. There should be silence when a woman hears of her husband's death.

It was the associate director of national security, Mediterranean District. He was calling to report the arrest of a certain Monsieur Richard Hart, who claimed to be a citizen of the United States and a temporary resident of the defunct municipality of St-Etang. The charges were trespassing with suspicion of espionage. Madame was advised to retain counsel. While Vivian sobbed out the news of Lily's disappearance, beseeching the officer to inform her husband, Rosalie told Hugo Justin's story. While the police officer took the line to confer with the security director, Hugo passed the word to Vivian. While Vivian tried to wrench the police officer away from the telephone and back to the search for her missing child, Hugo went to use his car phone to call his friend the former prime minister and ask him to arrange the release of this silly American trespasser. Thus he was the first to greet Peter and Ariel when they pulled up with a bedraggled but now jaunty Lily in the backseat.

In the confusion that followed, nobody paid much attention to what was going on outside the house. Vivian was smothering Lily with kisses while attempting to talk to Richard on the phone. The gendarme was trying to get a statement from Peter while ogling Ariel. Peter was proudly recounting his heroic exploits, while Hugo kept interrupting to tell him about the children's game of treasure hunting in the pond. Justin, to his great embarrassment, was crying again.

Rosalie, looking ahead, foresaw that at some point everyone would stop talking and want lunch. Perhaps the spike-haired horse of a girl who had been doing the laundry could be inspired to prepare something. Failing to find Clotilde in the kitchen, Rosalie moved to the back door — then stopped to watch the extremely strange procession visible in the distance. First there was the spike-haired girl, followed by an immensely fat woman old enough to be her mother. Both of them were carrying shovels. Behind them came a man in a forest green uniform who drove his motorbike right into the field. Next came a man in farm clothes, carrying a long-handled rake, and two more women wearing lurid satin nightgowns, each clutching a handful of plastic garbage bags to her well-exposed bosom.

As Rosalie stared, they passed in single file between the stubby rows of scalped lavender bushes, heading resolutely out of sight. She was turning to report these new arrivals when three men in safari vests, cameras slung around their necks, came jogging in their wake. Photographers, she was sure. This, at least, was a breed Rosalie understood. Abandoning all thoughts of food, she hurried back to the salon.

"You need to show us this pond right now, Justin," she said firmly. "A party seems to be gathering there, and we don't want to be late."

An Early Exploration of the Holy Site

B Y THE TIME they got to the pond, Clotilde had stripped down to her red bikini panties and waded out to the middle of the water, where she was vigorously turning up objects with her shovel and hurling them onto the bank. The two whores who worked at the truck stop were gathering Clotilde's dripping finds and packing them into the plastic bags. Marianne Renard, squinting in the unfamiliar sunlight, dug in the mud along one edge of the pond while shouting curses at Monsieur Maudit, the farmer from Apt, who was using his rake on the other side and stuffing unknown quantities of loot down the front of his pants. The photographers, Richard's friends down from Paris, had followed the crowd and were shooting as fast as they could, intent on capturing every bit of the action. There would be time later to find out what was going on. The forest ranger stood silent, one manly, sun-brown hand on his motorbike and the other on his twill-clad hip.

"Oh, my God," Hugo groaned. "Now we'll never know what an intact site might have looked like. The research people will kill me."

"This is the pond," Justin whispered.

The gendarme blew his whistle. Vivan sat down abruptly on the ground and started to laugh, which was what finally stopped Clotilde.

"Who is in charge here?" the detective asked.

"I am," answered the forest ranger in a loud, clear baritone. "I am the legal guardian of Marcel Ducasse, resident of Oppède-le-Percée, the owner of this land. Whatever is found here belongs to him."

A Sense of History

MUCH, MUCH LATER — after Clotilde had dried her legs and the whores had reluctantly handed over their plastic bags, after Hugo had managed to get Richard released and back to his family, after Vivian had absorbed the astounding news that her own children had been placing a trove of ancient treasure on the market, provoking envy and intrigue among art historians of two hemispheres — after all of this had come to pass, Madame Renard surprised everybody by insisting they all return to the truck stop café, where she fired up a gas-powered outdoor grill to cook them a special dinner.

The smoke from the grill rose to join the smoke from the forest fire, now safely contained in the distant hills but still casting its pall over the region. As sunset turned the clouds brilliant shades of violet and sienna, Clotilde brought out blankets so the children could lie down within sight of their parents. Richard, drowsy from painkillers, soon joined them. The forester, having explained in great detail the intricate history of local inheritance by which Renard's brother owned the farmhouse but Marcel owned the land, had gone off under a tree to join the police in an interesting discussion of the prosecution of vandals.

By morning, the first reporters would start descending on St-Etang, followed soon enough by an international throng of curiosity seekers. Richard's friends had already rushed back to Paris to sell their pictures. Renard was in his office placing urgent orders for extra food, wine, beer, film, batteries, tents, insect repellent, and anything else he thought he could sell to the new invaders. Guards had been posted to protect the pond, already officially designated a site of national patrimony, as stipulated under the code of the Republic of 12 Brumaire. The group still gathered around the picnic table seized the last calm moment any of them would know for some time and began the difficult task of deciding what it was Lily and Justin had found.

"Just for the sake of conversation," Hugo started, "let's assume that these children have stumbled upon one of the greatest hoards of Celtic gold ever uncovered, two thousand years old and not disturbed since it entered the water. That still leaves a number of questions. Who made it? Who owned it? And why did they leave it here?"

It was like being in school. No one wanted to be called on.

"Come on, Hugo," Peter said at last. "You know what it is. I saw the report you got from Arles and the fax from London. Probably this was the scene of a bloody battle, the carnage hidden by rising water. This was a war zone, you know. Julius Caesar. Domitius. Marius. Vercingetorix. All those first-century B.C. heroes. You remember them, don't you?"

"Not so fast," Hugo objected. "Think about what you're saying. A band of Celtic warriors is massacred, then left to lie in state, still wearing their golden armbands and amulets? It's hardly likely that the Roman army would accord their victims full burial honors, complete with immersion in the sacred waters."

Peter shrugged. Much as he hated to admit it, Hugo was right.

"What I like so much about this discovery," Hugo continued, "is that it confirms the absolute connection of art and commerce. It's exactly as I told you, Peter. Trade routes! Trade routes are the key! The Druid priests ordered it, the goldsmiths shaped it to their patrons' taste, and the whole shebang was shipped off for sale overseas."

"If it's all about trade," Peter objected, "why are there bodies?"

"Business is brutal," Hugo answered smugly. "Haven't you heard? Roadside robbers, perhaps. Quite common, I imagine."

Peter was squashed by the weight of Hugo's logic, but not Vivian. Fatigue and ignorance always made her eloquent.

"You're both missing something," she announced grandly. "We've all been blind, in fact, and no one more than I."

She paused to glance around the table, daring anyone to agree with her self-condemnation. She continued, her voice made throaty and compelling by the smoky air. "We've all been overlooking what we should have considered first, which is the physical context of these hidden events."

Site examination. Even Peter could live with that. What followed, however, was a subject covered in no manual of scientific excavation.

"We stand here at an intersection," Vivian began, using the deceptive simplicity that had always served her so well at Malcolm College of Knowledge. "An intersection of past and present, and also an intersection of violation and regeneration. The gold that was once wrested from the earth was thence returned, only to be snatched again from the mother's embrace. What is the story the earth is telling us? That is the question we must ask to know which route our inquiry should take. We must turn to Gaia to learn the answers of the earth."

"Gaia?" Rosalie asked. "Isn't she the younger daughter of the king of Greece?"

"Mother Earth," Ariel whispered. "The planet as a female organism."

"Oh. That Gaia."

Slowly, but with mounting passion, Vivian presented her case. She leaned forward, pulling her audience with her, showing them the scene as clearly as if it were being reenacted before their eyes. She made a sweeping gesture that took in the picnic table, the truck stop, the highway, the fields, and the encompassing sky.

"People complain about the Autoroute de Soleil." She sneered, her eyes glowing with an eerie blue reflection of the gas grill. "They say it spoils the natural charm of Provence." No one contradicted. Certainly this was a complaint Vivian herself was fond of making. "But the trucks are nothing compared to the brutal desecration by the Romans, the first rapists of the landscape. Yes!" she repeated defiantly, though Hugo's raised eyebrows were the only objection she could see. "Rapists! What else can we call them? The Romans ravaged Provence, carving roads into the soft flesh of the earth to remind the natives that all routes led back to Rome. They defiled the authentic landscape with their ecologically disastrous aqueducts and their pernicious keystone arches."

Ariel glanced at Peter. He seemed dumbfounded.

"The Romans thought they conquered with military force," Vivian continued, "but it wasn't the chariots and catapults that defeated the Gauls. It was only by driving the Celts from cover that the Romans could defeat them, and it was only by destroying their land that they could hold the conquest.

"Consider the arena!" she commanded, spreading her hands over the picnic table to mark the space where their imaginations should go to work. "Imagine this vast monument to Roman regularity, frigid offspring of granite and geometry, imposing itself upon nature, denying the changing, irregular, organic qualities of the earth. Now imagine the forest grove that must have been here two thousand years ago: small, dark, private, fragile, a sacred place not made but found, a sanctuary so easily reduced to cow pond and firewood, lost for centuries while the cold stones of Rome remain."

Peter thought with satisfaction of the well-constructed Roman contributions to the local architecture. He wondered what Vivian meant by "pernicious" keystone arches.

"The Celtic strategy was to stay hidden," Vivian confided in a thrilling murmur. "But the Romans cut down the forest, rerouted the rivers, destroyed their world. We remember the conquerors not because they were so wise but because they left so much garbage strewn along their path of conquest. Think of it! Bridges, columns, public baths, statues of Augustus, mosaic portraits of the tax collector, broken jugs, toga pins, green glass stoppers from perfume vials, still scented with a hint of cinnabar. Even anger turned to litter; when they wanted to curse someone, the Romans etched their maledictions on a sheet of lead and tossed it into the public bath, where it could lie intact for centuries and still poison the water. The Celts were cunning, but they made the mistake of leaving few traces on the land. History, I fear, belongs to the one who cares the least about the planet."

Another View

FOR A MOMENT everyone was silent. Even Madame Renard, who spoke no English, had been nodding to the hypnotic rhythm of Vivian's words. Then there was a loud snorting noise from Hugo's corner.

"I'm sorry," he said, though he didn't sound as though he meant it. "But, really, that is the biggest load of nonsense I've heard in a while!"

"Now, Hugo," Rosalie chided. "I think you could be a bit more tolerant of other people's views."

Hugo leaned back in satisfaction, looking up to where Rosalie stood behind him, rubbing his neck. Suddenly, Ariel realized that Rosalie had never been her rival. Rosalie was in love with Hugo. Rosalie wasn't thinking of Peter at all.

"Here's what I think happened," Hugo said loudly. "This was a trade war, different parties struggling to control the most profitable routes of distribution, and the most valuable article in question was gold. The invasion of the Romans threatened the gold route, the east-west road from Ireland through Britain and on to France and Germany. What we have here is a well-preserved casualty of the marketplace. That's the story I'm backing. It's going to be the winner in the end."

Maybe it was that she was so very tired, Ariel thought, but listening to people make up any theories they liked was much less interesting than she had been led to believe. She remembered her professor in Paris, and how sure he had been that concrete knowledge was irrelevant in understanding the past. Then she thought of the Nazi officers, drinking coffee and eating pastries in the synagogue at Cavaillon, thinking it was nothing more than a tearoom. The building had been saved because of their ignorance, but that didn't mean that the ignorance itself should be glorified.

"Excuse me," she said hesitantly. "I think there's something you're leaving out. These things weren't *stashed* here, you know. This was a ritual site."

She looked around the table, then started again in a firmer voice. This was not speculation. This was a fact. Over the past week, Ariel had continued her reading and had learned a great deal about the rituals of the early Gauls.

"The pool was at the center of an oak grove, always considered a sacred zone. The gold was cast into the water to please the gods. Holy men and women were killed here, their necks broken with the garrote, their throats slit with a sacred blade, their bodies tipped into the water to become part of that holy space. And when they died, they wore their gold, because only the highest were worthy of being killed."

Ariel remembered the strange gold circle she had found in Lily's backpack. It was covered with secret emblems, and a portrait of a goddess figure. She had forgotten all about it. It would show what she meant.

"Imagine a Druid princess," she continued, "led at midnight to the sacrificial grove. She wears a crown with an image of the goddess worked into the metal, a talisman that shows her connection to the gods. She welcomes her death, eager to become one with the sacred landscape. She wears her gold to show she is worthy."

Why didn't I think of that? Vivian wondered. I'll have to put it in my notes tonight.

"But my dear child," Hugo interrupted. "There was no such thing as a Druid princess. Have you become convinced by your own novel? Do try to stick to the facts!"

Ariel looked over at the blanket where Lily was sleeping, curled up back to back with her father like a pair of mismatched bookends. In her sleep, Lily was clutching the backpack that held the proof of Ariel's theory. She would have to wake her to get it. And what would happen then? Lily would cry, rub her eyes, and complain that the golden circle was hers. Vivian would comfort her and defend her rights, and some policeman would probably arrive at that moment to start making noises about confiscation of patrimonial treasure. Hugo, no doubt, would have some way of showing that this piece was the absolute confirmation of his views of the art market, ancient and modern. As for Peter . . . well, she wasn't sure what Peter would say, but she wanted to have time to find out without forcing a crisis. And so she let her speech trail off into silence, without proof.

Rosalie Bartello reached across the table and patted Ariel's hand. "It's not as though we'll ever really know what happened here," she observed. "Not for certain. We have the gold, and we have the bones. We have some records of the general events of the period, but they're not very reliable and they're not at all complete. As for what took place in this particular place on that particularly day" — she glanced at Ariel — "or night — well, we're all just giving educated guesses."

"There you have it," Hugo interrupted. "*Educated* is the keyword. We have to get better informed. You're absolutely right about those rituals, young lady, though I don't think they contradict my basic point at all. If you're making it for the Druid priest, it's still being made for a customer, and thus is still an item of trade. Commerce, I tell you, commerce is the key."

Rosalie and Ariel

FURTHER ARGUMENT WAS drowned out by the noise of the minister of culture's helicopter, passing close enough over the picnic table to raise everybody's hair before moving off to land in the flat space behind the gas pumps. Hugo bustled off to greet him and give him an immediate tour of the site, clearly visible now that a crew had arrived with the generators to power the floodlights.

Peter, still offended by the lack of recognition for all his contributions, joined the party. The forester slipped after them, intent on protecting Marcel's rights. He had watched out for his simple-minded comrade since childhood and had no intention of deserting his interests now. Richard woke and announced he was going to take pictures. The children were stirring, too, so Vivian took them back across the highway to their beds.

Left alone, Ariel and Rosalie waited in companionable silence. From time to time a fire plane, its belly fully of water, flew by on its way to extinguish some lingering pocket of flame. On the highway the trucks continued their journeys, as they did every hour of every day. After two weeks of wondering about Rosalie's relationship to Peter, mentally rehearsing various confrontations with her rival, Ariel was not even surprised that their first real conversation was about historical uncertainty.

"Don't be too insulted by my husband," Rosalie said. "There's nothing wrong with your interpretation, you know. If you were a fancy professor, Hugo would probably want you to write an essay for a catalog. But you have to remember, there's nothing wrong with Hugo's interpretation, either. Even Vivian Hart has a nugget of truth to what she says. If you were not there — and none of us was there in the past — you can never know for certain why events happened as they did. We should be grateful that we know they happened at all. We console ourselves by spinning theories, and it helps to chase the demons from the dark, but in the end, we'll never really know."

What Ariel's professor had presented as the triumph of intellectual independence Rosalie saw as an inescapable human limitation.

"Is that what matters?" Ariel asked. "Consolation?"

"Among other things," Rosalie answered. "Kindness helps, too, and generosity. And, if possible, love. You shouldn't underestimate the obvious, you know."

Ariel was too tired to argue. Was it only last night she and Peter had been dancing at the village fair? Was it this morning that they had chased after that ragged man? And would they ever find out where he had gone?

Seeing how late it had become, Rosalie insisted on driving Ariel back to Gordes. On the way, she managed to find out all the factual details of Ariel's real life, which she presented in lucid synopsis to Peter the next day. The past might be a shrouded enigma, but the future was something Rosalie always felt would benefit from her shaping influence, and never more so than when there was a possibility of romance.

Vivian

AFTER A SEASON of disappointment and confusion, a time when every route seemed to lead in a meaningless circle, Vivian hardly knew what to make of the events of the last twenty-four hours. As she lay in her big brass bed, she tried to put the chronology back together. Her daughter had fled from an unknown monster who had in fact captured her but then somehow let her go unharmed. Her husband had survived a near-fatal bicycle accident, had been arrested for espionage, and still had enough time before bed to take pictures of a midnight excavation that for all she knew might be the breakthrough subject of his career. Her children had been so unhappy that they had gone digging for treasure to finance an escape back to New York — a state of misery and rebellion Justin felt perfectly comfortable explaining to Rosalie Bartello but hadn't revealed to his own mother. And the director of the Metropolitan Museum of Art — the man she had been secretly hoping might hire her to give a series of interpretive lectures — had laughed out loud at her theories.

There were parts of the story that still astonished her. She was amazed that Justin and Lily had been getting their gold to market right under her nose, and that big, slow-witted Marcel, of all people, was their salesman. For that matter, she couldn't believe that Marcel was a landowner, or that Renard, under the watchful eye of the forest ranger, had been paying him a weekly rent for all these years. Then there was the Lion Man, a character Vivian had always assumed was a figment of Lily's overheated imagination but who apparently was real enough to have taken the child from

Goult to Lacoste. None of this was plausible, but all, it seemed, was true.

The children had insisted on sleeping in their own beds, in the dormitory room above their parents. Richard, beside her, snored in deep, powerful snorts. He had taken another pain pill and fallen into the sleep of the drugged. Vivian, however, had reached that plateau of nervous exhaustion where she was too restless even to close her eyes. Climbing out of bed, she went to the living room and turned on her computer. If she put it all in her journal, it would start to make more sense.

She began by recording all the arguments over dinner. Even allowing for the natural presence of hot air in such discussions, she had to admit she had sounded weak. To make herself feel better, she switched to her private journal to record some observations on the police detective who had been harassing her when her family was left for dead. A bondage episode should do the trick. She imagined him handcuffed to the headboard of her brass bed, wriggling in masochistic ecstasy as she interrogated him.

It was almost 2:00 A.M. when Vivian returned to bed. Five hours later she was roused by the noise of a helicopter landing in the courtyard in front of the house. Outside her window someone was talking in English on a portable phone, barking out orders for dry ice and cryogenic packaging. Giving up on sleep, Vivian moved off to the kitchen to make a large pot of strong coffee.

Richard woke a few minutes later and realized he was still wearing the green-and-yellow racing costume of forty-eight hours before. Peeling off the filthy jersey, the torn shorts and bloodstained socks, he was about to step into the shower when he saw a camera lens poking through his bedroom curtains. The popular press had arrived. Turning his back, Richard bent over in a universal gesture of contempt. He would call the police if this continued. These photographers were really intolerable.

This Is Going to be Big

P ROMPTLY AT NINE, Hugo Bartello returned to the farmhouse, shaved and pressed and looking as though five hours
of sleep was all he ever needed in life. He brought with him the
minister of culture, who had readily agreed to become Hugo's
houseguest once he saw the hotel situation in St-Etang. Rosalie
came, too, trailed by a plainly-dressed woman carrying a hamper
of supplies. She hoped she wasn't intruding, Rosalie said, but it
had occurred to her that Vivian might not have had a chance to
get to market. At the sight of the Bartellos' cook unpacking a platter of croissants and a glistening white jar of orange marmalade,
Vivian burst into tears of joy. It was the breakfast she had been
wanting ever since they arrived in France. She was so happy she
didn't even notice that Rosalie had thrown up her hands and fled
outside.

While Vivian and Richard ate, Hugo and the minister of culture cut deals. The two men would spend a few minutes in furious conversation, then turn away to place urgent calls on their
respective cellular phones. After a few rounds of this, the minister flew off in his helicopter and Hugo went out to consult the fax
machine in his car. When he returned, he was actually rubbing
his hands in glee — a gesture Vivian had never before encountered outside the pages of Victorian novels.

"This is going to be big!" he boomed in the general direction of
the coffeepot. "This is going to be very big! I've counted fifty-
three new pieces already, plus the fourteen that have already been
authenticated!"

Vivian blinked in amazement. Her children had sold fourteen pieces of Celtic gold, and she hadn't even noticed? And how had they missed so much of the rest?

"This is going to be as big as King Tut," Hugo announced proudly. "Bigger! After all, Tut was fifty years out of the ground before we ever got it, while this is entirely new. Plus it will piggyback on all this millennial mystic nonsense! I could not be more delighted. A simple exchange should do it — maybe I'll get away with loaning the Louvre that insipid pink Fragonard for the next ten years. Lucky for us that the Louvre just had that Celtic show and didn't want another so soon! What a deal!"

Then he was off to make a few more telephone calls. Smiling wanly, Vivian took her coffee and moved outside to join Rosalie by the pool. She couldn't stop Hugo's triumph, but she didn't have to watch it.

"A fantastic show — art, religion, guided tours of Provence, the whole world of first-century B.C. France re-created right on Fifth Avenue! And then the mother of all gift shops!"

Hugo turned to Richard, who was licking his fingers to get up the crumbs from his second croissant. He was not the most attractive confidant, but he was the only person around.

"What is so wonderful about this trove," Hugo told him, "is that it doesn't necessarily have to do with human sacrifice. I know they've been turning up all sorts of bones, but the pieces themselves don't appear to be about killing."

Richard looked up, bewildered. He had an uncomfortable sense that some crumbs had lodged in his new beard. Still talking, Hugo turned toward the opposite end of the room.

"That makes a significant difference in the reproduction market," he explained. "We learned that lesson with the Peru show, thank you. Sacred Gold of the Inca Empire. People lined up all right to see the originals, but as for an electroplate repro of a panther disemboweling himself, well, it didn't move. I hate to say it, but we have to consider the bottom line."

Richard nodded in agreement, one man of the world to another, but Hugo had already moved out to his car to wait for his latest fax. Then he returned to the farmhouse to find his wife.

"I'm afraid I'm off to Paris," he said apologetically, when he finally located her by the pool. "More heavy negotiations on the cultural exchange dimension. They want some Watteaus, now, too, and it looks as though I may have to throw in the Unicorn Tapestries for six months. It will have to be handled in person. Do you want to come?"

"Does this count as part of our honeymoon?" Rosalie asked.

"No, my dear, it does not. This counts as part of our life. The honeymoon will wait, but the museum calendar won't. If we really hustle, we can have the goldwork on display in two years."

"What about the children?" Vivian asked, breaking into the conversation. They were the true discoverers. Surely they deserved some credit. She recalled reading somewhere about a museum in Germany paying a three-million-dollar finder's fee, and that was for something that had been stolen.

"The children?" Hugo looked blank. Was this bizarre woman suggesting they stop now and work out an educational tie-in? Then he noticed Lily, rubbing her eyes and stuffing her mouth with buttered bread. "Of course! The children! *Your* children."

Hugo gave Vivian a look of sincerest sympathy. "Don't worry," he said softly. "I'm not really up on the penalties for appropriating French national treasure, but I imagine we can get them off on the grounds of childish ignorance. I'll get our lawyers working on it right away. Maybe the State Department can help. Try not to fret about it too much."

St-Etang

IT MIGHT HAVE BEEN ancient gods and it might have been commerce; whatever the reason, the stirring of the old pond had brought St-Etang back to life. By the following Saturday, the first construction workers had arrived to build a new motel next to the truck stop. Bertrand, the forester, had resigned his position to manage the legalities of turning Marcel's land into a tourist destination — a show of authority that Renard graciously tolerated in light of the news that he was dealing with his future son-in-law. Commercial development would be on Renard's side of the road, and the educational and recreational elements would cluster around the old farmhouse — slated to be the information center and thus, once more, saved from demolition. The lavender field would be dug up to hold a newly built replica of a Celtic Village, with Druid ceremonies — minus the blood sacrifices — staged every afternoon during the summer season. There was even talk of reopening the old road over the mountain to Oppède-le-Percée.

Much had changed since the official discovery of the pond (as opposed to the unofficial discovery, made by Justin and Lily and treated by everybody in charge as an unfortunate incident best left forgotten). The planks over the irrigation ditch had been replaced by a double-width reinforced-steel bridge, brightly lit throughout the night and protected at all hours by a gate that was raised only when the guards received proper authorization. To prevent forced entry, the gate was controlled by another guard stationed in a little fiberglass hut next to the new helicopter landing pad. Paving over the gravel driveway had been the first order of work. The minister of culture had seen to that. The site itself, now protected by a steel-mesh fence ten feet high, was guarded around the clock by a patrol made up equally of French soldiers and American civilians, mostly ex-Marines, hired by one of Hugo's trustees.

Other changes had followed. The swimming pool had been drained, scoured, purified, deacidified, and lined with nonreactive plastic film so it could be used as the initial rinsing chamber for objects recovered from the pond site. Metalwork went to Zurich for electron spectrometry. Teeth, bones, and other human remains were shipped to a laboratory in Kentucky that specialized in historical DNA analysis. A FedEx truck banged across the steel bridge every evening to pick up the day's haul.

The main room of the farmhouse had been taken over by the team of archaeologists and conservators, who could hardly be expected to do their paperwork outside, under eternal threat of a sudden mistral. They had appropriated the telephone line, too; from now on calls to the Harts (never many) were shunted to the office line at the truck stop, where Renard would take a message and pass it along at his leisure. At all hours, it seemed, the courtyard was occupied by the police, and the fields by a large division of the international press corps. The one item nobody was clamoring to claim was the Hart family. Everyone wanted them out of the way, but no one felt moved to help them leave.

Given few other options, they retreated to their bedrooms. Lily had refused to be interviewed by anybody, even *Inside Edition*, and wouldn't go downstairs if there was anyone in the house besides her immediate family. To Vivian's surprise, Justin had agreed with Lily. The two of them spent four days upstairs, eating their meals on trays and playing endless games of Monopoly and Life. Whenever their parents asked what they wanted, the answer was always the same. We want to go home. Now.

It seemed like divine intervention when Renard called Vivian to the telephone on Wednesday afternoon. It was their tenant, the

German lawyer, calling from New York. His case had settled un-expectedly early. Would it be a problem, he wondered, if he va-cated the apartment before the lease was out? Not knowing that Vivian's silence represented joy, he added that he would of course pay the rent in full.

Home

THEY COULD GO home. They could return to their own village of West Eighty-sixth Street, to the shabby apartment
with the storage room in the basement and the living room window that overlooked the French Touch Dry Cleaner. Vivian could
get a cappuccino and a croissant any time she wanted from Star-
bucks. Richard could meet his comrades for a drink at the end of
the day without having to risk his life in traffic. The children
could play with friends their own age and go to school in September.

Now everyone was happy. Justin and Lily began to pack as
soon as they heard the news. The conservators could have the
farm to themselves and pay Renard's brother four times the former rent. Rosalie knew somebody at Air France who was able to
change their tickets. They would leave at the end of the week.

The peculiar thing was that, in the midst of all this confusion,
both Richard and Vivian were getting unusual quantities of work
completed. Spreading his slides out over the big double bed,
Richard had culled them to a set of thirty spectacular landscape
photos. He would hand-carry the original slides to New York, but
he took advantage of the FedEx truck to ship his agent a set of
prints, processed in Aix-en-Provence, so there would be no question that he had completed the assignment. The agent also got a
set of proof sheets of the Clochard Series, as Richard was calling
his photographs of drunken derelicts, with a long philosophical
preface "from the artist," for giving to galleries, and a separate letter of instructions on how the portraits were to be hung. As a
joking gift to Ken, his agent, Richard included a set of prints of

the photos he had been taking for Lily, her record of Barbie in Provence. Then he put his slides in their special carrying case and started to pack.

Inspired by Richard's example, Vivian closed herself in the bedroom all day Thursday and went over her computer files. To her joy, she discovered there was at least the germ of a book already in there. Not much in the way of substance but certainly a lot of impressions and opinions. Slapping a chapter number on each disjointed fragment, she copied her files onto a floppy disk, banged out a cover letter, and gave it to the FedEx driver who stopped by every day to pick up bones from the archaeologists. It would be in New York before she was.

Marcel

THE WEDNESDAY AFTER the great discovery, Marcel walked to St-Etang as usual to cut and mount his cousin's watercolor pictures, and also to collect his rent. Everyone else might be in a flurry, but Marcel liked to keep to his routine. He noticed Renard calling the American lady to the telephone, but he kept to his work.

After he finished, he took the old tunnel under the highway, the one the construction workers had dug, to visit the boy and girl in the farmhouse. This was the day of the week they always gave him shiny jewelry to sell. Marcel waited for Justin and Lily to appear. After a time he started playing with his rope and kicking idly at the soft dirt in the bottom of the dry ditch. He dislodged a small, flat rock, and then another. Spying something bright in the hole he had made, Marcel put down his rope to explore. Soon he had uncovered a tarnished fragment of a necklace set with beautiful blue stones.

He stayed another thirty minutes, but his friends never appeared. Marcel put the jeweled fragment in the pocket of his faded overalls. He would sell it on Saturday, and he would keep all the money for himself.

Recognition

THE HARTS WERE TO LEAVE from Marseilles Saturday afternoon. Very early Saturday morning, as Vivian was struggling to separate her family's possessions from the encroaching goods of the archaeologists, Clotilde pounded on the door to deliver an urgent telephone message. She must call her literary representative right now. *Tout suite.* Collect.

Bouncing off the satellite connection, Kirstin's words were distorted, randomly loud and soft in ways that had no relation to natural emphasis. ". . . *book* . . . fabulous . . . sex . . . *changes* . . . auction . . . *sex* . . . reality of *modern* woman . . . sex."

Then the connection improved and Vivian could hear as clearly as though she were speaking to Clotilde — though Kirstin never spoke as clearly as Clotilde. The central story had obvious mass-market potential, Kirstin whispered. They would have to drop the front chapters. The academic apparatus was totally unnecessary. A natural storyteller like Vivian didn't need to hide behind all that pseudo-intellectual crapola.

Mass-market appeal? Pseudo-intellectual? Crapola?

"Also," Kirstin continued, inserting a sliver of steel in her tiny voice, "We have to change the title. 'The Rape of Gaia' was fantastic in itself, of course, but way too . . . intellectual. Besides, the, um, narrator, is so sexually confident, everyone in the office agreed that *rape* was the wrong word."

Narrator? What was she talking about?

Kirstin whispered on. She had collared her boss, the agency director, and absolutely insisted he read the middle chapters. He agreed right away that this was going to be next summer's big book and was hot for an auction, maybe as soon as Wednesday. They'd been printing out text all day, using every computer in the office and running shifts to the copy shop downstairs. Even as they spoke, manuscripts were being hand-delivered to editors across the city. Kirstin would take a few sets out to the Hamptons tonight. She would hang on to the movie rights for a separate deal. Unless, of course, Vivian objected.

No, Vivian did not object. Vivian could barely understand. It didn't matter. Across the ocean, Kirstin kept chortling about subsidiary rights and first serial deals and auction points. She was pitching it as a cross between *Fear of Flying* and *A Year in Provence* and predicted big bucks indeed for her newest star. She advised Vivian to refer all interview requests to her.

"I *adored* your rendezvous with the plumber after the party." She giggled. "I mean, when he started doing all that stuff with the hand-held shower — it was a total turn-on. Does your husband know?"

The plumber? With a sudden thump of understanding, Vivian realized what had happened. In her hurry to copy her computer files and send them out, she had included her secret journal on the disk. That was the book Kirstin wanted to sell. As for the "un-necessary apparatus," the "crapola," that was the book she had considered the distillation of her highest thoughts and deepest convictions, the testament to her long years as a cultural prophet in exile.

"So what do you say?" Kirstin was asking. "It's fast, but we really need to move on this. Trust me. I know how it goes."

"Of course," Vivian agreed. "Cut the front chapters. Change the title. I rely on your judgment completely. And, by all means, hold out for a separate deal for the screen rights. That's definitely the way to go."

Peter

NOT QUITE SUBMERGED by the sudden high tide of television crews, radio interviewers, churning fax machines, chirping cellular phones, and humming Internet connections, three pieces of extremely old-fashioned mail gradually washed ashore.

All were for Peter Wall. The first was a notice from the Yale School of Architecture, postmarked the beginning of May. It reminded him that his leave of absence could not be extended and his progress toward his degree would be forfeit if he did not enroll for the fall semester. Since he had not preregistered last spring, he would have to appear during new student week to establish his residency. New student week started on Wednesday, August 5. It was now Wednesday, July 29.

The second letter was from the minister of foreign nationals, informing Peter that his student visa had expired and he would have to leave the country unless he could show proof that he was currently enrolled in a certified program of advanced studies. An appendix, printed on a separate sheet of paper, noted that under the new budget of the Ministry of Education he would not be allowed to register at a French university unless he could show proof of French citizenship. The third letter, on thick white parchment bearing the seal of the French Republic, commanded him, as an adult male who had spent two years as a resident of France, to report for military service within the next fourteen days.

Reading these letters in the post office at Gordes, a stone-walled room built into the base of the castle and no doubt originally intended for a dungeon, Peter considered his options. He didn't want to become French. He didn't want to join the army. He didn't want to continue fixing up houses for Mirielle, and he certainly didn't want to go back to Castroville to watch the artichokes grow. What he wanted to do was build beautiful structures that would last forever and introduce inhabitants and passersby alike to the meaning of symmetry and grace. To do that, he had better get back to Yale and take that course on concrete.

Having made that decision, he walked down the stone street to the house where Ariel still lived alone. Their relationship had greatly improved over the last three days. Letting himself inside with his newly cut key (a gift from Ariel and a total violation of her employers' instructions), Peter made two important telephone calls. First he called his parents in California, where it was still the night before, and told them he was returning to school. Then he called Rosalie to tell her she should start looking for a new caretaker for the villa.

That done, he walked down two flights to the terrace, stepped outside, dropped on his knees, and asked Ariel to marry him — a proposal so startling she almost sent her laptop into the lap pool, which would have deep-sixed her novel. From his position at her feet, however, Peter was able to reach out and save the machine. It was a gesture at once so practical and so romantic that Ariel realized she couldn't imagine anything she wanted more than to spend the rest of her life with this guy, and she said so.

What were they thinking? They had known each other so little time, to make so serious a commitment. The answer was simple. They were thinking of passion and fulfillment, of sharing their hopes and dreams and forging together a future more glorious then either could hope to achieve alone. In some small, selfish corner of their individual minds they were also thinking about regular sex, and wedding presents, and not having to eat dinner alone. The similarity of these base calculations goes to show that they were, in fact, soul mates. And if not, they were old enough to make their own mistakes.

And so, one last time, they got out the map and made their plans. If they left tomorrow, they could drive to Paris and collect Ariel's things before her employers left town, and still get a flight to New York that would give them a week to get settled in New Haven. They would get married there, they decided. Everything was so much easier in America.

When Ariel called Paris to announce her resignation, the editor was dumbfounded. To lose one au pair to sudden marriage was understandable, but to lose two in a row defied logic. Now his wife's mother would have to bring the girls to Gordes, and then she would want to stay and probably go back with them to Paris, too. And they would have to agree, because where would they find someone at this short notice to be with the girls in the afternoon? Life was really extraordinarily inconvenient, he thought, before heading off to the Wednesday editorial conference. He sincerely hoped his editors had some new ideas to put forward. All these proposals on Celtic rites were becoming so stale.

Farewell to Provence

A ND SO ALL THE Americans left Provence. Peter and Ariel set out for their new life in New Haven. Rosalie and Hugo found their interrupted honeymoon much more private in Paris, where nobody they knew was in town and they could stay in bed all morning if they wanted. When negotiations threatened to fall apart, Hugo flew back to New York, a tactic that served the double purpose of irritating his French counterparts and impressing his trustees with how hard he was working to make this once-in-a-millennium show possible. Rosalie took this opportunity to fly with her friend Mirielle to an Israeli spa that was reputed to have the best cellulite people on the planet.

At St-Etang, too, the visitors were departing. Didier Renard, busy with his construction, with the great increase in customers for his restaurant, and with preparations for his daughter's impending marriage (which was to be a far more elaborate affair than Peter and Ariel could either contemplate or afford), forgot until almost the last minute that his tenants were leaving. Hastily rolling up the blueprints he had been studying, he drove across the highway and into the courtyard just as Richard was, for the last time, backing the lime green sedan out of the drive. The plan was for Renard's niece to pick it up at the airport parking lot.

As they were saying farewell, exchanging insincere promises to keep on cycling and sincere ones to always remember the adventures of the past five weeks, the forester came blasting up on his motorbike. "Come to the café," he ordered Richard. "There is a man on the telephone who must speak to you before you depart.

He says it's a question of art," the forester added scornfully. "He sounds drunk."

Both observations were true. Ken, Richard's agent, was calling from San Diego, where he was attending the annual meeting of the Calendars, Religious Art, Posters, and Postcards Association. More precisely, he was calling from the boat Extended Vistas Press had chartered for the weekend. In the background, Richard could hear an equally drunk companion demanding that Ken close the deal or forget the whole thing, because he wanted to find some girls and party.

"I got you a contract," Ken was saying. "Extended Vistas is doing a new line of calendars for discount superstores — puppies, cowgirls, hot rods, that kind of stuff. They love your work."

"The Provence scenes?"

"No, not that junk. That's for the artsy, upscale markets. This is for farmers' wives. The last thing they want to buy is pictures of a field!"

"Barbie?" In his secret heart of hearts, Richard had thought his fashion doll arrangements very avant-garde.

"Get real." Ken snorted, his good humor ricocheting from a satellite somewhere over the North Pole. "That was so last year, I'd be ashamed to show it! This year is urban grit. They want the Clochard Series right away, and then a contract for at least three more dirty old man calendars, in different settings, to follow. The Caribbean is next, I think. Then either Africa or Japan, they're not sure right now. But you have to give me an exclusive right now or the deal's off. And I have to tell you, the numbers are too good to turn down."

Richard's hope for a gallery show were dashed yet again, but at least, for once, his timing had been right. He didn't even argue the terms. It was time to get to Marseilles if they expected to catch their connecting flight to Paris.

While waiting for boarding at Charles de Gaulle, Richard and Vivian stopped at the airport bar for one last cup of French coffee.

Richard, feeling flush, gave all his change to the children to spend at the newsstand. As Justin thumbed through the Asterix comic books, he suddenly thought about the golden circle, the first thing they had dredged out of the pond. The Lion Man hadn't taken it, Lily said. It hadn't turned up in any of the piles of stuff the curators were cataloging. Nobody had mentioned it at all, and Justin had a strong suspicion that Lily was still keeping it. He hoped the little dummy hadn't done anything totally stupid like put it in her backpack, where the metal detectors would find it.

"Remember that crown with the naked lady on it?" he asked suddenly.

"You can't have it," Lily answered. She was busy counting her coins and comparing them with the cost of a Barbie doll in a red satin can-can skirt cut high in front to show her underpants.

"I don't want it," Justin retorted, though in fact he thought it was just as much his as Lily's, and he meant to say so sometime soon. "I just wanted to make sure it wasn't going through the metal detector. Because if you have it in your backpack, you're toast."

Lily nodded impatiently. Everyone always thought she was such a dope, just because she was the youngest. The crown was in her suitcase, packed in with her party tights, her frilly slip, and her pixie wand, and the suitcase had long since vanished down the conveyor belt.

"Come on, Justin," she ordered. "You gotta help me figure out if I can afford this. It's the prettiest thing I've seen in France."